# PAINTED BLIND

# MICHELLE A. HANSEN

ISBN: 1469972859
ISBN 13: 9781469972855

Library of Congress Control Number: 2012901650
CreateSpace, North Charleston, SC

*For Nathan*

*"Love looks not with the eyes, but with the mind,*
*And therefore is wing'd Cupid painted blind."*

-William Shakespeare

# PROLOGUE

I t was always a bad sign when his mother arrived before breakfast. The horses were in the courtyard. She hated waiting, so the young man slowly poured himself a glass of orange juice and cut another slice of warm cinnamon bread.

He existed; that was enough to anger her. She could rage all she wanted. He didn't really care. When the glass was empty, he dragged himself off the stool and adjusted his sash. Before leaving the kitchen he set his shoulders back and made his expression pleasant.

His gait was confident. Most would say he inherited his mother's pride along with her beauty, but the young man disagreed. His character was molded by humble hands not of his blood, and he was forever indebted. "Mother, to what do I owe this unexpected visit?"

The sun glistened into a halo on his mother's hair as she took him by the shoulders and kissed his cheek. If only she were as angelic as her face. "I don't need a reason to visit." But she always had one. She'd traveled without maids. A personal matter. Only her bodyguard, Theron, stood beside her.

Theron was not welcome here, and she knew it. He was closer to the young man's age than her own, and that was the least of his flaws. His greater crimes were known by all and spoken of by no one.

The mother sank onto a pillowed chair in the parlor. There was no need for pretended niceties. "Have you seen this?" She motioned to Theron, who pulled from his cloak a fashion magazine made by mortals. He offered it to the young man open to a dog-eared page.

The spread was a modern take on a familiar scene, and the girl on the page was stunning, even to immortal eyes. "It's just an advertisement," he said.

His mother's expression went hard. "It's an insult." She smoothed a lock of hair from her face. "I want you to avenge me."

"Me?" He glanced at Theron, confused. Dirty errands were her lover's specialty. The young man wanted no part of it.

"I went to see her, but she was gone," Theron replied, clearly disappointed.

The son looked at the photo again and tried to stifle the shudder in his chest. This mortal girl had no idea how lucky she was—how close she'd come to living her worst nightmares. Other mortals had not been so fortunate.

Theron offered him a card. There was a name and address printed on it. Now he understood why they were here. He owed his mother nothing. "And if I don't?"

"I'll send Theron to deal with it." She threw an affectionate glance at her bodyguard, who grinned.

"Not in my kingdom."

His mother stood. "She's mortal. Technically, it's not your…" She broke off when her son's fists balled and his shoulders tightened. He was hot-blooded, and it pleased her. That made him even angrier, so he sighed and stood expressionless as she drew nearer. "You'll do as I ask," she whispered.

He had no legal recourse when it came to mortals, and he wouldn't allow the girl to be brutalized. "What do you want me to do? Dust her?" He laughed. Really, it was ridiculous. All of this over a stupid photograph.

"I want you to dispose of her to the most despicable creature you can find."

Ironic choice of words. The most despicable creature alive was standing right in front of him holding his mother's cloak. "Fine." His mother waited until he muttered, "Yes, I'll do it," through gritted teeth. It took great will for him to offer, "Will you stay and dine?" as the cook entered with a tray for the guests.

"Thank you, but no." As soon as she got what she wanted, his mother retreated quickly. "Before the next moon, or we'll deal with it ourselves."

He didn't see them out. When they were gone, he showed the advertisement to the cook. "Local girl. Familiar name, too."

"Are you going to do it?" Her expression tossed a dagger of guilt into his heart, but he nodded.

The alternative was worse.

# CHAPTER 1

I swore my dad would never find out about those photos, but I felt kinda sick facing him.

He was waiting for me in baggage claim, just past the giant bronze grizzly meant as a welcome to Bozeman, Montana. Dad was clean shaven, and across his forehead was a light streak where he usually wore a baseball cap. This time of year, his skin was always deep brown. After unloading the bag from my shoulder, he hugged me with his other arm.

I hugged back hard, unwilling to say how much I'd missed him. I pulled away feeling stupid as the alarm blared and bags slid from under the segmented plastic curtain.

Evening sun slanted through the skylights and threw a blinding rectangle on the wall. Outside the air smelled of smoke, and the eerie pink haze of fire season marred an otherwise cloudless sky. As we crossed the parking lot, Dad said, "How does a fresh rib-eye sound?"

"With your signature barbecue sauce?" Heavenly. "I've been dying for a good steak."

"I can tell." He lifted my suitcases into the bed of a diesel pick-up that carried the words "Middleton Concrete Contracting" on the door.

"C'mon, Dad. It's only seven pounds, and I'll probably put them back on tonight."

He grumbled, "Let's hope so," and climbed into the driver's seat.

As we traveled the familiar streets, the threads of anxiety knotted in my chest finally started to unravel. Half a mile past the hospital was a giant Quaking Aspen, the landmark of our street. I'd never been so glad to see the weathered gray paint on our house.

After hauling my luggage upstairs, I settled into a chair on the deck while Dad lit the barbecue. Of all the things I missed while I was away, his cooking topped the list.

He began with the obligatory first question, "How's Jill?" He never called her my mother anymore.

"Fine." I wanted to avoid the subject as much as he. There were things I didn't tell him in my emails. Jill's sudden absence was one of them.

She called last spring and said her friend had a job for me. The modeling agency offered to pay my airfare to and from Italy as well as my living expenses. Dad was dead set against me modeling, but Jill said, "Oh, Psyche. At the very least it's our chance to see Europe for free." I was naïve enough to believe "our" meant she was staying. With visions of us strolling through Rome, I agreed to the job, a decision I regretted more than he could know.

"How's business?" I poured two glasses of lemonade and handed one to Dad.

He leaned against the deck railing and took a sip before answering. "I had to turn down a contract for fifty condominiums."

"For what?"

"A mini mall." Though he worked manual labor, my dad had a good head for business. We lived modestly, but it was more a choice on Dad's part than a necessity.

"Nice." The mall contract would pay nearly twice that of the condos.

Dad poked at the sizzling steaks, then moved them aside to put down foil and sauté fresh vegetables.

Somewhere down the block a lawnmower buzzed. On the breeze drifted the aroma of fire-grilled steaks and freshly cut grass. This was the summer I gave up to model abroad, and I wished I had come home sooner.

In the largest cottonwood tree an ancient tire swing drifted to and fro, a tribute to my spent childhood. Dad had gotten rid of the swing set and the outgrown bicycles, but the tire swing remained, its rope captive in branches that grew up with me.

My stomach grumbled when Dad set a steaming plate in front of me, even though I ate in Minneapolis and had a snack on the plane. Nothing in an airport compared to this. "I guess you won't have to borrow from my bank account." I knew he wouldn't do that, even if he was starving.

"No, I'm doing just fine." He settled into his chair and passed me the barbecue sauce. "Speaking of your bank account... You kept the rules we set, right?"

It was just one rule: no nudity.

Dad's idea of nudity and my agent Blair's were a wide, rocky river apart. Technically, I had not done any nudity, but my ears burned when I thought of the shoot with the waist-length wig. I choked on my answer, "Yeah." Did he know somehow? Could he see it in my face? "Why?"

"Do you have any idea how much money is in your account?"

With all my expenses paid, I rarely touched the money and had the statements sent straight home to Dad. "No."

"Fifty-seven thousand dollars," he said slowly, like the numbers stuck on his tongue.

"No way." I knew Blair booked me as one of her premiere models, but I didn't know how much that meant per hour. I didn't shoot catalogs or soap commercials; I did designer advertisements and runway. That's why I had to lose seven pounds. For the runway they wanted twelve, but seven was all I could manage. "I guess college is paid for."

When he looked up, I saw the real question in his eyes: What did you have to do to make that kind of money? He didn't ask, but it hung there in the air between us.

I cut a big chunk of steak and chewed slowly. When I left three months ago, I vowed not to disappoint him. It was one advertisement. He didn't read fashion magazines. He would never see it. Still, I knew I'd let him down.

Dad's cell phone rang, a corny, country-music chime. "It's the guy who owns the mall. I should take this."

"Sure." I ate while he talked, and before he hung up, I fled to my room. There my luggage stood like soldiers guarding my secret summer.

No one but my parents knew I was in Europe. Even my best friend Savannah believed I spent the summer on my grandparents' farm in South Dakota. A box on my dresser helped maintain this story. Grandma Dee didn't understand why I was so fond of Mount Rushmore key chains and T-shirts, but she was happy to send them to me.

Since most of the clothes I brought home were dirty, unpacking was easy. I grabbed the heap and dumped it into the dirty clothes hamper. I was careful to bring home exactly what I took with me. The only exceptions were packed in plastic at the bottom of the largest suitcase: two designer dresses. One for homecoming and one for prom. Buying both had been wildly optimistic. I had never been asked to any dance ever. I took the dresses carefully by the hangers and slid everything aside to make a place for them at the back of the closet. If I hadn't worn them by next summer, I would sell them on eBay to someone who actually dated.

I was picking through my portfolio updates and postcard collection when Savannah texted me that she'd picked up my class schedule and reserved our lockers side by side.

**Get ready for the best year ever!**

I didn't text back. Instead I piled the stuff into a box with my boarding passes and other souvenirs from Europe. I stashed it on a shelf in the top of the closet before collapsing onto the bed. When I closed my eyes, stars spun behind my lids. I knew it was jetlag. Still, I slept in fits. I dreamed of Dad and Savannah in a room stacked with magazines and nowhere for me to hide from my lies.

# CHAPTER 2

I sat in my car as minutes blinked away on the digital clock. I didn't mean to be early, but Dad roused me for a pancake breakfast just after six to celebrate my senior year.

There was nothing to celebrate. I hated school. The learning and the homework and the grades were fine. Even the rules were okay with me, but going into a building with hundreds of my peers—that was torture.

The door facing the parking lot led to the senior hall. When the weather was warm, everyone hung out on the grass and the waist-high retaining wall that flanked the door. Perched right in the center of the wall was Travis McDowell, two-time state champion in the 100-meter butterfly. Every summer he life-guarded at the city pool during the day and trained after the gates were closed. The petite blonde with her head against his shoulder was Savannah, unusually tan. From the looks of it, she spent a lot of time at the pool this summer. Anything beyond eight weeks was out of Savannah's usual guy cycle, but she and Travis had been dating since April.

The warning bell blared, and I grabbed my backpack with a groan. It was officially time to start a new school year. The crowd dispersed, but Savannah lingered at the wall.

"About time," she said when I approached. Travis held the door open for us, and she continued, "We were just talking about the Last Bash Carnival." We moved down the hall toward our lockers. "It's tomorrow night." There was a suspicious tone in her voice. The Last Bash was the Montana State University fraternities' tribute to the end of summer, and Travis's brother was a Kappa Sigma. "It's going to be *so* fun." She paused. This was the part I was dreading. "And this year, you are coming with us."

"Yeah, right," I replied.

Travis nodded at two boys coming our way. "I'm heading to class." He kissed Savannah on the forehead.

She waited until he was down the hall before saying, "Hunter just dumped his girlfriend."

"And I care because...?"

"Oh, come on, Psyche."

"A Kappa Sig?" My dad would go into convulsions. He could barely handle me attending a co-ed high school.

By then we were in the middle of senior hall, which made it impossible to continue our conversation. Every two feet someone said hello to Savannah, and she went into full Homecoming Princess mode, greeting everyone with a smile and a compliment. Savannah thrived on attention and, therefore, loved school.

Savannah and I had only third hour Chemistry together. The rest of the day was a blur of slouching in back rows trying to be invisible. Last period I had second year drawing. Instead of giving out a course overview or reciting the rules, Mr. Mayhue handed us each a sixteen-by-twenty-inch sheet of drawing paper and a handful of pencils.

It was the first time all day I felt completely at ease. I sketched the art classroom in perspective while sitting in the corner farthest from the door. I continued sketching after the bell rang. When the din in the hallway ceased, I handed in my sketch and went to my locker. Now the school was just the way I liked it—completely empty.

The parking lot was dotted here and there with cars. With a sigh I dropped my backpack onto the seat of my Subaru. One day down, a hundred seventy-nine to go, I thought as I pulled onto Main Street toward the bank to exchange the Euros I brought home from Italy.

Traffic was painfully slow. Friday would mark the beginning of Labor Day weekend, then a break in the tourist season until snow fell thick enough for skiers. This week the sidewalks bulged with shoppers, and not one parking space emptied as I inched east between the brick buildings of old downtown. I parked behind the bank then walked along the side street toward the front. I rounded the corner and froze.

A new billboard stood at the end of the block. The perfume ad was a look-alike of Botticelli's *Birth of Venus*, and there in the center, beneath a waist-length wig, was me. Stark. Freaking. Naked.

On Main Street. I choked on my breath. That one mistake, the one photo I swore my dad would never see was *right there*.

The photo didn't show how my eyelid twitched or that my armpits were dripping sweat. It didn't show the excruciating pain in my chest that made my arm numb. No, my face and body were dusted with gold, and my fearful expression looked half innocent, half seductive. A scream of panic pushed at my ears. My dad would see it. Every guy in town would see it. Savannah would see it, too.

My lunch jumped into my throat. I stumbled to a trash can and hurled.

Thunder cracked overhead. I looked up and that's when I saw the guy down the sidewalk staring up at the billboard, hands on his hips. He spun around shaking his head, but he stopped when he saw me. Even from a distance, he was dazzling. I felt his gaze like a punch in the chest that struck suddenly and sent my pulse screaming. His eyes narrowed, and in that momentary glance, he looked past the ratty jeans and oversized T-shirt. He saw Venus, and it made him clamp his jaw tight and glare. Rain pelted the sidewalk between us, but I couldn't pull myself away until he turned and disappeared around the corner.

Absently I walked into the bank, unable to free my mind from the angry set of his jaw. I set an envelope of Euros on the counter and saw surprise in the teller's eyes when she looked at my face. She made a quick glance out the window and back to me again.

"It's not me." My voice was unconvincing. I studied the dark spots made by the rain on my shoes. I didn't hear her reply. My mind saw only the guy who hated me without even knowing my name.

I was doomed. There was no other way to put it. By morning everyone would know about the billboard. Tonight I had to explain to my dad. Maybe if I told him what happened before he saw the billboard, he would understand. On the way home I gripped the steering wheel with both hands to keep them from shaking.

I watched out the upstairs window for Dad's pickup on the street. Soon a truck came into view, but it wasn't his. It was a company truck driven by the foreman. It pulled slowly into the driveway, and before it came to complete stop, my dad jumped out of the passenger seat and headed toward the front door with long, determined steps. He knew. It was too late. I ran to my room.

The footsteps coming upstairs were hard and fast. A moment later my bedroom door was thrown open with so much force it ricocheted off the stopper and came back to slap my dad's ready hand. His eyes narrowed on me in wrath so fierce, my knees actually wobbled.

"I rear-ended a Volvo on Main Street," he growled. He didn't have to say where. I knew it was somewhere around Church Street, in full view of the Venus billboard. I didn't know which was worse—his fury or the humiliation of knowing he saw it. "You promised me." Disappointment made his voice crack.

Tears pushed at my eyes. "I can explain..."

He cut me off with a wave of his hand. "Find a ride to school tomorrow. I'm taking your car." Then he turned into the hallway, and I rushed after him.

"I can't go back to school. Everyone will be talking about me."

"That is your own fault! You will go to school. No excuses." It was pointless to argue.

I went back to my room and threw myself on the bed. Tomorrow was going to be the worst day of my life.

It was probably suicidal to disobey him, but I made no attempt to find a ride to school. A slow and painful death sounded better than school.

Mid-morning he returned and caught me sitting on the couch. "I thought I told you to find a ride to school," he said.

I tossed the remote onto the ottoman. "I didn't."

"Get your shoes on." Dad flicked off the television. "I'm taking you."

Reluctantly, I gathered my books and gave my teeth a quick brushing before following him out the door. He dropped me in front of the school and left me to face my fate alone. I waited until the Subaru was indiscernible down the street before I turned and pushed myself through the door to the office.

The secretary wrote out my admit slip with raised eyebrows. She wanted to say something, but she didn't have to. All her condemnation was right there in her pursed lips.

I grabbed my slip and went to the senior hall. I was fifteen minutes late for third period, and I was in no hurry to face Savannah. As I stood fiddling with the combination of my locker, a boy named Rory Keene came around the corner wearing a bright green lanyard dangling a rubber chicken, the hall pass from our third period class.

Years ago Rory lived across the street from me. The first snowfall each year, we built a fort against the picket fence of his front yard and waged war on the neighborhood. Just about the time I got strong enough to heave a snowball from my front yard into his, Rory's parents divorced, and he moved across town. Rory now held a place in the social outcasts category, which he earned with greasy hair and the worse case of acne I had ever seen. He still talked to me occasionally, but today I wasn't in the mood. I turned my back to him.

Savannah must have put an air freshener in her locker because the air held a hint of cinnamon and orange. Something else, too. Salty, like the sea. Just as I lifted the handle, a voice behind me whispered, "Perfect!"

I spun around, ready to give Rory a verbal beating. "What did you say?"

He was still ten feet down the hall. Startled, Rory paused. "I didn't..."

Someone sneezed. Rory and I said, "Bless you" at the same time, then looked around. There was no one there but the two of us, and neither of us sneezed.

Rory muttered, "Weird," and continued down the hall.

As I grabbed my books and walked away, I heard a string of whispered curses that started with "stupid" and ended in a language I'd never heard in my life.

It took three steadying breaths before I could open the classroom door. I took Advanced Chemistry not because I was good at science, but because Mr. Billiard wore Coke-bottle glasses and called me "Ron's girl." All of us were just a blur to his ancient eyes—the children of students he loved in better years. However, to my utter disappointment, Mr. Billiard was spending the semester drinking coffee in the staff lounge while a student teacher named Michael Darling taught Advanced Chemistry.

When I opened the door, Mr. Darling turned from the class and said, "Look, everybody! Venus has arrived."

A guy in the back whooped, "Yeah, baby, take it off!"

My armpits grew damp. My eyelid twitched. I told myself not to overreact and hurried to my seat. I clenched my teeth as Savannah turned to me.

"South Dakota?" she said. "Then how do you explain *this?*" She opened the September issue of *Cosmopolitan* to a two-page spread of the Venus ad and held it out to me.

I swiped the magazine and closed it as fast as I could. Getting harassed by a teacher was bad enough. I didn't need it from my best friend, too.

Back from his errand to the office, Rory filled the seat in front of me, but he didn't mention the strange sneeze in the hall.

"I don't know how you could have done it," Savannah whispered. "You won't even wear a skirt to school."

I picked stray shavings off my pencil and stared at the desktop. I should have told Savannah about modeling, but she wouldn't have understood why I needed her to keep it a secret.

"There are no modeling agencies around here. How did you ..." She broke off and answered her own question. "Jill."

It bugged Jill to no end that she had a head-case for a daughter. Modeling was her grand scheme to cure me. She came from L.A. the last week in May and flew with me to New York. We stayed a week while her friend put together my portfolio. Then we left for Milan. Jill helped me decorate my apartment and went with me to my first two modeling sessions. All I needed was confidence, she said. I would learn to feel more at home in my own skin. A week later she slipped out while I slept. She was halfway to New York when I found her note. It said she was *so* proud of me. I tore it to shreds.

I wanted to go home, but I'd signed a contract. If I quit, I had to repay all the expenses the agency incurred to get me there. Too proud to tell my dad what a fool I'd been, and unwilling to let him foot the bill for my stupidity, I stayed and I worked. Blair kept me booked double sessions nearly every day. I finished my contract and refused to stay longer, even though she offered to find me a private tutor or pay for a school abroad. I missed my dad, and I wanted to be a normal high school student. Even if I wasn't normal.

"I'm still mad at you." Savannah reached across the aisle and swiped the magazine from my desk then dropped it into an oversized purse she used as a backpack. "On the upside, you'll be famous."

I grunted without meaning to. It was impossible for her to fathom how famous could be a bad thing.

"What did your dad say?"

"He rear-ended a Volvo and took away my car. Can I have a ride home after school?"

"*Of course,*" she replied before Mr. Darling called on her to read aloud from the overhead projector.

I should have noticed the devious look on her face, but Mr. Darling caught my eye. He focused on me so intently, I wanted to ooze into the desktop. I slouched behind Rory the rest of the period.

When the bell rang, I grabbed my books and darted out the door. The crowded hallway offered no refuge. A junior in a football jersey bumped against me and ran his hands down my sides before I could shy away. My pulse was racing and my peripheral vision took on dark clouds. I needed some air. Now.

I reached my locker. Somehow my fingers turned the combination. I dropped my books inside, then turned toward the nearest exit, tucked my head and charged through the crowd. I shoved people aside as I went.

Outside I gulped a saving breath, but it was too late. Halfway across the parking lot, pain exploded in my chest. Students streamed out of the building for lunch. I looked around for a place to hide.

I ran to the neighboring strip mall. When I reached the sidewalk I slowed, then swerved into a sporting goods store. It was the middle of the day, but no one was at the front register. Behind the gun safes and hunting gear were the fitting rooms. I locked myself in one of the stalls and stood there clutching my stomach. Pain spread down my arm.

The first time this happened I was thirteen and sitting next to Savannah at a basketball game. A few months later it happened at school. Mrs. Radcliff, the school counselor, called it a panic attack and assured me I wasn't dying. I was sure she was wrong. The pain was so intense. It wasn't in my head. I couldn't breathe; I couldn't feel my fingers.

I wished and prayed for my dad to come and find me now, but he was too angry to care if I died in a mustard-yellow stall in the sporting goods store. I couldn't risk the long walk home. Someone would recognize me as the slut from the billboard. I stood there shivering at my pathetic reflection in the mirror.

I heard the scuff of shoes across the tiled floor. The door to the next stall creaked ever so slightly. I pressed my back into the corner and tried to quiet my pounding heart. I waited. The air grew perfectly still.

I peeked down. No feet showed under the divider. My breath came in bursts. I inhaled slowly and tried to clear my mind. My pulse kept pounding, but the pain dulled.

Satisfied that I was in control, I stepped up on the bench and looked over the divider. The stall was empty, but a slight aroma of cinnamon made me pause and look again. Something brushed my face. It was warm, like a caress.

I yelped and stumbled. My foot slipped from the bench and sent me tumbling backward. My back smacked the opposite wall. I flailed and grabbed for a handhold, but there was nothing to break my fall. I landed on my butt on the tile, and my head bounced off the partition.

I was alone. And going completely insane.

# CHAPTER 3

I didn't attend any of my afternoon classes. When the bell rang to end the school day, I was sitting in Savannah's car, trying to shake the feeling I was being watched.

Half the parking lot was empty before Travis and Savannah left the school. As soon as they were out the door, he caught her by the arm and pulled her to his chest. Travis kissed her opened mouthed right there on the sidewalk.

I looked away. I should have been happy for her. A better friend would have been. I was just so empty that joy for someone else's happiness was hard to come by. Savannah had boyfriend after boyfriend since seventh grade, but not one guy had ever leaned against my locker and tried to make me laugh. No matter how much I denied it, that simple truth carved a deeper hole as I watched Savannah fall in love again.

A radiant smile plastered on her face, Savannah dropped into the driver's seat. "Travis said he'll meet us at the carnival."

"You're kidding, right?" I could not show my face at MSU. College guys, alcohol, dark corners and crowds. It was a nightmare from start to finish.

"Relax. It's at night. You'll have fun." She tried to sound convincing. "You have to come with me," she said, "unless you want to walk home." To make sure I couldn't, she put the car into gear and sped out of the parking lot.

By seven o'clock the temperature had dropped into the fifties. A cool breeze blew from the west, but it still felt more like a summer evening than fall. For that I was grateful. I borrowed a pair of fleece-lined leather gloves from Savannah and pulled up the hood of my sweatshirt.

Sixth Avenue in front of the Greek houses was closed and lined with booths. The carnival was supposed to be Mardi Gras themed, but that amounted to little more than masks and beads on guys wearing Wranglers and cowboy boots. The music blaring from the lawn of one house was country-western, not jazz or blues, and the Tippet Brothers' barbecue wagon was parked on one corner. Tri-tip steak and long racks of ribs sizzled over the flames. Bud Tippet had beer on tap and mostly forgot to check IDs.

We saw Travis and his brother Hunter near the art club's face-painting booth. Hunter slugged Travis when he saw Savannah. "You're still hanging out with this creep?" Hunter asked.

Travis put his arm around Savannah. "Have you met Savannah's best friend, Psyche?"

Hunter held out his hand. "I don't think we've...." He looked into my face and his mouth dropped open. I looked away, but Hunter moved to the side, following my line of vision. His eyes narrowed. "Wait. Are you the girl in ...?"

"The billboard?" Savannah offered.

Hunter's eyes made a pass down my body, and I felt my face getting hot. Recovering, he offered Travis a wad of tickets. "The first bunch is on me. I've gotta get back to the house." He looked at me again. "Come by if you get bored."

As Hunter turned to go, Savannah threw me an encouraging smile. I don't know what she expected me to do—call him back or tag along after him? I just stood there as he walked away.

Travis broke the silence left in Hunter's wake. "Food or games?"

"Games," Savannah replied. "Think you can win one of those giant teddy bears for me at the ring toss?"

"With four tickets or less," Travis replied confidently.

I didn't believe him and folded my arms cynically as he exchanged a ticket for three plastic rings. The first ring bounced off and landed on the ground. The second fell between the bottles, but the third settled onto its target in the center. As the attendant pulled a huge panda bear from the line for Savannah, I congratulated Travis, "I've never actually seen someone win."

After a quick glance in my eyes, he said to the ground, "Did you want one, too?"

"No, you'd better save your luck for Savannah's next whim."

As if on cue she pointed to an enclosed canvas booth. "Let's go there."

Over the door hung a sign that said: *PALM readings. TAROT cards. KNOW your destiny.* As we drew closer, a smaller sign warned us not to disturb the session in progress. Palm readings were two tickets. Tarot card readings were three tickets, and for an extra ticket, we could know our luckiest days of the month. It was all hogwash, but Savannah loved this stuff. Travis tore off tickets for each of us while we waited for the curtain to open.

The pungent odor of incense struck me as the three of us stepped inside, and I swallowed a cough. The fortune teller was seated at a folding table, over which hung a tattered tablecloth. Her violet dress and dangling pearl earrings looked like something straight out of a costume catalog. "One at a time." She looked up from the deck of cards on the table. She was old enough to be my grandmother, but there was a peculiar beauty about her.

"You go first," I offered. "Travis and I will wait outside."

Savannah kept hold of his hand. "I don't mind if Travis hears my destiny."

I sighed and waited outside alone. It took all of a minute, and Savannah came out smiling. I supposed fortune-tellers were prone to offering good news, since they'd probably go broke telling people their lives were going to suck.

"Your turn," Savannah prodded.

I moaned and stepped through the canvas curtain again. My mind was already rolling over the cheesy fortune lines she'd feed me. "You have strong life lines. You will fall madly in love sometime this year. Beware the twelfth of the month." Anyone could think up this garbage. I sat in the cane-backed chair opposite the woman.

"What can I do for you?" She looked up and smiled mischievously. "Venus."

"Psyche," I corrected. "Palm reading, I guess." I put my hand out palm up, but she didn't move to take it.

Instead, she rested her chin on her folded hands and studied my eyes. The canvas curtain whipped to the side. "Please wait outside," she said automatically.

I looked at the empty doorway. "Must have been the wind."

The gypsy looked toward the door and mumbled something I couldn't understand. Her eyes were wide when she turned back to me. "It is you, isn't it? One might consider it a mockery of the original." Her eyes had a depth that struck something inside me. It was like she could see the frayed edges of my lonely soul.

I pulled my hand away. "On second thought, I don't want a palm reading."

She grabbed me by the wrist, so I couldn't run. Her eyes darted to the back of the tent and came back to me with a warm smile. "What is it you want most?"

"I want to be normal." I tried to pull away, but she held on tighter.

"I will tell you this: Love like you cannot imagine awaits you if you have the courage to find it."

"No offense, but I'm not much of a believer." Not in love and not in cheap gypsy fortunes.

"Maybe there's someone who can make a believer of you."

"Yeah, whatever."

She shrugged and released my arm. "It's your destiny and your heart. What more shall I say?" She smiled at the back of the tent, then put her business card into my hand.

"What do you keep looking at?" I asked. When she gave me a puzzled look, I stuffed the card into my jeans pocket feeling stupid. "Never mind."

"Do you smell citrus?" she asked. "And the sea?"

"How'd you know about that?"

"I smell it, too, sometimes." She began sorting tarot cards on the table in front of her. "It's okay to believe in things you can't see. Isn't that what people say? The best things in life are unseen."

I paused in front of the door. "I thought the best things in life were free."

"That too, I suppose. Next!"

Utterly confused, I stepped outside and realized Travis and Savannah had ditched me. After scanning the crowd and not finding a sign of them, I wandered down the street. Fortunes and incense had given me a headache.

I stopped at a booth where a cartoonist sketched a couple kissing. The girl had her hair tucked around her ear so her profile showed. She sat on her boyfriend's knee, and his arm was casually wrapped around her waist. I pretended to watch the cartoonist's picture take shape and stole glances at the couple.

During the summer I shot two sessions with a male model named Holden Valentine. He was twenty and had recently ended a tumultuous and well-publicized relationship with a pop starlet. Our work together would become a Guess ad sometime next spring, romantic black and whites of a beautiful couple. For the shoot, Holden wrapped his arms around my waist and put his face to my cheek. The photos looked like we'd been in love our whole lives, but for me it had been more awkward than ice skating in soccer cleats. I was so inept at falling in love, I didn't even know how to let a guy touch me.

The fortune-teller's words floated through my mind again. *Love like you cannot imagine awaits you if you have the courage to find it.*

I didn't have the courage. It was just that simple.

I was half a block from the Kappa Sigma house when the first string of beads hit my feet. Whoever threw them disappeared into the crowd before I saw him. I picked up the purple plastic stars and ran my thumb over their sharp prongs. Across the street a lanky guy studied me while smoking a cigarette. He came forward. Instinct told me to run, but I froze as he approached. He took his time looking me up and down before his eyes locked on my face.

He pulled a mass of beads from his neck and draped them around mine. "For you."

"Don't even think I'm going to flash you," I said icily.

He shook his head. "A gift." He dropped the cigarette onto the street and smothered it with the toe of his boot then moved away and was lost in the crowd.

"Um, thank you." He didn't hear me, but someone did. Two more guys passing in the crowd pressed beads into my hand. That familiar, anxious churning started in my chest. I searched for somewhere to hide. I pushed through the crowd, but ran into a solid body. I looked up and cringed.

"Psyche?" Mr. Darling wore a fraternity sweatshirt. He reeked of beer and way too much cologne. "Couldn't stay away from your favorite teacher, huh? Let me show you around."

"I'm meeting someone," I replied.

He took hold of my arm and used it to steer me through the crowd. "C'mon. Let's have some fun. I'll get you a beer."

All the sirens in my blood went off. We reached the curb. I shoved my weight into him, and his foot struck the cement. Too much beer in his head, he stumbled, and I pulled free.

I took off into the crowd, but Mr. Darling shouted, "Stop that girl! She's Venus!"

All around me, people turned. "It is her," someone said. "She's the girl in the billboard."

The crowd closed me in. Suddenly I was trapped in a circle of bodies, all shoving and grabbing at me. I felt the breath slipping out of me. My chest constricted. I tried to scream, but nothing came out. Strong arms grabbed me from behind.

I fought hard. I was not going to be dragged into some frat house.

"Don't be afraid," a voice murmured in my ear. "I'll get you out of here."

I saw the sleeves of a black leather jacket and a hand that bore a single gold band around the first finger.

Then we disappeared.

# CHAPTER 4

"What the..." I stammered, too shocked to believe what just happened. My body, my clothes were just... gone.

"Shhh," he whispered. "I'll take you to safety."

People looked around bewildered. "Where'd she go?"

He kept his arms around me as he pulled me through the mob. I struggled to walk, unable to see my feet. Bodies parted and jostled as we passed, but no one saw us. Some girls on the edge of the crowd stood on their toes to see what happened. We moved past them, hidden from their sight and mine. I felt the leather of the glove as I touched my face, but I could see nothing.

I struggled against him once we were free of the crowd. "Let me go!"

"Around the corner here." We turned into an alley between two houses. Thick trees blocked the light of the streetlamps and the moon. In the shadows my body reappeared, and he let me go.

I spun around, stumbling away. "How... what did...who *are* you?"

"I'm sorry I grabbed you. I didn't want to lose you in the crowd." He kept his distance now. He was half a foot taller than me with broad shoulders. In the darkness, I couldn't make out his face.

"What did you *do* to me?" I insisted.

"I hid you from them. It's a talent I have." He spoke softly, an alluring voice that made me want to lean closer and glean the rise and fall of it. But I didn't dare get within arm's reach again.

"A talent? You call being invisible a *talent*." I suppose I should have thanked him, but he seemed as dangerous as the mob.

"I'm not exactly like you."

"No kidding."

He was unmoved by my sarcasm. "Did you drive?" He was either oblivious to my alarm or he just didn't care. "I can give you a ride home," he offered. "You probably don't want to brave that crowd again."

"I came with a friend." There was no way I was climbing into a car with him. He might disappear after slitting my throat... or worse.

He moved to a motorcycle I hadn't noticed before and pulled a helmet over his head. "Climb on."

"I'm not going to..." My protest was drowned by the engine, a smooth growl of speed and power.

"Before they find us."

I climbed on behind him, not needing the peg to lift me. When he hit the gas pulling onto Fifth Avenue and nearly dumped me off the back of the bike, I curled my arms around his waist and squeezed tight. "Pinecrest."

He knew the way without directions. The street lamp at the end of the block lit my driveway and half the yard. I hoped to finally see his face, but he didn't take off the helmet, and with the dark visor down, he was completely hidden.

"Thanks for the ride. I'm Psyche, by the way."

He revved the engine on the bike and dropped it into gear. "Good night."

I watched him drive away. There was something familiar about him. On the porch steps it hit me. The smell. I almost missed it because of the leather jacket, but it was definitely there, a hint of cinnamon and orange on salty air. It was him. He could make himself invisible, but I could smell him, and so could the gypsy. I had smelled him at school and heard him sneeze. He had followed me into the sporting goods store.

I stepped into the house and nearly collided with my dad.

He stood with his arms folded across his chest. "Was that a motorcycle that dropped you off?" He pulled the Subaru keys from his pocket and tossed them into my hands. "Don't ever let me catch you on that bike again." Dad started toward the couch in the living room. "Who was that anyway?"

What could I say? I didn't even know his name.

The next day I was zoning in Mr. Darling's class when a breeze blew by me. The air smelled of cinnamon and subtle but expensive cologne.

"Are you bored yet?" His whisper startled me. I nearly swallowed my pen cap. After the horrible coughing fit passed, he drew even closer to my ear. "So, that guy is your teacher?"

Before I could reply, Mr. Darling called my name. Holding out the dry erase marker, he said, "Come up and balance this equation."

"I haven't finished yet," I said.

"Come forward," Mr. Darling insisted.

I slowly untangled myself from the desk. While I struggled to place numbers on the equation, the student teacher stalked around me like some hungry carnivore. A hand rested on my shoulder, and I cringed, but it was my invisible savior who whispered, "Five $H_2O$, six carbon."

Mr. Darling paused directly behind me, and I wished I'd worn a longer shirt—one that completely covered my backside.

"Two nitrogen." The hand moved away. "I'll take care of him."

The equation finished, I set the marker on the ledge of the board and went to my desk, unable to look at anything but the floor. I slid into my seat and slouched behind Rory.

Mr. Darling scanned my work. "Correct," he announced. Then he tripped on some unseen obstacle. His body flung forward with unnatural force and his face smacked the whiteboard.

The class laughed when Mr. Darling stood, shaking his head like he didn't know what happened. He sniffed, and his nose dribbled blood. He tried to wipe it away with his hand, but smeared it up the sleeve of his shirt. "Okay," he said, acting nonchalant, "everyone start on the next problem." Pinching his nose at the bridge, he managed to stem the tide for a moment, but as soon as he let go, the stream was worse than before.

Five minutes passed and his nose was still bleeding, so Mr. Darling twisted up two tissues and shoved one into each nostril. The ends hung over his lip, making a white mustache that fluttered when he breathed.

Savannah giggled into her worksheet.

A moment later the counselor, Ms. Hubble, appeared in the doorway. "Could I see...." She broke off when she saw our teacher. "Michael, what happened to your nose?" she asked.

"Perfect timing," came the quiet whisper over my shoulder. The air whipped away.

"Ah chew!" Mr. Darling sneezed and sent the bloody tissues flying. "Excuse me," he mumbled. A new red trickle started down his lip. He looked at Ms. Hubble and the expression on his face shocked us all. He eyed the counselor like he eyed me just a moment ago. Then his features softened, and he gave her the most pathetic puppy-dog eyes. "I bumped my nose on the board. It won't stop bleeding."

The counselor stepped forward, all her motherly compassion surfacing right there in front of our class. "You poor thing." Then, "Ah chew!" and we all gasped as she lit up like a forty-year-old flashlight. "Just come to my office after class." She winked on her way out.

"You have got to be joking," muttered a girl in the next row. "She's like fifteen years older than him."

"Oh, that is just wrong," Savannah whispered before the bell rang to dismiss us.

I hurried out the nearest exit instead of meeting Savannah at our lockers. Today was bright and too warm for long sleeves. That was the mystery of fall in the mountains; it alternated between Indian summer and winter.

I knew I wasn't alone, but I didn't want to be seen talking to myself, so I pulled out my phone and put it to my ear. "Hey, are you here?" I asked and sat cross-legged in the grass under a cottonwood tree.

"You mean me?" the quiet voice answered.

"What did you do to my teacher? He looked like he was completely in love with Ms. Hubble."

"Some guys like older women. They'll get along fine for the next year or so."

"The next *year*! You're ruthless."

He chuckled a deep, chesty sort of laugh that made my insides do cartwheels. "And I enjoy it so much." I guessed he was leaning against the trunk of the tree, but I couldn't be sure. He didn't cast a shadow. "He deserved it for humiliating you." He paused, then added more quietly, "and for last night."

"Who are you talking to?" Savannah crossed the lawn then stood over me, hands on her hips.

"Hold on a second." I covered the phone, like I didn't want him to hear. At the same time I felt him settle onto the ground beside me. "Just a friend."

"Does he have a name?"

"Who said it was a guy?" I asked innocently.

"You were grinning from ear to ear. What's his name?"

"Oh, his name is... It's..."

"Erik," he whispered in my ear.

"Erik. His name is Erik." That tiny bit of knowledge fluttered on my tongue. Erik saved me from a mob.

"And?"

I held the phone to my ear. "I'll call you back." I pushed the end button on the already lifeless phone. "And what?"

"Is he cute? How old is he? Is he the reason you blew off Hunter?"

"Don't get all excited, Savannah. It's not like I'm dating him."

Her eyes narrowed. "Whatever. I saw the look on your face when you were talking to him. He's probably gorgeous."

I shook my head. "He's not much to look at." I felt a pinch in my side and tried not to squirm.

"Then he must be funny."

"More like mischievous." With a laugh that could tilt my world, but that was knowledge better withheld from both of them.

She sniffed the air. "What is that amazing smell? It's like... cinnamon ..."

"And the sea."

"Yeah." She inhaled deeply. "With some sexy aftershave mixed in."

"Air freshener." That wasn't entirely a lie. He did freshen the air wherever he went.

"You sprayed air freshener outside?"

"No, I... spilled it... on my backpack."

She waited for me to say more. When I didn't, she relented. "Well, I'm going to grab lunch. You want anything?"

I shook my head.

Savannah gave me a strange look, then held up her hands. "Okay, I'm leaving. You can call him back."

When she was gone, an awkward silence fell between Erik and me. He was sitting near enough to make the skin on my arm tingle. If I moved even slightly, I might brush against him, a prospect which thrilled and terrified me. His scent jumbled my thoughts. When I was finally able to speak, my words came out accusing. "You've been to my school before."

Anticipating my next question, he answered, "Looking for you."

"And the carnival?"

"The same."

My irritation grew. "Are you stalking me?"

He leaned closer. His breath warmed my ear as he whispered, "Do I frighten you?"

My response was completely unexpected. My eyes fell closed, and my head dipped toward the sound.

He jerked away. "Maybe we should get out of here before you give me away."

I snapped myself out of his spell, shocked at my own reaction. I should have felt panic rise in my chest. Where were the sweaty palms and the chest pains? He was a total stranger. And he was *invisible*. "I can't...I'm not ...going anywhere with you."

He stood up. I heard his feet shuffle, felt him towering over me. "I understand." Then his footsteps moved away.

It was the right thing to do—letting him go. But, what if he never came back? "Wait."

I stood and dug my car keys out of my pocket. This went against everything my dad taught me. I shouldn't go off alone with this guy, but he'd saved me from a mob and paid Mr. Darling back for last night. I could trust him enough to go somewhere safe and talk. "There's a trail by the river," I murmured as I crossed the parking lot. There were always joggers on that trail. I could scream if he tried to hurt me. "I'll meet you..." The door of my Subaru swung open, seemingly on its own.

"At the gazebo," he finished. The door closed after I dropped into the driver's seat.

I started the car and backed slowly out of the parking space, then slammed on the brakes. In my rearview mirror, I saw a streak of black. The bike zipped around me. Erik wore the same helmet and black leather jacket. He disappeared before I pulled onto Main Street.

There were three cars in the parking lot at the trailhead. I pulled into a slot and turned off the engine. A couple of moms with strollers chatted by the gazebo. I walked down the trail wondering how I was going to find Erik, but a moment later he fell into step beside me. His arm brushed against mine and made me jump.

"You seem to know your way," I said. "Are you from around here?"

"Not exactly."

I veered off the trail and I sat on a dry log. The sunlight reflected off the water in blinding glory. The river's steady rush soothed me, which I needed around Erik. "If you're some kind of alien," I said, "I'm not in the mood to be abducted."

He chuckled that irresistible laugh again. "You don't want to be the bride of some little green man with pointy ears?"

I knew he wasn't little. The green part, I wasn't sure about. "Why can't I see you?"

"Because I don't want you to." His voice was matter-of-fact, like there was no use pushing that point.

I stretched my legs. "You can't imagine the number of times I've wanted to be invisible. How do you do it?"

"It's sort of a mental capacity." Whatever that meant. He was good at being evasive. Maybe he saw the frustration in my face, because he relented and answered. "Our worlds inhabit the same space, but in different realms. We have the ability to block ourselves from your sight when we're in your realm."

"You're not invisible in your world?"

"No, and neither are you. Your kind doesn't posses the veiling power."

"Some sort of magic?" Here we were discussing the impossible like it was yesterday's lunch menu.

"More like physics than magic. There are basic laws of veiling. Once you understand the laws, it all makes perfect sense."

"Sure it does," I scoffed.

"Whatever I'm touching or whatever is touching me when I veil, veils with me. That's why you don't see my clothes wandering around without a body in them. That's why you became invisible at the carnival. I was veiled in the fortune-teller's booth, but I had to unveil in order to hide you. To the crowd I would have appeared momentarily and then disappeared. Luckily, they were all looking at you, and no one noticed me."

"Is Erik really your name?"

"It's similar to my name, and it's common in your language."

My mind was doing a weak calculation of the things I knew about him and the things I didn't. First, I didn't know what he looked like. The name he'd given me was false. He wasn't from my world and had the power to hide from my kind at will. But there was one sliver of instinctive knowledge that overpowered all the rest. I liked him. He should have scared me, but he didn't, and I wasn't sure why. "How did you get into my world?"

"We have portals."

"Like the Stargate?" I teased.

"Sort of like that, without the extraterrestrial metal and the weird watery doorway."

I was taken aback that he perfectly understood the reference. "And you're...human?"

"We live longer," he explained. "When I was a child, your world was very different. We used to interact with your people regularly, but they thought we'd enslave them, so they attacked our people, and we closed the portals."

"But you reopened it? The portal, I mean."

The log rocked as he stood. "Let's walk."

It felt like walking alone when he didn't speak. We wandered awhile, and I lost track of him until he spoke again. Then I was surprised by how near he was. Erik still had not answered the most important question. It took half a mile for me to get the courage to ask, "Why were you looking for me?"

He drew some branches aside so I didn't have to duck under them. "The billboard. When I saw you at the school, you weren't anything like I'd imagined. You intrigued me, so I followed you to the carnival."

I stopped in the trail and faced his voice. "The fortune-teller knew you were there. She could see you."

"She was one of us but chose to live in your world."

I remembered her face, the beautiful eyes and the golden skin tone. "Does that happen often?"

He nudged me forward on the path. "No, she was probably the first."

We reached the bridge, where the paved trail abruptly changed into dirt single-track that split in two directions. One trail went up to the sidewalk and across the bridge. The other went under the bridge among the boulders. I hesitated, then turned back. By now school was out, and I shouldn't linger here with him as dusk fell. I tried to walk slowly, but too soon I was standing by the gazebo looking at my lone car in the parking lot. Part of me wished he was a normal guy I could invite over to meet my dad. Knowing my dad, though, it was probably better if they didn't meet. Mostly I wondered why he wouldn't let me see him. "Where's your motorcycle?" I asked.

"In front of your car."

"But I don't..."

"See it?" he teased.

Already I'd forgotten the first law of veiling. "Whatever you were touching disappeared with you."

The gravel crunched under our feet as we crossed the parking lot. "May I visit you again?" he asked. As soon as I unlocked my car, he brushed my hand out of the way, so he could open the door.

"I'd like that," I admitted.

"Soon, then." He closed the door.

I started the engine and watched the bushes. Suddenly he appeared, already wearing the black helmet and straddling the motorcycle. He revved the engine, nodded a good-bye and pulled away.

It couldn't be soon enough.

# CHAPTER 5

It was fully dark by the time I got home. I grinned stupidly to myself over a date with a guy I couldn't see and failed to notice the extra cars on the block until I was on the sidewalk. Suddenly people ran at me calling me Venus. Two news cameras closed in. I spun around and was blinded by a flash. The photographer snapped three more pictures as I shielded my eyes.

From the porch I heard a sharp whistle and, "Get away from my daughter!" I bolted toward the sound. The next thing I knew, Dad's strong arms pulled me through the doorway and turned the lock behind us. "What was that?" he demanded.

I shook my head. "What do they want?"

The doorbell rang wildly. A guy with a microphone stood on the porch with a cameraman behind. He jiggled the button again.

"I'm calling Marty." Dad pulled the phone from his pocket and scrolled through the numbers.

Within ten minutes, a Ford pickup pulled into our driveway with the blue and reds flashing. Police Chief Marty DeWitt was the quarterback of my dad's high school football team. They still went elk hunting together every fall. Marty was six feet four inches tall and had packed on seventy pounds since his football days. He was out of uniform, but had his badge hanging from his jeans pocket and wore a shoulder holster over a gray T-shirt. Even without the gun, he was a presence no one took lightly.

He gathered the cameras and crews for a short meeting, which Dad and I watched through a crack in the office curtains. Then Marty came into the house.

"I can't make them leave," he told Dad. "As long as they stay off your property, they can be on the public street, but they can't camp there. I'll come back in the morning. If they are still here, I'll ticket them."

"That's it?"

Chief DeWitt held up his hands. "They have rights, too."

"Oh, come on." Dad shook his head, disgusted.

Marty's face didn't change. "Tomorrow's Saturday. Take a day off, Ron. Watch some football. They'll get tired of hanging around, and they'll leave." He glanced at me before continuing, "The Women's Club is petitioning to have the billboard removed," he said, "on the grounds it's pornographic."

"Amen to that," Dad muttered.

I made a quiet exit up the stairs. I didn't turn on any lights, as I closed the blinds then drew the curtains over them. It didn't make me feel better. Those reporters were violating our space, snapping photos of our house, telling everyone in the world who I was and where I lived. Now more than ever I envied Erik's ability to be invisible.

When my cell phone rang, I assumed it was Savannah, so I answered.

"Psyche, you've got to come back," Blair said. "My phone is ringing off the hook with booking agents who want Venus."

"I'm in school," I said flatly.

"You don't understand. I'm getting offers over fifty thousand a session."

"Tell them I'm booked until June." I wasn't willing to give up my last year at home, and things would be worse for me in a city. Around here a barn fire got more press than fashion. Once the hype from the billboard quieted, people would move on. At least, I hoped they would.

"Don't you have a winter break?" Blair asked.

"Yeah, two weeks in December, but..."

"Fine, I'll book you between Christmas and New Year's. At least give me a week."

"I have to ask my dad," I protested.

Blair would not be dissuaded. "I'll book two first-class tickets. Make sure he understands the kind of money you will be making. In the meantime, *do not* take any jobs behind my back. Are we clear?"

"Perfectly." I wandered into Dad's room, which faced the street.

"I'll get you an apartment in Switzerland. You may need it if they find you."

"If who finds me?"

"The paparazzi. Then your days as a normal high school student are over."

I peeked between the slats in the blinds. "You make it sound like I'm dodging a killer."

"Remember Princess Di, sweetheart. I'm out to protect you at all costs." She hung up.

I stabbed the end button, irritated and more scared than I wanted to admit. Much as Blair wanted to protect me, she was also out to make a fortune off me. That fame which promised misery for me was what her business thrived on.

Dad took Marty's advice and stayed home from work the next day, though he was probably up early making phone calls. By nine when I wandered downstairs only half awake, he was showered, shaved, sipping coffee and reading the sports page. On this trait we differed greatly. Dad was a morning person. I was not.

"Hot water on the stove," he said as I passed.

After mixing a cup of hot chocolate, I collapsed into a chair at the bar. "Are they gone?"

"Nope." He closed the paper and moved into the kitchen, where he began frying bacon and eggs.

I dropped bread into the toaster. "Did Marty ticket them?"

"Yep, but they aren't leaving."

"Great." I wondered why I bothered getting out of bed. I was a prisoner in my own home.

With the bacon browned and the eggs sunny-side up, Dad set a plate in front of me. "I guess I never gave you a chance to explain the billboard."

I shrugged. "Doesn't matter now."

"I'd still like to hear it." The body shop took only a day to repair the headlights and grill of Dad's truck. With his moving office back in service, he returned to the level-headed, diplomatic father I was used to.

"I was wearing a bikini under the wig, but where it showed, they Photoshopped it out. That's not my cleavage."

He coughed on a piece of toast. "Too much information."

"Did your crew see it?" It made me sad that all the guys who respected him probably thought I was a total sleaze.

"I'm pretty sure they all drove down Main Street this week, but none of them said a word to me."

I laughed, my mouth full. "If they value their lives or their jobs."

After breakfast Dad balanced his books and made another hundred phone calls. I went upstairs and soaked in a hot bath. The cameras robbed me of the emotional high I felt after hanging out with Erik. I closed my eyes and tried to hear his voice in my head.

My fingers turned into white prunes, but the water was still warm, so I stayed there rewalking the trail, repeating my questions until I was nearly dozing with my head against the side of the tub.

"Psyche." Dad rapped on the door and startled me from my daydreams. "The phone is for you. It's a boy." His voice sounded strained by that last part. "He says his name is Erik."

I splashed out of the tub, scrambled to get myself covered in a towel and nearly knocked down the door trying to get the lock to release. Opening the door a mere three inches, I held out my hand palm up.

"I could have him call you back," Dad offered.

"No!" I waved my hand frantically. "Just give me the phone."

When he set the receiver in my hand, I pulled it into the bathroom and slammed the door. I sounded out of breath as I said, "Hello?"

The reply was that chesty chuckle that drove me wild. "What exactly were you doing?"

There's no way I would admit I was naked in the bathroom dripping wet. It wasn't a mental picture I wanted to encourage. "How did you get my phone number?"

"It's in the phonebook. Right next to your street address."

"You have a phone." I didn't mean to say it aloud. I was trying to figure out how normal he was while also trying to dress. Multitasking generally wasn't difficult, but my mind went a little haywire at the sound of his voice.

"I'm not a complete moron. I can function in your world as well as you can."

I apologized, thoroughly embarrassed. "I didn't mean to insult you."

"It takes more than that to insult me," he replied. "I'd like to see you today."

I peeked out the window at the unwanted vans on the north end of the street. "I'm kind of trapped at home." I began toweling off my hair, keeping the phone balanced on my shoulder.

"Tonight," he replied unmoved.

"I don't think I can sneak out."

"Why would you need to?" He hung up before I could answer.

I dressed in a rush and dried my hair. Then I paused in front of the mirror wearing a pair of cargos I bought last year for school. At the sight of them Savannah had rolled her eyes. "Could you find anything less flattering?" she'd said.

I dug through the dresser, but it was all pretty much the same. Jeans, cargos and more jeans. The second drawer held T-shirts and hooded sweatshirts. All of them were baggy, and most looked worn. At the bottom was a shirt with a wrap bodice and three-quarter sleeves that Grandma Dee had sent me. I pulled it on over a tank. That was as good as it would get.

Hours passed. Dad didn't want to leave me home alone, so he had his crew foreman bring a stack of DVDs to our house. Dad stretched out on the couch with a bowl of popcorn and started the first movie. I slumped on the loveseat growing depressed. How was I supposed to see Erik tonight? He couldn't ring the doorbell and come inside. He couldn't drive up on the motorcycle then turn invisible as soon as he stepped in the doorway.

It was silly to be miserable over an invisible guy from an unknown world. I needed to get a grip—possibly some antipsychotic meds.

No sooner had I decided he wasn't coming, than I felt a hand rest on my shoulder. I jumped and let out a squeal.

Dad furrowed his brow at me. The movie had barely started. No one had died yet.

"I'm not in the mood for movies."

"Plenty of left-overs in the fridge if you're hungry," Dad said.

Erik squeezed my arm.

"Starving." In the kitchen I dished a double helping of enchiladas and set them in the microwave. Returning the pan to the fridge, I asked, "Anything else look good?" An apple climbed off the shelf and into my hands. I poured a large glass of milk and grabbed a bag of pretzels from the cupboard. Then I stood at the bar with all that food and wondered aloud, "How am I supposed to carry all this to my room?"

Inexplicably the apple and the bag of pretzels disappeared. I offered forks to the air and they disappeared, too.

Upstairs with the door closed I could still hear the soundtrack of the movie playing. We could talk without being heard. The apples, pretzels and forks reappeared in mid-air and settled onto the dresser.

"Explain the disappearing fruit," I said.

"I put it in my shirt."

"Your shirt is invisible. It shouldn't hide a perfectly visible apple."

"No, that is the second rule of veiling. Items covered in a veiled substance become veiled." He opened the bag of pretzels and drew one out. It seemed to float in the air. "Now I'll close it in my hand." The pretzel vanished and reappeared a moment later.

"Does the same rule apply to food you put in your mouth? Because I don't want to see stuff getting chewed up and swallowed."

"Same rule applies." The pretzel disappeared with a crunch. "Those enchiladas smell really good."

I put a fork on the plate and offered it in his general direction. "Help yourself. They're hot." I watched as the fork took off a chunk of cheesy tortilla and chicken, lifted into midair and the food disappeared. He ate three more bites before he gasped. The fork clanked onto the plate. The glass of milk rose into the air and was completely drained in a matter of seconds. "I warned you," I said.

He whistled quietly. "I thought you meant temperature. Are you hungry? Do you mind if I finish these?"

There was a whirlpool in my belly, but it had nothing to do with food. "You'll need more milk," I answered.

In the kitchen I filled the glass to the top and had to walk carefully not to spill. My thoughts were already upstairs, where the plate of enchiladas was empty when I returned. "I suppose you need this?" I held the glass of milk in front of me and watched as it was lifted from my hand.

"Thank you."

"My dad is an amazing cook."

"Your dad?" he asked when the milk was gone.

"I suppose I should have been paying attention all these years, but mostly I've been enjoying it." After he set the glass down, I lost track of him until he spoke again.

"You don't have a mom." He was somewhere near the dresser, probably looking at the photographs stuck with poster gum on the outer edges of the mirror.

"She left when I was four."

"I'm sorry," he said with surprising sincerity.

"I see her two weeks a year. That's enough."

"My mother didn't raise me either, but she meddles in my life plenty." There was a hard edge in his voice, but he quickly recovered. "So, I'm curious. You modeled all summer, and you kept nothing?" He was closer now, but I couldn't tell where.

I wondered if he knew that models kept a copy of their portfolios in case a client wanted to see it. There was another, larger portfolio in Blair's office, but since I worked overseas, I needed my own. "They're in a box at the top of my closet."

"May I?"

I hesitated. Granted, a portfolio was made to be seen, but outside the industry, no one had ever looked at my tear sheets—not even my dad. There was something deeply vain about photos that showcased your looks without your memories.

The closet doors opened and clothes shifted to the side. Two boxes came down from the shelf. The first held childhood mementos, and after lifting the lid, Erik set it back in its place. The box of photos and postcards hovered in front of the closet as he let out a quiet exclamation. "What is this?" One of the dresses I brought home from Europe appeared from behind my other clothes.

"An irrational purchase."

"It's a Valentino."

"I wore it on the runway." That didn't explain why it was hanging in my closet, but I didn't feel like laying down my pathetic Homecoming history.

He set it back in its place and moved my other clothes to cover it again. "I'll bet it got rave reviews." His weight jostled the bed as he sat next to me, and the box holding my secret life emptied onto the comforter. He opened the manila envelope and slid out the most recent photos. Four were fashion ads for various labels. One was a close-up advertising the sunglasses that were pushed back in my hair, and one was a black and white of Holden and I. "Who's the guy?"

I couldn't decipher the tone. Was it merely curious or was there something more? "His name is Holden Valentine. He used to be my Apollo."

"Your *what?*" There was inexplicable contempt in his voice.

"You know, like my standard of beauty. Apollo was supposed to be the most beautiful of the Greek gods."

"Supposedly."

"You couldn't be jealous?"

"I'm not jealous of Apollo." His voice was still tight.

"I meant Holden. How could you be jealous of Apollo? He's a myth."

"Right." The photo of Holden and I rose in the air, like he held it at arms length. "The two of you look very comfortable together."

I snorted. "Fiction is always convincing."

"You hated it."

I shrugged.

"You cringe every time a guy touches you."

There was no sense denying it; Erik had already seen proof. I'd cringed under his hand half a dozen times, mostly out of surprise. It was a reflex, an unconscious defense I developed over the years. The only exception was my dad, and he rarely touched me anymore.

He slid the photos back into the envelope and tucked them in the box. "It's the eyes that frighten you."

I shot a surprised glance in the direction of his voice. I never told him that.

"How do you do that? You looked right at me."

"I can see you," I lied.

"*What?*"

I laughed. Seriously, he sounded panicked.

He let out his breath audibly and chuckled. He took the box and stowed it in its hiding place. A moment later the bed shifted, but I didn't know where he'd gone until the pillow slouched under his invisible head. "You have questions?"

"Many." I grabbed another pillow and stretched out next to him in the opposite direction, so I was looking at the empty pillow. "You said you live longer, and you made it seem like time is different for you."

"Not different entirely. The days are the same length. Time passes in my world at the same rate as it does here, but because we live so much longer months and days seem much shorter. We measure the phases of the moon like you would measure hours."

"When I was little, summer seemed to last forever, but now it's three short months that pass in a blur."

"You've lived longer, so the time in each week seems shorter." Relaxed and quiet, his voice had an irresistible gentleness.

"How old are you?"

"I'm nearly eighteen."

He wasn't like any seventeen-year-old I knew. I wondered if he was lying. "In my time?"

"It would be like you measuring your life in minutes."

"Give me a rough estimate," I said, not hiding my irritation.

"Instead of days, we measure time in seasons. Four seasons is an annum. A hundred annum makes an age. My age is seventeen."

"You're a hundred and seventy years old?" I asked.

"You are in serious need of a math tutor," he replied.

I felt my face flush. A hundred years was an age. "You're seventeen *hundred* years old!"

"We are the same age, essentially."

We were not even close to the same age. He had lived over a thousand years, and I couldn't do simple math in his company. He probably thought I was a complete imbecile. "Except for your long white beard and wrinkly skin."

"I'm in my youth," he said defensively. "Now I'm going to touch you." He took my hand, turned it over and drew my knuckles across his chin, which was perfectly smooth. "No beard." Then he moved my hand up his cheek. "And no wrinkles." He released my hand and moved away.

My hand felt warm from his touch. I struggled to find my voice. "Why do you live so long?"

"We're a superior race." He nudged me playfully with his foot. "And, there's a fruit in our world that keeps us from aging. Our mythology says it's the fruit from the tree of life, but who knows for certain?"

"From the Garden of Eden?" It seemed strange that he'd heard of the Garden of Eden. I guess I expected every world to have its own beliefs that didn't cross into one another, much like primitive cultures had all worshiped different gods before being conquered by powerful, god-wielding empires.

"The same."

"So, you believe in God?"

"Don't you?"

"Well, yeah." We went to church most of the time and celebrated Christmas. "Do your people die?"

"Eventually."

I considered the vast experience and knowledge that an old person in his society could hold. Nearly ten thousand years of history in a single mind, experienced firsthand. It was beyond comprehension. "What else is different about your world?"

"Children are uncommon. My mother has been married for ages, and I am her only child. Many couples never conceive. The only exception is… well, never mind."

"No, tell me. What's the exception?" I grabbed a handful of pretzels and popped one into my mouth.

"A man of my world and a woman of yours would produce a child."

"You mean, could."

"No, would. Guaranteed."

I paused with a half-chewed pretzel on my tongue. "I seriously hope that's not why you're here." All my defenses shot up. Would Dad hear me if I screamed?

"Absolutely not!" he exclaimed. "Seducing a mortal is illegal. I would lose everything." He sounded indignant.

"Really?" I asked, relaxing a little. "It's against the law?"

"Yes, and it carries grave consequences. In the past there were problems. Men of my world seduced mortal women using the veiling power and their …*charm.*" He chose the word carefully, like he wanted to say something else, but decided against it. "The council—that's the governing body—outlawed the practice and affixed severe penalties."

"Not that it would happen, but I'm curious. If getting involved with me would bring disaster, why are you here?"

He did not answer for a moment. "I should go. It is getting late." This simple evasion pacified me. He was safer for me than any man on earth. Maybe he didn't know why he was here. Maybe he was instinctively drawn to me, like I instinctively trusted him.

I hauled myself up and pulled on my shoes so I could step onto the back deck for some fresh air and conveniently leave the door open. It was time to wake up and face reality. My moments with him were brief and private. No one could know. They would think I was crazy.

Erik seemed to read my expression. "I'll be back to comfort you soon."

"At the next full moon?" I said sarcastically.

"The next full moon is only eight days away." He said it sadly, like he was dreading it. Then he brushed my face with his finger-tips. "You didn't flinch."

I shrugged and looked at the carpet. "Maybe I'm getting used to you."

Outside he squeezed my hand and came very near. "Good night, lovely Soul," he whispered.

I was surprised he knew the true meaning of my name. "Most people think the psyche is the mind—Freud and all."

"I know better." He touched my cheek again and was gone.

# CHAPTER 6

E ven though I hid at home, my story was all over the news. Every Billings network carried a story about me. They dug up my school mug shots and a handful of print ads I shot over the summer. It was Labor Day weekend, however, and the crews outside my house seemed reluctant to spend the holiday in their cars. By Sunday afternoon we saw them milling around talking to one another. Soon afterward they left.

Dad took advantage of their absence and cleared a mess of boxes and tools from the garage to make room for my car. Nothing could keep him away from work for more than a few days, and he didn't want them to know when I was home alone.

I enjoyed a single day of peace and quiet, unmolested by fame, before returning to school on Tuesday. I checked the front sidewalk three times to make sure I wasn't going to be ambushed. I opened the garage door and started the engine. An early frost had fallen overnight, and for one crisp morning I had no windows to scrape. I supposed this was why some people actually used their garages.

Before putting the car in reverse, I double-checked my backpack and realized I forgot my Calculus book. I dashed upstairs to retrieve it. When I slid back into the driver's seat, a patch of fog appeared on the windshield like a spot from someone's breath. An invisible finger drew one curved side and then the other to form a heart.

"Erik," I whispered.

"Did you miss me?" he asked from the passenger seat.

The answer ran hot up my cheeks. "Not really."

"Liar." He brushed my cheek with his fingertip, which was cold from the windshield.

I hesitated before pulling out of the driveway. "Are you coming with me to school?"

"Yes."

The day would be entirely wasted. How could I concentrate when he was near? Plus, he'd already wreaked havoc on my Chemistry class. Who knew what kind of mischief he would concoct given an entire day? "Just don't get me in trouble."

The street was clear. Every car on the block belonged to one of my neighbors.

"How would I do that?" he asked innocently.

"How do you make them fall in love?"

He laughed. "Not love exactly."

"Why do they sneeze?"

"It's dust," he said lightly.

I snorted, visions of Peter Pan in my mind. "Fairy dust?"

"I'm not a fairy!" His resentment made me laugh aloud.

"C'mon, Tinkerbell, you don't have to be ashamed."

"Oh, I'm going to get you expelled today," he threatened.

I knew this threat was real. "Don't you dare!"

"I will just for spite." He leaned closer, and my skin grew hot. I blinked, trying to focus on the road. He pulled away with a chuckle.

"If you get me expelled, I'll have to move to Switzerland and return to my wayward career."

"Then I'll just get you kicked out for awhile. What do they call that?" Before I could reply, he answered his own question. "Suspended."

As we approached the school parking lot, Erik exclaimed, "Turn around!"

The sidewalks around the school were packed with people. Some carried picket signs that said, "We love you, Venus!" Along a side street were seven news vans, all clearly marked and surrounded by groups of people. They were interviewing students, taking shots of the high school and waiting for their story. Savannah stood in front of one camera with a microphone held to her lips. I should have known.

I braked and surveyed the scene. It was crazy. How could they all be here to see me? On the sidewalk someone shouted and pointed at my car. A group of guys jumped off the sidewalk oblivious to traffic. I swerved into the left lane and stomped on the gas. In the rearview mirror, I saw a van pull out and follow. It was gaining fast.

"What should I do?" They all knew where I lived, and Dad wasn't home. There aren't a lot of places to hide in a small town.

"Go south into the mountains," Erik said. "The portal is there. I'll get you out of here."

I turned toward the freeway, which would circle me back to downtown. I ran the light at the on-ramp and zipped in front of an eighteen-wheeler. Its horn roared at my taillights. Cursing the stick shift in the Subaru, I revved the engine high in fourth and hit ninety shifting into overdrive.

"If we were on my bike, they wouldn't have a chance of catching us."

"And we wouldn't have four-wheel drive." I took the first access into the mountains. Three vans crowded my rearview mirror. I dug through my purse while trying to keep one eye on the road. My phone had settled at the very bottom. When I tossed it into the passenger seat, it disappeared into Erik's hands. "Call my dad."

"Why?"

"If we dump my car in the woods, those reporters are going to find it. They'll tell the whole world I'm missing."

"I can hide the car. They won't find it."

"He still needs to know where I am. We'll run out of service as soon as we hit the forest."

The phone lifted into the air, and the phonebook came onto the screen, the curser scrolling down. Using the speed dial, Erik sent the call and handed me the phone.

"Psyche?" Dad answered.

I replied in a rush, "The school was crawling with reporters this morning. I have three vans tailing me. I'm headed into the mountains. Erik's family has a place up there, where I can hide for awhile."

"Erik?" He sounded incredulous. He said something more, but the service cut out.

"I'll call you later." The call was gone before I finished.

"Pull over."

"They're less than a quarter of a mile behind us."

"I know where I'm going. Let me drive."

"You're invisible!" That's all I needed—the news showing footage of my car magically driving itself.

"This isn't the interstate. Get out of the driver's seat!" Erik demanded.

"Fine, take the wheel." Without braking, I unbuckled my seat-belt and climbed into the back. The car slowed briefly, then down-shifted, revved high and sped forward throwing gravel. He could drive a stick. I guess he wasn't lying when he said he could function in my world as well as I could.

We took another road that wound up the mountain for three miles. It was a rutty, dirt path that would only allow one car at a time. Most likely the vans didn't see where we turned off, but if they found this road, we were boxed in. I watched out the back window, but I couldn't see anything beyond the dust in our wake. Erik turned through a clearing, where the dirt was worn in a single tire tread.

The trail ended at an outcropping of rock cliffs overlooking a hundred-foot gulley. On the other side was a steep face of forbid-ding rock that climbed straight up. "We're trapped," I said.

"Out you go," was his reply and the door opened. "Climb up on that rock."

It was too close to the edge. I balked. "I'm afraid of heights."

"This is going to be difficult." He took hold of my hand. "I promise you won't get hurt."

I climbed onto the rock, unable to look down and irrationally terrified I would fall to my death.

"Now follow me." He pulled hard toward the drop-off.

"NO!" Momentum flung me forward. My foot hit the air beyond the rock and stopped. "How is this possible?"

"There's a bridge here. It's veiled. It leads to that cave on the other side. The portal is in there."

"Once we go through the portal, where do we go?"

"You will go to my home."

I walked two steps and looked down to see nothing beyond my feet except far-away rocks and tree tops. My stomach twirled. "I can't do it."

"Close your eyes and hold onto the railing." He put my other hand onto the invisible, metal railing. With it and Erik's hand, I crossed the bridge and descended into the darkness of the cave. "Well, you're here. Just walk straight ahead through the wall."

"The *stone* wall?"

"The portal is open." He sounded irritated. "I can see the woods on the other side."

"Aren't you coming with me?"

"It's morning, and I can't veil myself in my world."

"Then don't." All the secrets and the hiding could end right here.

"I'm not ready for you to see me."

"But you see me. It isn't fair," I protested.

Erik whispered so softly, I had to lean closer to hear him. "Love looks not with the eyes, but with the mind..." He ruffled my hair. "This is all I want. Don't ask to see me, and I'll give you every desire of your heart."

"I'll never see you?" It cut deeper than I wanted to admit. Too many hours I'd lain awake trying to imagine what face belonged to that intriguing voice.

"When I'm ready."

I didn't know which was worse: not seeing him or being exiled into his world without him. "I'll just go back. I'll face the reporters. It is me on that billboard. I'll just deal with it."

"It wouldn't be that simple, and you know it. You're safe in my world." When I shook my head in refusal, he promised to join me at dark.

"I don't know anything about your world. I won't be able to find your house."

He chuckled. "It's easy to find, and you won't be alone. If you promise not to turn around, I'll take you through the portal."

"I won't look at you," I promised, but it was torture.

He stood behind me and took hold of my shoulders, then pressed me forward. The wall was nothing more than air, and we emerged at the edge of a forest. The trees around us had enormous trunks comparable only to ancient redwoods in protected forests. The forest opened onto a valley in full bloom with flowers I didn't recognize. Their sweet fragrance mingled with the wood and moss. In my world, autumn pressed into the valleys. Here it felt like summer, alive and pulsating in glorious color. To my right was the familiar bullet bike with a black helmet resting on the seat.

"How'd you get to my house this morning?"

"I caught a ride," he answered evasively. "My home is straight ahead over the next rise." He pointed, and I forgot to listen to the rest. He wasn't wearing a jacket.

My fingers shook as I touched his arm. Its fair skin was tanned golden. The band on his index finger glistened in the sunlight. He brought his hand down and let me examine it. Around the band was an inscription in hieroglyphics. Erik's smooth, narrow fingers were nothing like my dad's rough, wide hands. I traced each of his fingers with mine.

He breathed huskily and pulled his hand away. "As I was saying, Pixis will take you there."

"Who's Pixis?"

Erik dropped a whistle into my hand. It was hand-whittled from a narrow branch. The sound of it brought a whinnied reply and a flap of wings. Pixis landed a few yards away and came toward us.

"A Pegasus? That's impossible."

"Winged horse," he corrected. "Pegasus was a single creature. Your world used to have them, too. But like everything that is rare and beautiful, they were hunted and destroyed. We used to have your ordinary horses here, but no one breeds them anymore. Winged horses are as common in my world as cars in yours." Erik put out his hand for the horse to nuzzle. "Hello, Friend. This is Psyche. Please take her home."

He moved his hand lightly over my shoulder. "These horses are very intelligent. It's proper to introduce yourself. Say hello, Psyche."

"Hello, Pixis," I replied awkwardly. Pixis put his head down like he was bowing.

Erik nudged me forward. "All that I have is yours. I'll be back when the sun goes down." Behind me, he slipped through the portal.

My fear of heights somehow did not equate to a fear of flying. The solidity of Pixis's body under me, the majesty of his enormous wings, and the rush of air in my face as we soared over the valley replaced all my fear with awe.

A glistening river wove its way through newly harvested fields to dump its wealth into the expanse beyond—the sea. The distinct odor of salt and fish floated on the air long before I could see the water. I leaned over, my fingers wound tight in Pixis's mane, and said, "Will you show me the sea?"

He tilted the tips of his wings and veered in a sweeping curve that ended over the beach. Waves crashed against a reef a hundred yards off shore, but the beach was calm with sudsy fingers rolling onto the sand. It was here, soaring over the beach, that I first glimpsed a structure in the distance. "What's that on the mountainside?" I asked the intelligent, but mute beast.

Pixis whinnied and took two deep thrusts with his wings. We flew toward a marble palace perched on the cliff. In front the palace overhung the cliff supported by angular pillars anchored in the rock. It seemed to be a single, expansive room and covered balcony sitting in the air. This room faced the valley, and open on the balcony were double doors and windows with heavy wooden shutters but no glass shimmering in the sun.

In back the palace followed the natural plateau of the mountain. Beyond its massive rooflines were extensive gardens and orchards. Tiny horizontal lines made a winding path from the palace to the valley below, and as we drew near, I saw that they were hundreds of marble stairs.

In a courtyard with perfectly groomed flowerbeds, Pixis landed and folded his wings. He crossed to a fountain, dipped his head and drank. At the center of the fountain was a marble statue of a woman with flowing hair. Her left arm reached to the east, while her right arm cradled a chubby infant. The marble was carved into delicate folds on her dress, and a pendant around her neck showed the detail of cut gems and a crest.

I slid from the horse's back and touched one of the child's hands, so realistic I half expected it to close around my finger. "It looks like Cupid, minus the wings," I observed.

Pixis snorted and made waves in the fountain's basin. He turned abruptly and galloped a few steps before launching himself into the air.

"Hey, where are you going?" I called after him, but he disappeared over the roof.

I moved toward the enormous house. "Hello? Anyone here?" When no one answered, I ventured into the open-air foyer. My steps echoed on the stone floor. "You've got to be joking," I said aloud. "*This* is Erik's house?"

Still hesitant, I moved through the foyer into the massive hall, where the high ceiling was held by marble pillars. I found a ballroom, a dining room with a table to seat fifty and an enormous service kitchen. Though elegant with shimmering white stone and dark-wood furniture, the palace was oddly cold in a climate so warm. My footsteps and whispers echoed off the walls. It felt like a museum, so different from the rugged comfort of my dad's house.

I spent the whole morning exploring and still didn't see the entire palace. A hallway behind the stairs housed over a dozen doors. I stopped at one and turned the knob. Inside was a large bedroom with a poster bed and matching armoire, both masterfully carved.

The walls of the bedroom were frescoed with scenes of a village in summer. The houses lining the street were small with tidy yards and low fences. The women in the fresco wore drape gowns reminiscent of the ancient Greeks. The men were similarly dressed in half-robes. Over their shoulders they wore colored sashes belted at the waist. Their skin was golden. Most had light brown or blond hair.

Watching the scene from a tree perch was a child about five years old. His gaze held a mixture of wonder and intelligent study. The painter illustrated the child's profile with a small nose, smooth golden-brown hair and a slight curve of the lips, not quite a smile. He was larger than the other people, closer in the perspective of the painting and clearly the focal point. This one fresco was as magnificent as any work of art I had seen in Rome or Florence, and it was innocently hidden in a bedroom off the dim back hall.

I wandered out and found other bedrooms, all furnished the same with magnificently frescoed walls.

The last door in the hallway was a vast storage room. Oil paintings draped in canvas lined one entire wall. I pulled back a single drape to reveal a dozen paintings, all framed. I lifted one from the row. It was an ocean scene. The one behind it was a still life of a kitchen window with herbs growing in the background. I continued down the rows. The paintings grew more accomplished with each row.

The last row included a battle scene with a fierce figure at the center. His flowing golden hair contrasted sharply with his severe expression. At the soldier's feet were half a dozen bodies, and his raised sword glowed red. The figures weren't dressed like the ones in the frescoes. These wore tattered, dark pants and loose shirts. They were from my world.

In the lower right corner of the painting was the artist's signature. It was not a name but an ornate E. I sifted through the stacks, pulling paintings randomly: a pastoral, a winged-horse in flight, a ship on a stormy sea, more still lives, several portraits. All had the same signature—the decorative E.

"Erik?" I wondered.

On the other side of the room various sculptures and busts cluttered shelves along the wall. One sculpture was of a woman's hands. Each knuckle and vein was represented in perfect detail, as if the hands had been cast and the statue molded from the forms. When I lifted it from the shelf, I was sure it was marble. It had been carved. Under the base was the same ornate E. I carefully set the statue back on the shelf and continued through the room. I found stacks of hand-written musical compositions, discarded instruments, whittlings in wood, dozens of bows with quivers of arrows, and a sword with a handle inlaid with gems. It was enough stuff to stock a museum, and everything was marked with that single initial.

By the time I wandered from the storage room, my stomach was grumbling. I guessed it was afternoon, but I wasn't wearing a watch, and there was not a single clock in the house. Adjacent to the service kitchen I found a smaller kitchen which contained brick ovens, shelves of pottery and a work island. Herbs grew in the window boxes. Rolled strips of cinnamon bark were hung to dry on one wall, and a door at the back of the kitchen opened into the orchard. The trees were laden with citrus, and that sweet scent mixed with the spice in the kitchen. Erik carried the scent of this place with him when he came to my world.

I ate bread and cheese, which I found in a pantry. I was about to venture into the orchard for oranges but I heard voices, and I hid in the doorway.

There were seven boys ages about ten to nineteen. The older boys pulled wooden crates along at their feet, then hoisted the younger ones into the branches of the trees. The smaller boys picked the fruit and rolled it down a heavy sheet of fabric into the crates below. They were speaking a strange language and laughing as they worked their way up the row toward me. They all had golden skin and flawless features.

The most handsome among them was about fifteen with sandy hair and bright blue eyes. As I leaned on the window sill to get a better look at him, he glanced up and saw me. Caught, I jerked out of sight. When I ventured another peek at the window, he was no longer in the orchard, but standing right outside, setting oranges on the window sill.

My cheeks felt hot. I kept my back to the wall so he couldn't see me and waited until he was gone before I grabbed one of the oranges from the ledge. Now I moved more carefully through the palace in case there were maids lurking in the vast rooms.

Upstairs I found where Erik actually lived. There were six large rooms on the upper level. One was a grand living area with the coolest piece of furniture I'd ever seen. It was as long as a couch, but stretched forward like a chaise lounge. Pillowed on the back and sides, it became a combination between a huge comfortable chair and a bed. I couldn't help throwing myself down on its inviting cushions. Next to the couch were high-backed chairs and a table stacked with books. I pulled a stack of books onto my lap and inspected the titles. One was a modern suspense novel—a New York Times bestseller. Another was a college mythology textbook. The other three were printed in a script I couldn't read. I assumed it was the written language of Erik's world. If I thought the library down the hall was just for decoration, I now knew otherwise. In addition to being an accomplished artist, Erik was well read in both our worlds.

Not knowing what else to do, I opened the novel, the obvious choice over textbook mythology, but somewhere in the third chapter I fell asleep.

"Psyche?"

At the sound of his voice, I sat up with a start. It was dark, and he was silhouetted in the doorway. I had slept for hours.

He joined me on the couch, stretched out his long legs beside mine and shed his leather jacket. Even in the dark, I could tell he was wearing jeans and a T-shirt, which was oddly comforting after a day in a strange world.

"This is some house," I said.

"Cozy, isn't it?" he replied.

"You forgot to mention that you were a prince."

"I'm not. Why are you sitting here with the windows closed?"

"They're open," I said and pointed to the two small windows at the end of the room.

He chuckled. "You've missed the best thing about this room, and the entire reason for this couch sitting here." He stood and walked the length of the room, drawing all the floor-to-ceiling curtains to one side. It was too dark to see what lay behind them until he opened the latches and they swung outward, revealing that the far wall was not a wall at all, but three sets of massive double doors. "The view."

From the couch I could see the waves crashing on the reef. The white caps glowed in the moonlight. Most surprising was how forcefully the sound traveled into the room without the thick doors. If I closed my eyes, it sounded like I was standing on the beach with the waves rushing at my feet.

Erik settled beside me with a sigh. "There's something hypnotic about watching the waves roll in." He picked up the book I left open beside me. "Did you go to the beach today?"

"No."

"Tour the kingdom?"

I didn't answer.

His voice grew irritated. "You didn't go to the village or explore the valley?"

His anger stole my voice, and I whispered, "No."

"You just stayed in the house alone all day?"

"I didn't know if you wanted anyone to see me," I answered, recovering myself.

"Don't expect me to believe that," he said sharply. "The truth is *you* were afraid to be seen." He tossed the book onto the table and leaned back on his elbows. "What could possibly have held your interest all day?"

"There was one peculiar storage room downstairs full of paintings..."

He groaned. "Of all the places to snoop, you chose that room."

"You're an amazing artist."

"I am not!" he scoffed. "Those are stored behind closed doors for a reason."

"I've been through the Louvre and the cathedrals of Italy. Don't tell me I don't know a masterpiece when I see one."

"A masterpiece in your world maybe. Consider this. The greatest painters of your world lived sixty or seventy years? If they began painting in their childhood, they would paint fifty or sixty years at the most, right?"

"I guess so."

"And you attend school for twelve years?"

"Thirteen," I corrected, "if you count kindergarten."

"Thirteen years, plus four or five years for a bachelor's degree. Add another two to eight for advanced degrees and you would attend school for twenty-six years. You'd be highly educated as far as your society was concerned."

"Yeah," I answered, thinking that twenty-six years sounded like an unbearably long time, and that maybe I'd just stick to high school and a bachelor's.

"Here we are educated from age five to age fifteen. Fifteen is the legal age to buy property, marry and choose a profession."

"A thousand years?" That was a lot of homework. "But why? If you grow up in a single age and then live forever..."

"No, I thought I explained this to you. It takes a child five hundred annum to grow to the stature of your five-year-olds. To us, your world lives at the speed of light."

I thought of the baby in the fountain. "You were in diapers for a *very* long time."

He held up his wrist and pressed a button to light his watch. "Speaking of time, I should take you to the portal. It's getting late, in your world, that is."

"And here?"

"Here time doesn't matter."

He led me through the hallway to the large door at the end. "What's in here?"

"This is my room."

The dark recesses of the room spread before us on all sides. "It looks big." I balked at the doorway.

"We're just passing through." He tugged on my hand with a chuckle. Across the room stood another open set of wooden doors, which revealed the balcony I'd seen overhanging the cliff.

"Way out of my comfort zone now," I said.

"That fear of heights is inconvenient. Stand here against the wall. There's no railing and we're hundreds of feet above the valley floor."

"That's kind of stupid." I clutched the wall, but there was no good hand-hold on the slick stone. "Why would you have a balcony with no railing hundreds of feet over a cliff?"

In reply Erik blew his wooden whistle, and a shimmer of white flew through the night. Pixis landed with a rush of wind and clatter of hooves on the balcony. "You first." Erik offered me his hand, but I grabbed a fistful of Pixis's mane and swung my leg over without help. "The advantages of being tall," he mused as he pulled himself up behind me. Erik gripped Pixis's mane with both hands and squeezed me between his arms. "This is the fun part. Hold on."

I was already holding onto Pixis's mane, but I was completely unprepared when he dove off the balcony. I screamed, my entire body tightening in terror, until the horse unfurled the fan of his wings and caught us with a mighty whip of air.

Erik squeezed me tighter. "I've got you. Don't worry." He was holding on as much with his legs as with his hands. His knees pressed against mine to keep me balanced on the animal's back. "Please take us to the portal, Pixis."

We soared over the valley, but all that showed below was the river sparkling in the moonlight and an occasional lit window. The stars shimmered so close I imagined I could catch one in my hand. At the edge of the woods we landed, and Erik took my hand.

He went with me through the portal and showed me where he'd stashed my Subaru. He veiled himself until we were inside the car and he'd put out the dome light, then he appeared like a shadow beside me. Halfway down the mountain my cell phone regained service, and I pulled over to call home.

Dad picked up on the first ring. "Psyche, are you all right?"

"I'm fine, Dad. Is it safe to come home?" I asked.

His voice grew angry. "No! There are hundreds of people on the street. They've been chanting, 'We want Venus.' Don't come anywhere near this house."

"Okay, I..."

He interrupted, "You should stay with Savannah tonight."

Erik caught my arm and shook his head.

"Savannah would probably march me into the street so she could be on camera," I replied. "No one will find me here in the mountains. There are extra bedrooms at Erik's house."

Dad let out his breath slowly. In my mind I saw the worried lines across his forehead deepen.

"Dad," I said softly. "You can trust me."

"Are you sure his parents won't mind?"

Erik snorted.

"His parents won't mind at all."

After telling me he would call the school and pick up my homework, my dad lingered over good-bye and finally let me go. I turned to Erik. "Looks like you're stuck with me for awhile."

"Sheer torture, but I think I'll survive.

# CHAPTER 7

"There's so much I want to know about you."

"Besides what I look like?" He stretched himself over the couch. His legs reached to the end while his arms spanned the breadth of it. Of all the things I liked about Erik, this was the oddest: he made me feel small. For a girl who is five foot ten, that was no small feat. Erik was taller with thick arms. His hands could span my waist, although he said his housekeeper would make it her mission to put some meat on me.

"Have you always lived here alone? Why didn't your mother raise you? And what's that crazy dust you go spreading all over?"

He nudged me lightly. "Take a breath. We have all night."

"You're being evasive." I folded my arms. "Why bring me here if you don't want me to know anything about you?"

"I want you to know everything about me." He leaned closer and whispered, "I just don't want you to hyperventilate."

"Then stop touching me."

With a chuckle he leaned back. Since I hung up the phone with my dad, the atmosphere between Erik and I changed. We were no longer on a deadline stealing quiet moments to get to know each other. The whole night stretched before us. No parents, no curfew. It was liberating and showed mostly in Erik's tone. His voice was light and casual, obviously more at ease.

"We'll start with the dust," he suggested. "My mother discovered it." His voice floated softly through the darkness. I leaned closer to hear, and he drew me under his arm. His touch still jolted me and, caught in the crossroads between elation and terror, I shivered, but Erik didn't let go. "You're safe with me," he whispered.

My mind believed him, but my body was slow to forfeit its deep-seated defenses. I let my head rest on his shoulder, and Erik breathed into my hair. "The dust," I prodded.

He lifted his head. "Near the caves on the other side of the mountain, my mother collected a small flower, which she intended to transplant at home. When she unwrapped the plant and shook out her skirt, her maid swooned at the sight of the gardener. The maid was all of seventeen, and he was nearly three times her senior. My mother believed the flower had done it, so she potted it, delighted by the prospect of inducing love with this simple potion."

"To make mischief, like you?"

"No, she wanted it for herself. Her marriage was arranged by my grandfather, and while her husband is devoted and kind, he is not at all handsome. She was fond of him but completely indifferent to him physically. She was willing to resort to any sort of witchcraft if she could make that missing attraction bloom in herself. But the flower did not make her love him. She tasted the pedals, inhaled the fragrance, rubbed the plant on her skin to no avail.

"She decided to get rid of it. In the garden, she pulled the plant from its pot and shook the soil free from the roots. The gardener sneezed, fell to his knees and declared that he would be her slave if she would love him. Stunned, my mother called for a stable hand and another maid. They hauled the poor man away, and when they returned, my mother got the wild notion to try the experiment again. She stood them facing each other and threw a handful of dust between their faces. They both sneezed, looked up, and their faces burned with newfound passion. That evening when her husband returned, my mother threw a handful in her own face, sneezed and looked on the man she had married."

"And she loved him," I finished for him.

"No. Somehow she was immune to the dust. She tried everything—breathing it, eating it, bathing in it. Nothing worked, yet all around her, the household was wild with love. Believing she was immune to passion, she fled her husband's kingdom and came here, where she'd discovered the flower. There was a little cabin here then, not a palace, and the land belonged to her father. One day she wandered to the far reaches of the estate, sat upon the stone wall and wept. She did not hear a man approach her, nor had she ever seen him, though she would have known his name if he had introduced himself. He simply said, 'Beautiful lady, why do you weep?'"

Erik's voice grew harder as he continued. "My mother looked up and her life changed. Before her was this beautiful man, and she felt the kind of attraction for him that she should've had for her husband. A handful of the dust was in her apron pocket. Without thinking she tossed it into his face. So began a secret affair that ended when I made my miserable appearance into this world."

"You are the child of her infidelity?" I'd made him retell this story to appease my curiosity, and now I was sorry for adding to his pain.

"They were both married. My mother's husband and my father were on the brink of war when my grandfather intervened. He purchased peace with the arrangement you see before you. Half of my estate belonged to my grandfather, the other half to my father. My grandfather purchased the land at an exorbitant price, built this palace overlooking the valley and made an agreement with my mother's husband. She would live here until I was born, stay an additional summer and return to him, fully repentant, in the fall. I would remain here and never burden him for support. My mother would live with me each summer."

"She agreed to leave you? You were just a baby."

"It was either agree or have two kingdoms ravaged by war. Eudora was born only a few months before me. Her mother nursed us both and became as much a mother to me as my own—more actually. But if you ever met my mother, you'd understand that what belongs to her is hers, and she won't let anyone forget it."

"What about your father?"

"He denied that I was his, but when I was born, it was obvious. My father has very distinct eyes, and I inherited them. Still, he wanted nothing to do with me. He only sees me when matters of the kingdom require it."

"I'm sorry," was all I could say.

He shrugged. "I've been a menace from the very start." Then he added, "By choice, of course."

"And the dust?"

"It's only found on my estate. My grandfather had the caves blocked off, but I tore down the walls and started mining it as soon as I was of age to manage the estate myself."

"And it's made you rich?"

"No, the kingdom generates its own income, and I live on a portion of it. I've never sold the dust. I just use it to entertain myself."

I giggled into his shoulder. "And take revenge on unsuspecting student teachers."

"Very deserving student teachers. It produces desire, but it doesn't take away a person's power of choice. I once dusted a man whose love was of a different religion. Though they were passionately attracted to one another, they separated and each married someone of their own faith. Their relationships with God meant more to them than their passions, and they chose accordingly."

"The effects of the dust wear off."

"In my kind, they always wear off. In your kind, it depends on the dose. Dust someone well enough, and it will last a lifetime."

"Do you ever do that?"

"No, mortals are too fragile. I give them a passion that lasts a year or two, and if they fall in love for real, they never notice when the dust wears off."

This brought us to the most pressing question of all. "Did you dust me?"

"Of course not. It wouldn't work unless you saw me." He pulled me closer. "Your passion for me is all genuine."

"Who said I had a passion for you?" I replied.

He put his fingers under my chin and found my pulse. "Feverish, irregular breathing, racing pulse? Either you love me, or you need a doctor."

I elbowed him in the side. "I'm just nervous—strange world and all."

When the night's blackness gave way to blue, I was dozing against Erik's shoulder. He shook me awake. "I'll take you to your room. It will be light soon."

I was too tired to argue.

He guided me down the hallway and walked me to the bed, where I pulled down the covers and fell in, clothes and all. Erik drew a finger across my forehead. "Sleep well."

The perfume of summer roses, a scent long dead in my world, wafted through my dreams. When I opened my eyes, I found three pink buds resting on the pillow with a sprig of lavender mingled among them. The window was open to a square of cloudless sky. The sun was high overhead. I guessed it was almost noon.

On the nightstand was a folded letter with my name printed in exquisite script on the front. The message inside was written in the same beautiful hand.

*My Lovely Soul,*

*There are fresh clothes in the armoire and sandals in the drawer below. In the boxes on the dresser I've left gifts. A guest, such as you, should be properly adorned when roaming my kingdom. The smaller box contains a pendant. It is a token of my affection and will guarantee that no other man in the kingdom will bother you. It must be worn on your forehead not your neck. (I'll explain that later.) My friend Aeas will gladly show you around the kingdom today.*

*The bathing area is on the lowest level. Take the narrow stairs next to my bedroom door. If I've neglected anything, ask Aeas.*

*Stop hiding and enjoy yourself. I'll return at dark.*

The signature was the elaborate E on the paintings downstairs.

I opened the armoire, expecting regular clothes, but found white gowns. The fabric was thicker than cotton jersey but softer than silk. They were all floor length, flowing and sleeveless. I chose one with a halter-style bodice that tied behind the neck. In the dresser I found silk underclothing. After digging through eight pairs of sandals, I finally found a pair that would fit my size ten feet.

The gifts Erik left were frighteningly expensive. In addition to the pendant, there was a gold belt adorned with amethyst stones, a gold arm cuff, and a bracelet, which was roughly twelve carats of amethysts strung together with twisted gold chain.

After bathing and dressing in the silky gown, I put my hand through the arm cuff and slid it above my elbow, where it spiraled around my bicep and shimmered in the light. Next I fitted the belt around my waist. On the smallest setting, it threatened to slide onto my hips. The bracelet clasp gave me the most trouble, but I finally got it onto my wrist.

Properly dressed, I ventured upstairs. My stomach rumbled, and if Erik's housekeeper wanted to make it her mission to fatten me, this morning I was willing.

The scent of baking bread coaxed me into the kitchen. I turned the corner expecting to find a middle-aged woman elbow deep in dough. Instead, a young woman looked up from dicing vegetables and let out a squeal. I turned and fled, while she ran to the back door and shouted for help.

I was halfway up the stairs when a boy called my name.

"Please, wait. She didn't mean to frighten you."

I wasn't scared. I was embarrassed, a trespasser in their world.

The boy's face was familiar. He was the one with blue eyes who caught me looking at him in the orchard. He offered me his hand and said, "I'm Aeas."

I shook his hand awkwardly. "Thanks for the oranges."

"You're welcome." As he led me into the kitchen, he asked, "What's in your hand?"

The pendant drew surprised smiles from him and the cook.

"Now we know why he was plucking roses from the garden before dawn." Aeas's eyes brightened. "Are you going to wear it?"

"If you think it's all right," I answered.

"All right?" Aeas laughed. "It's a miracle."

The girl stepped forward and took the token from my hand. She smiled with glee as she fastened the chain around my head. The pendant hung on my forehead. A second chain went over my head from ear to ear to keep the first from slipping.

"This is Eudora," Aeas said. "She's learning your language, but she doesn't speak it well."

"Erik's surrogate sister?"

"Yes, but if you ask her, she'll say she's just the cook and housekeeper."

She was more beautiful than any of the models I worked with this past summer. Her dark hair hung in curls down her back, and on her neck hung a similar pendant—the same gold crest, but a different cluster of stones.

"Her pendant is on her neck," I observed.

"She's married." Aeas pulled a stool to the island, where Eudora had been working before I interrupted her. "Are you hungry?" he asked.

"Starving."

Eudora made scrambled eggs and offered me thick slices of bread, while Aeas fed orange halves into a press until he'd filled a pitcher with juice. "We have to take her to the village," he said to Eudora. "No one will believe us otherwise."

When she squinted in confusion, he translated.

He turned to me and continued, "He did say to show you around today. He wasn't happy that I let you hide in the house all day yesterday."

"I don't know," I protested. "I don't like crowds."

Aeas brushed away my concern with his hand. "The villagers will love you. Most have never seen a mortal. Although, you don't really look like one."

"The dress?" Maybe I wasn't wearing it right.

"No, your face."

"Oh." My voice fell flat.

To Eudora, he said, "In her world they call her Venus."

I choked on a gulp of orange juice.

Aeas stuffed the last of his bread into his mouth. "I'll send for the horses."

"Aeas, what's his name?"

He paused in the doorway and gave me a teasing smile. "I believe we're calling him Erik these days."

Grudgingly, I finished my eggs under Eudora's wistful gaze.

I recognized the village from the frescoes in the palace. Several more shops had sprung up along the main road, and there were more house-lined streets in the rear. Still, it was recognizably the same. Even the people matched the likeness in the painting. The fashion of clothing hadn't changed. Neither had their market. Yet, most of the frescoes were painted when the palace was built. That meant the village had been here almost two thousand years.

We landed at the edge of the town and dismounted. The horses pranced away and gathered in a field adjacent to the road. At least a dozen other winged horses mingled there. Like horses from my world they were a mixed assortment of sorrels and bays, a few white ones, a black and a grey. Each had its wings delicately folded at its sides. Individually, they were impressive. Collectively, they were downright spectacular.

With Aeas on one side and Eudora on the other, I walked tentatively down the cobble-stone street toward the first row of shops. Eudora carried a basket for the goods she planned to buy. Sensing my discomfort, Aeas promised to translate everything people said to us.

We were approached by one of the boys from the orchard—the oldest. "That's not your pendant," he said to Aeas.

"No, it isn't," Aeas replied with a smile.

The guy looked closer before the realization struck him, and his eyes widened. "I don't believe it." With an embarrassed laugh, he took my hand. "Forgive me." He bowed and kissed the first knuckle of my hand. "Welcome, Lady." After politely excusing himself, he ran down the street carrying the news.

Fear ran up my spine. This scene was looking familiar, like the one that began with someone shouting, "Stop that girl! She's Venus!"

I grabbed Aeas's arm. "Don't take me into a crowd."

He put his hand on my shoulder and steered me toward the shops. "It will be all right." We went through a gate to the court-yard of the first shop. There cloaks, dresses and men's half-length robes hung on display. A table nearby held colored sashes and sandals. "You should choose a cloak," Aeas said. "The evenings are growing cooler."

"I don't have any money."

He rolled his eyes. "You have no understanding of what it means to be a guest. They all know who to charge."

Eudora took two cloaks from the rack. "You like them?" she asked in hesitant syllables.

"I like this one." I held up a plum-colored cloak with gold trim. "What do you think?"

They exchanged a momentary look that I couldn't decipher. "It's expensive, isn't it?"

"It doesn't matter." Aeas spoke briefly to the shop keeper, then turned to me. "Why did you choose that one?"

"I like the color. It matches the stones I'm wearing."

The shopkeeper draped the cloak over my shoulders and fastened the gold clasp in front. She gazed at the pendant and spoke to me in words I couldn't understand.

"She says she would have embroidered more detail if she'd known you were destined to wear it."

"Tell her I like it just the way it is," I replied.

A small crowd had gathered near the shop. Women pretended to admire dresses and sneaked glances at us. When we turned to leave, a few of them approached. Aeas murmured a warning, then translated their words.

"We are so happy for you both," said the first.

"We welcome you to the kingdom and pray for your happiness," said another.

The third offered her question with a crooked smile. "Shall we plan a celebration for summer?"

Aeas reply was gentle, but seemed a rebuke nonetheless. He did not translate it.

"I don't understand," I said as he led me away.

"Weddings are a private matter, but usually there's a celebration within the month after."

"And in this case, it would be a big celebration?" I asked.

"A *very* big celebration. It's been nearly three ages since he became eligible for marriage. Everyone wants to see him marry." Aeas motioned to Eudora. "Finish your shopping, and we'll meet you near the bakery."

As she walked away, I lifted my chin toward a pair of young women at the jeweler's cart, who eyed me with pinched expressions. "Everyone except them."

Aeas followed my gaze. "The ocean would freeze before he would give his pendant to one of them. This way. You have to try the sweets at the bakery. They are like scones in your world, only better."

After stopping at the bakery, we sat at a table in the village square. Aeas bought a pastry for each of us and wrapped a third in paper for Eudora. I broke off a corner of the treat and tasted it. It was so light that it melted the moment it hit my tongue. The soft flavors of citrus and cinnamon were baked into the buttery crust. "This *is* really good," I admitted.

"There's nothing like ..." The friendly ease dropped from his face as a man approached us.

The man was a bit younger than my dad with strawberry-blonde hair and stunning eyes of the strangest color. Violet. Ignoring Aeas, the man touched the center stone on my forehead, an amethyst, and spoke to me in what sounded like Greek.

Through his teeth Aeas replied, and the man relented. He spoke to Aeas and let him translate.

"A gift for the lovely lady, with my congratulations," the man said. He laid open a small wooden box that contained a pair of hair combs with diamond accents. I was no jeweler, but they looked real, and the gold was braided over the stones so delicately, I was sure it was done by hand, though I couldn't figure how.

Aeas's jaw clenched tight, and I tried to understand why.

"Thank you," I said and Aeas gathered his composure enough to mutter my reply.

The older man bowed slightly and walked away.

An awkward silence followed. "That was nice of him?" I offered.

"It was sly of him."

"Who is he?"

"He's from another kingdom. Erik will not be happy that he spoke to you." His eyes fell to the open box on the table between us. "The gift will not please him."

# CHAPTER 8

T he sun sat on the horizon when we arrived at the palace. It would still be an hour before dark fully fell and Erik ventured back into my company. I went upstairs alone. I ran my hand along the wall to find the dial for the lights in the living room. Erik's society didn't have electricity, but the upper floor of the palace did. I learned from Aeas that Erik installed the system himself. He diverted a stream into the lower levels of the palace to create the bathing area, and the excess water fell to the valley floor after turning hydroelectric turbines. It wasn't enough power to run a village, but it was enough for six rooms upstairs.

Sea air blew through the living room. The day had been pleasant, even with the strained encounter in the square, but it was all just a prelude that left me restless. I couldn't sit.

At the far end of the room was a large cabinet, a built-in that looked like a closet. Curious, I crossed the room and pulled open the door. "Oh, yes!" I exclaimed.

Blessed be Erik's love of my world. The cabinet contained a stereo, DVD player, and a flat-screened television. Six shelves on one side were lined with CDs, while the four on the other side were crammed full of DVDs. An iPod sat on the shelf in front of the stereo.

I scrolled through Erik's music, found a song I really liked and set the iPod into the dock of the stereo. The acoustics in a plaster-walled living room weren't great, but somewhere hidden around the room were surround sound speakers. Music flooded toward me.

The thumping bass soaked through my skin and ran into my blood. Outside day dimmed. I threw a glance over my shoulder. Below was only the orchard and the sea—no homes, no people. Though the windows were open, I was alone, and I let myself get lost in the movement of the music. I had never needed so much to break free from myself and live in a song. I experimented, letting my body remember lessons from long ago and testing the limits of my older, longer limbs.

Sweat trickled down my spine and dampened my waistline. The familiar chorus gave me predictable strings of chords. I danced until the music grew distant and finally still.

In the silence between songs, I heard laughter in the orchard.

How could I have been so stupid? Embarrassment ran hot through my arms and left me chilled. I switched off the music and doused the light.

It was Erik's voice I heard next, low and indiscernible.

Aeas said, "Wait. There's something I need to tell you." He switched back into their language for the rest. If I was going to visit often, I definitely had to learn that language so I knew what people were really saying about me.

"And he spoke to her?" Erik replied.

"In Greek."

"What did he say?"

"A flourish of compliments, mostly of her beauty."

Erik let out a growl. "Bastard." When Aeas snorted, Erik added, "Oh, yeah. That's me."

"He gave her these." I saw Aeas hand over the diamond hair combs. "She doesn't want them if they make you unhappy."

"What else did she say?" Erik asked.

"That he had beautiful eyes."

Erik tossed the box back to Aeas. "Just what the old dog wanted, I'm sure."

"You should let her see you."

The reply was sharp. "Absolutely not."

When Erik's footsteps climbed the stairs, I was waiting on the couch trying not to look like a guilty eavesdropper.

"He wasn't laughing at you." He pulled me to my feet.

I didn't want to talk about it.

"Honestly. You can *move*." His hands inched lower on my waist, then stopped.

"I was a clumsy kid. A neighbor suggested dance, so Dad signed me up. Stayed in for seven years." I muttered it all in a rush.

"You can dance for me anytime."

I turned my face away and shook my head. That was the problem. I could dance perfectly in private but not for an audience.

"You have amazing body control."

"Came in handy on the runway. Six-inch heels? No problem."

"Six-inch heels," he mused. "That would put us eye to eye."

"You have eyes?"

He pinched my side. "And fangs and big burly paws."

I touched his fingers, finding the metal band on his right index finger. "I'm terrified." That wasn't entirely sarcastic. I traced the curves of his arms to his shoulders and then ran my tentative fingers over his chest.

My breath caught. "You're not...Where's your..." I tried to back away, but he closed the gap between his hands and held on.

"Shirt?"

I managed some ultra-intelligent sound like, "Uh," my mind scrambled by the feel of him, taut and smooth and so warm it made my fingers tingle.

"I was in the kingdom today." He wore what all the men of this world wore—a waist-to-knee robe with a shoulder sash, but somewhere he'd ditched the sash. "Did you enjoy the village?"

"They *did* stare. I was having frat party flashbacks."

"Poor thing," he said, completely unrepentant. "Would you like to go to the beach?"

"Not if it means another dive off the balcony."

"From the courtyard?"

"Sure." I moved to the couch and felt around until I found my cloak, which I draped over my shoulders. The soft lining caressed my bare arms.

As we descended the stairs, Erik put his arm around me. "This is nice," he said, fingering the cloak.

"You bought it."

"I hope so. You'd disgrace me if I didn't."

After I climbed onto Pixis's back, Erik slid his arms around me and held on tight. "I'm not going to fall," I said. "I'm getting used to flying."

He didn't let go as we launched into the air. "I'm not the least bit afraid of you falling."

Pixis landed in the cove with a great flap of his wings that threw mist in my face. Erik slid off and helped me down. Since the first moment when he appeared tonight, Erik kept at least one hand touching me. By never breaking contact, he didn't catch me by surprise and make me shudder.

We wandered in silence. All day I logged questions I wanted to ask him, but as his shoulder brushed against mine, my curiosities drifted off insignificantly. It was enough just to have his fingers gently curled around my hand.

I tugged him toward the water, and he resisted.

"Give me your sandals and your cloak. I'll catch up."

I tossed him my shoes as he backed away. Then I ran toward the surf, hiked up my dress and let the waves crash into my knees. "It's warm!" I exclaimed.

"The current brings the water straight from the equator. That's why our climate is so mild." He pulled off his shoes and set them on a rock out of the water's reach.

"We aren't near the equator?"

Beside me now, he answered softly. "We are at the same longitude and latitude as we were in your world."

"Then they can't be the same world, or the landscape would be the same."

We continued walking where the water lapped at our ankles. "It's a phenomenon no one can explain. We are the same distance from the sun, the same distance from the equator."

"What about the stars?"

He slid his arm around me once again. "The stars are in the exact location here as they are in Bozeman, but where you have mountains, we have a sea. Where you have seas, we have vast continents of land. It is a mystery to even our brightest scholars."

"Who'd have thought you could grow oranges in Montana?" I mused.

"Not exactly Montana, or Butte would be somewhere out there." He pointed to the ocean.

All that showed of the moon in the overcast sky was the silver outline on the clouds. Erik stopped and tugged on my hand. We had wandered far, and I assumed he wanted to turn back. I turned, but he stood still and brought me into his arms.

"Does this bother you?"

"No," I answered honestly. He was familiar to me now, and I relished the feel of his skin on mine.

Erik brushed his lips against my temple and lingered there before dropping his chin and softly kissing my cheek.

I turned my face to him, and our lips touched feather light and warm for an instant before he pulled back.

He didn't quite push me away. It was more subtle, the way his hands dropped from my waist, and he put three or four gaping inches between us. It might as well have been a canyon, the way I felt the void open and myself falling into it.

Erik kept hold of my hand as we returned to the cove, but the intimacy of it was lost. I had overstepped the bounds, wanted too much, and the sting of his refusal rang in my ears louder than the surf. Embarrassed and confused, I wished he would disappear. If he would just vanish, I could curl up on the sand, cover my head and own my shame.

His gate quickened slightly, and his posture stiffened. "It's late," he said. He wanted to be rid of me.

Storm clouds threatened the horizon. The air smelled of rain. I could see nothing of his face, but I knew what was there: a strained jaw line and tight expression, the same things I felt in my own face.

I swung onto Pixis's back without Erik's offered hand, and when we landed in the courtyard, I entered the house before he left the grass. In my cowardly retreat I felt his dismissal like needles in my back.

"Psyche." His voice softened now.

I stopped and listened. When he didn't say more, I moved on without answering.

The wooden door closed behind me with a comforting thud. I leaned against it in the solitude of my room. His footsteps passed to his bedroom. The rooms stood too close together for the distance between us now. It had all been so fragile, the trust and the intimacy. One false step, and it was lost.

I rummaged through the dresser and found a modest nightgown, which I pulled on, then left the dress and the cloak and all of Erik's gifts on the dresser by the door.

Pain, I could handle. Failure, too, was easy to live with, and loneliness was simply a fact of life for a girl so different from her peers. But misread intentions and offering something of myself that wasn't wanted—that was unbearable. I crawled under the covers and closed my eyes. My only consolation was that I would never have to face him in the light of day.

I lay there unable to sleep and helpless to stop the silent trickle down my cheeks. Somewhere in the distance thunder bellowed, and a flash of lightning showed through the open window.

The door slid open, and Erik crept past. He closed the window and locked the latch, then turned and stood over me. I lay perfectly still and slowed my breath to convince him I was asleep. He sat on the edge of the bed with a sigh and touched my hair. When his fingers hit on a damp spot on the pillow, he drew a sharp breath and stood. I waited for him to slink away, but he drew back the blankets. He slid his arms under my shoulders and knees and lifted me to his chest.

"What do you think you're doing?" I pushed against him, trying to wiggle out of his arms. Rain struck like hundreds of soldiers marching across the roof.

"It will storm like this for hours," he replied as he carried me toward the hall.

"I can walk."

"I know my way around the palace without looking." The hall was completely black and so was the living room. Even the foyer downstairs had been closed off with heavy doors. I could see nothing as he moved toward his bedroom. When the door opened, the blackness stretched unbroken before us. He moved through the dark and set me against a pile of pillows on the bed.

Another clap of thunder rumbled on the mountainside, closer and more fierce than before. We were in the master suite, which hung over the cliff.

"Wouldn't we be safer downstairs?" I protested.

"We're perfectly safe here." He moved to the other side of the bed and sat down, easily able to keep his distance, because the bed was huge. He waited in silence, then, "Here it comes."

Suddenly a rush of water swept overhead. "What was that?" I asked. "It sounds like we're under a river."

"A waterfall," he corrected. "All of the rooflines divert water over this room, where it runs off the balcony and falls into the valley. If you were standing in the valley, it would look like the palace disappeared completely under a wall of water." With that he fell silent again, and I wondered if he, like me, was thinking of our botched embrace on the beach and those stupid tears on my pillow.

Apparently he was, because he said, "I didn't want to hurt you."

I forced a laugh. "I'm fine. Seriously."

He touched my arm unexpectedly, and I flinched. He slammed his fist into the bed between us. "We were past this."

I folded my arms across my chest. What right did he have to be angry? He was one who drew me closer and put his lips to my face. Refusal was my right at that moment not his, but somehow the whole thing fell apart.

He moved toward me. His hand felt around where my arm had been and didn't find it there. He found my shoulder, slid his fingers down my arm and tugged on my elbow until I released my grasp. "That isn't what I meant."

"Whatever." I tried to pull away, but Erik's grip tightened.

"I kissed a mortal once," he said. "She collapsed. Unconscious." He stroked my arm. "I didn't want to hurt you." He chose his words carefully and spoke them with regret. "But this pain seems worse somehow." It was possibly all the apology he could muster. After all, he was the ruler of a kingdom, a boy who'd grown up without parents. He answered to no one.

"Was she hurt?" I muttered.

"I don't know. I fled." Then he added, "I was only thirteen."

"I'm not afraid of you," I replied, the storm nearly drowning my words.

Erik put his lips to my ear. "We both know that isn't true."

I couldn't keep my head from dipping toward him or my face from brushing against his. Carefully, he raised my chin and pressed his lips to mine. For a moment he paused, and I thought he'd pull away, but he drew me into his arms and parted my lips with his.

Something inside me burst, sending sparklers glittering through my body. His kiss overpowered me with a sense of perfect well-being and... *love*.

My grip on his shoulder slackened; my body grew weak. If I'd been standing, there's no doubt my knees would have buckled.

"Psyche." His voice was frightened.

I didn't lose consciousness, but I was too weak to speak. All that came from my lips was a sigh. He pulled me to his chest muttering curses, some in English and some not.

The fog in my head parted. "I'm fine."

"You nearly fainted," was his sharp reply.

"It didn't hurt."

He pulled away. "Explain," he demanded with all the irritated authority of the prince he claimed he wasn't.

I tried, honestly, I did, but I could only manage a few flustered sentences and a single adjective.

"May I clarify this?" he said. "You nearly fainted because it was..."

"Wonderful," I repeated, my voice stupidly dreamy. Maybe he didn't believe me, but it was true. People were overwhelmed by pain all the time; somehow he did the opposite to me.

A mischievous laugh escaped him, and he drew me to his face. "Squeeze my arm when you start to go."

I never understood the laws of attraction. Occasionally, I would do a double-take, catch a glimpse of some guy at a distance and feel the inherent need to see more of him, but on closer inspection, everyone was flawed, if not physically, in deeper, more significant ways.

Holden, for example, was the epitome of masculine beauty, but he was intolerably conceited. At our joint photo shoot, he was visibly pleased by my looks and made my skin crawl with every touch. At this he smirked, sure I was reveling in the pleasure of him, when all I wanted to do was run away.

Here in the dark, however, I came to understand that attraction had so little to do with sight. The brush of Erik's skin against my arm made me shiver. From a single deep and unrestrained kiss flowed a thrilling tide that could take us under. Since I'd never seen him, he allowed me to see with my hands, which was so much more dangerous. I lay with my head against his shoulder and traced the ridges of his chest and abdomen with my fingers. He was a varied landscape, dips and valleys between mounds of muscle. My fingers slid up to his shoulder and over the bulk of his bicep. I wrapped my hand around the bulge and couldn't make it halfway as he tightened his arm into a stone.

My fingers moved onto his collarbone and the dip of his neck, where his scent always drew me closer. When I raised my hand, he turned his chin away. "Not my face."

I dropped my hand to his chest and drew my cheek across the hollow of his shoulder.

He raised up on his elbow and dumped me onto the pillow. "Is it my turn?"

"Definitely not."

"You don't trust me," he said, more amused than offended.

I didn't trust myself. It would be too easy to let the thrill of tonight run away with me.

He laid against the pillows, stretching his long arms over his head. "It's just as well. You need to understand our marriage customs before you offer anything of yourself to me."

"I thought I was the forbidden fruit. Isn't it illegal to seduce a mortal?"

"Things are different now. You're here, and you've worn my pendant. The counsel would frown on it. They'd give me grief, but..." He chuckled. "I've made a nuisance of myself with the dust. Mortal or not, they'd happily dispose of me to any woman."

"You and your dust."

"Me and my lust."

"Present company excluded, of course."

He snorted. "What*ever*."

I yawned without meaning to.

"Are you sleepy?"

"How could I sleep through this ruckus?" The thunder and the rain still pounded an angry cacophony on the roof.

"Good, then let's talk marriage."

"Whoa, horsey."

"In general," he reassured me. "Did you notice Eudora's pendant today?"

"The crest was the same, but the stones were different from the one you gave me. And she wore it around her neck because she's married. Aeas told me."

"Do you remember what stones were in the pendant?"

The largest was a sapphire. There was a center onyx and two side stones, but I didn't remember what they were.

"One is an emerald and the other is an aquamarine. The crest represents the kingdom, and the gem cluster is a signature."

"The woman in the fountain is wearing a different crest," I remembered.

"It's my mother. The crest on her pendant belongs to her husband's kingdom. Every pendant in the kingdom bears the same crest, but each adult male has an individual gem signature. The signature Eudora was wearing belongs to my head shepherd. I had to purchase two hundred sheep from the neighboring kingdom to bring him here, but she wouldn't have anyone else." He rummaged around the pile of pillows and pulled down the covers. "Crawl under, it's getting cold."

"Not a good idea," I protested.

"I told you, you're safe with me."

"Oh, but are you safe with me?" I teased.

Erik pulled the blanket over us. "Molest me. I dare you, but not until I finish explaining what would happen if you did."

I faced his voice. "The pendant is a token of courtship. I get that."

"A man presents his pendant to a woman and, while she wears it, no other man will try to court her. It would be dishonorable. Courtship is a public matter."

I wasn't sure I liked the sound of that.

"Everyone in the village knows who is courting a girl by the gem signature she wears. They know the duration of the relationship by how long she's been wearing the pendant. Their courtship would not be like dating in your world—two young people going off at night to date in private. Here they spend time together with their families, because if they are to form any serious attachment, the families must love and accept the new member."

"I suppose that makes sense, but you don't want to meet my dad."

"I didn't say I wouldn't meet your dad. I just didn't offer to let him see me."

"Gee, I really think he'll go for that, Erik."

He ignored my sarcasm. "Back to our hypothetical couple. Before they marry, they need a home. The whole village gathers to build it, unless he has one that he's inherited from his family."

"Like yours."

He grunted in disapproval either at my interruption or the mention of his inheritance. "When the home is complete, the man moves into it. They spend time alone now. Most likely she'd move into the home, too. One night they marry, and she begins wearing the pendant around her neck. Everyone knows they're married because of the pendant."

"What happens if she decides she doesn't want to marry him?"

"Then she gives him back the pendant, and everyone knows it's over."

"So, the ceremony is private? Just the couple and a priest?"

"No, Psyche. Just the couple. In this world, the consummation is a marriage contract."

"*Oh*. That is different from my world." Most the girls in my senior class would be married by that standard, including Savannah I suspected.

"So, if you seduced me tonight, you'd be my wife."

That put a whole new spin on commitment. "I think I should go back to my own room."

I felt him shrug. "If you want, but I meant it when I said you were safe here. It's not something I take lightly." He settled onto a pillow, fluffing it and getting comfortable. "Good luck finding your way back in the dark. And, don't bang your toes on the foot post. It hurts."

Just to prove I could, I climbed out of bed and moved toward the doorway, which I could barely make out in the dark. I went two steps and my foot hit solid wood. I yelped in pain.

"Foot post," Erik murmured.

I clenched my teeth to keep from swearing. My toes throbbed.

He caught my wrist and pulled me onto the bed, then felt around to find my foot. "This one?"

I groaned a reply, and he rubbed the wounded toes.

"I should take you home in the morning," Erik said softly. "Stay with me until the storm blows over."

"You'll be here in the morning?"

"Silly mortal." He tickled my foot. "I'll be waiting for you at the portal."

# CHAPTER 9

A flood of light pulled me from deep sleep. I moaned, shielded my eyes and saw Aeas opening the windows.

He spun around and gasped. Then he dashed out of the room mumbling an apology.

I sat up and rubbed my face. Here I was in a nightgown in Erik's enormous bed. This looked bad.

My own clothes were in a pile in the other bedroom. I pulled them on and ran a brush though my hair before I ventured downstairs to the kitchen. The conversation I overheard was exactly what I dreaded.

"... so mesmerized he fell off the wall watching her. Then, this morning she was in his bed," Aeas said quietly.

"It's ..." Eudora searched her knowledge of English to find the right word. "Sudden."

"She's mortal. Everything moves faster in their world."

I stepped into the kitchen and made my defense. "It wasn't what it looked like."

Eudora turned away, and Aeas's head dropped, so I could only see the crown of his head as he replied, "You don't have to explain yourself to us." He looked up tentatively. "Why are you wearing those clothes?"

"I'm going home."

His eyes widened. "Now?" He seemed genuinely alarmed.

"I need to go back to school, and my dad worries about me a lot."

"Eat," Eudora prodded.

I thanked her and accepted warm biscuits and fruit. "I don't suppose there's a toothbrush around here that I could use?"

Aeas looked at me like I'd asked for a rocket ship. "What would you do with that?"

"Clean my teeth," I answered, which was much nicer than the "Well, duh" I was thinking.

"Oh. He probably forgot to put one of these in your room." Aeas went to the window and drew a potted plant from the sill. "We call it lover's breath." He scooted it across the table to me.

I looked at the plant and didn't move. Somehow this was supposed to be the equivalent of a toothbrush.

Seeing my confusion, he explained. "You sleep with a leaf under your tongue. It cleans the teeth." He took another bite of biscuit, then plucked a leaf from the plant and offered it to me. "You can also chew on them, but don't swallow. They make a nasty stomach ache."

"And, this keeps you from getting cavities?"

"What are cavities?"

"You know, rotten teeth."

"Rotten teeth? You have those in your world?"

"I've got a whole mouthful of them."

Aeas leaned closer. "They look fine."

"Of course. I've been to the dentist." At their confusion, I waved the subject away. "Never mind." I popped the leaf into my mouth and chewed. It tasted like parsley, but fizzed and bubbled. Sort of reminded me of pop rocks—grass flavored. When I spit it in the trash, my teeth did feel cleaner, although I'd much rather have had mint-flavored mouthwash.

Aeas downed the last of his orange juice and stood to go. "Pixis is in the courtyard. Can't you stay? This school of yours could wait."

"But my dad can't. If Erik lets me, I'll come back." I thanked Eudora for breakfast and turned to go.

When I was in the hall, I overheard Aeas mutter, "If he lets her? More like *begs* her."

Eudora shushed him. "Don't discourage them. He seems very happy."

"Yeah," he said flatly. "Let's hope it lasts."

After two days in Erik's world, reality seemed stark and raw. The cold was more chilling than I remembered. Each honk and rev in the street rang louder than before. The sky seemed washed of color. Low clouds hung over miles of pavement, parking lots and commercial buildings, all individually painted, but somehow blending together in a sea of blah. It unnerved me. Never in my life had I thought Montana was ugly.

I found my cell phone and dialed my dad's number.

He answered on the first ring. "Where are you? I was starting to worry."

"I'm on my way to school. I didn't have service at Erik's place, so I didn't get your messages."

"The crowds are gone and there haven't been any more vans parked outside the house. The school hasn't seen them either."

I turned into the high school parking lot and had to drive to the far end before I could find an empty slot. "I'm here, and I'm late, so I'll call you later. Okay?"

"Sure. See you tonight." There was a nervous edge in his voice. Dad had never had to deal with a boyfriend before. It was new territory for both of us.

After checking in at the office, I made my way to class. I spent the day paranoid. I avoided the crowded hallways and was late to every class. By last period my shoulders were strung tighter than a guitar, and I had a headache.

In art I managed to relax a little. When I asked Mr. Mayhue how to make up for the days I'd missed, he went to his cabinet and began rifling through the mess.

"We are moving into charcoal," he said. "You need to turn in four sketches by the beginning of next week."

"What kind of sketches?"

"Yours. Original."

"Doesn't matter if they're landscape or still life or whatever?"

"Whatever." He found the box of charcoal pencils he was looking for, and handed one to me. "As long as they're fully developed and properly shaded."

Mr. Mayhue was my kind of teacher. I slid into my seat and began sketching the still life on the front table. Since he'd given me the weekend, I might be able to do my drawings in Erik's world, which put a bright spot on this miserable day. Narrowing Erik's world into four sketches was impossible. I was struggling with a lopsided apple on my paper when the bell rang.

I dumped my pencils into my backpack and headed for the door. The crowd thinned quickly. Students slammed their lockers and hurried out the nearest exit, but standing still and oblivious to the crowd were Travis and Savannah.

She shook a crumpled piece of paper at him. "Six months and you scribble a note saying it's over. Don't you think I have the right to hear it face to face?"

He shrugged, his answer quiet. "I need a break. It was fun while it lasted."

"It was *fun?*" Savannah's expression hardened. "I wish you would have told me in June that all I was to you was *fun.*"

He reached for her. "Savannah."

She jerked her arm away. "Go to hell."

Travis bit his lip. He mumbled something too low to hear.

Savannah shook her head. "Whatever." She stood there shell shocked, as he walked away. Then her jaw tightened. She looked up and saw me. Her lip quivered. I reached for her hand.

"No," she warned. "Just get me out of here."

I grabbed her purse and backpack from the ground and pulled her by the arm toward the door. By the time we reached the parking lot, Savannah ran without my help. We dodged traffic to the far end of the parking lot, where my Subaru sat alone. I unlocked the doors, dumped our junk in the back seat and shoved the key into the ignition. Savannah dropped into the passenger seat and slammed the door. By the time I pulled onto Main Street, tears threatened her eyes.

"I loved him," she murmured.

"I'm sorry, Savannah."

"I knew it was coming ..." She stared at her open hands in disbelief. "I meant nothing to him."

I drove to my house and sent her to my room while I rummaged through the kitchen for comfort food. Mascara drew wicked lines down her face as I sat beside her and tore the lid off a pint of Ben & Jerry's.

Without saying anything, she took a big scoop and skimmed off the top with her lips. Her gaze fixed on the carpet, faraway as her thoughts. "He told me he loved me." She blinked, as if seeing those intimate moments flash across her mind. "I wanted to believe him, but I always wondered. I was so afraid to let myself love him."

I understood that more than I wanted to admit.

"He used to compliment me every day, then one day he just stopped. It was like I stopped being pretty to him. Then he got a little farther away every day."

"You didn't change, Savannah. He did."

She nodded. "The harder I tried to pull him back, the farther away he got. There were so many times I wanted to talk to him, but I wanted more of him than he was willing to give. And I was so stupid. I tried to give him everything he wanted." She forced a bitter laugh. "So stupid."

"Everyone makes mistakes," I said softly. "I'm the queen of stupid mistakes. At least yours isn't hanging over Main Street."

She laughed and sniffed the tears away. "It's beautiful, though. You look really good in it."

I shook my head. "I never wanted anyone to see it. Now it's national news."

Savannah took another scoop of ice cream. "When you ran away, Erik hid you?" There was a suspicious note in her voice. "I want to meet him."

"I don't know..."

Her eyes narrowed. "Don't try to fool me. You say he's too shy to be seen with you. I don't believe that. What's really going on?"

"He's different than most guys," I replied. It would be impossible to explain all the ways he was different.

She looked hard into my eyes. "Different in an imaginary friend kind of way?"

My mouth fell open. "You think I invented him?"

Savannah leaned back on her elbows. "Prove you didn't."

I slowly reached for my cell phone, only to realize he'd never called it. The only time he called me, it was on our home phone. "I don't have his cell number," I said, which I realized sounded completely stupid. If I was dating a normal guy, of course I would have his number.

"Then call him at home."

"It's clear up in the mountains. There's no service up there."

"Uh huh." She nodded. "And I bet you don't know when you'll see him again, but tomorrow you'll come to school and say he mysteriously dropped by."

"Actually, he's supposed to drop by tonight."

"Great," she said. "I'll wait."

I felt my heart drop into my belly. If she stayed, he wouldn't come. She'd think he didn't exist, and I wanted to be with him more than anything.

When my dad came home a few hours later, Savannah and I were hanging out in my room with the stereo blaring. He pushed the door open a few inches and squinted at that noise.

"Did you miss me?" I yelled over the music, then turned it down.

"Less now than before. Hi, Savannah."

"Hey, Ron. What's for dinner?"

He scratched his head waiting for inspiration to hit. "How about grilled chicken with a mushroom Alfredo sauce and pasta?"

Savannah squealed with delight. "Can I marry you?"

"Gross!" I threw a pillow at her.

Dad turned to go. "Dinner in half an hour."

When the phone rang in the middle of dinner, Dad and I looked at one another. He slowly reached for the phone and checked the caller ID. "Unknown name," he said. "Could be a reporter."

"Could be a contractor calling to offer you a million-dollar job," I replied.

He smirked and answered. His expression turned suspicious. "May I tell her who's calling?" Then he held the phone across the table. "Erik."

Savannah jumped from her chair and grabbed the phone before I'd put my fork down. "Hi, Erik," she said sweetly. "This is Savannah Schofield, Psyche's best friend. I was just telling her today how excited I am to meet you. She said you might be stopping by."

Dad wiped his mouth with a napkin. "Really? I'd like to meet him, too."

"Oh, that's too bad," Savannah said. "Another time, then. Yes, it was nice talking to you, too." She held the phone out to me, and turned to Dad. "He's working late and can't make it tonight."

I grabbed the phone and headed into Dad's office, where I shut the door before answering. "Erik?"

"You have company." He sounded disappointed.

"Yeah, sorry. She wants to meet you and decided to stay until you showed up. Where are you?"

"Nearby. Mind if I sneak in later?"

I looked out the window, and wondered how near he really was. "It would make my day."

"School was that bad, huh?" He chuckled. "I feel your pain. My mother visited today."

"Your mother visiting is as painful as a building full of teenage boys?"

"Worse."

Nothing would make me happier than being near him. "Call me when you're here, and I'll take out the garbage or something."

"Unnecessary," he replied lightly. "I'll surprise you."

After he hung up, I sat with the phone in my hands and a smoldering hope in my chest. Trying to look disappointed, I returned to the dining room, where Dad and Savannah eyed me curiously.

"So?" Savannah prodded.

"He has to work. Are you satisfied?"

She finished her last green bean and wiped her mouth. "For now."

Dad stood with his empty plate. "I still want to meet him."

I rolled my eyes, but Savannah leaned closer. "Sexy voice. Does he always sound like that?"

"Yeah." His voice was nothing compared to the feel of his arms. His kiss.

"I hate you."

I shrugged. "You and half the school."

She smiled and shook her head. "I should go. I have purging to do."

"We aren't talking about the pasta, are we?"

"No." She sat back in her chair and pressed a hand to her belly, which she'd stuffed with a second helping. "I'm going to purge my life of that heartless lifeguard."

"Purging is healthy." I forked up the last cold mushroom from my plate. "And tomorrow?"

"Tomorrow I'm wearing my white leather mini."

"That a girl. You want to take my car and pick me up in the morning?" We piled our plates into the sink. "Is that okay with you, Dad?"

He poured dish soap into the sink and turned on the water. "Sure. Don't rear end any Volvos."

"Saw the porn, did you?" Savannah gave him an understanding nod.

I punched her in the arm, but my dad laughed. "Wish you'd gone with her this summer. Maybe she would have made better choices."

Savannah's eyes twinkled. "I'd be happy to go next summer. I'd be a *very* responsible chaperone."

"*If* I go back next summer." Maybe I'd disappear into paradise instead.

She thanked my dad for dinner, and we walked outside. It had gotten windy, and I hugged my arms as we crossed the lawn. After pulling my coat and backpack out of the car, I waved as she backed out of the driveway. "Don't be late," I called.

Dad was scrubbing dishes, so I picked up a dish towel and started drying. With only two of us, he'd never bothered to buy a dishwasher. "Been a long time since Savannah's been over here," he observed.

"Her boyfriend dumped her this afternoon."

"Oh." He pulled another plate from the sink. "I still remember when Patricia Wallace dumped me my senior year. Right next to the trophy case in the foyer." He smirked at the memory. "After she walked away, I turned around and saw her picture there in the trophy case, all smiles and pompons. It took everything I had not to put a fist through the glass."

I tried to imagine my dad in love. If he'd loved my mother, I was too young to remember it.

"I heard she moved back and took a job at the university a few years ago." Dad turned on the water and rinsed a couple of plates, which he set in the drainer for me. "She married some lawyer and had a few kids. He had an affair, and they divorced."

"Sad."

Dad shrugged. "Happens to the best of us."

"I'm sorry, Dad."

"Don't be." He dumped a pan into the water and scrubbed it clean. "I'm not sorry I married your mom. I got you out of the deal."

"But I'm graduating. Then you'll be alone."

The lines around his eyes crinkled as he smiled. "Don't think your crotchety old dad can manage without you?"

"Of course you can manage, but do you want more?" Until now I'd never considered that probably he didn't date because of me.

"Do I want to get married again?" He rinsed the pan and turned off the water. "I've liked our life. I didn't want to throw a third wheel into it. You're easy to live with. Some women aren't." By this he meant my mother, but I supposed it was true of other women, too.

I'd never begrudge his happiness. Was the same true for him? If happiness for me meant leaving someday and not coming back, would he want me to live without it?

Upstairs I took pajamas from the dresser and was about to pull off my shirt, when a voice said, "I don't think you want to do that in front of me."

I spun around. "Where are you?"

Erik fluffed a pillow, and I could see the indentation of his head as he laid it back down. I dove at him, and he grunted as he caught me. "Happy to see me?"

"I've never seen anyone so handsome." I settled beside him. "How long have you been here?"

"Since Savannah left. You really shouldn't leave the door open like that. You never know what kind of trouble will blow in." He pressed his lips to my forehead. "The palace is empty without you. Aeas and Eudora scolded me for letting you leave. Top that off with my mother dropping by unannounced..." He groaned. "Come back," he begged, "and stay longer this time."

"I can't just disappear. My dad is worried already."

"It wasn't a problem before."

"Before there were reporters stalking me. And of course, I can't tell him the truth. He'd have me committed." I sat up as an idea struck me. "Unless..." I needed an ally. "Savannah wants to meet you."

"You know that's impossible."

"Yeah, but she could see the palace. She could vouch that I'm not insane. I didn't invent you or your world. He would trust her if she told him I was safe with you."

"No, Psyche. She could jeopardize everything we have together."

"Or she could make it easier for us. I want to be with you, and I don't want to lie about it. What am I supposed to do when he demands to meet you or forbids me from seeing you?"

Erik's voice was stern. "You come to me anyway."

"Erik, you grew up without parents. You don't understand how things work. I can't come and go as I please. I can't disappear for days on end."

"Or what? He'll throw you out? You lived on your own all summer. Why should he control you now?"

"Because he's my dad, and I live here now. That's just the way it is."

"Because you aren't willing to let go." There was a bitterness in his voice that hadn't been there before. "This world is cruel. You don't belong here."

"Your mother isn't the loving type, and I don't see you cutting ties with her."

He took my hand with a sigh. "We seldom allow mortals into our world. I took you there because I want you to be a part of it. I don't trust Savannah."

"She's my best friend. And, honestly, I could use a second opinion. I'd like the assurance that it's real."

"It's real." He touched me gently. "I'm real, and my love for you is real."

"I need this."

He was silent a long time before answering, "I'll allow her to visit briefly. A few hours is all. She may be at the palace only, not in the village or anywhere else in the kingdom, and I will send all my people away. You will take her there with Pixis, stay a few hours and bring her back. Agreed?"

"Yes." I was so excited, I could hardly wait to call her. What a relief it would be to share this secret with someone!

"I'm not comfortable with this. I don't like it at all."

"I understand." I didn't like him being invisible, so I moved across the room and switched off the light. He appeared in the dark when I returned to him. "Erik, there's one more favor I'd like to ask you."

He moaned. "What will this cost me?"

"Can I stay at the palace Friday night? I want to sketch your world for my art class."

"What happened to being committed?"

"Mr. Mayhue will think they're fantasies. I'll need your help with the shading."

"In the dark?" he asked.

"We could do it here on Sunday."

He pulled me down on the pillow. "I don't tutor for free." His lips brushed my face as he whispered, "Try not to faint."

I was lost in Erik's kiss and didn't hear Dad's footsteps until he was right outside the door. Then I pulled away with a start.

We vanished.

"Erik!" I whispered. "You took me with you!"

Dad's shadow blocked the light coming from under the door. The knob turned as Erik dropped to the floor behind the bed. I reappeared and squinted into the light from the hallway.

Dad looked around suspiciously then flicked on the overhead light. "You're going to bed already?" he asked.

"Uh, yeah. I'm tired."

"Aren't you going to change?" Dad's eyes scanned the room—the closed window, the ruffled pillows, the guilty expression on my face. He was nobody's fool.

I grabbed my pajamas and headed for the bathroom. Pausing in the hallway, I saw him check the other side of the bed. He didn't go so far as to look under it, but I'm sure he wanted to.

"Where are your curtains?"

The window blinds were half closed, but the curtains next to the bed were gone. "They were dusty," I lied. "I threw them in the wash."

He seemed satisfied and headed toward his bedroom. "Well, good night."

"G'night, Dad." I closed the bathroom door and leaned against it, my heart thumping. I changed and brushed my teeth then returned to my room, where I closed the door and doused the light. I crawled into bed. Soon I heard the shower running in the master bathroom.

Erik slid under the covers next to me silently laughing.

"That was too close."

"Sorry about the curtains. I didn't know they were touching me." They mysteriously reappeared while I was in the bathroom, but Erik was veiled.

"Now do you see why I need Savannah's help?"

Erik let out a slow breath. "Yes, I understand."

# CHAPTER 10

I pulled a bagel from the toaster and started across the kitchen with my plate. An unseen finger slid under my hair and across my neck. I squealed and tossed the plate. It should have shattered on the floor but stopped mid-air and caught the bagel before it hit the tile.

"I thought you left at midnight like a respectable date," I said.

"I came back." The plate settled onto the bar.

I reached toward his voice. My hand lighted over a cotton shirt and the contours of his muscled chest. It was a good thing I couldn't see him, or I would have ditched school. "After school I'll bring Savannah through the portal."

His reply was an indiscernible murmur. A horn honked outside, and I turned to go, but he caught my wrist and kissed my hand.

By some unnatural twist of fate Savannah was on time. As promised, she wore the leather mini skirt and a blue sweater that played on her sapphire eyes. "You're early."

"No, you're late." She put the Subaru in first and let out the clutch too quickly so we jerked into motion.

"I should drive," I said.

"I just need a little practice. I haven't driven a stick since my brother totaled the Toyota a few years ago." At the stop sign she made a smooth start. "See. No problem."

All morning, between swirling memories of Erik, I'd been trying to figure out how to approach the subject of the palace without sounding completely crazy. "I talked to Erik last night after you left," I said finally. "You won't be able to meet him today, but he agreed to let me take you up and see his... house."

"When?"

"After school. There won't be anyone there except us. And, you'll want some pants."

Savannah nearly sideswiped an oncoming car. "Why?"

"Just trust me and wear jeans. And, I'm staying at your house tonight."

"Really?" Her voice brightened. It had been awhile since we spent any real time together.

"No, but I can't tell my dad that I'm staying at Erik's."

"Psyche, don't," she pleaded. "You..."

"It's not like that," I said emphatically. "I have my own room. You'll see."

After school Savannah followed in her car toward the Forest Service access road. By driving separately, I could stay and send her home when the sun went down. I parked in the turnout.

"Isn't this all National Forest?" Though suspicious, Savannah had relented and changed clothes. She had a pair of jeans in her car from a fit of indecision last week. When all else failed, she brought both outfits to school. Now she wore tennis shoes and jeans with her blue sweater.

"It's not actually in the forest."

"Then where is it?" She followed me to the rock outcropping. "Okay, it's a cliff. What the heck is going on?"

"I didn't quite know how to explain this to you. Erik isn't from our... world."

"You're dating ET?" Her voice was cutting.

"No, he's human, but there are some differences."

"Like?"

"Like this bridge you can't see." I ignored the mocking expression on her face. "I hate this part," I muttered as I inched closer to the rock ledge feeling for the railing.

"A bridge. In the air. *Right.*"

My fingers found the cold metal. "Here." I gingerly stepped onto the bridge, testing its solidity before putting any weight on the invisible structure. "It's here. Look." I stepped onto the bridge with both feet.

Savannah screamed, then gaped wide-mouthed as I stood in the air. "Impossible."

"Give me your hand." When she reached out, I put her hand on the railing. "The bridge leads into that cave. Follow me." I closed my eyes and crossed the bridge. I knew I was at the cave when the railing ended and my feet landed on solid rock. I stepped away from the opening and looked back. Savannah stood in the middle of the bridge looking in wonder at the air all around her feet. It made me woozy just watching her. "C'mon," I prodded.

She stepped into the cave grinning. "What a rush."

"This way."

"Where? There's nothing but solid ..."

I stepped through the back wall of the cave and emerged in the meadow. Looking back, I could see Savannah blinking at the wall. "Trust me." My voice echoed in the cave. Savannah put her hands out, closed her eyes and stepped forward. I grabbed her hands as she came through the portal.

"What the...?"

"Now you see why I didn't tell you. You wouldn't have believed me."

"I still don't believe it. It's warm here."

"Yeah. Come into the meadow, and I'll call Pixis."

"Pixels?"

"Erik's horse. Wait until you see him." I pulled the whistle from my pocket and blew. He whinnied a reply. He was waiting nearby and trotted over to nuzzle my shoulder.

"No way. He has wings."

"Aren't you glad you ditched the skirt?" I turned to Pixis. "Savannah's never seen a winged horse before. Maybe you should show her all your glory before I ask you to take us to the palace."

He gave a throaty nicker that reminded me of Erik's chuckle, then stepped back, reared and unfurled his wings with a mighty flap that threw wind in our faces.

"I can't get over how gorgeous he is," I said.

"A Pegasus," Savannah said in wonder as Pixis curled his wings and knelt for us.

"Winged horse," I corrected. "Climb on."

With Savannah settled behind me, I leaned closer to Pixis's ears. "Will you please take us to the palace?"

Pixis flew a straight course from the meadow to the palace and landed in the courtyard. I slid from his back and offered Savannah a hand.

"Erik lives here?" She turned a circle to take in the whole court-yard and the open foyer. "Of course, you'd land a guy that was sexy *and* rich," she muttered.

I started the tour in the foyer then went to the kitchen. We picked oranges in the orchard then sat in the shade and ate. Afterward we toured the bathing area, the living room and my bedroom. I showed her the gown I wore and the sandals that matched.

Savannah's eyebrows arched. "Well, it's not high fashion, but the fabric is nice. What's this?" She touched the wooden boxes on the dresser.

"Erik's gifts. I'll show you." I drew out the amethyst belt, the arm cuff and bracelet and put them on.

"Those are some hefty stones."

"I was afraid I'd lose one, but Erik said the stones don't have the same kind of value here as they would in our world. This is the most amazing part." I held the pendant to my forehead. "It's a token of courtship like a promise ring."

"Some ring." She turned away. "So, you stay in this bedroom when you're here. Where does Erik stay?"

"Down the hall in the master suite."

"Let's see it."

I wasn't sure if snooping through Erik's bedroom was included when he gave me permission to show Savannah the house. Still, I was determined to satisfy her curiosity so she'd help me convince Dad that I was safe here.

The hallway was dim, and the massive door to Erik's room was closed. I felt for the knob and pushed open the door. It wasn't like we'd get caught. He promised the house would be empty.

Straight ahead were the closed doors leading to the balcony. At one end of the suite was the poster bed with heavy velvet curtains wound around the posts. The headboard was nearly buried in pillows. The comforter over the bed was crimson velvet, embroidered in the center with Erik's crest. The top of the comforter was turned down revealing silky sheets in the same fabric as the gowns, but dyed to match the crest.

All of the furniture in the room was walnut and each piece was beautifully carved. Savannah ran her hand over the back of a chair near the doorway. A flying horse was carved into the wood. Its wing was slightly raised and gave depth to the carving. On one table sat a vase painted with a storm scene. I ran my fingers over the glaze and remembered cracks of thunder and the mighty rush of the water cascading from the roof. Mostly I remembered the feel of Erik's arms and his raspy murmurs in my ear.

Savannah went to the two enormous closets that stood behind carved wooden doors. She threw them open and revealed a stunning array of clothes. It looked as if two separate people lived here—one mortal and one immortal. The first closet was full of his native robes, all white. Next to those hung sashes in every color, golden belts and over a dozen cloaks. Several pairs of sandals were lined up on the floor beneath them.

The other closet belonged to the wealthy mortal. Savannah took a pinstriped suit off the rack. She whistled softly. "This is an Armani." She hung it next to three other suits. "These are *all* Armani. His clothes are worth more than our cars." She slid the hangers down the rod. There were dozens of shirts, jackets, slacks and jeans, all with designer labels. Now I understood why he liked the Valentino in my closet.

At one end she found the leather jacket. I pulled it from its hanger and held it to my nose. "It smells like him." I didn't want to put it back.

"So, where's the catch? He's rich, sexy and has amazing taste. Oh, and he's given you a *promise* thingy. This is unbelievable. Your first boyfriend, too." She didn't try hard enough to hide the irritation in her voice.

"There's no catch. This is Erik."

"When do I get to meet him?"

"I already told you, he's shy."

"He didn't sound one bit shy on the phone, and no one with this kind of money hides it. He should be knocking down your door, convincing your dad that he is God's gift to mankind."

"Erik isn't like that."

"What is he like?" she prodded.

"He enjoys making trouble, but he didn't get rich in crime. He inherited all of this."

"I bet he looks amazing in this suit."

"Yeah, of course." My voice fell flat, and Savannah's expression brightened.

"What color are his eyes?" she prodded.

"Blue," I lied.

"How tall is he?"

"Half a foot taller than me." Not a lie. He'd said so himself.

"Build?"

"Medium and muscular." And indescribably enticing, but I didn't tell her that.

"What's his nose like?"

"It's... a ..."

She nodded like she was getting somewhere now. "How did he make the bridge disappear?"

"I don't know." Erik had only made things disappear when he was touching them, but the bridge was invisible all the time. I'd never asked him why.

"How did you really meet him?"

"The MSU carnival. Remember, I told you. I got caught in a crowd and he pulled me out."

"He pulled you out of a mob? How? He would have gotten caught in the crowd, too."

"He... he made me... us... disappear."

"Invisible, like the bridge. He can make himself invisible." The dangerous gears in Savannah's brain were clicking.

"Not in his world, only in ours."

"And when you're here, he isn't with you, is he?"

Sudden fear made my voice hoarse. "He comes at night."

"Oh... my... gosh. You have never seen him."

"I've kissed him. He held me in his arms. I stayed right here with him through a storm!" I said in a rush.

"And when you woke in the morning?"

"He was gone." My voice broke. To speak it aloud made it seem so absurd, but I knew him even though I'd never seen him.

Savannah came forward, smoothing her voice into understanding. "Psyche, I know you want him to be everything you've dreamed of, but he's not."

"You don't know that!" I snapped.

Her eyes softened. "He would only hide from you if he was monstrous. Even an average-looking guy with this kind of money would let you see his face. Something is terribly wrong with him."

I shook my head, unwilling to believe her.

"Have you asked to see him?"

"He said I could see him later."

"How much later?" she demanded.

"After..."

She grabbed me in alarm. "After what?"

I didn't answer.

Her eyes widened. "He's trying to trap you! Can't you see what he's doing? He's winning you over with gifts and this palace, but he's hiding who he really is."

"I love him, Savannah." It was the first time I'd actually said the words, but it was true. I loved him.

Pushing hair out of my face, she dropped her voice into a murmur. "You don't have to stop loving him, but you can't go on blindly. You have to know who he is. That is your right."

"I can't betray him."

"You can't betray yourself!" she snapped. She took a deep breath, calming herself, as she squeezed my hands. "Listen, you're staying here tonight?" I nodded jerkily. "Okay, you go to bed in your room like you usually do. He'll be in here, right? You wait a few hours, and you come down the hall." She pointed to the dresser. "You don't have to turn on a single light. There's a candle right there. That bit of light shouldn't wake him. You light the candle, see his face, and blow it out. If he's a man you can go on loving, fine. If not, you come home that minute. Don't let him trap you here. Don't let him hold you captive."

"He's not a monster," I cried.

"He hasn't been honest with you either." She closed the closets and looked around once more. "If he's what you want, you'll be the luckiest girl in the world." Her tone didn't make that sound like a good thing.

Savannah bid me luck as we parted at the portal. It was dusk when I returned to the palace alone. I changed into a gown and put on Erik's gifts, but Eudora and Aeas didn't come.

I rummaged through the kitchen and found bread, cheese and smoked fish for dinner. My stomach churned, and I tasted nothing. Much as I tried to convince myself that Savannah was wrong, I doubted Erik myself in the beginning. He seemed to offer the kind of love I'd always dreamed about, but it wasn't fair for him to ask me to love him blindly. It might be a trick. I craved more of him every day. If I was going to break free, it had to be soon.

As the light waned, I grew more restless. I longed for his company and hoped he wouldn't come. I didn't want to betray the only guy who had ever loved me, but then again, maybe it was a lie. He had seen my face. He had seen more than that on the billboard. Maybe like every other guy in the world, he just wanted what he saw and all of this was an elaborate ploy to take what didn't belong to him. The fish threatened to come up.

I found mint sprigs and munched on a leaf to settle my stomach. Eudora told me it made the food settle better. I hoped she was right.

The palace grew dark, and my mood followed. I didn't know which was more crazy: to betray him or to believe him. I waited in the stillness with a stormy heart.

"Psyche?" As soon as Erik said my name, I knew something was wrong. His voice was deflated. My dad sounded like that on nights when he ate left-overs and went straight to bed.

I wondered if Erik somehow knew my doubts. "Are you all right?" My voice quivered.

"Exhausted."

"Too much mischief today?" I forced lightness into the words.

A half-hearted laugh was all he could manage. He came forward and rested his head on my shoulder.

"I'll have Pixis take me to the portal," I offered. It was better to run away than betray him.

"No, stay with me." He fingers slid down my arm and took my hand.

I thought he would throw himself on the lounge and doze, but he led me through the hall to his bedroom. I balked in the doorway.

"I just want you near me," he said.

A pillar of moonlight slid through the open window, but it cast beams on the far side of the room, away from Erik and his bed. He coaxed me forward, then lay down with a moan. I gave in. I snuggled up next to him and let him wrap his arms around me. Within moments his breath turned heavy in my hair.

The moonlight climbed higher overhead and cast fewer beams into the room. It was very late now. Was it possible the gentle arms curled around me belonged to a hideous face? He was sound asleep. Should I put my fears to rest?

Erik didn't stir as I slid out of his arms. I crept past the foot post of the bed and felt my way to the dresser where the candle stood. Beside it was a box of matches. I opened the box and struck a match. The hiss of the flame seemed to echo through the silence. I froze, listening for him to wake, but his breath remained steady. As I lit the candle and shook out the match, I noticed a heart-shaped silver box on the dresser. It was closed by a looped clasp. I slid aside the clasp and eased the lid open. Inside was fine pink dust.

Erik murmured my name. I turned to face him. He was sound asleep, and he was no monster.

Delicate skin smoothed over his high cheekbones. His full lips were naturally coral, and thick lashes adorned his closed eyes. Even Aeas, who would be gorgeous in my world, didn't compare to Erik's beauty.

He wore the robe of his world wrapped around and tied at the waist. His bare chest was rippled with sculpted muscle. From his broad shoulders to his ridged abdomen, he took perfection to a level beyond imagination. I was mesmerized, unable to pull my eyes from his glorious personage. Most surprising, I had seen him once from a distance on the first day of school. He was staring at the billboard of Venus when he turned around and saw me.

I moved closer, compelled to touch him and reassure my senses that he was not an illusion. I forgot I was holding the candle and the box of dust. I leaned closer. The hot wax dripped on his flawless shoulder.

He awoke with a start. I jumped and sent a cloud of dust into my face. I coughed and sneezed, and when I looked at him, heat flooded my veins.

"You fool! What have you done?" He jumped up, fury in his eyes. They were violet and the most beautiful that had ever looked on me. "You're covered in dust." He snatched the candle and the box from my hands.

"It doesn't matter. I loved you before I saw you." I reached for him, but he pushed me away shaking his head.

"Love cannot live without trust."

All the little droplets of knowledge I'd gleaned about him— this place, the dust, the winged horses and the robes—finally pooled into understanding. "Eros," I whispered. "You're the god of love."

"I'm no god, and it isn't love. It's just dust," he spat. "Now you're under its power."

"So are you! I heard you sneeze the first time you came to my school!" I threw my arms around him.

He peeled me off his body and dragged me toward the balcony where he threw open the doors. A sharp whistle cut from his lips. "Pixis!" The horse landed on the balcony and Erik pushed me toward him. "Throw her back into her own world, and close the portal."

"No!" I clung to him. "Give me another chance."

"Another chance to betray me?" He tried to force me onto the horse's back, but I put my feet out and pushed against him. In frustration, Eros caged me in his arms. "Down," he ordered.

The horse unfurled his wings and leaped off the balcony. Before I understood what was happening, Eros launched me after him. I screamed as I fell through the night, but Pixis came up under me. I seized a handful of his mane and clung to him. He bobbed in flight, which set me onto his back, then he flew full speed toward the edge of the meadow. He didn't land in the clearing where he usually did, but barreled through the trees. He tucked his wings and glided through the dark cave, then gave a mighty flap to cross the ravine. On the rock outcropping, he landed. A full moon outlined the familiar woods and mountains. Cold prickled up my arms.

"No, I won't leave," I protested.

He knelt on his left knee. When I didn't move, he put his ears back and whinnied. I felt his muscles tense. I relented and slid off his back. Pixis brushed his nose against my cheek, then he put his head down and nudged me hard. I tumbled off the rock and fell into the frosty grass.

He bucked and his hind feet struck the invisible bridge.

"No!" I lunged toward the outcropping, but it was too late. I heard the bridge crash to the rocks on the other side of the ravine. Pixis looked back at me one last time before stretching his wings and crossing the ravine.

"I'll wait here in the cold!" I cried. "I'll never give up."

The words echoed back to me from the opposite cliff, but the horse was gone. I collapsed on the rock shivering and wrenching with bitter regret. Eros hid his beauty from me so I would love him instead of his face, and I turned out to be as shallow as every guy who gawked at the billboard. I'd wanted the shell instead of the pearl inside.

The night grew colder, but I refused to move. Pixis might return. Eros might relent and let me come back. Even as those thoughts came to mind, I knew it was impossible. He wasn't going to forgive me. I waited until the moon fell in the sky. I shivered uncontrollably. Curling into a ball preserved some of my body heat, but I was no match for the mountain. Near dawn it started to snow, but by then I was no longer cold.

# CHAPTER 11

The crack of a rifle tore through my consciousness. There was
light all around me, but I couldn't open my eyes.

"I hit him in the shoulder. There's a ravine ahead. He won't
get far." The voice was unfamiliar. Not Dad. Not Erik. The last
name was painful, but I couldn't remember why. Didn't matter.
Too sleepy.

"... a green Subaru in the brush. Hope he doesn't start tracking
my buck." The voice was soft but near. "Check for blood." The next
sentence was a string of profanities even my dad wouldn't say.

"Blood trail?" asked another voice farther away.

"No, it's a girl. The car must be hers." His breath smelled like
chew. I felt his hand, but I couldn't move. "She's ice cold, but I
found a pulse. See if there's ID in the car. I'll get the truck."

I struggled to speak, but he was gone. A pickup rumbled closer.
He pulled me into his arms. My limbs wouldn't struggle. "No..."
I managed. I didn't want to go.

My protest was lost. I felt warm air and scratchy seat covers.
Coats and blankets wrapped around me. The other voice returned.
"I found a backpack and high school ID. It says Psyche Middleton.
Think she's Ron's girl?"

"Yeah, the girl from the billboard."

The pickup bounced down the road. "What the hell was she
doing up here? Did you see what she's wearing?"

I didn't hear more. The warmth put me under.

I felt a hand in my hair. "Erik?" I whispered without opening
my eyes. It must have been a dream. I fell asleep in his arms and
had nightmares.

"Hey, kiddo."

"Dad?" I pulled my eyes open. My throat felt like sandpaper.
The room was beige with muted curtains and sterile tile floors.

There was a TV mounted on the wall. A hospital room. "What happened?" I croaked.

He turned to the table behind him and came back with a plastic mug. He put the straw to my mouth. "I was hoping you could tell me. A couple of hunters found you this morning. I thought you were at Savannah's house."

"Erik," I murmured. The memories hit me like a crashing wave—how I betrayed him and he threw me out.

"You were with Erik last night? Why did he leave you in the snow, and where are your clothes?" My dad's expression turned hard. "I've got plenty of questions for Erik."

I let my head fall back on the pillow. "Save it. I'll never see him again."

"He'd better hope *I* never see him, or I'll put him in the ground."

My nose itched, and I reached to scratch it, only to hit my face with a mess of bandages. "My hands."

"Frostbite. You were lucky. You won't lose any fingers."

"My face?"

Dad brushed my cheek with his fingers, and his eyes got a little moist. "Still perfect."

"Has Savannah been here?" I had no idea how long I'd been out.

"She called this afternoon, and I told her you were here. She's worried." He squeezed my arm. "I'll call and tell her you're awake, then you're going to tell me exactly what happened. You understand?"

I closed my eyes and nodded. My mind was too foggy to lie, but the truth wasn't an option. I put a bandaged hand to my forehead. The pendant was gone. Maybe it was lying in the valley below Erik's balcony. No, his name wasn't Erik. Eros was so much more, and he was no longer mine. The words he whispered to me that first day I crossed the portal came into my mind. I'd heard them before, but couldn't remember where. "Love looks not with the eyes, but with the mind..." The rest of the stanza from *A Midsummer Night's Dream* now came into my mind, "...And therefore is wing'd Cupid painted blind."

He tried to tell me, but I was too afraid to listen.

I'd heard the phrase "broken-hearted" thousands of times, but until that moment, I didn't realize it would actually hurt, that the anguish of losing his love would make my chest ache and my lungs constrict so that even breathing was painful. I was glad it hurt—glad my body could vouch for my suffering. For my stupidity.

I remembered Eros's glorious face and those angry violet eyes. No matter how long I lived, no one would compare to his beauty. His image was seared onto my memory where it would haunt me indefinitely. Every other face would be flawed, every other voice flat. If I was empty before he loved me, I was a desert now, a barren heart with no hope of rain where there had once been a valley full of lush tenderness. My hands ached under the bandages, and I wanted to cry. But how do you pull tears out of dry sand?

"What happened to you?" Savannah rushed into the room with my dad following somewhere behind.

I blinked awake and held out my arms. She hugged me. "I did what you said. I lit the candle and looked at him."

"He was a monster?" she whispered.

"No! He was a thousand times better than Holden."

"Holden?" It took a moment for the name to register. "You're on a first-name basis with Holden *Valentine*?"

"He was like a mirage, beautiful beyond belief. I reached out to touch him." My voice grew weak. "The candle wax dripped on his shoulder. I burned him. Literally." I was aware that my dad was standing at the foot of the bed listening, but I didn't care.

"So he did this to you?" She touched the bandages.

"He threw me out, but I couldn't leave. He has to come back sometime. He has to!"

She nodded. "Yeah. I'm sure he'll come back. You can apologize."

"He threw you out of his house?" Dad interrupted. "Then why were you in the forest?"

I met his eyes. "There's a portal between his world and ours. It's in the forest."

"A portal?" He shook his head.

"Savannah has been there. Tell him, Savannah."

She looked at my dad and back at me with wide eyes. "Ron, could we have a moment?"

My dad gave me a suspicious look and trudged out the door.

As soon as he was gone, I grabbed her arm. "You make him understand, Savannah. You have to."

"You've been through a lot. Just give this some time." She looked around the room. "You were wearing the stuff from his world when they found you?"

"Yeah, and I don't know what happened to the pendant. Will you see if you can find it?"

"Sure." She went to the closet and pulled out the plastic bag with "Personal Belongings" on the side. She drew out the dress and laid it on the chair next to my bed. Then she pulled out the sandals, belt, bracelet and arm cuff. At the very bottom was the pendant. She held it up for me to see.

I snatched it from her hands and brought it to my lips. "Thank goodness. It's all I have left of him."

"I could stash this stuff at my house until you get out of here?" she offered. Savannah folded the dress and placed it in the bag along with the sandals. Then she carefully wrapped the belt around her hand, slid it off her fingers and set it on top with the bracelet and arm cuff inside. She looked up and waited for the pendant.

I studied the amethyst in the center of the signature. "I know his name now. It's not Erik. It's Eros."

"Eros, as in the... God ...of *Love?*" She blinked. "I guess that is a thousand times better than Holden Valentine." She held out her hand, and I dropped the pendant into her palm. "This pendant means you belong to him?"

"Not anymore."

Savannah considered the pendant, then placed it on top of the other things in the bag. "I'll keep these safe." She squeezed my arm. "Let them pamper you for a few days. You deserve it." With the bag in her hand, she left the room and closed the door. Through the window, I saw her talking to my dad. She held up the bag for him to see, and made a small gesture toward me.

I sank back relieved. She was explaining. He wouldn't think I was crazy, and maybe he wouldn't ask too many painful questions about Erik. It would be all right. When I got out of here, I would go back to the portal. I would find a way to cross the ravine, and I would get to Olympus. I wouldn't stop trying until he forgave me. Whatever it took, I would win Eros back.

When Dad returned a few hours later, he had a sandwich and a bottle of chocolate milk from the cafeteria. He didn't ask any questions, for which I felt a profound gratitude to Savannah. He settled in the chair and picked up the television remote.

"How long do I have to stay?" I asked.

"Overnight." He frowned at the football game on the screen. MSU was losing. "They want to run some tests."

"For what?"

The offense fumbled the ball, took a timeout, and the screen went to commercial. Dad turned to me, his expression softer. "I just want you to get better." There was genuine sadness in his voice. He wasn't talking about hypothermia or frostbite.

The hospital released me the following afternoon. Dad drove through the wet streets. Snow clung to the upper elevations, but it rained in the valley. As soon as I got home, I called Savannah's cell phone. It went straight to voice mail. I called a dozen times over the next few hours but she didn't answer.

I called her house, and her mom answered on the first ring. "Psyche?"

"Is Savannah around? I tried her cell, but I got voice mail."

"I was just going to call you," Katherine said. "I thought you knew where she was."

"I haven't seen her since she visited me in the hospital." I waited, but she didn't reply. "Katherine?"

"I need to go. I'll tell her you called."

After she hung up, I called Travis, but he hadn't spoken to Savannah since Friday morning at school. I debated calling the police, but her parents beat me to it. An hour later a couple of deputies showed up at the door.

"Are you Psyche Middleton?" the deputy asked.

He was young, and I didn't know him, but when his partner came trudging up the steps after him, his face was familiar. "Hey, Todd," I said.

"Your dad around?"

"No. He went to check on the job. You want me to call him?"

Todd nodded. "We need to ask you some questions about your friend Savannah Schofield, and we'd rather he was here."

I pulled the cordless from its charger on the kitchen bar. "Do you guys want to come in?"

The younger officer started through the doorway, but Todd set a hand on his shoulder. "We'll wait in the car until your dad gets here."

When my dad's truck pulled up half an hour later, Todd and his partner crossed the wet grass toward the driveway. From the living room window I watched the three men approach the house. Something was definitely wrong.

The officers sat facing us in the living room, and the scene looked oddly like something from my dad's favorite cop show. Todd took out a pocket spiral notebook and a ballpoint pen. "When was the last time you saw Savannah?"

"She came to visit me at the hospital." I looked at my dad for help. Time had passed in blips and blurs. There wasn't clock in the hospital room.

"It was about one o'clock yesterday afternoon. They released her today around noon."

"Have you spoken to her since?"

I answered, "No. I've been trying to call her. She took some of my belongings from the hospital for safe keeping, and I want them back."

"What kind of belongings?"

"A dress, sandals, and some jewelry." At my answer, Dad's brow furrowed, but he didn't speak.

"What can you tell me about this?" Todd reached into the pocket of his coat and drew out a plastic evidence bag that held a sheet of notebook paper, which he turned over for me to read. "Her parents found this in her room just before they made the missing person's report." The letter was in Savannah's handwriting.

*Mom & Dad,*

*I know you'll be worried about me, but you shouldn't be. I'd tell you where I'm going, but you wouldn't believe me. I can only say that Psyche has been there, and it's completely safe. I was devastated when Travis broke up with me, but now I realize it was for the best. There is someone better for me, and I'm going to be with him. I'm sorry I can't tell you more. Just know that I'm going to be happy (and very rich).*

*Love you,*
*Savannah*

"No, she wouldn't," I stared in disbelief at the paper in my hands. It was impossible for my best friend to betray me so completely. I had known her since preschool. She wouldn't do this to me. But the dark reaches of my mind conjured involuntary images, like eighth grade when I confessed I had a crush on the guy who sat in front of me in English. The next day I caught Savannah talking with him at her locker. I accused her of telling him my secret, but she swore she didn't. Two days later they were a couple.

"What can I say?" She'd shrugged. "He likes me, not you."

Todd interrupted my thoughts, "Do you know where she might have gone?"

I wanted to hurl all over the coffee table. "She's going after Erik. I can't believe it. She has my pendant." She wasn't keeping it safe for me. She was using it to win him for herself. I hated her with more vehemence than I believed myself capable.

"Psyche," Dad said calmly. "Savannah said you rented that costume and that the jewelry was hers. She said you invented Erik's world."

"She lied," I said coldly.

He wasn't convinced. "I don't know what to tell you, Todd. I had her blood tested before we left the hospital."

"Tested for what?" Apparently everyone was taking to betrayal these days. "I'm not on drugs, Dad. And I'm not crazy!"

Todd eyed my dad kindly. "And?"

"Clean," he replied.

"Duh," I said.

"Here's the thing," said the younger cop. "Whatever the story, did Savannah believe you about this Erik?"

"Yes."

"So, you know where she might have gone?"

"The same place they found me, but if she got through, she won't be there. Her car will be, though."

Todd stood. "We need you to take us there."

My dad and I drove in silence. It was hard when he was mad at me, miserable now that he thought I was insane. Eros told Pixis to close the portal. The bridge was gone. Savannah couldn't possibly cross to the cave. I said a hundred silent prayers that she would be standing there on the rocks unable to get across. The thought of her in the palace basking in Eros's beauty made my whole body ache.

"Here." I pointed to the clearing in the brush. Twin tire tracks in the snow forged through the pines and junipers.

Dad parked the pickup on the road, and the police car pulled in behind us. We followed the tracks to Savannah's car, where all three men inspected it with their eyebrows raised.

"My Subaru is over there," I said. It obviously hadn't moved since the snow fell Saturday morning.

"So, where's the portal?" Dad asked meekly.

"See the cave on the other side of the ravine? The portal was in there. There used to be a bridge across the ravine, but it's gone now."

The young officer started toward the rock outcropping facing the cave. "You say there was a bridge? There's no trace of where it attached to the ... Todd!"

Both Dad and Todd ran to the ledge and looked over.

"What? What is it?" I demanded.

"It's Savannah," Dad said quietly.

I rushed toward the ledge, but Dad caught me by the shoulders. I pushed him away and grew woozy looking over the edge. Savannah lay on her back at the bottom of the ravine with her eyes open. She wore my white gown and the pendant around her neck. I teetered; the rocks spun.

My dad pulled me away from the ledge and hugged me to his chest. "I'm sorry, Psyche." I felt him shiver. "I am *so* sorry." He led me back to the truck and ordered me to stay inside.

I stared blankly at the dashboard. The young deputy found a path and hiked to the bottom of the ravine, but we were too late. Savannah was dead. The news went into my ears and stayed there, unable to penetrate the rest of me. I waited for a paramedic to say we were mistaken. She was badly injured, but she would come around. I turned my face away as they loaded the body bag into the coroner's van.

My mind swirled in irreverent courses. I wondered how Travis would take the news and what her parents would do with all her shoes. Would they blame me for her death? Mostly, I wanted someone to tell me whether I was angry or sad. Her last act in life had been to betray me. Did that somehow cancel thirteen years of friendship? Could I hate her and miss her at the same time? Could I survive high school without her?

Savannah wasn't afraid when we crossed the bridge the first time. She didn't know it was gone. The police report would list her death as suicide, but I knew better. She tried to march across a bridge that was no longer there. She wouldn't have stopped to test it like I had. No, Savannah was always supremely confident that what she wanted, she would get. She had set her course for Eros, and she died for it. I wondered if he knew.

"I'll pick up your car later," my dad said quietly as he put the truck in gear. He drove far off the road to get around the police and emergency vehicles.

The ride home was bumpy. My vision blurred. I found myself at home sitting on the bed but didn't remember getting there. I changed into pajamas and stared at the ceiling.

My dad came and went. In the morning he brought breakfast and put it on the nightstand. At night he gathered up the full plate with a sigh and put dinner in its place. Sometimes I slept. Mostly I just lived in my mind with Savannah and Eros, unwilling to see a world beyond the walls of my room that existed without them.

# CHAPTER 12

I woke to a crash and found my dad standing over me, a shattered plate on the carpet and taco casserole splattered across the wall. "Get up! It's been three days. I will not let you die with her!" He pulled me out of the bed.

I tried to jerk away.

"Get in the shower and go to school. People die, Psyche. You have to deal with it."

"No." I tried to crawl back into bed, but Dad moved in front of me.

"Take your clothes. You will shower, you will eat, and you will go to school."

I stared blankly at him.

"Or I'll check you into a hospital."

I searched his eyes for some sign of uncertainty, but it wasn't there. He meant it. Go to school or he'd ship me off to the funny farm. With clenched teeth, I moved past him to the dresser, where I dug out clean clothes. I slammed the bathroom door so hard the fixtures rattled. After scalding my skin in the shower and yanking the tangles out of my hair, I finally relented enough to go downstairs.

On the bar lay a circle of familiar items: a gold belt, an arm cuff, an amethyst bracelet and Eros's pendant. "What are these doing here?"

Dad put a plate of pancakes in front of me. "Savannah's parents said they'd never seen them before. They wanted you to have them back."

I fingered the pendant as I slid onto a bar stool.

"The funeral is tomorrow," Dad continued. "You should go." When I didn't answer, he added, "I'll go with you."

I nodded jerkily and poured syrup on the pancakes. I took a bite, and my stomach lurched at the intrusion. "Did it hurt when she left?"

"Jill?" he asked, confused. He sank onto a barstool opposite me and folded his hands. "I asked her to leave."

I should have known he wouldn't understand. "I wish they hadn't found me."

"No, Psyche." He put his hand over mine. "You can get through this."

How could I tell him that I didn't want to get through it? I wanted to bury myself in a dark hole where I would never have to look into the eyes of another man or wonder if I might have been happy if I'd never seen Eros's face. I wanted to hide from the fact that I led Savannah to that ravine, and that it was my fault she was dead.

Dad gathered up his keys and a stack of contracts. "Go to school. I'll check back later."

I nodded out of habit not obedience. After scraping the full plate of food into the trash, I left the house, but I didn't go to school. I found the wrinkled business card for the fortune teller at the MSU carnival. She'd been one of the immortals. She was my only hope of finding Eros again.

Her shop was in a shabby section downtown, a rundown neighborhood where several houses had been turned into businesses. Between an accountant's office and a used bookstore was a bright blue bungalow with a wooden sign over the door. The door was locked, and the sign said it was before business hours, but I pounded relentlessly until she opened the door.

"You have to help me," I said through the sliver in the doorway.

She gave me a scowl, but didn't fight as I pushed the door open and went inside uninvited.

"You were one of them. You're the only person who can help me get him back." When she didn't answer, I begged. "I'll do anything—pay any price."

A fraction of compassion entered her eyes, and she motioned me into a small room at the back of the shop where she poured me a cup of tea and made me drink half of it before letting me speak again.

My words came in a tidal wave that splashed all my secrets onto the dingy wooden table. I held nothing back, not of the time I spent in the kingdom or the tenderness I found in Eros's arms.

The woman listened without flinching, and when I finished, she lit a cigarette and considered me quietly. "You won't be able to get into Eros's kingdom," she said finally. I opened my mouth to protest, but she raised a hand to silence me. "He is very careful about opening portals into his land. He'll move it, and there's no way you could find it." She took a long drag and blew the smoke away from me. "He doesn't keep a permanent residence here either."

"Others do?"

"Fewer now than used to, but some of them cherish the worship they get from mortals."

"One of them can help me," I said.

"Aphrodite frequents this world more than ..."

"Tell me where to find her," I demanded.

The fortune-teller—her name was Gina—shook her head. "You don't understand. She will *hate* you for that billboard. Plus, you won Eros's love then betrayed him. If there was ever a girl in this world Aphrodite would despise, it's you."

"I don't care. I have to find a way to reach him."

Gina's expression grew darker. "Her bodyguard is dangerous. He may kill you on sight."

I was unmoved. "Better dead than living like this."

Something in her face changed, a shadow of understanding. "Okay," she said quietly. "I'll tell you how to find her mortal palace. It's on an island in the Tyrrhenian Sea, northwest of Naples." She smashed the cigarette in an ashtray and lit another.

"Those things will kill you, you know."

Gina scowled. "So they say, but I've lived nearly eighty years in this miserable world." She went to a cupboard and took out a world Atlas. "Of course the island isn't shown on this map, but it's there. Only a quarter mile wide and two miles long. No one is allowed on the island except Aphrodite's guests." She pointed to the location, then scribbled the coordinates on a piece of paper.

"I wish you would reconsider," Gina said. Then she leveled her gaze at my desperate eyes. "Take the pendant as proof of who you are. It may soften her stone heart."

"She's supposed to be the goddess of love and beauty," I replied.

Gina's eyebrows arched in amusement. "Mortals wrongly believed that love and beauty went hand in hand. She's beautiful, but her love is always self-serving."

I thanked her and turned to go.

"Did you meet Aeas?" she asked as I reached for the door.

Confused by her question, I muttered, "He showed me around the village."

"How is he?"

I shrugged, not really knowing what to say. "Fine, I guess."

She nodded sadly. "I still miss him. Every day." She turned away.

Another day I might have asked her why, but today I was too consumed with my own loss, so I left her stooped over the table clearing teacups.

Without any other plan than to catch the next flight to Europe, I packed a duffle bag with jeans, two shirts, a couple pairs of underwear, an extra bra, a toothbrush and a hair brush. As an afterthought, I threw in some socks. The clothes mattered little. The most important things I laid on top: the amethyst belt, arm cuff, bracelet and Eros's pendant, all proof that I was his betrothed.

The back of my old travel itinerary listed the airline's phone number, which I dialed on my cell. If I was flying on my own dime, I wasn't booking first class, and the thought of being packed into coach made me cringe. I was still on hold listening to corny music when I heard the front door open. True to his word, Dad was checking back, and I was caught at home.

I pocketed the phone and tossed the bag into the closet before my dad came upstairs. I slipped my passport into the back waistline of my jeans and covered it with my shirt.

"You're supposed to be at school." His voice was stern, but his eyes betrayed him. He was more sympathetic than he let on.

"I'm not in bed," I protested.

He leaned against the doorjamb and waited.

"I left the house...but I didn't... go there."

"You have to face it eventually."

"After the funeral." I was able to meet his eyes then, because I wasn't lying. By the time I got home, the funeral would be over. I couldn't tell my dad I was flying to Italy to meet a mythical Greek goddess. I couldn't think of anything I could tell him that would make him agree I should take this trip. I decided it would be easier to ask forgiveness than permission.

Before catching the plane, I made a substantial cash withdrawal at the bank, most of which I tucked into the front pockets of my jeans. Somewhere over North Dakota, I sent my dad a text message: `I'm fine. There is something I need to do. I'll be home in a few days. Love you, Psyche.`

I turned off the phone, so he couldn't call back.

# CHAPTER 13

I typed the coordinates of Aphrodite's island into a search engine. After scrolling through a bunch of garbage travel sites offering tours of Italy, I found a site dedicated to the island known as "The Fortress of the Goddess." Photographs of the island showed high stone cliffs surrounding most of the island. In the background were white, marble-like cliffs. If I hadn't been to Eros's palace, I would not have realized that the cliffs were more than they seemed. They were the exterior walls of Aphrodite's palace, so well set into the background of the island as to become part of the landscape. Plus, to the record of mortals, the island had always looked that way. The website reported that references to the Fortress of the Goddess were found in buried Pompeii.

Legends claimed the island was inhabited by gods. No mortal could step foot on the island uninvited, though a few sailors reported they had delivered goods to its shores. Three small vessels over the past hundred years reported making deliveries to the Fortress. All agreed on their means of delivery. They were directed to the northernmost shore of the island, where there was a small strip of beach. They dropped their goods on the beach at night and left immediately. In his journal one sailor recorded that he received payment in cash by post, and it came with instructions about how to deliver the items wanted by the gods. If he stayed at the beach past the delivery hour, he would be struck dead. If he ventured off the beach onto the island, he would be struck dead. He was instructed never to tell anyone about the delivery. Over fifty years he kept the secret. After he died, his children found the account. He wrote that he kept the secret out of gratitude because the gods paid him more than two years' wages for one night's work.

I clicked off the Internet and went downstairs to the front desk. The clerk, a man in his mid-thirties with wavy hair and a five o'clock shadow, smiled widely at the sight of me. "What can I do for the beautiful lady?" he offered.

"I need to go somewhere tomorrow night..." I looked at the clock on the wall. It was three o'clock in the morning here in Naples. I awoke sweating and disoriented a few hours ago. "I mean, tonight, and I don't have a dress to wear. I'm looking for something very specific—a white silk or satin dress like the goddess Venus would wear. Do you know where I might find such a dress?"

"Something *very* nice, yes?"

"Yes, high quality and it must look like the goddess. Understand?"

He nodded. "Of course."

From my pocket I took a hundred dollar bill and laid it on the counter. "If you find me this dress, I will be very happy." I slid the bill across the counter and smiled.

"As soon as it is morning I will call the best shops." His English had the most charming accent. He was probably used to American women swooning over him.

"Size four. Have it sent here and charge it to my room?"

"Yes. I will call when it arrives."

From the desk beside him, I pulled a city bus brochure. "I want to go to the docks before the fishing boats go out for the day. Will the bus on this route take me there?"

"Oh, no." He shook his head furiously. "I mean, yes, the bus would take you there, but a beautiful woman should not be roaming the streets alone before dawn. I will call a cab."

After thanking him I waited with the doorman. The air was warm. Fall here was temperate compared to home. It gave me hope that Aphrodite would understand I made a mistake and I really loved Eros. She would give me a chance to apologize to him. With optimism brewing in my chest I went to hire a ship to the Fortress.

None of the fishing vessels wanted to take me to the Fortress, and my efforts to bribe them failed. A few of the fishermen didn't speak English at all. Most of the others got the gist of what I was saying and adamantly refused, even with a handful of green-backs in front of them. Frustrated and nursing a splitting headache, I sank onto a bench near the pier at war with myself. The rational part of me said to catch a cab back to the hotel, sleep off the headache, then take the next flight home. The stubborn, love-sick part of me wouldn't move and kept gazing across the water wondering if redemption waited in the serenity of the sea. The turquoise water reminded me of Eros's kingdom and made me ache. I hauled myself up, not knowing what else to do but admit defeat.

From down the pier came a trill, someone whistling with skill. A man sauntered along the planks, coffee cup in one hand and a set of keys in the other. He wore khaki shorts, a dark T-shirt and loafers.

I moved toward him unnoticed until I was standing at the edge of his vessel. He balanced the coffee on a ledge and unlocked the cabin. The boat bore Italian words on the bow. "You're not a fisherman?" I said.

He spun around, then stared at me while I squinted into the sun.

"And, you're not Italian?"

"Swiss," he said finally. "I run a shuttle."

"How much to hire your boat for the next twenty-four hours?"

He sipped his coffee and stowed the keys into his shorts pocket. "That depends on how far you want to go."

"Twenty-four miles."

Moving toward me and really studying my face, he replied, "It won't take all day to travel twenty-four miles." A month ago this close study would have creeped me out, but I saw in him curiosity more than longing. Eros taught me that most men were cowards. I needed to be cautious, but not afraid of everyone.

"I need to make two trips, one this morning and one tonight. I want the assurance that the boat will be available." He nodded and quoted me a reasonable price, so I agreed without haggling. "You'll accept US dollars instead of Euros?"

"Of course," he answered.

He might have been forty, but his unkempt hair and casual clothes gave him a more youthful appearance. I supposed he was handsome. It was hard to say anymore. My sight was tainted. "You have GPS?"

He set his hands on his hips and grinned at my checklist as I rattled it off. "Yes."

"Binoculars?"

"Yes."

I narrowed my eyes at him. "Do you believe in ghosts?"

"No," he answered with a chuckle.

I stepped aboard. "Well, that's good, because I want you to take me to the Fortress of the Goddess. A fisherman told me that seven men have gone missing near its shores in the past two years." Handing over the coordinates, I continued, "This morning I want to see it from a distance. Tonight I'll have you take a crate ashore for me. By the way, do you know where we can find a large delivery crate?"

"What will be in the crate?"

Now it was my turn to smile. "Does it matter?"

We circled the island but kept our distance. The photos on the website were accurate. There was only one way onto the island, and it was the small strip of beach on the north shore. The west, sea-facing side of the island had large caves cut into the cliffs, but there was no way to explore them without being seen. From a quarter of a mile off shore I studied the beach with binoculars. There was too much foliage to clearly see how the cliff tapered down, but I was willing to bet there was a trail leading to the white, marble walls.

I handed the binoculars to my shipmate and asked, "If you were guarding that island, where would you put your look-outs?"

He threw me an incredulous look.

"Humor me," I insisted.

After a long study of the north shore, he answered, "You could place men anywhere along the upper cliff, but they would be seen. If you wanted to guard it without being seen, you'd have to place them in the trees along the ridge."

"We wouldn't be able to see them. Don't you know? The gods can make themselves invisible." I told him about the accounts of deliveries to the island, the strict protocol followed on each sailor's delivery. "The thing is, this is not an expected delivery. There won't be someone waiting on the beach. It's a scout from above you'll have to worry about."

"You think they'll shoot me?"

"Not with bullets. Plus, you're simply delivering a crate. It will catch them by surprise. Hopefully, it'll make them curious instead of angry."

"Are you coming with me for this delivery?"

"Yes." I didn't say more. If all went well, I would leave the island another way. If things didn't go well, I wouldn't be leaving at all.

Two dresses waited for me at the hotel. The desk clerk was just heading out the door at the end of his shift when he saw me and ushered me with enthusiasm toward a closet in the office. "They are very nice. Yes?"

Both dresses were white. One had a halter bodice similar to the one I'd worn in Eros's kingdom. The fabric was white satin, and the waistline was fitted with a back zipper.

The second dress had a drape neckline that was set with sequins and rhinestones. At the waist was a gaudy gold belt. I handed it to the clerk. "Send this one back. I'll take the satin one."

He agreed, and I took the elevator upstairs, where I immediately tried on the dress. The label was a designer I recognized. I wore his clothes on the runway, and without standing in front of the mirror, I knew the fit was perfect. He was a lesser known designer whose line focused mostly on the Italian market, so the dress cost a fraction of what the Valentino had.

Though I tried to sleep, I couldn't. I thought of ordering room service, but I knew I wouldn't be able to eat. In the early afternoon I ventured out to buy sandals to wear with my dress. It was fall, and the shops were pushing leather boots for winter, but I found some strappy, gold sandals on a clearance rack.

The breeze lifted my hair. The smell of coffee and baking bread floated in the air. Of all the places for me to seek Aphrodite, I was glad it was Italy to which I'd come. Though the city was different, and I didn't speak much Italian, it felt familiar. I didn't realize until now how much I enjoyed Milan. Italy was my home away from home, and I found some solace here.

I probably could have used a strong cappuccino, but I ordered a pastry and herbal tea at a café. I didn't want to be any more jittery than I already was. While I waited for my order, I wrote a short letter to my dad explaining why I came to Italy. I apologized for running away, told him I loved him, and asked that he not hold a public funeral for me if I never returned.

Nightfall came slowly. I stood at the window of my hotel room and wished I could reach out and push the sun down. I was dressed in jeans, a black T-shirt, and tennis shoes. My duffle bag lay at my feet. The clothes I'd packed for the trip were strewn on the bed, and now the bag held only the white dress, sandals and Eros's gifts. I left instructions at the front desk to mail the letter to Dad if I didn't return by tomorrow night.

The Swiss was waiting on the shuttle, also dressed in dark clothes and probably hoping it would make him a more difficult target, not that he believed there was really anyone on the island. A large wooden crate sat on the bow of the boat. The print on the side said it contained furniture. After checking that it was secure, I tossed the duffle bag inside. "How do you plan to unload this?"

The man shrugged. "I can run aground on the beach and drop it off the front. The cargo isn't breakable is it?"

"No, that will be fine."

The engine's roar drowned the lap of the water on the pier and the music wafting from a bistro down the street. I stood near the steering column taking calming breaths while he drove. The trip to the Fortress took just under a quarter of an hour. When the shadow of the island came into view, I told him to cut the engine. It was time to load the crate. He watched dumbfounded as I climbed inside.

"Oh, come on. You had to have guessed I was the package?" When he didn't answer, I continued. "Just make sure you get me onto the beach. Don't dump me in the water. Then get the heck out of there." I paid him the rest of his fee.

He looked down at the bills and shook his head. Then he stowed the cash in his pants pocket and pressed the lid down on the crate. A moment later the engine roared to life again.

My heart pounded a hurried rhythm as the motor softened. Shards of moonlight slanted through the lid of the crate. The bright moon made the boat easier to see. We glided slowly to the beach. I felt a sudden jerk as the bow struck sand. We were there.

# CHAPTER 14

He grunted and heaved the crate. I tumbled backward. The crate rolled twice and landed on the lid. I rocked hard to the side so I wouldn't be trapped. Then I waited. The boat's engine rumbled low until it cleared the shallow water near the beach, then jumped full throttle in the distance. That was my cue. If someone watched from above, now he would leave his post to inspect the crate. I had only seconds to move.

I kicked the crate open, crouched low and ran into the shadow of the cliff. There I stripped down to my underwear and pulled on the white dress. In my hurry, the zipper gave me trouble, but I managed to get it up and the neck tied. I slid into the sandals while pulling on the belt and arm cuff. The bracelet was too difficult to clasp in the dark, so I put the pendant on first. It was the most important part of this costume. As I fastened it on my forehead, I heard voices above. They were coming. I threw my clothes and the bracelet into the duffle bag and hid it in the bushes. Then I stumbled onto the beach, where I could be seen, glowing like an apparition all in white.

I hoped they weren't veiled, or my ruse was off. I went toward the voices, and just as they broke from the trees, I reached out to them and let myself collapse on the sand.

With an exclamation in Eros's language, the two young men ran toward me. I let my eyes flutter open and saw their concerned faces. Like Eros's servants they were in their late teens. One shook me, asking me questions. I closed my eyes and let my head fall limply. He took the bait. He gathered me into his arms and carried me toward the palace.

The entrance to the palace was hidden in the foliage. We entered a cave, crossed through a doorway, then climbed a circular stairwell before breaking into the light of the palace foyer. Once inside, the other man shouted, "Theron! Theron!"

We passed through the foyer into a great, round room. Though my head dangled against the man's shoulder, I kept my eyes half-open. Eight pillars held up the frescoed ceiling. White chairs and lounge benches stood in clusters around the room. Onto one of these benches I was laid. The guy who carried me shook me gently, then took my face into his hands until I opened my eyes fully. I blinked at the brightness of the room.

He asked me something, probably, "Are you all right?" or "What's your name?"

I did not speak.

A man in his late twenties came to see the cause of all the commotion. He wore mortal clothes like he had been on the mainland. With light hair that fell in unruly waves around his forehead, he would have been inhumanly handsome if it hadn't been for his menacing eyes. This was Theron, the bodyguard Gina warned me about.

At his approach, the others offered brief, muttered explanations before retreating halfway across the room. Theron knelt before me, looked closely at my face, then reached out with one flawless hand. He caught me by the throat and squeezed just hard enough to threaten without cutting off the air. He rocked back on his heels, rose and took me with him.

Now that I stood before him, he released my throat and inspected me. His eyes took in the belt, the arm cuff, skittered over the pendant but settled onto the bodice of my dress. He walked a circle around me, touching my shoulder as he passed, then drew his finger across my back to the zipper. I was caught. The immortals didn't use zippers.

"Which part of 'No Trespassing' don't you understand?" he whispered. His English was as flawless as his beauty.

"Please," I answered softly, "I came to see Aphrodite."

At the mention of her name, he spun me around, threw me against a massive column, and held me there with a forearm across my chest. He pulled a knife from his belt and brought it near my cheek. He glared into my eyes. "How dare you come here and further insult the goddess? I have every right to kill you." Over his shoulder he called to the other servants, "You fools brought a mortal into the palace."

When one protested, Theron grabbed my hand and sliced the blade across my palm. I yelped in pain as the cut erupted angry red.

"Immortal blood is clear," he told me. "Aphrodite will have nothing to do with you."

Pain flared my temper. I shoved him hard and freed myself from the pillar. "I would have told them what I was if you'd given me the chance!" I squeezed my hand into a fist, trying to slow the bleeding. "I'm Eros's betrothed," I said, "and I seek an audience with the goddess, Aphrodite."

Theron looked more closely at the pendant. His eyes twitched slightly as he recognized the signature. Then his jaw set in frustration. Apparently the pendant carried more sway than he let on. "This way."

He pressed the knife against my back as we passed through the vast rooms. The windows were shuttered so they gave no light to the exterior. The mansion was very old, but electric lighting and indoor plumbing had been added. The pipes and conduits showed along the ceilings and walls, but these were the only things that dated the interior. The furnishings were lavish and new. The hallway floor was marble. Hammered bronze chandeliers hung from the ceiling, and matching sconces lit the hallway.

On the upper level we stood before double doors, and Theron told me to open them. White wall-to-wall carpet spread between the pale blue walls. A woman rose from a pillowed chair with her back to us. "Did you get rid of the trespasser?"

"I thought you might want to see her," Theron replied.

She turned, and he motioned to the pendant. Her mouth flattened into a line as she approached.

"Did you know they were one and the same?" Theron asked.

Aphrodite studied my face then the signature on my forehead. "I assure you, I did not."

I was no scholar of Greek mythology, but Aphrodite wasn't what I imagined. She was beautiful, of course—amazingly so—but she held her features with a hard edge. Like her bodyguard, she had piercing blue eyes. She'd passed her high cheekbones and radiant skin on to her beautiful son. She was as tall as me, slender, and would be hard pressed to pass for forty, so ageless was her face.

"What is this?" She gestured to the hand dripping blotches of red onto my dress and leaving a puddle at my feet. "Theron, fetch some rags and bandage this." As soon as the door closed behind him, she asked, "Why did you come? If you knew the way, you must have known the risk."

"I didn't care about risks. I have to talk to Eros." I stepped forward, but was caught by her quick glance, which told me plainly I had not been invited to move. I retreated onto the square of marble just inside the doorway. "He didn't give me a chance to explain. I was afraid, but I love him."

"I doubt he would believe that, even if I told him."

"There must be a way," I pleaded, "for me to prove myself to him."

Theron returned with bandages. After he slapped some gauze on the wound, wrapped it with a long strip of cloth and tied it snugly, Aphrodite spoke, "I'll propose three tasks. If you complete them, I'll grant you an audience with Eros." I agreed without hesitation, but Aphrodite held up her hand, and Theron chuckled like I'd agreed to swim the Atlantic.

"If you don't complete them, you will never again hear Eros's voice or see his face. You will live your life as if you'd never met him."

Her offer stank, but there was no other way. I couldn't find him on my own.

"We'll have this down in writing, so it's legal." She took sheets of parchment and a calligraphy pen from the drawer of an antique desk. She wrote two copies of the contract and offered them to me.

I shook my head. "In English. I won't sign something I can't read."

Aphrodite let out an exasperated sigh, then offered the paper and pen to Theron. "In English."

He sat at the desk and translated her writing into beautiful English script, then offered the contracts to me. I read both and found they laid out the terms exactly as she spoke them. She added that refusal to perform a task was deemed a forfeiture. I took the offered pen and signed my name under the terms of the contract on both copies. My hand left a smudge of blood next to my name.

Theron fingered the smudge. "Even better."

Aphrodite read the contract again. Satisfied, she signed her name, then she turned to me. "I'll keep the pendant as collateral in our agreement." She held out her hand.

"You have a contract signed in blood. You don't need collateral."

"I think I do."

Before I could shy away, Theron snatched the pendant from my head taking a handful of hair with it. I growled in pain, and his eyes glistened with satisfaction. He passed the pendant into Aphrodite's hand. She slipped it into her pocket and went to a bedside table. From the drawer she took a magazine. Across the room I recognized the cover, and I knew what was inside—the Venus ad.

She thumbed the pages and she came toward me. "You openly mocked me in print. You stole the love of my only son, and then you burned him." She stopped on the full-color, double-page spread of the Venus advertisement. There was no kindness in the set of her shoulders now.

That contract was going to be the death of me.

"How many of these are there?"

I didn't answer.

"At least a million," Theron offered.

*Cosmopolitan*'s U.S. circulation topped three million, but I wasn't about to tell Aphrodite that.

"And, there are billboards," Theron added.

There was noticeable frustration in her voice. "How many?"

"Only a handful," I interjected. I wanted to elbow Theron in the gut, but he'd probably break my arm.

"Your first task is to rid the mortal world of this despicable Venus painting."

"Photograph," Theron corrected.

"You don't know even how many there are," I said. "Even if I got every one, you would lie and say I failed. No, you pick a number. Tell me how many you want, and I will get them."

Aphrodite's cheeks blushed with rising fury. "One million..." Her eyes searched Theron's face for help. From the corner of my eye, I saw him lift his chin. "... four hundred thousand of these little ones." She held up the magazine. "And, a dozen billiards."

"Billboards," Theron muttered.

"Those. I'll give you a month," Aphrodite replied. "Don't ever come ..."

"A month if you pick them up," I interrupted. "Two months if you want them delivered." I wasn't Ron Middleton's daughter for nothing. I'd seen him negotiate terms a hundred times.

Theron moved forward, ready to inflict bodily injury, but Aphrodite set a hand on his chest. "Delivered." She turned to her bodyguard. "When is the new moon?"

"The day after tomorrow," Theron replied.

"We don't use your calendar," Aphrodite said to me. "Your time begins the day after tomorrow. They must be delivered by the second new moon. Theron will contact you. See her out." With that dismissal she returned to the pillowed chair, where she held up the pendant and watched it sparkle in the lamplight.

We followed a conspicuous red trail back downstairs. "You'll return home?" Theron asked. "To where?"

"Bozeman, Montana. You know where that is?"

He nodded. "You have a cell phone?"

The question caught me off guard. We stood in the timeless palace of a Greek goddess, but like Eros, Theron understood modern life. "It's at the hotel."

"What's the number?"

I rattled it off, and said, "Do you want me to write it down?"

"I'll remember."

The two young men who brought me inside the palace waited in the round room murmuring to one another. At the sight of us they straightened into silence.

The older of the two looked about twenty. He stood as tall as Theron with dark hair, olive skin and full lips. I caught him looking at my hand, where the blood had already soaked the bandage bright red.

"Change clothes and return her to the mainland," Theron said to dark-haired guy.

"I left a duffle bag on the beach," I said.

Theron sent another man to fetch it, and when he returned, so had the dark-haired guy, who wore cargo shorts, a half-zip sweater and sandals. Ironically, standing between him and Theron, I looked the least mortal, except for the blood on my dress.

They led me down a hallway that descended out of the marbled halls of the palace and into rough hewn passages within the island cliffs. Eventually we met a wide wooden door. Beyond it was a stairwell that descended into darkness. Theron threw a switch, and a single row of dim bulbs appeared to guide us down.

The young man and I entered the stairwell, and Theron closed the door behind us. The metallic *clunk* of the lock said there was no going back. I walked blindly for five or six steps before my eyes adjusted to the darkness. The dampness clung to my skin, and the musty air felt stale in my lungs. Still, it was easier to breathe now that a locked door separated me from Theron.

We descended about thirty steps before the stairway widened into a cave. On either side were iron bars which made cages of the lesser caves. The cages were more shadowed than lit, but on one wall hung a pair of iron shackles.

The air felt colder, and I stifled a shiver. I knew my guide was watching me.

"That's where you would have ended up if Theron decided to kill you. If you're wise, you won't cross Theron."

I held up my hand. "I've been warned already." I kept walking and hoped the next bend in the corridor wouldn't be worse.

The stairwell narrowed and the steps grew steeper. My sandal slipped on the stone, and I instinctively reached out to catch myself. My wounded hand hit the stone, and the sharp pain nearly made me sick.

My companion offered a hand to steady me, but I didn't take it. "Keep it above your heart," he murmured.

Of course, I knew that, but I wasn't doing it. I discreetly tucked my hand through the haltered neck of my dress. The bandage felt hot and sticky on my collarbone, but in a few minutes the pain lessened to a dull throb. I wanted to cry, but I wouldn't allow myself the luxury of tears until I was alone. "Will you be punished for taking me into the palace?"

"Most likely." He slowed his pace to match mine. He carried my duffle bag on his shoulder.

"I'm sorry for getting you in trouble." I realized how costly that mistake might be. What would Theron do to him?

"Less trouble than you." He motioned to the contract in my hand.

We were close to the water now. Its gentle lap echoed in the stairwell, and the air smelled of fish and rotting seaweed. "They expect me to fail," I replied.

"Of course they expect you to fail. No mortal has ever succeeded at Aphrodite's tasks." He shoved a hand into his pocket angrily. "I can't believe Eros betrothed himself to one of your kind."

I suppose I should have been offended, but I appreciated his honesty.

"Don't do it. Forget Eros. Walk away from here and pretend you never met Aphrodite."

He made it sound so simple, but there was no way I could forget Eros. I would rather roam the country collecting a million magazines than forget those violet eyes. "I can't."

He caught my arm and stopped me. "He dusted you, didn't he?"

I jerked my arm from his fingers. "No, he didn't." I could tell he didn't believe me, but I didn't care. It was none of his business. He was Aphrodite's servant. Anything I told him would be repeated upstairs once I was on the mainland. But wait, maybe that was a good thing. "He didn't have to," I confessed. "I loved him without seeing his face." Tell that to your mistress, I thought. Make sure she knows I will complete these tasks.

The stairs ended inside a huge cave with a semi-circle walkway around a small bay. A speedboat bobbed softly in the water. "Get aboard," my companion said.

On the other side of the bay a giant wheel was attached to thick chain and some kind of pulley system. As soon as I was seated in the boat, he doused the light. I heard the wheel churn into motion. The stone slab separating us from the sea rose and revealed a narrow passageway to open water.

He drove us out of the caves and headed a quarter mile toward the open sea before looping back to Naples. I wondered what hazards lay beneath the water that made him take this route, but it didn't matter.

If I ever returned to that island, Theron would kill me for sure.

# CHAPTER 15

I was camped out in a plastic chair for the two-hour layover in Chicago when I finally gathered the courage to power on my cell phone. The flight home went from Naples to Chicago before connecting to Bozeman. Since I was only a few hours from facing my dad, I wanted to know what to expect when I got there.

The inbox of my voicemail was full, and every message was from Dad. The first few were worried, then angry, desperate, and finally, remorseful. "Psyche, I'm sorry," he said. "Whatever I did that drove you away, I'm sorry. Please, just come home."

I hoped that meant he wouldn't ground me forever.

The downstairs lights were off when I pulled up to the curb. I'd hardly eaten all day. After dropping my duffle bag on the dining room table, I ransacked the fridge for left-overs. I found chicken pot pie and a can of root beer.

There was a rumble of feet down the stairs. "Psyche?"

Hands full of food, I turned and held my breath.

Dad crossed the kitchen and pulled me to his chest. "Where have you been?"

I hugged him back briefly, then I waited for him to let me go. "It's probably better if you didn't know."

He stepped back and said, "You're gonna tell me anyway."

"I'm hungry." I put the food in the microwave and opened the root beer.

Dad waited unmoved.

I was a terrible liar, but I did my best. "There was someone I needed to see."

"Who?"

Yeah, right. I couldn't tell him that. "You don't know her." As an afterthought I added, "A client." It was sort of true. I was doing her bidding now.

"You're modeling again?"

I shrugged as the microwave beeped. I pulled the container out and blew steam off each bite, but I still burned my tongue.

"Psyche, where *were* you?" Dad demanded. He eyed my bandaged hand. I'd put fresh gauze on it, but it soaked through again.

"Naples."

"Florida?"

"Italy." Four bites, and I was no longer hungry. I set the food on the counter. "I charged some stuff on the credit card..."

"And you'll pay back every dime of it," he snapped.

"I wouldn't have it any other way." I stepped past him, grabbed my duffle bag and started upstairs. I'd been up for twenty hours. If he wanted to punish me, I was too exhausted to argue.

I'd missed about a week of classes. I couldn't even remember what day of the week it was, much less the date. Time had shifted and stalled for me since Eros threw me out.

Fallen flower pedals littered the floor in front of my locker, remnants of a shrine left to Savannah, which had been cleared by the custodian. The front of her locker remained wallpapered with post-its and photographs that students left in her memory. "We miss you!" one said. Another said, "You were always nice to me. I'll miss your smile." Near the bottom was an index card taped on three sides. I pulled it off and read the back. "I never told you I loved you." It was signed by a junior boy I barely knew. I carefully set it back in its place.

"Why'd she do it?" Travis's voice startled me.

Later I learned it was his first day back at school, too. I faced him, not knowing what to say.

He usually avoided my eyes, but now he looked at me like he was trying to find absolution somewhere in my face. "I loved her."

I thought of her tears after he broke up with her and how she said she meant nothing to him. "She knew that." I would never tell him how Savannah betrayed me.

"She left her sweatshirt in my car," he said absently then wandered away. I wondered if I should have tried harder to help him, but I was too consumed with my own heartache.

When I reached first period, I found out it was Tuesday. Tonight was the new moon. I had exactly sixty days to complete the first task.

While the class copied notes in chemistry, I nudged Rory's shoulder. "What are you doing for lunch?"

He turned his head sideways and muttered into his shoulder, "Same as every other day. PBJ and Robert Jordan in the caf."

"Who's Robert? Is he a senior?"

Rory dropped a paperback novel onto my desk. "Fantasy."

I scribbled intently while Mr. Darling passed our row. When he crossed the room, I whispered, "If I buy, will you ditch Jordan and have lunch with me?"

Rory slowly turned in his chair with suspicious eyes. "Serious?"

I copied the last of the notes and looked up. "Yeah. I need a genius. Thought you'd be the guy to ask."

"I'm flattered." He looked around and added quietly, "You sure you want to be seen with me?"

"As long as you don't mind being seen— possibly photographed—with me." I wasn't kidding about the paparazzi. The crowd and the news crews had moved on, but a few photographers remained to torment me.

One was sitting at the edge of the high school parking lot with a zoom lens when Rory and I crossed the street to a Mom & Pop burger joint.

I ordered my usual out of habit—a mushroom-Swiss burger and vanilla milkshake—but when we took our seats at a window booth, I could only force down a single bite. Like the toast I ate this morning, the burger tasted like cardboard in my mouth and threatened to come up after I swallowed. I pushed the food aside and thumbed through Rory's novel. "Do you believe in this stuff?"

Rory took a bite of his double cheeseburger and answered with his mouth full. "It's obviously called fantasy for a reason."

"Yeah, but I mean the fundamentals. Good always triumphs. The knight saves the lady in distress."

"Damsel," he corrected.

"What?"

Rory licked ketchup off his finger. "Damsel in distress."

"Whatever." I turned the book over and studied the cover. Words were harder to come by than I expected.

He sat back and thought while sipping his Coke. "I believe you can overcome insurmountable odds with fortitude and a little luck."

I tossed the book to him. "You're definitely the guy I need."

"For what?" Rory paused with a fry poised in front of his mouth. His gaze was somewhere across the restaurant. He looked over his shoulder and across the room in the other direction.

I slid lower in the booth. That little knot of anxiety churned in my chest.

Rory swallowed his last few fries and reached for mine, which where untouched. "People are staring at us," he whispered.

"We should go." I started to pull up the hood of my sweatshirt, but Rory stopped me. I wanted to kick his shin under the table when I realized he enjoyed people staring at us.

"You didn't answer my question."

"I need to collect one point four million copies of the Venus ad."

"Why?"

I told my dad a fraction of the truth, and he had the hospital test me for hallucinogens. "I can't tell you."

"Why not?" When I didn't answer, Rory grew irritated. "But you want my help." He tossed wrappers and used napkins onto the tray. "Sorry, but if you can't trust me, I can't help you. We're late for class." He dumped the trash and walked out the door.

I should have known Rory wouldn't help without knowing all the details. The clock was ticking, and it looked like I was going to lose.

That night I slept in fits. My mind wouldn't let me rest. Every time I drifted off, I dreamed of Eros's voice, his palace and his fury at my betrayal. I slept half an hour here, an hour there, but my dreams shook me awake, more exhausted than when I lay down. By three-thirty I was restlessly dozing. In my dream I was trapped in the meadow surrounded by dogs, all barking and nipping at me. I opened my eyes and realized one of the dogs was real. He was in the neighbor's yard outside and barking relentlessly. I was about to get out of bed and shout out the window at him, but I realized I wasn't alone.

I lay motionless and watched the top dresser drawer slide open on its own. The veiled intruder searched beneath the clothes. He found the amethyst belt and bracelet but pushed them aside and kept searching.

"Eros," I whispered.

The hidden person stopped moving.

"I know you're there. Don't hide from me."

"I'm sorry, Psyche." It was not the voice I hoped for.

I sat up. "Aeas?"

He appeared in front of the dresser still holding a pair of my socks.

"What are you doing here?" I demanded.

"He sent me for the pendant," he answered softly. "May I have it, please?"

"No." My voice was cold and flat, sort of like my heart lately.

"I've never seen him like this." Aeas slid the drawer closed. "He abandoned the kingdom for days and when he returned, he demanded I get that pendant."

I glared at the shadow in front of me. "Tell him if he wants it back, he can come get it himself."

"Psyche," Aeas pleaded. "He'll be furious if I return without it."

"Even if you search this whole room, you won't find that pendant, and I won't give it to you. Now get out!"

There was a pause in my dad's snoring down the hallway. We fell silent and waited for his door to open, but he started snoring again.

Aeas disappeared before my eyes. "I didn't want to come."

Saturday morning was deceptively bright. Sunshine streaked through tufts of clouds and gave the illusion of a warm day, but the moment I stepped outside, cold nipped at my fingers and nose. I pulled gloves out of the pocket of my coat and carefully slipped one over my bandaged hand, then used my teeth to secure the other one before heading down the driveway to my car. A van was parked across the street, and a telephoto lens reflected sunlight as I climbed into my Subaru and locked the doors.

The photographer followed me to Rory's house, taking more pictures while I knocked on the door, and he answered. "Can we talk inside?" I stepped through the doorway. "Sorry. We're being watched."

"We are?" Rory stuck his head out the door, spotted the van and waved. "Have a nice day," he shouted.

I was irritated, but I tried to keep my voice friendly. I really did need his help. "I came to apologize. You'll think I'm crazy, but..."

Rory interrupted, "Uh, why don't we go somewhere more private before..."

"Rory," a woman's voice called from the kitchen. "Was someone at the door?" She came around the corner drying her hands on a dish towel and blinked at the sight of me. "Oh, hello."

"Mom, you remember Psyche Middleton?"

Her gaze went from Rory to me and back again.

Rory cleared his throat. "She needs help with homework." He jerked his head toward the hallway and strode off.

"It's nice to see you again, Mrs. Keene." I followed him down the hall.

"I'm baking cookies," she called after us.

Rory opened a door and motioned me inside.

I crossed the threshold into a castle. The gray walls had been lined to give the illusion of stone. Dark carpet, velvet drapes and a mahogany poster bed made the room look like a small royal chamber. A sculpted dragon stood on the dresser, and a green stuffed version stood waist high on the floor next to the bed. One entire wall was filled with floor-to-ceiling bookshelves, and in the corner sat a computer desk equipped with two large monitors. Here was a guy that spent a lot of time reading and a lot of time gaming.

After a nervous glance down the hallway, Rory shut the door. "Let me just say two things. One, most of this," he gestured around the room, "was my mom's doing, and two, I've never had a girl in here, so it never mattered before."

"I like it." I fingered a velvet curtain. "It's cool."

His shoulders relaxed. "Thanks... I like it, too."

Rory dropped into the computer chair, and I sat on the bed. We used to play together in his room all the time when we were little, but this was beyond weird. Rory looked out the window; I looked at the carpet.

Finally I broke the awkward silence. "So, you probably heard how they found me in the mountains?"

"You almost froze to death," he replied. In a town like this, it's pretty hard to keep a secret, especially when you end up in the ER.

"I was seeing this guy, and he threw me out." I wasn't sure which part of that surprised him more, but there was obvious confusion in his eyes. I went on undaunted. "I want to talk to him again, but I can't. So, I made a deal with his...uh, mom." I reached into my messenger bag and drew out the rolled parchment tied with ribbon. "Aphrodite." I offered the contract to him. "See for yourself."

He snatched the document from my hand, but the ancient characters she'd written stopped him dead. His eyes widened on me, and he quickly scanned the English text. "So you're trying to..."

"Win back Eros, the god of love."

Rory fingered the signature. "Aphrodite. She exists. You've seen her?"

I nodded. "She looks younger than our parents."

"Incredible." He rolled the document closed and offered it to me. "Collecting one point four million ads is the first task. What are the others?"

"I don't know. I have to complete one to get the next. She probably figures I'll fail at this, and she won't have to bother with the rest." And she was probably right. Even with Rory's help, the task was impossible given a year. With only two months, we were grasping at straws. I explained the details of the task then said, "I called my agent yesterday. The ad debuted in *Cosmopolitan* and will run in Vogue this month. She said sales were up. Cosmo's circulation spiked to three and a quarter million." I rolled the contract carefully and returned it to my bag. "I wondered if we could get a lawyer to order a recall. It totally violated my contract."

Rory sat back and folded his arms. "How so?"

"It was right there in the paperwork I signed: no nudity."

"If your contract said 'no nudity', why'd you pose for it?" Rory's tone was cutting.

My temper flared. "I wasn't nude, and I have the original to prove it!" I pulled it from my portfolio this morning. Now I handed it to Rory. The original was completely different from the billboard. The background was a swirl of blue, and I was standing in an open clam shell, but all the other features of the painting had been added later. In the photo it was obvious I wore something under the wig. The strings of the bikini showed at my neck, across my chest and on my hips. They'd posed my hand to cover most of the bikini bottom, but the flesh-colored fabric stood out behind my fingers.

Rory studied the photo, and when he handed it back, he didn't meet my eyes. "I'm sorry I thought..."

"It's what everyone thinks," I answered.

"I don't think they will issue a recall. They edited the strings off, but it's not like they put your head on someone else's nude body. It *is* you, and you're basically covered. Legally, I don't think you have a case. Plus, the courts are slow. You'd miss your deadline."

I stuffed the photo into my bag and felt myself crumbling from the inside. There had to be a way, somehow.

"I think we should have a contest," Rory said. His hand swept across the air like a headline. "Win a date with Venus. The entry fee is one copy of the ad. Enter as many times as you like."

No one had ever asked me on a date. What made him think guys would buy magazines to go out with me? I'd probably have more luck going door to door.

"We could offer, like a hundred entries for every billboard," Rory said. His eyes shimmered as the ideas hatched in his mind. "We could make a video and upload it to YouTube, so people know it's legit." He turned to his computer and typed furiously. "And, I'll post it on Dragonslayers Anonymous."

"Dragonslayers?" I muttered.

"It's a website for fantasy junkies like me. A million members, well over half are in the U.S."

That knot from yesterday threatened explode. "No way." I hated that Venus ad. I didn't want to attract more attention to it. This was exactly the sort of thing that would bring on a panic attack. "I can't." Plus, the press might show up at my doorstep again.

Rory's voice softened. "When we were kids, I told my mom how you were afraid of stuff."

"Stuff?" I said sarcastically. If he wanted to parade my paranoia across the room, he might as well be accurate. I wasn't afraid of small spaces, the dark, fast cars or wild horses. I'd ridden every roller coaster at Seven Flags when Dad took me there. I was afraid of heights and...

"People. It told her how you were afraid of strangers and crowds." He had large, light-flecked eyes and a nice chin. They were small things I'd never noticed before. If it weren't for the terrible acne, he'd be more handsome than Travis McDowell. "She said it was probably because your mom left you. She told me you'd grow out of it."

"Guess what?" I grabbed my bag and headed for the door, angry and disappointed. "I didn't."

My dad was in the kitchen when I got home. As long as I lived I would always picture him with his sleeves rolled up standing at the stove. He didn't look one bit like those pompous chefs on cooking shows, but my dad was a genius in the kitchen.

"What's on the menu tonight?" I asked as I dropped my bag on a bar stool.

"Wild mushroom ravioli with pesto." He looked up, and his shoulders relaxed. "I bought a new cookbook." When he smiled, the little lines around his eyes crinkled, but that was about the extent my dad had aged. He was still lean and broad shouldered. "Where've you been?" he asked lightly, but his eyes betrayed him. He was worried.

"Rory Keene's house."

Dad set the lid on a pot and wiped his hands on a towel. "The boy that lived across the street?"

"He's in my chemistry class." I guess I learned the art of evasion from Eros.

"Homework is a good distraction."

"Yeah." I wished homework was the extent of my worries. In fact, I totally forgot about the mountain of make-up work that wasn't getting done.

The food smelled good, but when we sat down to eat, I lost my appetite. I ate a small serving to satisfy my dad and prayed it wouldn't come back up. I'd never been like this before, jittery and restless, unable to eat or sleep. Something in me was off, and I couldn't fix it.

I spent that night and most of the next day trying to catch up on school work. I struggled to concentrate and had to redo one assignment twice. Sunday night brought another bout of restless sleep so I woke Monday morning more exhausted than the night before.

I felt miserable. My belly swam with depression-induced nausea, a constant murmur I was getting used to. I was groggy when I dragged myself to the shower hoping to kick-start my system. There I realized something was different. Gone was the oversized bandage on my hand, and in its place was a gauze wrapping, which was now soaked from the shower. I pulled at the end and started unwinding, tossing the long strand over the shower curtain as it unraveled. When I pulled the last of the gauze away, there was no gash—not healed into a scar, but *gone*. I opened and closed my fist, then checked the other hand just to be sure. It was as if Theron never cut me. My awe sprang into panicked hope. Someone had done this, and it wasn't a mortal.

I switched off the water and threw on clothes, barely pausing to dry. Did Eros come himself after all? I paused at my bedroom door and listened for even the slightest movement. I sniffed the air. Did I imagine that hint of cinnamon? I crossed the room and pitched forward over an invisible foot. The body groaned as I landed with a thud on top of it. I jumped to my feet, and Aeas appeared clutching his abdomen.

"Good morning to you, too," he muttered.

"I told you to get out."

"And I left," he answered, "but I'm back."

"You're not welcome here."

He was sleeping under a wool cloak with only a sash over his chest.

"Why are you wearing your native clothes?"

"Eros didn't give me time to change before he threw me out." Aeas sat up. "I can't step foot in the kingdom without the pendant." His skin prickled with goose bumps, and he rubbed his arms to warm them. Fall in Montana was no time to be wandering around shirtless.

I dug jeans and a sweatshirt out of my dresser and tossed them to Aeas. "I don't have the pendant anymore." I showed him Aphrodite's contract. "She kept it as collateral."

He started to read then sat on the end of the bed. His eyes went over the words several times before he leveled his gaze at me. "How did you find her?"

"The fortune teller. She used to be..."

"You've seen Alia?" he interrupted.

"She goes by Gina now."

Aeas drew his brow together and studied the contract again. "She had no right to send you to Aphrodite."

"Look, I know you're his friend and all, but she did me a favor. He moved the portal, so I couldn't come back." I slouched onto the opposite side of the bed feeling defeated. "Anyway, you can take him the contract and tell him his mother has the pendant. That should get you back into the kingdom. Or you can fly to Naples and ask her for it yourself."

Aeas threw off his sash. "She wouldn't give it to me. I doubt she'd give it to Eros until your bargain was over." He held the jeans up in front of him. "Are these women's clothes?"

"The sweatshirt is unisex. The jeans are men's actually."

He and the jeans disappeared. "Why do you wear men's pants?"

"They're less flattering."

"Always hiding, just like him." He reappeared wearing my clothes. "How do I look?"

"Like a freshman." He gave me a puzzled look, but I didn't explain. "So what are you gonna do?"

"There is only one thing I can do—stay and help you complete the tasks."

"Stay where? Here? My dad will skin you alive if he finds you here. Eros will understand once you show him the contract. He'll let you back into the kingdom."

Hands on his hips, Aeas replied flatly, "No. He won't."

The alarm on my phone buzzed. "We'll have to talk about this later. I am going to be late for school."

"Then let's go."

"Oh, no. You're not coming with me." Been there, done that with Eros. He caused enough trouble.

"Well, I'm not going to stay here and let your dad skin me." Aeas pulled his leather shoes onto his feet. "You won't even know I'm there."

I lost track of Aeas the moment we got out of the car, but he'd promised to stay with me all day and not cause trouble. The morning passed in a blur. I was too restless to hear anything my teachers said. I kept my head down and bided the time until third period when I would see Rory.

"I've been looking for you all morning," Rory said when I slid into the seat behind him. "Thought you might have skipped."

I considered it, but I was too far behind in my classes already.

Rory set his arms on my desk and murmured. "I surfed around the Internet last night. That picture of you has gone viral. Did you know you already have fan sites?"

He might as well have punched me in the stomach. My mouth watered like it does right before I puke.

Rory saw the look on my face. "That's not a bad thing, Psyche. It makes your task easier."

I looked around, not knowing where Aeas was. "The seat next to me was Savannah's," I said quietly. "No one sits there anymore."

Rory wrinkled his eyebrows in confusion. He thought I was talking to him.

"*Beauty* and the *Beast*," a girl sang as she passed Rory and I hunched over my desk.

"Hailey," I snapped, "why don't you pick on someone with an IQ as low as yours?"

"Hot off the presses." She tossed a magazine onto my desk. There smeared across the cover was that same headline, "Beauty and the Beast," with a close-up photo of Rory and I leaving the burger joint last week.

My eyes burned at the cruelty. "Rory, I'm sorry."

He forced a smile. "I can't help it if I'm beautiful." He turned to Hailey. "You can keep your gossip rag. Psyche and I know where we were this weekend." He winked at me.

"Fame is dangerous," I warned, trying to match his playful tone, but I was amazed he could shrug this off. "It's going to your head already."

"You need a new lab partner," he replied, "since we already established that the seat next to you is empty. My partner's gone. Wanna pair up?"

"Yes," I replied. Chemistry just got a lot easier.

Rory skated through our lab like it was remedial freshman science. I stood back and watched as he filled the beakers, mixed, measured and made careful notes.

"Do you really think I can get over a million magazines with a contest?" I asked.

Rory stirred a substance on the burner. "Most definitely."

"You realize this is a total nightmare for me. What if he's some nasty truck driver with no teeth?"

"Is that what you're worried about?" Rory dropped his pen onto the lab notebook. "We'll rig it," he whispered. "We hold the contest, then you can pick whoever you want in the drawing."

"But I would have to pick someone," I muttered. Rigging the drawing had never crossed my mind. My dad raised me to be fair, but it was the only safe option, even if it was dishonest. I felt a twinge of guilt but even more relief. "Okay," I relented. "Win a date with Venus. I know I am going to regret this."

# CHAPTER 16

I drove through at the nearest taco place and ordered the ten-taco combo. I held a handful of tacos up between the seats. "Aeas, meet Rory. Rory, meet Aeas."

Rory looked at me like I was crazy until a hand appeared and took the tacos from me. Then he spun around and looked at the boy in the back seat. "Where did he come from?"

"He's been with me all day. Veiled."

"Veiled." Rory repeated. Quietly he added, "He looks kinda young."

"Don't let that fool you. Aeas, what are you? Fifteen?"

He chewed and swallowed before speaking. "I'm thirteen annum shy of sixteen."

"Which means he's by far the oldest person in this car. For every year of his age, he's lived a hundred of ours. He's thirteen years shy of sixteen *hundred*. He probably speaks five languages."

"Eight," Aeas corrected. "Wish you guys would settle on one and use it forever like we do."

"Phenomenal," Rory whispered as he started munching a taco. "So, have you spent much time in our world?"

"Not as much as Eros, but a fair amount. He sends to me to deliver messages and sign all his legal documents. I go places he can't be seen."

"Eros is always invisible?" Rory wadded up a wrapper and started on another taco.

Aeas shook his head with a laugh. "He prefers not to be seen. Pretty much every woman who sees him wants to have his child."

Rory turned to me. "Have you seen him?"

"Once, without his permission, which is why I'm in this mess." I saw a flash of curiosity in Rory's eyes, and it made me defensive. "I didn't offer to have his child," I said emphatically. "I didn't offer him anything."

In the mirror I saw Aeas's expression sadden. "That's why he loved you."

After school I took Aeas shopping so he wouldn't have to keep wearing my clothes. My hands gripped the steering wheel tighter as I pulled into the mall parking lot. Another crowd. Another chance for people to gawk at Venus. "No dallying," I warned. "We grab, pay and dash. Got it?"

"Got it," Aeas replied.

"Don't you dare disappear on me." I took a deep breath and marched into the store. I headed to the men's section where I pulled cargos and jeans from the racks and dumped them into Aeas's arms. My clothes fit him, so I bought the same sizes.

When a sales guy headed our way, I crouched toward the bottom row of shirts and kept my face turned away. "Can I help you find something?" the employee asked.

"We're good, thanks," Aeas replied without hesitation.

"Nicely done," I murmured, as the guy walked away.

"I'm an expert at running off unwanted attention. It's what I've been doing for him all our lives." He pulled a shirt from a rack. "I like this one."

"Good taste, too. Grab a few more and we're out of here."

"I'll pay you back," he said as we went to the car.

"Don't worry about it. Consider it a thank you for my hand."

"It was the least I could do since I came into your home uninvited twice. I hope you understand. I have access to Eros's accounts, but I could never steal from him."

I hadn't known him very long, but I knew Aeas was loyal and honest. Eros trusted him completely. "Just stay out of sight when my dad is home."

"If you don't mind me asking, what is this Venus ad you were talking about?"

I decided to show him rather than explain. We hit a red light a block from the billboard, and Aeas's mouth actually dropped open at the sight of it. "The birth of Venus," he whispered. "You saw her face to face?" He turned to me in disbelief. "And she didn't harm you?"

"I had the pendant."

"Still..." His voice trailed off. "You know that story mortals tell about Aphrodite blinding a man because he saw her bathing?"

"Yeah."

"It's true. Theron did it for her."

"Now, that I believe. I also believe if we succeed at this task, the others will be harder."

"And more dangerous," he added. "Are you sure we need Rory's help?"

"With this task we most certainly do."

"I don't like the way he looks at you."

I stomped on the gas when the light turned green. "That isn't your concern. He's helping me out of kindness. You're only helping me because you want to go home." That shut him up. Facing Aphrodite's tasks, I had no room for testosterone bickering.

Rory pulled into the driveway just as we climbed out of the car. "I borrowed a friend's camera. It's better quality than mine," he said. "And I typed up a press release during fifth period." Rory turned to me. "But, there is one magazine I thought you would collect yourself."

"Why would I ..." Then I saw it in my mind—Savannah opening the magazine in Chemistry to show me the ad. "Yeah, I'll talk to her mom."

Rory opened the front door, stood a moment and inhaled. "My mom's been baking."

"I never say no to brownies," I answered as I crossed the doorstep, but my thought was lost as the scent hit me—cinnamon and oranges.

"Smells like home," Aeas added. "Psyche!"

I heard his voice but couldn't answer. My knees buckled; the living room blurred and went dark.

"She's got a knot on her forehead from the door jamb." It was Rory's voice. A moment later something cold covered a throbbing spot on my forehead.

"That doesn't look like ice," Aeas replied.

"Frozen peas," Rory said. "Is she coming around?"

I tried to open my eyes—I'm fine; stop fussing—but my eyes stayed shut. Murky shadows played with little sparks of color behind my eyelids. Must have whacked my head pretty good.

"It's possible this is a side effect of the dust," Aeas said.

"Dust did this to her?"

Irritation slid into Aeas's voice. "What do you mortals call it? Cupid's arrows?"

Rory scoffed. "Whatever."

"This isn't a joke." Aeas lowered his voice to a whisper. "A mortal could die from this."

I managed to push myself up on my elbows, though my eyes were still a little blurry when I opened them. "I'm not going to die. How long was I out?" I was lying on the bed in Rory's room with one boy on each side. The two of them scowled at each other over my now-conscious body.

"Just a few minutes," Rory answered. "You okay?"

"No, I'm not okay. I just swooned like some helpless maiden. I'm mortified." I fingered the goose egg on my forehead. "Bet that's pretty."

"Flawless is boring, right?" Rory offered me the bag of peas. "What happened?"

Aeas answered, "It was the smell. There's an orange grove outside the palace, and we dry cinnamon in the kitchen. But, I don't understand why." He frowned at the bump on my head. "The dust usually doesn't work like that."

Rory crossed the room to his computer chair. "You mean to tell me that Eros put some kind of love spell on her then threw her out. The guy sounds like a complete jerk if you ask me."

Aeas jumped to his feet. "No one asked you, and you will watch what you say."

"I can say whatever I like in *my* house." He leveled his gaze on me. "Is he worth the trouble of collecting these ads? Give me one reason why we should bother. The guy messed with your head then tossed you aside. He doesn't care one bit about you, or he wouldn't have put that dust on you."

"He didn't," I admitted. "I spilled it while he was sleeping."

Aeas's eyes widened. "How much did you spill?"

I shrugged as I shook the last stars from my peripheral vision. "I don't know, like, half the jar."

Aeas made a choking sound and spun around to face Rory. "There's your reason. A heavy pinch of dust is enough to make her love him all her life. No mortal has ever been exposed to a handful of it. She'll waste away, unable to sleep or eat, fainting like this at any reminder of him."

Rory looked at me. "There has to be a cure."

"Only one," Aeas said quietly, "and even if he forgave her, he can't come to her. He's bound by the contract as much as she is. It specifically says that she will never see his face or hear his voice until the tasks are completed. That contract is legal and binding to my kind in our world or yours. She cannot see him unless she succeeds at all three tasks."

"All right, you guys," I interrupted. "Enough. Nothing's changed. We complete the tasks as planned. I'm not going to pine away and die. So, let's get to work."

"I need to rent a storage unit," I said as Rory loaded the video footage onto his computer.

His eyes didn't leave the screen. "No, you don't."

"All that mail isn't going to fit in my *bedroom*."

"Not by a long shot." He saved the file onto two different drives, then turned to me. "I figured this out during school. If each magazine is half an inch thick, then it takes up 46.75 cubic inches, times one point four million is like thirty-eight thousand cubic feet."

"My dad's a cement contractor, Rory. Give it to me in yards."

"Fourteen hundred three cubic yards. You need a warehouse."

"Holy crap! We could *build* a warehouse with that!" And once we had a place to store it all, how would I deliver it to Aphrodite? "Any idea where we can find an empty warehouse?"

He grabbed his coat and keys. "Way ahead of you. C'mon." When Aeas stood beside me, Rory muttered, "I suppose he can come, too."

We drove past the fair grounds to a run-down building near the railroad tracks. It was made of cinderblock and used to be white. Now the sides of the building were covered in graffiti. The place had been empty for years. It was probably condemned. "I drove by at lunch and got the address," Rory said. "Then I called the county recorder to see who owns it." He led us to the office door, which had a broken doorknob. A padlock had been added at eye level. "I told the owner we needed it for a school project. He said to just come by and get the key." Rory unlocked the door. "It's ours rent free for sixty days."

The offices still contained old file cabinets and metal desks. An ancient phone hung on the wall. On the warehouse floor, there were odd tires, broken machines and an inch of dirt, but it was certainly large enough for the magazines. Most importantly, it had a mailbox on the loading dock, so we could have the magazines sent directly to the warehouse.

Around midnight, Rory sent me a YouTube link. Aeas was asleep and invisible in front of my closet. I pulled on headphones so I wouldn't wake him and clicked the link.

When my face appeared on the screen, I could barely see the knot on my forehead. We had covered it with make-up and hair. "My name is Psyche Middleton," I said, "and I'm Venus." The video cut to the Venus advertisement, but my voice continued. I said how flattered I was that the ad was so well received, and that I knew of six operating fan sites. "I want to give something back to my fans, so I've decided to take one fan to dinner." Then I explained how to enter the contest: send in a copy of the Venus ad with an index card containing your name, address, phone number and email address.

The next scene showed me standing on Main Street. I pointed at the Venus billboard and offered one hundred entries into the drawing for anyone who sent me a billboard. "But hurry," I said, "I will pick a winner six weeks from today."

Text appeared against a blue background. It said, "SEND ENTRIES TO" followed by the address for a graffiti-covered warehouse down by the railroad tracks. The next screen gave the deadline date. The screen went black, and I rubbed my sweaty palms together.

Rory sent this link to a dozen sites, including Dragonslayers Anonymous. He said not to worry. It would work.

All I could do was wait and see if he was right.

By five o' clock the next morning, my cell phone was ringing. I'd dozed off a mere two hours before and had to focus hard on the buttons to answer. "This better be important," I figured it was Rory.

"You are brilliant!" Blair shrieked in my ear. "I just heard about the contest. Cosmo's fashion editor called me personally. When are you coming back to work?"

"I'm in school, Blair." I yawned. "And, it's five a.m." I hung up and tossed the phone on the floor. Dad was clanking around in the kitchen, so I dragged myself downstairs.

"Came to see me off?" Dad joked as I slid onto a barstool. He went to the stove, poured water, measured, mixed and came back with a steaming cup, which he put in front of me.

The herbal concoction was fragrant and sweet. I sipped, grateful for the warmth. "What's in this?"

"Ginger. It settles the stomach." He split the eggs he'd made for himself, and dropped more bread into the toaster.

"You're too observant."

"Eat what you can. Grief does crazy things to a body."

I could not tell him that it was Eros, not Savannah, who was the root of my grief. Having someone you love die might be easier than having them throw you away. There were so many times as a child when I daydreamed that the mother who left me wasn't my mother at all. My real mother died of a tragic illness. My real mother would never have forgotten my birthday or abandoned me in Europe.

While I drank the herbal tea, Dad packed himself a lunch of wrap sandwiches, fruit and Oreos. Then he grabbed his keys and kissed the top of my head. "See you tonight, kiddo."

I locked the door and climbed the stairs. After the tea and a real breakfast, I fell asleep and didn't dream. By the time I pulled myself out of bed again, I barely had time to throw on some old jeans, brush my teeth and dash out the door to first period. The day dragged, and I was preoccupied by the sad task awaiting me after the final bell.

Katherine Schofield answered the door wearing a cashmere sweater with khakis. She had made great effort to cover the circles of fatigue under her eyes, but grief had marked her.

"Psyche?" She looked around in momentary confusion then offered, "Come in?"

I went with her into the living room, where Savannah's photo hung on the wall next to her brother's. If Savannah had been alive, I wouldn't have given the picture a second glance. It had always hung there. Each year it changed when the new school photos came out. Savannah took her senior pictures in the summer when her hair was streaked with sunlight and her skin glowed. I hadn't taken mine at all, unless you counted advertisements, which I didn't. Her brother's picture would eventually be replaced by a wedding photo and his future family, but Savannah would remain forever seventeen and smiling on the Schofield's wall.

Katherine stood next to me and studied the photo, too.

"It's a really good picture of her," I said.

"She wanted a different one, but this was my favorite." She didn't ask why I was there.

"I think I may have left... I think I..." I could not lie to a woman whose face held so much pain.

"Go ahead," she said. "I haven't touched anything." She went around the corner to the kitchen.

I walked down the hallway, half expecting Savannah to be sitting on her bed waiting for me as she had been the last Saturday in May, the beginning of Memorial Day weekend and also the first day of our summer break. The weather wasn't overly warm then. I was still wearing full length jeans and a long-sleeved T-shirt, but Savannah had broken her summer wardrobe out of hiding and was sitting on her bed in a yellow boat-neck top and fitted ivory capris. She was hunched over a photo album. I knocked lightly on the doorjamb and went in.

Savannah had looked up and said, "Remember last summer when I was dating Aiden?"

I merely nodded. It had been a whirlwind beginning and a bitter end. By August two things were painfully obvious—Aiden worshipped Savannah, and she was bored with him. I remembered how he bought her a dolphin toe ring and made her candy grams.

"I went swimming with Travis last night," she said. They had been dating exclusively for four weeks. I figured Travis was slated to be this year's summer fling and nothing more, but Savannah's expression changed. "It was amazing watching Travis swim. He goes under, and I swear, I thought he'd drowned he was gone so long. The whole time I'm treading water trying to see him. Then he swam under my feet and tugged on my toes." Savannah hugged her knees. Her gaze found a place on the far wall and saw nothing but Travis in the last rays of sunlight. She broke from her memory and looked up at me. "For some reason, it made me think of Aiden. He tried so hard, but it never did anything for me. But swimming alone with Travis at dusk—it was romantic." I should have known right then she would be different when I came back, but I could not have imagined it would end here with me turning the knob on her empty room.

The room was a wreck. Savannah wasn't a tidy person, and when her mom said she hadn't touched anything, she meant it. Clothes were strewn all over the floor. Savannah's make-up compact lay open on her vanity. Scattered across her dresser were textbooks and spiral notebooks. I opened one and found English notes written in Savannah's loopy handwriting. She had that stylish script that looked like it had been written in a rush. I traced her signature with my finger, the overlarge S through the four bumps of the double N's to the tall H with the broken-off tail. It was strange what you missed about people.

I made a neat stack out of the books, picked up all the dirty clothes and dumped them into the hamper by the door. Cleaning Savannah's room was a familiar job. Her parents always insisted her room be clean before she went to movies or basketball games on weekends, so I had spent more than a few Friday afternoons helping comb through her messes. Talented in so many other ways, Savannah simply did not understand the art of organizing.

On the shelf above the desk was a line of framed photographs. The photo of the two of us in a "Best Friends" frame was lying face down. Maybe she'd had trouble looking at it while she planned her betrayal. It didn't matter now, so I righted the frame and saw myself smiling back with my arm draped around Savannah's shoulders. At the center of the shelf were a dustless rectangle and a gaping hole, where a frame had recently been removed. I checked the garbage and found a framed snapshot of Travis sitting on the lifeguard's seat holding his hand out to the camera in the "I love you" sign. I hesitated, then placed it back on the shelf.

Beside the garbage can I found Savannah's backpack and the magazine I came to collect. The ad was still inside. In fact, she dogeared the page.

I took Savannah's books and the magazine to the kitchen, where I found Katherine staring at a grocery list like she'd lost the ability to read.

"I could return these to the school if you want."

She nodded. "That would be fine."

"Would you mind if I kept this, too?" I showed her the cover of the magazine.

Her puzzled expression told me she didn't have a clue what was inside. "Sure. Take it."

One ad down, one million three hundred ninety nine thousand nine hundred ninety-nine to go.

# CHAPTER 17

News of the contest spread faster than a forest fire. The school secretary gave me nasty looks every time she had to call me down to the office to pick up a stack of magazines. I purposely left my car unlocked at school, and most afternoons I found magazines littering the back seat.

After school Rory and I met at the warehouse. "So, where's your demigod today?" he asked as he unlocked the door.

"I don't know." Aeas left my house last night and didn't come back this morning. I didn't know how he got around town, but somehow he managed.

Usually there were envelopes stuffed in the mailbox and stacked on the loading dock, but today there was nothing. We had nearly six hundred, well short of the million we needed.

My mind chimed, "I told you so." Six hundred fans. That was all I could muster. Why had I believed we could get a million magazines?

I carried the ones in from my car. We pulled out the cards and dropped them into a circular kiddy pool Rory said was large enough to hold a million cards. Then we put the magazines in stacks of a hundred so they were easy to count. Today most of the back seat was covered in magazines. Our collection climbed to a whopping six hundred eighty-six. I felt like bashing my head against the cement floor.

"The video had seven hundred thousand views last night," Rory assured me. "Mail takes a few days."

"Yeah, sure," I mumbled.

"It's too soon to give up." Both Rory and I jumped at the sound of Aeas's voice. When he unveiled he was standing only an arm's reach away. He could have been there a minute or an hour for all I knew.

A fist pounded on the loading dock door. Rory stepped out-side to see what the commotion was. A moment later he returned. "Mail's late today." He removed the metal pins holding the door in place, then pulled hard on the handle. The rusty metal creaked and didn't budge. "Help me out here."

Aeas took hold of the handle, too. At first the old door screeched an inch at a time, then the rust on the wheels broke loose, and it rolled up its track until it was fully open. The sunlight and the smell of diesel exhaust hit me at the same time. Parked outside was a semi truck with a US Postal Service marking on the trailer. The blue-uniformed driver opened the back of the trailer. Inside the trailer were white mail bags piled to the ceiling. "All of this is yours," the driver said. He tossed me a bag, and the weight of it nearly knocked me over.

We emptied the magazines onto the floor of the warehouse. By the time the trailer was empty, the pile was twenty feet wide and four feet tall in the center.

"Um, Rory," I said. "We may need help sorting and counting."

He scratched his head. "This is just the beginning." He imme-diately started making phone calls.

Aeas and I pulled out cards and counted magazines into stacks. We'd barely sorted a quarter of the heap when we heard another knock. This time it was the regular door, not the loading dock. I moved to answer it, but Aeas moved faster. He nudged me out of sight before opening the door.

"Is this where we drop off entries for the contest?" The voice was familiar, but I couldn't place it.

"It is," Aeas replied.

"Here you go." He handed Aeas a box eighteen inches square and six feet long. Then he offered him a stack of index cards. "And here's my hundred cards."

Aeas thanked him and shut the door. "Our first billboard." He handed the cards to me. On every one was the contact information for Hunter McDowell.

A week before the contest deadline, we were two hundred sev-enty-five thousand magazines short, but we had fifteen billboards, and the kiddy pool was over half full. The counted magazines stood on pallets and filled half the warehouse. Along one wall were the billboards, which had been delivered in boxes that contained thick paper strips rolled together. If you unrolled them and laid them out on the floor, it gave you the whole billboard. On Main Street the *Birth of Venus* was replaced by a Budweiser. If nothing else came of Aphrodite's tasks, at least my dad would never have to see that billboard again.

Somehow Rory convinced two dozen Dragonslayers to help us, and they had taken over sorting, counting and stacking the magazines. They also turned the warehouse into a hangout. Two tattered couches and some plastic chairs sat in a corner next to a space heater. Someone paid the Coke truck to deliver soda pop to the warehouse. It showed up every Friday. On the open floor between the couches and the loading docks, some guys set up a launch ramp and grinding rail. Between mail deliveries, they skated and even convinced Aeas to try it.

"I feel sort of helpless," I said as the Dragonslayers moved through the day's mail. "They're so organized, like an ant hill."

Rory chuckled. "We ants live to serve the queen."

I punched him in the arm. "Seriously, is there something I can do?"

"Pizza. It's crunch time. Rally the troops."

"Okay, I'll be back in an hour with all the pizza my car can hold. Oh, and Rory, will you let me know how many eighteen wheelers it's going to take to deliver all of this? I told the trucking company I'd call tomorrow to reserve them. When Theron calls, I want to have everything ready to roll."

"We'll be ready," Rory said confidently.

We were still way short of the total number, but whatever we had, we would deliver to Aphrodite on time. I called two pizza parlors and ordered ten pizzas at each, I grabbed my keys and pulled on my coat. "Anyone seen Aaron?"

Rory, who was carrying a stack of magazines to the sorting table, grunted, but the girl at his shoulder smiled. "He disappeared a couple of hours ago. Said he had errands to run."

Her comment was funnier than she knew. Aeas kept his power to veil a secret. The volunteers believed he was just like the rest of us, only drop-dead gorgeous, unbelievably coordinated on a skateboard and downright mature for a fifteen-year-old. Several girls were openly smitten with Aeas, who went by Aaron among mortals. Most likely he was still around, but he'd stepped around a corner and hidden himself.

"Well, I'm going to pick up dinner, so everyone be hungry when I get back."

There was a general murmur of approval as I hopped off the loading dock and turned the corner to the parking lot. No one but me saw the passenger door open and close on its own.

As soon as I started the engine, Aeas appeared beside me. "You were looking for me?"

"I didn't want to haul all this pizza to the car myself."

His nod was slight and habitual. Servitude was ingrained in him.

I took great pains not to take advantage of him. He wasn't my servant. "If you ride shotgun, you get the first piece."

His voice seldom showed any hint of emotion. "That's a fair deal."

One step into the pizza parlor and my stomach was rumbling like a freight train. Had I eaten at all today? I couldn't remember. Until now nothing smelled good, but I knew I'd be lucky to down one slice of pizza before my body rebelled. Aeas was right about the effects of the dust. I couldn't eat or sleep normally. Against my will I was wasting away.

With ten pizzas stowed in the back seat and the aroma making me salivate, we drove to the other shop, which had our order ready. I paid, and as I carried half the boxes to the car, my cell phone beeped the receipt of a text message.

"What's on top in your stack?" I asked.

Aeas lifted the lid. "Looks like pepperoni and olives. What about yours?"

"Sausage and mushrooms."

"I'll take one of those," he said as we stowed the boxes on top of the others.

I took one for myself, too. Sitting in the driver's seat, I checked the text. The number was local, but unfamiliar. The message was a series of numbers. "What is this?" I showed the text to Aeas.

"Coordinates? Possibly your delivery point."

In reply I messaged: **Theron? Call to confirm delivery point.**

I pressed send and started the ignition. I really didn't want to hear his voice again. Just as we pulled into the warehouse parking lot, the phone rang. It was the same number. Slowly, I brought the phone to my ear.

"How's your hand?"

It felt like a cold hand gripped my spine. Theron was the most evil person I'd ever encountered, and his beauty only made him worse.

"I got the coordinates. Is there a street address, or would you like me to dump three million magazines on the roof?"

He chuckled. "The loading docks are on the south end. How will you be delivering?"

I had no idea where the location was, so I wouldn't commit to anything. It was an island for all I knew. "I'll get back to you. You'll be at this number?"

"I will." I heard the smile in his voice. "If every ad is not accounted for, I will personally let you know."

Aeas snatched the phone from my hand and disconnected the call. "The less you talk to him, the better," he said. "You must not let him threaten you." He tossed the phone into my lap and unloaded the pizza boxes.

I lagged behind toting the few boxes Aeas left in the car. I went straight to Rory, handed him the boxes and said, "Grab your laptop. We have the delivery point, and I need you to Google it."

A brush of excitement ran through his eyes. "When?"

"The text came while we were in the car."

He handed off all but one box then steered me toward an empty table away from the volunteers. There we powered up the laptop and typed in the coordinates. The delivery point was on the coast in New Jersey. When we brought up the satellite photos, we were able to pinpoint one warehouse in a long row near the docks.

"So, we deliver by truck?" I asked.

"Sure, if we have time," Rory said.

Aeas appeared at my shoulder munching another slice of pizza. "However you deliver, it has to be done swiftly and securely. This is Theron we're dealing with. He may sabotage the delivery."

"You should go with the shipment," I told him. "You can see Theron and his men when they're veiled. Plus, Rory and I have parents and school to deal with."

Aeas nodded. "Tell the trucking company we'll provide our own drivers."

"Will they do that?"

"They should," Aeas replied. "And I have people I can count on."

Over the next hour we finalized the trucking route and the shipment date. Aeas disappeared to arrange drivers.

I turned to Rory. Helplessness made me fidgety again. "So, between now and then, all we can do is wait and hope another three hundred thousand magazines show up."

"I'll send another email to the fan sites. Then, yeah, all we can do is wait."

Two days before the contest deadline, we were still two-hundred forty thousand magazines short, and Theron had not called again. The fleet of trucks was lined up outside the warehouse, all loaded and locked except the last two, which needed to be filled if I was to complete the task.

When the day's mail arrived, Rory's team jumped up ready to attack, but it was obvious there wasn't enough. The mail truck delivered ten bags, not even half a truckload.

Aeas appeared beside me. "Are you okay?" He had been sitting there for half an hour, but only now unveiled. He was strange that way. Maybe it was more habit than anything.

"Fine." I gnawed one fingernail down to the quick. I wasn't okay. I was spiraling into depression and dread. Theron said he would personally let me know if I'd failed. I knew what that meant.

Aeas had rented an apartment near the high school, and for awhile he stayed there every night, but as the deadline drew nearer, he seemed to be lingering. He claimed it was because he didn't trust Theron, but I wondered if it had more to do with the fact that my jeans would have slipped right off my hips if I hadn't stolen one of Rory's belts. My face was more angled than usual, and my arms were all sharp edges. I lived in a state of chronic fatigue and had become a caffeine addict, which only worsened the cycle. All this I knew, but my body was having its own rebellion, thanks to the dust, and my mind was unable to conquer it. And unwilling, too. When I looked in the mirror, I saw what I'd lost, not just Eros's love, but myself with it.

I think Aeas sensed I was slipping, losing the will to fight, and he was keeping a closer eye on me. I doubted it was for me as much as loyalty to his best friend.

Rory started to close the dock door, but from outside came the distinct honk of a truck. He paused. I figured the mailman found another bag. Rory stood with his hands on his hips and peered into the dark. Two tractor-trailers pulled into the warehouse parking lot. The first swung around and backed up to the dock.

"What's going on?" I hopped off a stack of pallets and joined Rory at the dock.

"No idea," Rory replied. He motioned the driver back until the trailer was inches from the dock.

The air-brakes hissed, and the driver opened the door. "Had trouble finding you," he said. He hopped out with a clipboard in his hand. "Who wants to sign for the delivery?" After I signed, he handed me a copy of the delivery slip. Then the driver unlocked the trailer and opened the doors.

I grabbed Aeas's shoulder in excitement. The trailer was full of pallets of magazines. Unlike the magazines coming out of our warehouse with tattered edges and dog-eared pages, the magazines on this truck had never seen a newsstand. Their vibrant covers lay flat and clean beneath the plastic wrappings.

I pressed my finger through the plastic and tore it enough to pull out a single magazine. It wasn't the September issue of *Cosmopolitan*. It was the November issue of Italian *Vogue*. I fanned the pages frantically, but the Venus ad wasn't hard to find. It was right at the center and a stiff subscription card made the magazine naturally fall open to that page.

As the pallets were unloaded, the driver set a large box at my feet. It was too heavy for me to lift. I knelt down and opened it. Inside were three hundred thousand honey-colored cards, professionally printed with embossed black ink. One card for every magazine in the two trucks.

A stranger named Tyson Ewing just saved my life.

The following morning Aeas shook me awake in the dark. "Your dad just left. Let's go."

He drove, because I was too groggy to get us safely to the warehouse before six a.m. Rory and the drivers were already there. The trucks were locked, and though they had been guarded all night, we checked them again. The magazines were stacked and packaged the way we left them.

"Call me eight times a day," I told Aeas.

He nodded amiably. "You can trust me, Psyche. I won't fail you." He climbed into the lead truck riding shotgun and took the radio into his hands. A moment later the trucks shifted into gear and rumbled toward the street forming a line.

Rory and I watched them until they turned the corner and the cloud of diesel exhaust cleared from the air. The next few days were sheer torture. Rory and I went to school like nothing changed. I copied notes and worked on an overdue lab report feeling like a caged animal ready to bash its brains against the bars.

When I got home from school on Wednesday, I found my dad unloading bags of groceries. "What's with all the food?" I asked.

He set a heavy bag into my hands. "On Thanksgiving don't we always make turkey, stuffing and your favorite—pumpkin pie with extra whipping cream?"

The task completely consumed me. I'd lost track of the days. Cursed be the dust for making me sick on one of my favorite holidays.

Because I couldn't eat normally, I celebrated Thanksgiving the way any girl who was wasting away to skin and bones would: I ate only mashed potatoes, gravy and half a pumpkin pie. Usually, that sort of binge was nothing for me. This time, I really thought I might end up with my head over the toilet all night. By sheer will, I kept it down, and I was able to sleep a few extra hours, too.

Early Friday morning, the *Lord of the Rings* theme blared from my cell phone—Rory's doing. I grabbed the phone hoping for Aeas, but I saw Theron's number instead.

"Are you ready to admit defeat?" he asked.

"Nope." I nudged the door closed with my foot so my dad wouldn't overhear. "You'll get them before the new moon."

There was a long pause. "We will count them. You can't trick the goddess."

I rolled my eyes. Aphrodite really liked the whole goddess bit, even though I knew better. "You can count them. I even sent you a few extra." I could almost hear him growing angrier. "What about the second task?"

"I'll contact you after we count the ads." The line went dead.

I shivered in the morning chill and got dressed. Rory picked me up half an hour later to film the contest drawing. Much as I dreaded it, it helped take my mind off the delivery.

The warehouse felt dead without the magazines and the Dragonslayers. The garbage bin overflowed with pizza boxes and empty soda bottles. The grinding rail and the couches were gone. All that was left was the kiddy pool full of cards.

I used a snow shovel to stir the cards while Rory videoed. "Okay." I looked up at the camera. "Time to choose a winner." I reached down, shoved my hand way into the mess of cards and pulled one out. It was honey-colored with *Tyson Ewing* printed in black. I held up the card and said, "Erik Savage." If you searched for Erik Savage on the Internet, you would not find a photo, just a description of the reclusive, billionaire CEO of Millennial Holdings, Inc. Erik Savage was Eros's current mortal identity. "Congratulations, Erik. I will be in touch soon."

I stuffed the card into my coat pocket, and Rory said, "Cut."

Eros would probably never see the video on YouTube, but if he did, he would know he was still the only guy in the world who mattered to me. As for Tyson Ewing, if I survived these tasks, I would fly to Italy and personally thank him.

For three full days Aeas was out of contact. I sent him a dozen text messages and tried to call, but his phone went right to voice mail. As the sun fell behind the mountains for the night of the new moon, I lost what little hope was left. Something happened. Aeas said he wouldn't fail me, but he did. I drifted into restless sleep and was jarred awake by music.

I felt around the blankets and finally found the cell phone.

"It's done, Psyche," Aeas said. "The shipment is delivered."

Two hours ago I wanted to kill him, but now I nearly wept with gratitude. "Why didn't you call?" I demanded.

"One of the trucks broke down. It took us all night to fix it, then we were running behind schedule."

"What about Theron?"

Aeas replied, "See for yourself." A moment later a picture message came through followed by two others. I opened the first picture and saw a mountain of magazines in the center. The next photo was of the drivers, unloading the last truck. The final photo was of Theron scowling at the delivery. The text said, Task Complete!

# CHAPTER 18

After my dad went to bed the following Friday night, Aeas appeared on the carpet of my bedroom. He leaned on his elbows with his legs stretched out and crossed at the ankles. His brow wrinkled at the screen of his new iPod.

"You said you'd never steal from him."

Aeas suddenly had money to spend and was blowing through it fast. He bought clothes and furniture then filled his apartment with electronics. He looked up, surprised. "I didn't." He held out the iPod. "Can you help?"

I scrolled through the menus and showed him how. When the music started playing in his ears, his expression brightened. "Are you going to explain?" I persisted.

"I sent for personal assets, then sold them for your currency."

"What kind of assets?"

"Diamonds." When my mouth dropped open, he added, "Only a handful." He pulled a wad of bills from his pocket. "For the clothes you bought me."

"Keep it. You have no concept of what it means to be a guest," I mimicked.

His mouth flattened into a scowl. "I didn't mean you had to do the same for me."

"So, you could stay long-term if you had to?"

"Yes, but I would have to give up my horse, and I really don't want to." So, that was how Aeas got around. He flew. "He stays in the back yard. But, don't worry," Aeas assured me, "he's under strict orders to relieve himself in the field outside of town."

I snorted. There was an invisible, winged horse living in my back yard. Could my life get any weirder? "I wondered why there were hoof prints in the alley."

"I hope your dad didn't notice."

"The horse takes messages to your family?"

He shook his head and thumbed through the music. "Eudora. I couldn't tell my parents I was banished. It would shame them."

"You think Theron will call tonight?" I asked.

"I expect him to give you the task soon. I hope he'll call." What he meant was, he hoped Theron wouldn't visit, which explained why Aeas camped out on my floor instead of watching high definition television at his apartment. Theron was prone to violence against mortals at any provocation, and I'd just made myself target number one.

Having Aeas on the floor by the closet did make me feel safer, but I tossed and turned until two a.m. before sinking into deep sleep. I heard voices in my dreams; one I had been aching to hear for weeks.

"Figured I'd find you here," he said. "Made yourself right at home, didn't you?"

"If you're accusing me, speak plainly," Aeas replied. Then he added, "You look like you've been to Hades and back."

"I'm fine," was the muttered reply.

"When was the last time you slept?" There was a pause, then the exclamation, "Judge of Olympus!" Aeas exclaimed. "You have it, too!"

"I'm *fine*. But you can't get enough of her, can you?" He made no effort to hide the jealousy in his voice.

"I want to go home." Aeas's reply was just as angry. "And I don't want her to die because of you."

"She won't die." Eros scoffed. "It was just a little dust."

*Eros!*

Suddenly wide awake, I scrambled out of bed.

"See for yourself," Aeas whispered.

"Aeas!" I felt around the room frantically. "*Aeas!*"

"Here." He appeared in the far corner. He stood rigid, fists balled and shoulders tight.

I grabbed handfuls of his shirt. "I heard… Is he *here?*" I sounded hysterical, but I couldn't help it.

"You were dreaming."

"No, I heard you talking." That voice pulled me out of my dreams. I didn't imagine it.

Aeas's expression hardened, and he peeled my hands off his shirt. "I was on the phone," he said finally, "with Rory."

"But I was sure..."

He shook his head.

Grief stole my strength. I stumbled back. My legs refused to hold me. Aeas made no effort to catch me as I slid to the floor against the wall. I clutched my belly and waited for the nausea to pass. "Did Theron call?"

"He sent a text. You're to meet him at nine o'clock. Local address."

"What time is it?"

"Almost eight-thirty," he replied.

I pushed myself off the floor. "I'll change. Wait in the hallway."

"You're going to undress in here?" Aeas asked as I pushed him out the door.

"It *is* my bedroom."

He tried to claw back through the doorway. "I think the bathroom would be better."

"Just wait out there." I pushed his hands off the doorjamb, then closed the door in his face. The dream seemed so real. I thought I smelled cinnamon in the air. Echoes of Eros's voice floated through my mind, jealous of Aeas. If only that were true. If only he were driven to fight for me. But there I was—dreaming again.

With Aeas in my room I slept fully dressed. I stripped off my T-shirt and flannel pants, then stood in front of the mirror in a bra and panties revealing what I hid under my clothes. My hips were all bones and no meat. There were deep dips above my collarbones, and every rib showed. Blair would be thrilled that I now had the skeletal build to work runway in earnest. Too bad I was never going back.

My face, too, showed the strain. My skin was paler, not an attractive translucent tone, just stark. Dark circles swept from the bridge of my nose past the center of my eyes. Gone was the healthy summer glow. I turned away and pulled on clean clothes.

Theron today, another task tomorrow.

"We have another problem," Aeas said when I opened the door. "I found these on your dad's dresser." He scowled at the window and placed a stack of pamphlets into my hand. They were hospital brochures from specialty centers around the country. One treated eating disorders, another specialized in post-traumatic stress disorder. They ran the spectrum all the way to schizophrenia.

"He's planning to send me away, but he doesn't know where."

"It would seem that way."

"If I'm locked up, I can't complete the tasks."

"Get better," Aeas answered flatly.

I pulled on my coat and pocketed my phone. "Yeah, I'll get right on that one."

The address took me to a two-story Tudor home with steep rooflines. A real estate sign in the front yard boasted "SOLD" in red across the bottom, but the information box was still hanging on the back. I crossed the grass and pulled out one of the brochures. The home sat on three lots and contained six bedrooms and four baths. The asking price was just under a million dollars.

The front door was slightly ajar, and entering put me into the two-story great room with a stone fireplace climbing one wall. Sunlight shimmered amber across the wood floor.

"Theron?" My voice echoed through the empty space.

I stepped lightly toward the kitchen. This had all the makings of a trap. I was walking right into a beast's lair, but I needed that second task.

Theron appeared on the other side of the bar leaning against the counter. He considered me a moment then said, "Follow me."

"You can just tell me the task, and I'll be on my way."

He moved toward the stairs. "If you want the task, come with me."

I waited until he was halfway up the stairs before I followed. A long hallway accessed the bedrooms. Theron stopped at the end of the hall and waited until I approached then eased the door open.

It was the master suite, and this one room was fully furnished. A sitting area just inside the door contained a small dining table and chairs. The table was laid with pastries, fruit, hard bread and sliced meat. An empty wine glass sat next to each place setting, and a rustic violet wine bottle sat between them. Theron motioned me to sit.

"I already ate," I replied.

"I doubt that. You're not looking well." He poured an opaque liquid into the glasses, took a pastry from the tray and bit off the edge.

"Same back at you."

My insult was met with a smile. "I can heal you," he offered. From the basket on the table, Theron plucked a piece of fruit. It was white, shaped like a pear, with a crimson blossom still clinging to the round end. He held it out to me. "You'll be well again tonight."

I folded my hands in my lap and eyed him coolly. "In exchange for what?"

"Quit the tasks." He tilted his head to the extravagant bedroom set behind him. "And give me what you didn't give Eros."

It took effort not to roll my eyes. "That's so original. No guy has ever wanted *that* from me before. What would Aphrodite say if she knew you were offering me immortality in exchange for my body?"

Theron rubbed crumbs from his fingers and took a sip of wine before answering. "When I look at you, I see the first woman who could tempt me from her side." A golden curl dropped onto his smooth forehead. His cold eyes shimmered.

"And when I look at you, I see every guy who has crossed my path since I was twelve—hungry eyes and a rooster strut."

Theron rose slowly from his chair like a storm gathering force as it creeps across the valley. "You're killing yourself with these tasks, but you'll never win him back." He stood over me. "You're pathetic."

"I'm pathetic? You're one to talk. How many ages have you been hanging around playing Aphrodite's boy toy?" I should have shut my mouth, but I continued, "Does she lie and tell you that she loves you? How does it feel when she goes back to her husband or some other lover?"

Theron grabbed the front of my shirt and hurled me into the wall with so much force I hit before I realized I was no longer in the chair. My head struck a mirror. The glass shattered. Pain blossomed in my head, and I saw stars. The shards jingled to the floor, and I landed on my hands and knees in the pile. Theron grabbed the collar of my shirt and jerked me to my feet. The frame hung crooked, the center gone, but sharp splinters of the mirror clung to the corners. I saw my reflection for a split second before Theron shoved my face into the glass. The shards dug into my cheek, barely missing my eye, and tore the flesh open. I screamed in agony. He jerked me back, tearing my face deeper, and laughed at the sight of me. "Will he love you now?"

I didn't even have time to breathe or pull away. Theron's fist slammed into my face with so much force, I felt it clear down to my hips. The blow drove me to the floor again. I tried to crawl away but was swept to the side by a violent kick in the ribs that knocked the wind out of me.

He knelt and reached for me.

All I could do was whimper and try to blink blood from my eyes. My skin had turned hot and sticky. The rusty stench of my own blood sickened me.

"'Unworthy, inconstant mortal,' Eros said. 'Should never have saved her from that crowd.'" Theron sneered. "You want the task? There it is." He pointed to a basket at the foot of the bed. "You're to fill it with silver wolves' fur."

"Then what?" It took effort to squeak out two words.

"Bring it to me here." Theron pulled me close so he could murmur in my ear. "When you fail at these tasks, I will come for you, and you won't find any pity in my hands."

I gritted my teeth against the pain. "And I pegged you for such a nice guy."

He growled. The last thing I saw was that violet wine bottle coming down on my head.

# CHAPTER 19

I surfaced in utter terror—disoriented, but fully aware that I lay helpless in Theron's grasp. I could only open one eye. The other was swollen shut. When I pushed myself up, shards of glass stuck into my palm. My entire body screamed in pain, and I collapsed back to the floor. The table was cleared, most of it broken on the floor around me. I fumbled in my coat pocket, found my cell phone and pushed the speed dial. A piece of glass lodged deeper into my thumb.

"Psyche!" Aeas answered.

I struggled to breathe. "I ... don't know ...if he's still here."

"I'm coming."

I sank into the reassuring dark, only to be pulled out again by Aeas frantically shouting my name. It echoed through the empty rooms and ricocheted around my head.

He knelt beside me cursing heaven and earth. I opened my eye and saw him turn away and vomit on the carpet. Then he pulled off his shirt and held it against my head. "I've never seen this much mortal blood before."

I was in too much pain to be embarrassed.

Aeas lifted me into his arms.

"The basket....it's the next task."

"I'll come back for it."

The stairs jarred my aching ribs as I leaned against Aeas. I couldn't keep myself from crying. He tucked me into the passenger seat of my car.

"I need to send a message home." Aeas dug through the compartments of the car. "Do you have paper and pen?"

"Glove box." I tried not to breathe, because it hurt. There was glass embedded in my hand, and I didn't dare touch my face. From the corner of my eye, I saw a piece of flesh hanging from my cheek. The pain was so raw that it consumed me.

Aeas found a pen and scribbled a message on the back of my car registration. Then he vanished. When he reappeared, he threw the basket in the back and climbed into the driver's seat.

Halfway across town his cell phone rang. He ignored it. The call went to voice mail, and the phone started ringing again. Aeas answered with, "I can't talk to you right now," then hung up. It beeped again immediately. This time it was a text message.

"Watch the road." I struggled to read the print. "It says, 'Answer me. Was it like the others?'" The number was local, but not Theron's. I didn't recognize it. "What does it mean, like the others?"

Aeas gripped the steering wheel tighter. He didn't look at me. Across his face and bare chest were red smudges of my blood. "Theron has attacked mortals before—several of them."

"And the others were...?"

"Raped," he whispered.

"This number. Is it Eros?"

He bit his lip. His eyes stayed fixed on the road.

I smeared blood all over Aeas's phone as I typed the reply, **What do you care? She's just an unworthy, inconstant mortal.** I powered off the phone.

It was afternoon. I didn't know how long I had lain unconscious in Theron's bedroom. My shirt and jeans were covered in glass and blood which dried into dark splotches.

Bitter wind whipped through the valley and blew snow around in the air. Luckily, it wasn't sticking, so my dad was still at work. Aeas carried me upstairs and rummaged through the bathroom cupboards for first aid supplies. He came back with water, gauze and tweezers.

From the feel of it, I guessed I needed a surgeon—a very skilled one—or I would be monstrous for life.

"I sent for medicine," he said, "but the glass has to come out." When I offered him my hand, he shook his head. "Forgive me. It will hurt." Aeas's face was stark white, but he clenched his teeth and went to work. He pulled five shards of glass from my forehead and another three from my cheek. He dabbed the blood as it ran down my face and apologized every time I winced.

"How bad does it look?" I probably didn't want to know. It was bad enough to make him sick.

"Your hand isn't scarred, is it?" he murmured, and held up a piece of the mirror he'd just pulled from my face. It was half an inch long.

Downstairs the door opened and closed with a slam. I jumped away from the tweezers. "My dad!"

"I'll see." Aeas disappeared and closed the door on his way out.

I turned away from the door. I would rather die than let my dad see me like this, but I was too weak to cross the room and lock the door.

There was some scuffling and arguing in the hallway, all in whispers. The door opened. "It's not your dad. It's the medicine I sent for."

I turned toward Aeas, and an invisible person made a choking sound. The door wobbled as he fell against it. A piece of Aeas's shirt disappeared as the other grasped it to steady himself. I was nightmarish enough to make an immortal swoon.

"You should leave," Aeas muttered. He pulled away and came to me. "We need to get the rest of the glass out." He pulled a vial from a small leather pouch. "This will make it easier."

I drank it all and handed the vial back. Aeas cupped his hand around the back of my neck to steady me as I lost consciousness.

I woke in the dark. The house was quiet. Dad might have been at work or already in bed. The lamp on the table cast a small circle of light at the side of the bed. Unseen hands bathed my wounds with cool, sticky liquid. The skin tingled and itched, but I felt no pain. The person beside me sucked short, grieved breaths.

I could open my eyes completely now. The swelling was gone. "Thank you," I whispered.

A gentle hand stroked my hair. He pressed his lips to my forehead and left warm tears there.

The gesture surprised me. Aeas never laid a finger on me unless he had to, but his kindness was touching. I reached for his hand, and my fingers found a metal band on the first finger.

It wasn't Aeas.

There were so many things I promised myself I would say if I ever got the chance, but all that came out was, "I'm so sorry."

When he pulled me into his arms, it opened a floodgate. I cried so hard, I couldn't speak. My hands moved over his familiar shoulders and his muscled chest. It was him. My Eros. I buried my face in his neck. "I was helpless. I couldn't get away."

He tenderly kissed my healing face, but bound by Aphrodite's contract, he never spoke. When he brought my mouth to his, love poured into me and brought the life back into my soul. I felt it from my toes to the tips of my fingers, sparkling and alive. Apology accepted; we still belonged to each other. I squeezed his shoulder, but he didn't pull away. He kissed me deeper. I held on and willed myself not to faint.

When our lips parted, he sighed the way he did when he was irritated, probably because his little trick didn't work. He touched my eyes and slid them closed.

"If I fall asleep, you'll leave," I whispered.

He held my hand to his face and shook his head. His arms folded around me and laid my head on the pillow. I clung to him, afraid that if I let go, I might lose him again forever.

Morning loomed in shades of blue when I felt Eros stir. As he untangled himself from me, I whispered, "Don't go," but he did.

Before climbing out my window, he dropped my cell phone into my hand. A few minutes later, it vibrated. I opened the text message.

`Will return soon. Love you. E.`

I grinned at the text then fingered my face. The skin was smooth and unmarred. Happy for the first time in weeks, I rolled over and went back to sleep.

When I trudged downstairs, my dad was sitting on the couch reading the newspaper. He wore a flannel shirt and khakis. It took a moment for the clouds to clear and me to realize it was Sunday. I curled up on the couch next to him. "Is it really one o'clock in the afternoon?" I asked.

Dad didn't take his eyes off the article. "Yeah."

I slept almost twenty-four hours. "Will you make me waffles?"

He glanced sideways, then went on reading. "Only if you're going to eat them."

"With strawberries and whipping cream?"

"Out of real cream." He folded the paper at the center crease. "Have to settle for the frozen stuff."

I grinned. "I'll eat four of them."

"You will not. You can't eat more than two when you're not…"
He caught himself. I don't know what that last word would have
been: sick, mental, anorexic maybe?

"You'll never know unless you get in there and start cooking."

He rapped me on the side of the head with the paper as he
stood. "You'd better eat at least two."

Dad watched as I forked down my sixth waffle. He kept up with
me until three, then he sat back in his chair with a cup of herbal tea
and a crooked smile pulling at his mouth. The waffles were fluffy,
perfectly brown, and loaded with strawberries. I couldn't remember when food tasted this good.

The fork poised for another bite, I stopped and let it clank onto
the plate. "Okay, that's enough."

Dad sipped his tea. "You'd better not get sick on me."

"Not bulimic, Dad." I yawned. "I'm ready for a nap."

"You just got up. Maybe you should do homework." He reached
over by the phone and pulled out a folded sheet of paper, which he
slid across the bar to me.

The school's letterhead showed through the paper. I unfolded it
with dread. My midterm grades were not pretty. The letter reported
eight truancies in addition to seven excused absences I earned since
the beginning of school. I slid the paper back. "What good will A's
do me in a hospital in Maryland?"

"Is that what this is about?" He gestured toward the remnants
of waffles on my plate.

"It's about me getting better, if you'll give me a chance." I couldn't
tell him why I was better. Eros's silent visit cured the ill effects of the
dust. I was still completely under the dust's power and more attracted
to Eros than ever. Instead of love sick, today I was euphoric. And starving. My body was ready to take back what it lost over the past month.
"I just need some time," I told my dad. "I'll get my grades up."

He looked down at my empty plate. "Okay," he agreed.

Outside it began to snow. Heavy flakes threw themselves at the
window then slid down the glass and melted. Soon snow would pile
up on the sills. "How much are they predicting?" I asked.

Dad went to the window. "At least a foot."

It was a perfect day for napping or doing homework, so I
trudged upstairs and emptied my backpack onto the bed.

"I'm sorry, Psyche," a voice said quietly. "I failed you."

"Aeas?"

He appeared in the corner with his head hung.

"How long have you been here?"

"I never left." He looked more sick now than when he found me. "I should have gone with you. I should have protected you."

I shook my head. It wasn't his fault. "I had to meet Theron alone. You know that." I looked down at my clothes. I was wearing the gray T-shirt and yoga pants I slept in, but I didn't change before losing consciousness the night before. Where were my blood-stained clothes from yesterday?

"Did you...?" I motioned to my clothes.

"Well, uh...." He wouldn't look into my eyes. "We didn't want your dad to see you covered in blood."

I was grateful but embarrassed nonetheless. They healed my shattered face and bruised body. I wasn't sure how their medicine worked, but even my ribs, which I thought were broken, were better today. Both Aeas and Eros had seen the billboard, but it was different knowing they'd undressed me.

Aeas cleared his throat. "So, the task?" He sat on the corner of the bed.

"Fill the basket with silver wolves' fur."

The way his brow wrinkled reminded me vaguely of Dad. "Wolves are vicious and somewhat reclusive, but this task seems easier than the last."

"They're protected animals in my world. We can't kill them for their fur. I don't even know where to find a pack of wolves. Somewhere in Yellowstone, but the park is huge. They could be anywhere."

"You're sure there are wolves in the Yellowstone Park?"

"Yeah, it was a big deal when they were reintroduced. How many do you think it would take to fill the basket?"

He shrugged. "It depends on how big they are. Two or three at least."

"Maybe we can find someone who's seen them recently. Still, once we find the pack, what do we do?"

"We'll have to catch them. Winter's coming, so they'll have thick coats. We could brush the fur off them."

"These are wolves we're talking about, not golden retrievers." We would have to knock them out. Forest Rangers had tranquilizer guns. We needed something like that, but I didn't know if we could buy that stuff. I found my phone and scrolled through the numbers. I bet Rory could find a tranquilizer gun.

Aeas caught my wrist before I pressed the send button. "We don't need Rory's help."

"We needed him last time."

"But now you have Eros."

# CHAPTER 20

"**W**hat's next?" Rory asked. We stood at our lab station in chemistry. I sorted beakers and he measured the first compound.

"Wolves," I answered quietly. In explaining the task to him I left out the part where Theron nearly beat me to death, Aeas healed me, and Eros spent the night in my bed after I cried myself silly. "I have a lead." I showed him the text I received in first period: **Dr. Nancy Bonner.** During English class I googled her name. "Local wolf expert. MSU professor."

Rory lit the Bunsen burner and handed me a graduated cylinder. "So, when do we go see her?"

"Today." Dr. Bonner's schedule was posted on her homepage. She had office hours every Monday and Wednesday from two to four.

I looked up and caught Rory watching a girl across the room. Her name was Vanessa, and she transferred from Kalispell last year. Her dark hair was cropped short, and she wore chic little glasses.

When he realized I was watching him, his attention snapped back to our experiment. "Can't today. I promised my mom I'd help set up the church nativity." He set the beaker on the burner and noted the time.

I couldn't wait two days. "I'll let you know what I find out."

Rory's eyes narrowed and his pen tapped the countertop. "I suppose you're taking Aeas."

If it were up to Aeas, I wouldn't go anywhere alone. After haggling most of Sunday afternoon, I convinced Aeas I was safe in my dad's house and at school. He was adamant that I not go anywhere else without him.

"I'm going alone," I told Rory. "I can handle introducing myself to a college professor without the two of you holding my hands."

Rory didn't answer.

"When we're ready for some real action, I'll let you know."

He avoided my eyes and stirred the compound. "Yeah, whatever." His glance went to Vanessa again.

I elbowed him. "In the meantime I think you should ask her out," I whispered.

He studied the lab instructions and muttered, "Says Venus."

At the end of last period I went to Mr. Mayhue's desk and told him I wanted to bring up my grade.

He leaned back in his chair and put his Birkenstocks on the desk. "I think there's something you need more than a grade." He smoothed the hair that fell from his graying ponytail.

I scoffed. "Therapy?"

Mr. Mayhue threw his head back and laughed. "I wasn't going to say it exactly like that." He leaned forward, and his expression grew serious. "Therapy doesn't have to be sitting down with a shrink and telling your life story. Sometimes it's just expressing what's inside you." From a bottom desk drawer he took a worn, leather-bound drawing book. "I have dozens of these." He fanned the pages, which were filled with detailed sketches. "Full of my own personal therapy." He smiled widely. "No advanced degree necessary."

"So...?" I wasn't quite sure how this related to my grade.

Mr. Mayhue shrugged. "Get one. Fill it. I'll give you an A."

"Seriously?"

"You'll never master still lives and perspectives until you harness the chaos in your head."

Sketch therapy and an A. Yeah, I could handle that.

Garland and wreathes hung over Main Street. Radio stations played holiday music, and bell-ringing Santas stood outside the department stores. I saw these festivities but felt completely disconnected from them. All I could think about was wolves.

I drove to Montana State University and parked in the visitor lot. Going alone seemed perfectly reasonable while I was at school. Now, as I watched students crossing campus in every direction, I instinctively scanned the crowd for wavy blonde hair and mean, powerful shoulders. I hated Theron for making me more afraid. I breathed hard against the knot in my chest then got out of the car and started uphill. I made a quick stop at the bookstore, where I purchased a sketchbook, before heading across campus.

For Dr. Nancy Bonner studying the Yellowstone wolf pack was a passion; sharing the knowledge she gleaned was her life's work. She was a professor in the Ecology Department, and her research focused on the impact of carnivores on their surrounding ecosystem. Photos of the Yellowstone wolves covered every link on her homepage. Her office was located in Lewis Hall, a turn-of-the-century brick edifice with rows of forward-facing rectangular windows.

It was three-thirty when I climbed the stairs and made my way down the tiled hallway past several other offices. Dr. Bonner's door stood ajar. Behind the desk stood a petite woman with curly red hair partially tamed by a barrette.

I rapped on the door. "Dr. Bonner?"

"Come in." She rummaged through the papers on her desk without looking up.

"I wanted to ask you some questions about the Yellowstone wolf pack."

"Packs," she corrected. "The nearest is at Mammoth, but there are several."

I rehearsed this a dozen times in my mind, but I still didn't know how to approach the subject of gathering wolf fur. "How many wolves are in the Mammoth pack?"

"Currently there are eight."

"Are they all silver?" I asked.

She looked at me like I stepped out of kindergarten with paint smudged on my face. I should have brought Rory. He was much better at talking to adults. But, here I was on my own and botching it up big time.

"One white, two black and the rest gray," Dr. Bonner answered finally.

"Do wolves move in predictable patterns?"

Dr. Bonner pushed the papers aside and sat down. She considered me silently as she rolled up the sleeves of her button-down shirt.

"I mean, is it possible to see them?" I stammered.

"Most people don't see them from the road, and if you are out hiking, you don't want to see them at all."

"But you've seen them," I said. "There are photos of them on your website."

She opened a desk drawer and drew out a compact photo album. She showed me the print on the first page. It was a close-up of a large white wolf. "These photos were taken from a hundred yards away while the wolves were milling about their den. They may seem cute and fluffy, but there's no meaner carnivore out there."

I felt myself swallow fear. "Where's the den?"

Dr. Bonner smirked and tossed the album aside. She turned her attention to a plate of sugar cookies covered in cellophane. "There's a bake sale at the Union—the first of many holiday fundraisers around campus." She pulled off the plastic wrap and took a frosted snowman from the plate. "Usually I steer clear of baked goods because of my allergies, but I couldn't pass on sugar cookies. Have a few." She eyed my baggy clothes disdainfully. "Seriously, you could use them."

I took a cookie from the plate. It was a reindeer with a red dot nose.

"You're not a college student."

"I go to Bozeman High," I confessed.

"Your teacher assigned a science report or a persuasive paper or something like that? All the things you need to know for your assignment are on my website." Dr. Bonner bit off the snowman's head then wiped cookie crumbs from her lips. "I have papers to correct. Have a nice afternoon."

Despite her dismissal I stood there a moment debating what to do. She raised her eyebrows and waited, so I thanked her for the cookie and went out the door. I bit off the reindeer head and chewed angrily.

Without Dr. Bonner's help, I couldn't complete the task. I needed information, and all I got was a sugar cookie. At least it was a good one. My grandma used to make sugar cookies like this with pistachios in the dough. I froze mid-step halfway down the stairs.

Dr. Bonner had allergies.

I turned and ran to her office. The door was still open. She stood there wheezing. Her neck and face were blotchy red. An oversized purse lay on the desk, and Dr. Bonner rummaged furiously through its contents. She swayed unsteadily. The swelling under her eyes made her unrecognizable from the woman who stood there minutes ago.

"What can I do?" I exclaimed.

She clutched her throat and collapsed into the chair.

I dumped the purse contents onto the desk. Caught in the folds at the bottom was an EpiPen, which fell out last. I didn't know how to use it, but the instructions were on the side.

Dr. Bonner's eyes rolled back as she lost consciousness. I pulled the cap off the EpiPen and jammed it hard into her thigh. The instructions said to leave it there ten seconds.

Was I too late? Would I have to tell campus police and the county sheriff that she'd been killed by a sugar cookie? I watched for her chest to rise and fall, but it didn't.

Suddenly she gasped and startled awake. She grabbed my shoulder and squeezed hard.

"Let me guess." I tried to make my voice light, but I was shaking. "You're allergic to nuts?"

The answer was labored breathing.

"Should I call an ambulance?"

She shook her head, still unable to speak. Within minutes the swelling in her face disappeared. As she gained strength, she touched her throat and looked away from my eyes. Finally she whispered, "What do you really want to know about the wolves?"

I dropped the EpiPen onto the desk. "I want to know how to gather wolves' fur without getting killed. It's a task I have to complete—fill a basket with silver wolves' fur."

"You're too young to get into a sorority."

"It's more serious than that." I forced a smile. "Almost as serious as pistachios in sugar cookies."

The natural color returned to her cheeks. A tiny circle of blood on her khaki skirt where the needle pierced her thigh was the only indication that she nearly died. "The only time I touched a wolf was when they tranquilized the pack to tag them. Once you've seen a pair of wolves take down a fifteen hundred pound moose, you realize they're best admired from afar."

I groaned. I didn't want to hear how the task was impossible.

"However," she continued, "your particular task is easier than you think." The fierce strength returned to her green eyes. "Between the den and the nearest stream is a blackberry bush—thorny and twisted. The wolves pass it every day on their way to water."

"And they leave fur behind." Hope quickened my heartbeat.

She nodded slowly. "Lots of it. All you have to do is wait until the pack leaves the den, then gather as much as you need. Grab a sheet of paper from the printer, and I'll draw you a map."

She explained the route through Yellowstone Park I would have to use to get there. "Go early in the morning and watch with binoculars from the hilltop." Dr. Bonner marked a star on the map. "Count them as they leave the den. One white, two black and five gray. When they're all out, make your way to the bush here." She marked another spot on the map. "Take some pepper spray in case you meet the pack. The alpha male is one mean S-O-B."

I folded the map and tucked it into my pocket. "You have no idea how much you've helped me."

"Ditto on that one."

"Are you sure I can't drive you to the hospital or something?" I offered.

"No, I'll call my son. He lives on campus."

I thanked her again and started to leave.

"Wait." Dr. Bonner gestured to the plate of cookies that nearly killed her. "Take those."

I finished the cookies on the way to the parking lot, and I was still hungry. I called Dad's cell as I drove home. "Are you home?" I asked.

"No. Where are you?" he replied.

"MSU," I answered. "I was talking to a professor."

"Gonna see if they'll take you with C's and D's?" He chuckled at his own humor.

I ignored the jibe and got down to the more important matter. "I was thinking maybe you could bring home Chinese—sesame chicken, beef and broccoli, egg rolls..." Just thinking about it made my mouth water.

"Still interested in food?" he interrupted.

"Starving." I arrived home and wondered if Aeas was in the house ready to chew me out. I'd gotten tired of him tromping in and out my bedroom window, so I copied my key and gave it to him, which made it harder for me to tell when he was around.

"Maybe I'm getting my daughter back after all," Dad observed.

I unlocked the door with the phone propped on my shoulder. "Is that a yes?"

"Yes, Chinese food." Someone hollered in the background. "Give me an hour." Dad hung up.

I locked the bolt and climbed the stairs. "Aeas?" No answer. I continued down the hallway and into my room. "Are you here?" The room was still. I sent him a short text: I know how to complete the task. He didn't immediately reply, which was odd.

I settled on the bed with my new sketchbook and smoothed the clean white page beneath my fingers. I picked up a pencil and started to sketch. There was only one image my mind wanted to create, and I could not get it right. I did five sketches, all from different angles but the same scene—Eros awakening with angry eyes. The room and the bedcovers I remembered well. The eyes I could sketch perfectly. The rest of his face I couldn't recreate. It was torture knowing it was somewhere inside my head, but I was unable to put it on the page. I turned to a clean page and tried again. This time I outlined a square jaw line and tufts of wavy hair. Onto this face I drew those angry eyes. The rest of the features remained blank. I tossed the sketchbook aside in frustration. Spilling my guts to a shrink might be easier than this.

I lay back and closed my eyes. His voice echoed in my memories, but his face didn't appear. Even in my dreams Eros remained veiled.

There was not a noodle or shred of cabbage left when Dad and I cleared the table. Whatever pamphlet Dad had on anorexia would probably be tossed in the trash. Soon my clothes would fit and my features would soften. Until then, I was enjoying the extra calories.

After dinner I found Dad's stash of cookies and sneaked the package upstairs. I decided to give the sketch one more shot. I turned to what should have been the first blank page but there, staring back at me, was a perfect sketch of Eros.

He wasn't angry. His eyes, though only rendered in pencil, were playful and matched the voice I remembered so well. A half smile tugged at his mouth. There was only one word to describe that expression: mischievous.

I'd never seen Eros's face when he looked like this, and it made me ache. I stood considering the sketch a moment, then looked around. "That explains why Aeas isn't here," I said aloud.

One of my cookies disappeared.

I sniffed the air. If he kept his distance, I couldn't smell him. Aeas must have told him what cinnamon did to me. I guessed Eros was showering at Aeas's apartment, so he was more anonymous. He didn't wear cologne anymore either. I would never have known he was there if it weren't for the disappearing Oreos and the sound of him chewing.

I dug through the drawers of the desk and found a handful of colored pencils. I carefully adjusted the shading on the sketch to accommodate first the flesh tone, then the violet of the eyes. I sat there contemplating the hair color when a light brown pencil rolled away from the others.

He fluffed the pillow and laid his head on it. Then he slid an arm around my waist. Maybe he stared at the ceiling or at me.

I turned the page and started another sketch. Eros lying silently and invisibly beside me was soothing, but I missed his voice.

When Dad tapped on the door a few hours later to say good night, Eros didn't stir. I thought he was asleep. I went into the bathroom and changed clothes. He wasn't there when I climbed into bed. Deep sadness pooled in my chest until he leaned down and kissed my forehead. He set my phone on the pillow. A new message was on the screen.

`I'll be gone for a few days. Don't get eaten by wolves`.

# CHAPTER 21

Three hours before sunrise on Saturday morning I drove with Rory and Aeas to Livingston. There we exited the freeway and went south to Gardiner. This was the north entrance to Yellowstone Park and only a few miles from Mammoth. Mammoth Hot Springs was one of the few areas in the Park that was open this time of year.

I followed Dr. Bonner's map and found the ridge overlooking the den. It was only ten degrees outside, but we came prepared with layers of winter clothing, shelter tarps and plenty of hot chocolate. An outdoor stakeout wasn't my idea of adventure, but if we could fill that darn basket in one morning and be done with the task, I was willing to sit in the snow for two hours until the pack woke hungry and ready to hunt.

Wolves were unpredictable. Sometimes they hunted at night, but they could just as easily hunt during the day. They didn't obey a set schedule, so our best chance of seeing them leave the den and not return for a few hours was right at dawn. As the light broke golden across the horizon, we heard a low howl and saw the first black wolf emerge from the den.

He wasn't the alpha. That male was gray, but the black wolf was regal and alert as he made his way around the den's opening, sniffing the air and the ground. This was why we were perched on a ridge a hundred yards downwind. One sniff and we would be given away.

The second wolf to emerge was the lone white in the pack. Beside me Aeas drew a breath. "Beautiful," he murmured.

"She may be beautiful, but we don't want white fur," I answered. "We want gray."

"Plenty of gray," Rory replied as the rest of the pack sauntered out of the den stretching their legs and yawning.

We watched for another forty minutes as the wolves milled around. The younger ones playfully sparred in the snow. At last, the largest of the pack, a gray we identified as the alpha male, threw his nose into the air and let out a howl. Rory turned the binoculars to a distant meadow.

"Buffalo," Rory murmured. "Maybe half a mile out." He handed the binoculars to Aeas, who turned them on the herd.

"Well, let's hope they put up a good fight. It won't take the pack long to cover half a mile when they're finished eating."

"We'll be quick. The basket isn't that big." I was trying hard to forget about the unsteady pounding in my chest. Wolves looked much more vicious in real life than in Dr. Bonner's photo album.

The pack galloped through the woods toward their buffalo breakfast, and we jogged down the hillside to the den. I slid off one glove and clutched the pepper spray canister in that hand. It was a few hundred yards to the stream. The gurgle of the water told us we were heading in the right direction. The trail tunneled beneath a twisted blackberry bush, and there the bush had taken on a knotted, furry skin. From a distance, it looked like mold, but it was the winter coats of the pack, brushed off their backs each time they shimmied under the thorns heading for water.

Aeas dropped the basket at the opening, and we switched winter gloves for heavy leather ones. The bush tugged at our clothes as we gleaned the silver fur from its branches.

"No black or white," I reminded them. "Only gray."

We filled the basket, packed it down and filled it some more.

"That should do," Aeas said finally. "Even Theron must admit this is full."

"Then let's get out of here," Rory said warily.

"Don't you want to see the stream?" I asked. "We've come this far. When will you ever be in this part of the park again?"

"Sorry, don't care. I don't want to be here when the pack comes back," Rory replied.

"It's only been half an hour. I'm sure they're not in that big a rush to come home."

"Let's just go, Psyche," Aeas answered.

"Okay, fine." We started back toward the den. Rory took the lead and moved swiftly up the trail. Aeas followed carrying the basket. I brought up the rear. We moved through the trees toward the ridge. Just as we started the ascent, I felt the hair on the back of my neck prickle. From behind me came a guttural growl. Armed with pepper spray, I turned slowly. One member of the pack had stayed behind. It was a yearling male. He lowered his head and bared his teeth. His youth and size made him no less a threat. He was hungry.

"Bad doggie," I whispered.

A tuft of fur on the back of his neck rose, and he growled again. Aeas stopped. I heard his heavy breathing behind me.

"Not so pretty now, is he?" I murmured. I backed another step away from the wolf, who crouched. I didn't wait for him to pounce. I opened fire with the pepper spray.

The dog's sensitive nose took the hit. He sneezed, yelped and rubbed his nose in the dirt. Then he pawed at his eyes and tried to rub them in the dirt, too.

I gave Aeas a shove. "Run!"

We ran up the ridge and all the way to the car. Rory dived into the back seat. Aeas hopped in shotgun with the basket on his lap. I jumped into the driver's seat and locked the door. Like a wolf could open it. We sat there listening to each other panting, then Rory erupted into hysterical laughter.

"That was too close," Aeas muttered without so much as a smile.

# CHAPTER 22

We stopped at a café in Gardiner for breakfast. The only other customers were two old men sipping coffee at a table in the corner. Bing Crosby's "White Christmas" blared through the overhead speakers, and a waitress stood at the counter rolling silverware into napkins. The aroma of freshly brewed coffee and frying bacon drifted through the air. Suddenly I was starving.

A sign instructed us to seat ourselves, so we took the window booth farthest in the back. Gold tinsel-garland had been taped around the window, and red balls hung from the top section. A sticker on the menu advertised eggnog and mincemeat pie through the month of December. I scanned the breakfast section, already knowing what I wanted.

The waitress came to our table carrying a coffee pot. She wore a plush Santa hat and had cork-screw curls that framed a narrow face. "What can I get for you today?" She gave Rory and I a quick glance, then her gaze settled on Aeas and stayed there.

Aeas, however, was preoccupied punching out a text message.

After taking Rory's and my orders, the waitress lingered over Aeas. She gave him a pretty smile, but he didn't look up to see it.

"Bacon and eggs, please." His fingers continued moving over the buttons of his phone.

"Do you want hash browns and toast with that?"

Aeas nodded, pressing send on his message. "Yes, and orange juice." He glanced up briefly and gave her a polite nod. "Thank you."

The waitress grinned and blinked. "You're welcome."

While we waited for our order, the reply to Aeas's message beeped through. He frowned at his phone and looked up. "Are you well rested?" he asked me.

"What kind of question is that?" I replied.

He waited.

"I guess," I answered.

The waitress returned balancing our orders on her arms. She set a steaming plate of pancakes in front of me.

I poured huckleberry syrup on the stack with slow precision. "We got up early this morning, but overall, I've been sleeping better."

"Of course you have," Aeas murmured and began typing out the reply.

"You are looking better these days, and you're eating." Rory unwrapped a set of silverware. "Why is that?"

I shrugged, and Aeas gave him a sideways glance but didn't answer. Rory didn't appreciate having things withheld from him, but the fact that Eros was visiting me by night was none of Rory's business. I wasn't willing to share one moment of that time with either of them. Rory would assume, erroneously, that Eros and I spent our nights intimately. Aeas understood the magnitude of such an act for Eros if not for me, and while he probably wondered if we let our passions get the best of us, he was happy being ignorant.

The waitress lingered over Aeas's plate until he looked up and met her eyes. "Can I get you anything else?" she offered.

"No, thank you." After she returned to the kitchen, he excused himself to the restroom.

"What would that be like?" Rory stabbed a sausage. "Girls falling over you everywhere you go."

"It's not as great as it seems." I should've been more compassionate, but I was tired of Rory's self-pity and his jealousy. It wasn't Aeas's fault he was beautiful any more than it was mine. It wasn't Rory's fault he had acne. We all had cards we were dealt, and we played our lives with them.

He chewed bitterly. "Yeah, right. And he's only fifteen. Think of what it will be like when he's twenty."

"Five hundred years from now?"

Rory's jaw went slack. "I never really thought about that."

My phone beeped the arrival of a text message. I was happy to see the now-familiar number of Eros's cell phone. Aeas slid into the seat across from me as I opened the message.

**Well done. Aeas has a message for you.**

I looked up. "What's going on?"

"He knows the final task already, and he's preparing." Aeas started to cut the bacon with a knife and fork, but I tapped his shin with my foot and made him use his fingers. With a shrug he relented. "We," he said, motioning to himself and Rory, "aren't allowed to accompany you. The task will take awhile, so you're to make an excuse to your father. You need to meet Theron early in the day, so you'll have time to complete as much of the journey as possible the first day."

"Journey?" I set my fork down.

"I don't know where," Aeas added.

"How long am I going to be gone?"

He shrugged. "I'm waiting for instructions. Most likely I'll get them after you see Theron."

It would be mean of me to leave a second time and not tell my dad, and if I didn't even know how long I would be gone or if I was ever coming back for that matter, what could I tell him? I hated hiding all of this from Dad.

My appetite waned. The thought of meeting Theron was enough to make me lose my breakfast without a dollop of deceit on top. I turned to Rory gravely. "If I can't complete the task, and Theron really does kill me, you have to tell my dad the truth."

"Me?" His eyes widened. "What about him? Let the demigod explain your disappearance."

"Psyche, now is not the time for doubt," Aeas said without emotion.

"Well, we ought to have a plan B just in case. I don't want to be some face on a missing poster whose parents never know what happened. You guys know what I'm doing. Someone has to be honest with my dad if I can't make it back."

"We wouldn't leave him wondering if you were never coming home," Aeas said finally. "It won't come to that."

"I'll be in the car." I scooted out of the booth and left cash on the table. "We're wasting time that I'm probably going to need."

I sat alone in the Subaru and dialed my home phone number. Dad was at work and wouldn't get the message until tonight. "Dad," I said, "I know you're going to be mad at me for taking off again, but there's something I have to do. I wish I could tell you more, but you already want to have me committed, so..." I sighed. Finding the words was harder than I thought it would be. "I love you. I hope you know that. I'll come home when I can." I hung up as Rory and Aeas came out of the restaurant.

"Will he check your story?" Rory asked, knowing I had just called home.

I shrugged. "It doesn't matter. I'll be halfway to who-knows-where before my dad gets that message." It saddened me more than I wanted to say. My dad was a decent guy. He deserved better than this.

The dashboard clock read 9:40 when I pulled into the driveway at Theron's house. Through the window I saw that furniture had been delivered since my last visit. It was trendy and perfectly placed, probably the work of a professional designer. I wondered if he would use the property as a lure for college girls, and the thought made my insides twist. It was a monumental injustice that someone so despicable would live almost an eternity.

I rang the doorbell, and an aging, butler-type person answered the door. I had never seen a household with a butler. It was beyond weird. "I need to see Theron."

He gave a short bow. "Just a moment, please."

When Theron appeared in the doorway, he was wearing faded jeans and a ribbed sweater that hugged the contours of his muscular body.

I offered him the basket without a word of explanation. There was no disputing it as completion of the task.

"Come in." He lifted the basket from my hands.

"I saw enough of your house the last time I was here." I tried to hide the fear in my voice. It was hard to look him in the eyes.

Theron set the basket on the ground, then crossed the living room to the fireplace, where he took something from the mantle. It was a small wooden box with an intricately carved rose on the top. A tiny gold lock held it closed. He offered it to me.

As I inspected the box, Theron pulled a card from his pocket and held it out between two fingers. Printed on the card was another set of coordinates: 28.7573°, 82.8588°.

"I'm to go to this location?"

"At high noon one week from today, Aphrodite's associate will be at that location. If you are there, he will lead you to the woman who has the key to this lock. Inside is your reward. He will not wait for you. If you're late, you fail."

196

"Anything else?"

"No other companions may accompany you beyond the meeting point." Theron looked over my shoulder and glared viciously at something across the lawn.

"And when I complete the task?"

"*If* you complete the task, we'll know."

We didn't exchange parting pleasantries.

I climbed into my car ready to zoom home and Google the coordinates, but a text message rang through: `Go to the airport, private hanger #3.` Apparently I didn't need to know where I was going, and I was leaving immediately.

The airport was only a few miles away. The clouds hung low and threatened more snow, but the roads and runways were clear. I parked outside the gate and jogged to the hanger, where I found an ultra-long range, high-speed business jet waiting.

True to Eros's anonymous nature, the jet had no markings but a stylish black stripe down the side and its model, Global Express, stenciled under the cockpit window. The engines were warming and the stairs were down awaiting passengers. I had a hard time believing this was all for me until I saw Aeas jogging toward me with a duffle bag in his hands. He met me halfway to the jet. The bag in his hand was mine, and it was only lightly packed.

"I thought you weren't coming with me?"

"I'm not. Here are some clothes." From his jacket pocket he pulled out a wad of cash, which he put into my hand. "In case there's something you need that we missed."

"Where am I going?"

"Nepal."

"*Alone?*" Europe was one thing, but Nepal? Did people in Nepal even speak English? I had no idea where the coordinates would lead me. "What about my passport? I don't have a visa." I unzipped the duffle bag and placed Aphrodite's box inside.

"It's being taken care of."

"It takes months..."

"Money goes a long way in a country like Nepal."

How silly of me. Eros would just bribe someone to give me a visa today, and I would land tomorrow.

Aeas moved me toward the plane. "Titus will fill you in once you're in the air."

"Who's Titus?"

A young man appeared at the doorway of the jet. He was dark haired and uncommonly beautiful. He found me on the beach in Italy and carried me into Aphrodite's palace. He returned me to the mainland after I signed my life away with these tasks.

I stopped dead. "Absolutely not! He's one of Theron's men. I'm not going anywhere with him!" I set my jaw obstinately, knowing full well that Titus could hear me over the hum of the jet engines.

Aeas took my elbow and turned me away from the plane. "When Titus returned to the Fortress, Theron beat him so severely that he abandoned his post and sought refuge in Eros's kingdom." He threw a glance over his shoulder and continued. "He told Eros about the tasks. Eros offered him a place in his household, but Titus refused to swear allegiance to Eros. Psyche, he's sworn his allegiance to you. He's your servant and bodyguard now."

"Why would he do that? I'm a mortal. I don't belong to your world."

Aeas shrugged. "I serve Eros before anyone else. Eros said I would be useless to you on this journey."

"Eros decided he's sick of me, and Titus is going to murder me before we land?"

Dragging me toward the stairs of the jet, Aeas replied, "I assure you he will not. He knows what punishment awaits him if he murders his mistress." When I balked again, Aeas grew irritated. "You're wasting time. Go."

Finally I trudged up the steps, but Titus had disappeared. He was probably veiled in a corner sharpening a knife. I tossed my duffle bag on the floor by the first leather seat.

The customized interior of the jet was nothing short of spectacular. From nose to tail the Global Express was nearly a hundred feet in length. Just under half of this was the cabin area. At eight feet wide and six feet four inches tall, the cabin might seat eighteen passengers, but this jet was partitioned to accommodate very few people. There were six leather chairs at the front of the cabin, then a narrow hallway through a full bath. At the back of the plane was the luxury stateroom, though I could see only part of it through the open doorway.

I sank into one of the leather chairs as the steps folded up and the cabin door closed seemingly on its own. Into the com system Titus murmured, "Package aboard. We're ready for take-off."

"Roger that," was the pilot's response. The "Fasten Seatbelts" sign lit at the front of the cabin, and the engines thundered.

"Titus," I said, testing his obedience, "show yourself."

Immediately he appeared, mid-stride as he moved to a seat across the aisle. "Lady?"

"Cut the crap, will ya? It's Psyche." I ignored the smirk he tried to hide with a bowed head. "What's in Nepal?"

"The Himalayas."

I swore without meaning to. "Of course, she's sending me up Mt. Everest. Experienced climbers die trying to summit."

"No, it isn't Everest. The coordinates are farther west. It's in the mountains for sure, but the location is at an altitude of only 4550 meters, about 15,000 feet."

"That doesn't make sense," I said. She could send me anywhere in the world. Why would she pick a mountain that was only 15,000 feet when one nearby was double that?

"It's only the meeting point. Yes, it will be difficult to get there, but we're led to believe the second leg of the journey will be harder. You'll either climb higher with Aphrodite's messenger or you'll be taken through a portal."

"Whose kingdom is it?"

"Apollo's."

I shook my head. "Theron said the messenger would lead me to a woman, not a man."

Titus's expression grew darker. "There is another possibility, but Eros is hoping he's wrong."

"What is it?" I was pressed back into the seat then by the forward thrust of the jet as we took off.

He refused to answer, even when I commanded him. "I won't worry you unnecessarily," he said. "The most important thing is that I get you to the location on time."

"We have a whole week. It will only take a day to fly to Nepal."

"It's primitive country we have to travel through. There are few roads, and once we reach the last village, we'll be on foot the rest of the way." When the seatbelt sign clicked off, Titus stood. "I'll show you to the stateroom, so you can rest."

Still wary of him, I asked, "Does the door lock?"

He rolled his eyes. "Yes, but before you lock yourself in, get some food from the refrigerator up front."

My stomach was full of pancakes. "Maybe later." When he tried to usher me down the aisle, I simply waited and made him pass in front of me. It obviously frustrated him. If I was his mistress and he my servant, then I was supposed to go first, but I wouldn't turn my back on him. He pointed out the shower, sink and toilet as we passed, then stepped inside the stateroom so I could pass from the tiny hallway into the room.

There was a queen bed and compact, latching cupboards on either side. The headboard was mahogany, and the cupboards, while made of vinyl, matched the color and the grain. Just over my shoulder, a flat screen television was mounted to the wall, and Titus informed me that the stateroom had Bose speakers and a built-in video library of over a thousand movies. He showed me another compact refrigerator, which was stocked with water, juice and soda pop. "Can I get you anything?"

"No." I had my bag slung over my shoulder. As soon as he stepped into the hallway, I locked him out then fell onto the bed more tired than I should have been.

Aphrodite was cunning to send me on a long journey. Over two months into her tasks, I was weary, but I couldn't abandon my resolve to see Eros. At his name my thoughts brightened. It was his jet and his bed. What were the chances they hadn't changed the pillow cases since his last flight? I threw the covers back, hugged a pillow to my chest and inhaled deeply. It smelled of laundry soap but not Eros. Disappointed, I lay back and pictured him as I closed my eyes. Thanks to his sketch, I could see him perfectly in my mind.

"Someday soon," I promised him. "I will see you again." I knew he wasn't there to hear me, but it didn't matter. The steady hum of the jet engines lulled me to sleep.

When I woke, it was strangely quiet. I had been jarred from sleep, but I was too groggy to remember exactly why. The window blinds of the stateroom were closed, and with the overhead lights off, it was completely dark except for a strip of emergency lighting which led to the door. Freeing myself from the blankets, I stumbled to the door and was nearly blinded when I opened it. Sunshine blazed through the cabin windows, and the jet was still. We were on the ground. I gathered my composure in the bathroom, where I splashed water on my face and rinsed my mouth. Then I ventured out. Titus was not in sight, and the cockpit door was open. One seat was empty. Sitting sideways in the other seat was a man with graying hair, who was reading a paperback novel.

"Hello?" I said.

At the sight of me he stood. "Well, hello. This is a change."

"What do you mean?"

He shook his head as if he'd misspoken, but he continued anyway. "I don't often get to greet my passengers." The pilot was mortal and couldn't see a veiled Olympian.

"How long have you been flying for Erik?"

"I've never met Mr. Savage, but I've been flying for the company over twenty-five years. This beauty…" He gestured around at the plane. "…rolled off the line almost ten years ago, one of the first of its kind. It's a joy to fly."

"So, you understand their, um, uniqueness."

He gave me a wide smile. "I've aged twenty years since I started flying for them, but Aaron hasn't aged a day. For the longest time I thought I was flying an empty jet all over the world, fully stocked, no flight crew, no passengers, but I came to understand I carried important cargo I simply couldn't see."

"Well," I said. "You can see me. I'm like you." Out the front windows of the cockpit I saw blue sky, beach and waves crashing onto the shore. "Where are we?"

"A privately-owned island in Hawaii. When traveling west, we usually layover here for fuel. The jet could make it all the way to the edge of Asia without stopping, but fueling here means one less government to deal with."

"Do I have time to look around?"

He escorted me to the cabin door. "We're scheduled to take off in an hour, but I won't leave without you."

I thanked him and made my way down the steps. There was no airport, just a landing strip. Across a small yard stood a cottage about the size of my dad's house. I started toward it. Before I reached the steps, the door opened, and Titus appeared in the doorway. "I wasn't sure if the landing would wake you." He gestured me inside. "Eros sent instructions for me to feed you well. Supplies have to be flown onto this island, but a delivery was made for us today." From one of several grocery bags on a nearby table, he withdrew an orange and tossed it to me. "You're thinner now than the last time I saw you."

"Are there macadamia nuts in there?"

"Yes." He pulled out a large can.

"Toss it here. I'll eat the whole can."

"You will not."

"Yeah, I will. I love these things." I set the orange aside. "Eros knows better than to send only fruit and nuts."

At this Titus grinned. "One entire bag is full of meat—beef jerky, pepperoni sticks, canned chicken, even sardines."

"Really?" I elbowed him out of the way and dug through the sack. "The sardines are for you." I didn't eat anything that smelled that bad. "But this," I said, drawing out one giant bag of pepperoni sticks, "is mine."

Upstairs the cottage had three bedrooms, each with a balcony. The sea-facing windows showed a long stretch of sandy beach and a rocky shore beyond. The inland-facing windows opened on a towering mountain scene. Though jagged and rocky, the mountain was green all the way to the top with leaves and vines swaying in the breeze. I preferred this view to the seaward one, and I wasn't alone in this opinion. This was the largest of the bedrooms, and upon opening the closets, I found casual men's clothing in sizes to fit Eros.

People might think it odd that someone who had enough wealth to buy a private island would not build a grand mansion on it, but that wasn't Eros's style. This cottage, like the upstairs rooms of his Olympian mansion, was a place of solace and peace. The furnishings were expensive I was sure, but not lavish like Aphrodite's palace. Eros did not build mansions to entertain guests. He found places he liked, and he lived in them.

By the time I boarded the plane, the engines were humming again. Titus had already stowed the food in the compartments of the cabin, and all that was missing was me. As soon as I was seated, we taxied to the far end of the runway, turned around and barreled ahead full speed. Through the window, I watched the trees next to the short runway whiz by, and I clutched the edge of my seat wondering if we'd run out of pavement before we made it into the air. A moment later I felt the nose lift, and we sailed effortlessly over the sea. Able to breathe easily again, I turned to Titus, who was fiddling with an electronic gadget.

"What's that?"

"A GPS device. The target coordinates are already programmed in. I need your cell phone."

It was futile to protest. We were at sea, and I didn't have service.

He plugged my phone into another, larger one and downloaded my contacts. "Keep this satellite phone with you at all times. I'm programmed into your speed dial. Just press and hold number two."

"I know how to use speed dial."

On the seat next to him was a stack of documents. "I have our passports, visas, maps and all the climbing permits we need. We have a reservation at a hotel in Kathmandu tonight and a car to take us as far as the road goes. Two of Eros's men are ahead of us. They will find us lodging in the villages along the way and secure a yak for the journey."

"A *yak*? Those big hairy cattle? We're actually going to use one?"

"You'll be glad when you don't have to carry all your gear." He looked up with a smirk. "I wouldn't think someone from Montana would mind."

"Cowboys ride horses, not Herefords." Both passports were issued from the United States. I reached to inspect them, but Titus slid them away from my grasp.

"Yes, I'm American now," he replied.

The time synchronized on two watches, our destination on the GPS device, and both satellite phones charged and working, Titus finally sat back and folded his arms.

We had a seven-hour flight ahead of us, and I wasn't going to sleep. I still couldn't believe I was stuck with Titus for the entire journey.

"I will never betray you," he said finally.

"Whatever." Words were cheap. I would find out on the mountain whether or not he could be trusted.

"Ask me anything. I will always be honest with you."

"You won't tell me what Eros suspects about the second leg of the journey."

"When we get closer, I will tell you, but we need to focus on getting there first."

Evasive, just like Eros. "I swear you immortals are all alike."

"We are more moral and principled than the men of *your* world." He was angry because he knew when I looked at him I saw one of Theron's men.

"What happened when you returned to the Fortress?"

Titus folded his hands together and leaned forward on his knees. "I never made it up the stairs. Theron was waiting for me in the dark with a lead candlestick in his hands."

Still unconvinced, I waited.

"He struck me twice, and I rolled down the steps to the marina before I managed to stand." Defiance flickered in his eyes. "I'm a trained fighter, but Theron is fast and ruthless. As a general rule, when he disciplines us, we aren't allowed to defend ourselves. We're left to suffer with our injuries for a few days, and then he heals us. But I'd had enough. My father died protecting Aphrodite's husband. When I fought back, it enraged Theron. By the time he beat me to my knees, I knew there was no going back. He was going to kill me, so I dove into the marina and swam for the mainland."

"It's salt water."

"Yeah," he said flatly. "It hurt."

It still didn't explain how he ended up here with me. "Why go to Eros? Why not Aphrodite's husband?"

"Because of you. I knew about the contract."

I remembered how he treated me that night. He tried to convince me to run away and abandon the tasks. "You refused his generosity."

"Not exactly. When I told Eros about the contract, he didn't believe me, but he sent someone to watch Theron anyway. Two months later when the magazines arrived, Eros went to see the delivery. That's when he offered me service in his household."

"But, you said no."

"There's a hierarchy among servants. No one is higher than the master's personal servant."

"Aeas?" I said. "He hardly seems like a bodyguard."

"He's not." Titus gave me a crooked smile. "Eros needs a babysitter more than a bodyguard."

His arrogance irritated me. "That's your boss you're talking about."

"Not yet. I'll get to that. Some of the serving class inherit their posts, like Aeas and me. Others, like Theron, serve under oath.

Aeas's and my loyalties are inherited by blood, but as the household was unkind to me, I have chosen to leave. It is my right. You are not of an Olympian household. No one will ever inherit loyalty to you. The only way you will have a loyal servant is by oath."

"Now, why would anyone swear an oath to a mere mortal?" I guessed at the reason, but I made him answer anyway.

"Because Eros wants you back, and you need an immortal's help. Once you marry Eros..."

"Only Aeas outranks you."

"Exactly."

If I was trying to paint a picture of Titus's character, and I was, these few details were telling. First, he wouldn't allow himself to be abused. Second, he wasn't above pitting one master against another if he believed an injustice had been committed. Third, he was willing to risk his time and reputation with me if it meant a raise in situation for him later.

I still didn't like him. He wasn't at all like Aeas. I'd never have to remind myself not to take advantage of Titus. He would probably start ordering me around. "I'm sure there are trained fighters in Eros's kingdom that he trusts more than you."

"Maybe, but they are all loyal to him, not you. And, I better than anyone understand the greatest danger to you."

At the same time we both said, "Theron."

"But, you're right," Titus added. "Eros doesn't like the idea of me being with you every waking moment, and he told me in no uncertain terms that if I ever tried to have the kind of relationship with you that Theron has with Aphrodite, the beating I received from Theron would seem merciful."

"If you so much as think about having that kind of relationship with me, I'll kick your sorry tail all the way back to the Fortress." Honestly, didn't Eros understand that the last thing I needed right now was another guy to deal with? "What if I fail at the tasks?"

"I'm led to believe that Aphrodite and Theron have an agreement. Once you fail, you're fair game. She wants you to disappear forever, and he's willing to oblige."

"He told me as much himself."

"No matter the outcome of the contract, I will stay with you until your dying breath. That was my agreement with Eros. No man in his household was willing to give up an age of his life guarding a mortal, but I will, and I'll make sure Theron never hurts you again." It was hard to doubt his sincerity. If we had one thing in common, it was a hatred of Aphrodite's bodyguard.

"You could be lying," I said. "You could lead me right to Theron and hand me over."

"Then my fate would be worse than yours, because I've sworn an oath to protect you, and if I betray you, the Judges of Olympus will condemn me as a traitor."

Aeas told me nearly the same thing when he put me on the plane. More importantly, I knew Eros wouldn't have sent me someone that couldn't be trusted. My reluctance to accept him was based on my run-ins with Theron, and I knew very well that Theron was an exception, not the rule.

"By the way," Titus offered, "Theron paid for what he did to you. Eros made sure of that."

I didn't ask how. I wasn't sure I wanted to know.

The jet was much faster than a commercial airline. Our actual flying time from Montana to Nepal was just under twelve hours, but we crossed the international dateline, so when we landed in Kathmandu, it was nearly noon on Sunday, over twenty-four hours since I received the task from Theron. I had lost one full day. After taxiing across the tarmac, we stayed in the silent jet. The pilot and copilot stood outside the cockpit.

"What's going on?"

"We're waiting to be boarded," the copilot explained. "Once they check your visas and passports, they'll let you be on your way without going through the airport."

I glanced at Titus, who seemed to expect this. Only I was unaccustomed to the lifestyle of the wealthy and privileged. Titus motioned me to stay seated as the airport security guard boarded the plane.

The guard was pleasant and spoke English. "Came to do some climbing, did you?"

"I hope we're not too late," Titus replied. "We are sticking to the lower elevations."

After glancing at our climbing permits, the man smiled. "That area is accessible year round if the weather is good."

"We'll hope for clear skies," Titus said amiably. "My girlfriend is quite a photographer." I threw him a glare, while the security guard looked at the passports. After the guard was gone, Titus stood to unload the overhead compartments.

"I am not your girlfriend."

"For now you are." He paused with a hand resting on the shelf above so he towered over me. "It's simpler. We don't look anything alike, so we can't pass for siblings. We say we're a couple, and no one gives us any grief."

"Why did you give him a fake passport?"

"It isn't fake. It's as real as the one you have back home, but in this one you're a year older. No minors are allowed to climb without a licensed guide."

"That's so stupid. I'm going to be eighteen in a month."

"Now you're almost nineteen." Titus told me his passport said he was twenty-one, but he had just passed the mid-point of his nineteenth age.

After airport security cleared us, two young men from a waiting car boarded. I recognized both of them. They had been with Aeas in the orchard outside the palace that first day I visited Eros's kingdom. They helped unload the supplies we picked up in Hawaii.

Titus spoke to them in Italian. "She doesn't like me," he told them. "Thinks I'm going to kill her when her back is turned."

One of them called Titus a name that roughly translated to "scoundrel," but the other put a hand on my shoulder. "Eros sends his love. He also sent Titus, so you can trust him." My Italian wasn't great, but I knew what he said.

"If you say so," I replied in English.

He nodded and led me down the steps into a hot afternoon. I spent yesterday morning staking out wolves in the snow. I had worn long underwear under my jeans, a thermal top under my T-shirt and a sweatshirt in addition to my coat. At the cottage in Hawaii, I shed all the layers except my T-shirt and jeans. My duffle bag was bulging with extra clothes. Here in Kathmandu, it was even warmer than Hawaii. I wasn't used to seventy-degree weather during the third week of December.

On the tarmac waited a mid-80s Isuzu SUV. The seats were torn and an old AM/FM radio sat in the dashboard. The seatbelts were broken. The steering wheel was on the right side, so the gears had to be shifted with the left hand. After being ushered into the back seat, I peeked into the cargo area and found it loaded with winter gear.

Titus climbed into the back seat with me. "Is there anything you want to see before we go to the hotel?"

I didn't know enough about the city to name a single landmark, which was sad. I had never been to Nepal, and I would very likely never return, but I wasn't here to sightsee. I didn't have time to act like a tourist, snapping pictures and sampling the local food. The jetlag was starting to hit me, too. I nodded toward the guys in the front seat and asked Titus, "Why do they speak Italian, but not English?"

"Anyone educated to have dealings in the mortal world learns Greek and Latin first. The romance languages are easy to learn. German and English are more difficult."

"You speak English perfectly."

He smiled at this compliment. "Aphrodite sent me to Oxford for two years. English is useful in Europe. She expects all her entourage to speak it fluently. Eros's servants are more likely to know the native tongues of the Americas, since that is their kingdom." He leaned closer, and whispered, "Actually, they do know some English. They're just embarrassed to speak it in front of you."

I had only heard of conditions in impoverished nations. I had never seen them firsthand. As we meandered through neighborhoods trying to dodge traffic, I saw crumbling stone houses with metal or warped wooden rooftops. Ragged children played along the street. Very few wore shoes.

One of the boys in front pointed to a building ahead. *"Il suo hotel."*

I expected modest accommodations, but we arrived at a luxury hotel. It was an American chain and offered all the amenities one would expect in the States including restaurants, an indoor and an outdoor pool, exercise room, and twenty-four-hour room service. It seemed like an eyesore, a temple built to pride, after the poverty we had just witnessed.

Titus checked us in while the other men oversaw the unloading of our gear. Standing in the enormous foyer, I felt myself growing dizzy. Stars streaked across the lights in front of me. We took the elevator to the top floor, where each suite lay behind a grand wooden door. Ours was midway down the hall. Upon opening the door we found that the exterior wall of the suite was all windows and showed a view of the city and majestic mountains beyond.

"We have separate bedrooms," Titus informed me. "Each has a private bath."

I teetered through the doorway.

"Whoa." He caught me as I collapsed.

"Don't touch me," I protested.

"I'm not," he answered as he scooped me into his arms. "You're walking." He carried me to a bedroom, where he poured me onto the bed and threw a blanket over me. "Sleep. I'll find you some decent food when you wake."

"I only need a few hours." My words were slurred. Even with my eyes closed my head spun. It was the worst jetlag I had ever had, and the worst possible time for it. I was completely worthless until I slept this off.

I awoke hot and threw the blanket off to find shoes still on my feet. Fierce late-afternoon rays beamed through the window. In my grogginess on the way in I didn't notice just how upscale the suite was. Hand woven carpets covered the wood floors. My private bath included a jetted tub and a walk-in shower. The countertops were granite. There was even a satin nightgown and matching satin robe hanging in the closet. I looked down at my faded jeans and worn T-shirt. The hotel staff probably wondered why a ragamuffin like me was staying in their nicest room.

Titus was inventorying our gear when I stepping into the living area.

"Don't you ever sleep?" I asked.

"You're just in time for dinner," he replied.

"I hope it's nothing too adventurous. I'm a meat-and-potatoes kind of girl." I picked up one sheet of the inventory list and was struck by the magnitude of the journey ahead of us. This was no day hike. We were packing snow shoes, crampons, ice axes and rappelling gear in addition to our tents, bed rolls, first aid supplies and electronic equipment. "I thought we were sticking to the lower elevations."

"It's still treacherous. We're going prepared for the worst." He handed me a pair of boots and a parka. "Yours. The pants are there next to you."

"How are we going to carry all this?"

Titus began rolling Mylar blankets into the first aid kit. "This is just our gear. We also have to carry enough food and water for the trip up and the descent."

"I think a yak is a very good idea."

"I thought you'd come around on that one." After packing the supplies into two titanium-framed backpacks, Titus pulled the hotel phone onto his lap. In the desk he had found the menu for a restaurant downstairs. He was thrilled to see that it specialized in European cuisine and offered several Italian entrees. "What do you want?"

"Steak, but only if they have beef. No yak meat."

When our food was delivered, I ended up with a ten-ounce New York steak while Titus had spaghetti and meatballs. We sat at the table, and the waiter served our plates. Before he left, Titus asked him to take our picture. "Make sure you smile," Titus said to me.

The waiter snapped two photos then wheeled his cart out of the suite.

"Why did you have him take our picture?" I cut a piece of steak and savored it. It wasn't a Montana Angus, but it was dang good.

"For your contest." He ate like an Italian with a spoon in one hand and a fork in the other, turning the tines of the fork in the dip of the spoon until the spaghetti was fully wrapped around the fork. "We both know Erik Savage never entered."

I broke off a piece of dinner roll. My cheeks flushed hot with embarrassment. "I was... after the tasks..." Did he know that Tyson Ewing saved my life? Did anyone else know that the honey-colored cards all belonged to that one man?

Titus set down his fork. He reached into his shirt pocket and pulled out a rumpled card with embossed black letters. "This fell out of your coat pocket."

Before going to the wolf den I shoved that card in my pocket for luck.

Titus set a blue passport booklet on the tablecloth and slid it toward my plate.

I opened it and saw his picture next to the name Tyson Ewing. "You?" I almost dropped the passport into my plate. I was too shocked to utter the thank you I should have. "Why?"

Titus picked up his fork and spoon. "You're not much good to me dead."

There was a knock at the door, and I was grateful he left the table to answer it. The delivery was a large manila envelope. Titus lingered in the doorway after the messenger was gone, then his eyes moved across the room.

"What is it?" I asked.

"Our travel itinerary and instructions. It lays out how far we need to go each day to reach the meeting point on time. We'll head out first thing in the morning and drive to the town at the foot of the mountains. It's only three hundred miles, but the trip will probably take all day." His demeanor changed. He pushed the papers aside with a wicked glint in his eyes. "Do you know about the billboard Eros stole from Aphrodite's warehouse?"

I continued eating and didn't look up. He moved from one uncomfortable subject to another just to torment me. I could not survive an entire week of this.

Titus dipped bread into the extra sauce on his plate. "You remember the doors in the upstairs room that overlook over the sea?"

"Behind the curtains."

"Eros hung the center portion of the billboard—the part that's you—behind the curtains on those wooden doors. Everyone thinks he sits up there for hours staring at the sea, but he's really just looking at you."

I set my fork down and sipped some water. What did Titus expect me to say? That I was flattered? I slid back from the table. "Then he'll be disappointed if he marries me. They edit photos to make them perfect. I don't really look like that." I tossed the napkin on the table. "I'm going to make use of that huge tub in my bathroom."

Titus's glance darted across the living room, and he stood. "Lock the door."

I turned on him, suddenly furious. He spent the entire day trying to convince me I could trust him, but when it came to me bathing, I had to lock the door to keep him out. "I guess you're not as trustworthy as you claimed to be."

He set his hands on his hips. "I am a man, after all."

"That you are," I muttered before slamming the door and locking it. I was too angry to admit he'd hurt me. I wanted to believe he would be my friend and my guardian, but it turned out he was just like every other guy in the world.

While the tub filled, I watched the last rays of sunlight linger on the rooftops before the mountains stole the light and sank the buildings into shadows. When the stars began to sparkle in the sky, I drew the curtains. For awhile, I just soaked in the hot water. Then I found the switch that turned on the jets, and I let the air massage the tension out of my back and shoulders. I stayed in the tub until my hands and feet were pickled and pale. With reluctance I finally wrapped myself in one of the plush towels embroidered with the hotel's crest.

Aeas only packed me a single change of clothes, two pair of underwear and some socks. The thought of Aeas in my underwear drawer was disturbing, but somehow my pride was being shredded on all sides since I had undertaken to win a god. I put on clean underwear and the satin nightgown from the closet. In the morning I would tell Titus I needed more clothes, but I didn't want to see him again tonight.

Today was the easiest leg of my journey. Tomorrow would be a long drive, and each day after would grow more difficult. I had to wonder if it was all futile. I wasn't especially strong or smart or athletic. There was nothing that uniquely qualified me to beat these tasks except my will to win and the help I received from certain, generous immortals. Were Eros's planning and his money and his servants enough? Once I met the messenger, I was completely on my own, and that was what I feared most. Alone I was weak. If I failed, there would be no one else to blame but me.

I fluffed the pillows and pulled the blankets around me, but I couldn't sleep. I listened for movement outside the room, but the suite had been built for privacy. It was a giant cocoon.

I thought I imagined the light *tap, tap, tap* on the door. I sat up and listened, then I heard it again, barely louder than the first.

"Titus?" I wasn't ready to forgive him, so if he was bugging me, it had better be important. "What do you want?"

*Tap, tap, tap.*

Aggravated, I climbed out of bed and pulled on the robe before opening the door. I expected to find Titus standing there. Instead, I saw the suite darkened and completely still. "Titus?" I stepped into an invisible body. A squeal of surprise escaped me before he put his fingers over my lips. The ring on his first finger brushed my nose. He held me immovable and kissed my cheek, giving me time to recognize him before he set me free. "You're here."

Of course, Eros didn't reply. He fingered the satin on my arms, then touched the thin strap of the nightgown that had fallen into view at my neck.

I snorted. "It was in the closet. Don't get any ideas."

He backed me into the bedroom, where he gathered me into his arms and kissed me.

I was so tired of being without him. I wanted to let him lay me down and marry me right there, except it probably wouldn't count since we were in the mortal world and we didn't have the pendant.

Eros, too, seemed complacent about keeping the boundaries between us. His kiss was long and hungry and deep. Standing there, completely lost in him, I didn't hear Titus approach until he switched on the light.

"Isn't that a violation of the contract?" He leaned against the doorpost rubbing his eyes with the ball of his hand. If we had wakened him, he was one light sleeper.

I spun around. To a mortal, I would have appeared alone in the room, but Titus could see the veiled Eros with his arms around me. "Technically, no." I forced myself to look in his face. I was supposed to be the master here, not him. "I can't see Eros, and he never speaks."

"Then, how do you know it's him?"

"I know."

"What if I said it wasn't him?"

Eros ran his hand over my hair. He leaned closer and drew his face across my cheek. I smelled his skin and knew the contours of his arms.

"You'd be lying," I replied.

Titus looked past me. "If you need a bed, take mine, but you're not sharing hers. Let her sleep. Her days are only going to get harder."

The arms around me tightened.

"You, of all people, should want what's best for her. Let us finish this."

My invisible love sighed, and he let me go.

"NO!" I reached for him, but my fingers found nothing but air.

Titus was jarred by a passing body and accepted the blow without flinching.

"Don't go!" I tried to follow, but Titus caught my arm and held on until the door out of the suite opened and closed. I jerked myself free and pounded a fist into his chest. "Don't ever send him away from me! He is *all* I want!"

Titus shook my shoulders. "Then win your bargain." He pushed me away. "So you can have him for real, not just these games."

Suddenly calm and so angry it turned me cold, I stepped forward. My nose grazed his chin. Though I was no physical threat to him, I felt his body tightening as I overstepped the bounds of his personal space. "Get out," I said slowly. "I do not take orders from you."

Titus backed away, bowing slightly. "Yes, Lady." He returned to his room and closed the door.

When he was gone, I found the satellite phone. Eros was programmed into the contact list, so I punched out an angry text.

`I don't know why you sent him. I don't like him. I don't trust him. He's worse than having my dad around.`

I waited almost an hour, but he didn't reply. Finally I relented and went to bed. By morning my head was clear. Get the map, finish the task and live with Eros, or die trying. There was no other option.

In bags near our backpacks, I found clothes intended for me—tough cargo pants, long sleeved undershirts and pretty T-shirts to go over the top. They were nice clothes and I liked them, but I was irritated that they were women's and fit the contours of my body, especially since I was stuck lugging Titus around everywhere I went. I carefully packed Aphrodite's box and the rest of my clothes into the metal-framed backpack, so I could leave the duffle bag in the car when we reached the climbing area.

We ordered breakfast the night before, and it arrived outside the suite promptly at seven o'clock. I had already eaten and was studying the map to the next town when Titus stumbled out of his room. "You're late," I said.

"We aren't supposed to leave until nine."

"I'm leaving now." I gathered my things and phoned the front desk to have our car brought around. A few minutes later when the bell boys arrived to take our luggage, Titus was eating with one hand and pulling on his shoes with the other.

Before the elevator closed to take me down, Titus dashed out of the suite with his duffle bag slung over his shoulder. He caught the elevator door with his hand, and pushed his way inside. "You can't ditch me that easily."

"Oh, that I would be so lucky," I muttered.

When we reached the foyer, he stayed a step behind until we passed the doorman. Then Titus sped up and tried to steer me around to the passenger side.

Instead I went to the valet. "The keys, please?" I held out my hand.

The valet handed over the keys and wished me good day.

I climbed into the driver's seat and started the engine. Titus was gritting his teeth when he climbed in next to me. Ignoring him, I programmed the location of our next lodging into the GPS. There was no way I could navigate the streets of Kathmandu without it.

"Would you please let me drive?" Titus said as I ground the gears pulling out of the parking lot. Shifting left-handed was harder than I thought it would be.

"When I get tired, I'll let you drive." I put on the blinker and turned left as I was instructed by the navigation system. A car in another lane honked, but let me in. "Why don't you just crawl into the back seat and disappear?"

Titus let out an angry breath. "If I thought for one moment that the two of you wouldn't have completely violated the contract, I would have left you alone."

"We've been alone dozens of times, Titus, without you babysitting, so just step down from that high, self-righteous horse you're riding."

He turned his face toward the window. It was going to be a very long day stuck in the car together.

# CHAPTER 23

There was a single highway from Kathmandu to India, upon which nearly all goods travelled. The term "highway" was generous. It was a narrow, unmarked road that accommodated traffic in both directions without laws of right of way, passing zones or crosswalks. Traffic consisted of everything from busses to hand carts, yaks and burros.

It took over an hour just to get out of Kathmandu. Unconsciously, I had anticipated a grand exit from the city and the speedometer suddenly climbing the way it does when you pull onto the freeway back home. This did not happen. We were stuck behind one slow-moving truck after another, inching our way west. We might have been faster on foot. When we finally reached a more rural area, I learned that if I honked as I came up behind slower traffic, they would let me through.

I thought I was driving fast when the speedometer said I was going a hundred, but Titus informed me with a grin that it was only about sixty miles an hour. The road was full of potholes and the pavement was warped. My dad would have harassed me about beating the shocks to death if we had been in my car, but I didn't care if the old SUV was worse for wear after this trip.

Titus did finally climb into the back seat and prop his feet up on the window. He fell asleep using our bags as a pillow. Somewhere in his dreams he disappeared, but I could still hear him breathing.

The GPS signaled me to turn right, but when I arrived at the road, it was little more than a dirt trail. I hit the brakes and felt the unseen body slam into the back of my seat. Awake now, Titus reappeared. "What's the matter?"

"I think we're supposed to turn here, but it doesn't look like a road."

He looked at the navigation system, then pulled out the map. Roads were not clearly marked, and neither were towns for that matter. One looked very much like the next. "I would trust the satellite. It's only supposed to be thirty miles to the village where we're staying the night."

"You can drive," I answered. I wasn't tired; I was starving. After he took the wheel, I found a bag of food and put it in between us on the front seat. The SUV was stuffy. With the windows down we gathered a lot of dust. I pulled my hair back as tightly as possible, but strands still whipped at my face. After peeling an orange, I offered half to my bodyguard.

He accepted it tentatively. "Does this mean I'm forgiven?"

I shrugged. I wasn't good at holding grudges. There was no one else to talk to for the next five days, so it was hard to keep ignoring him. "I don't think we should stop at the next village."

The orange gone, he opened a granola bar with his teeth. "Why not?"

"This schedule says it's another hundred miles to the village where we're getting the yak. From there we're on foot." I squinted into the sun, which was still high overhead. "There's no sense wasting an afternoon. We should go as far as we can tonight. It gives us more time to climb."

"You're the boss. I can't guarantee suitable lodging if you skip the village. You may end up in a barn with livestock."

"We've got camping gear. If worse comes to worse, we just pitch our tents." I was more concerned about finding suitable food. Would the villagers feed a couple of strangers a hot meal? I doubted there was going to be a restaurant, and I was getting tired of fruit and packaged snacks.

The road worsened with every mile, until I was clutching the window frame to keep from having my brain jarred loose. Titus navigated the rocky terrain well, and since he had spent more time in Europe, he was better with the left-handed gear shift. In all honesty, we probably would have made better time if I'd let him drive the whole way, but I would not admit it to him.

We were way beyond the popular tourist areas, and we were climbing fast. Steep, jagged peaks rose all around us. The road meandered between them. Outside the temperature dropped rapidly. Whereas in the city and on the lower roads, it had been warm, now the air carried a chill. Soon we would be in the lands of eternal winter.

The village, where we were supposed to stay, was made up of nearly a hundred buildings, mostly built of stone and mortar. The road cut right through a valley, and the town rose up in terraced steps on either side. We stopped for gas, which I wasn't sure we'd find. However, the village needed supplies, and the delivery trucks needed gas, so we did manage to find a working fuel pump. While I paid for gas, I sent Titus for food. If we could at least find some fresh vegetables and meat, we could build a cooking fire at the next stop.

He returned looking triumphant. "Fresh meat from the butcher," he announced. "And vegetables from the market."

"What kind of meat?" I eyed the package suspiciously. It was wrapped in newspaper.

"I didn't ask. It's red, though, so I figured you'd like it." He eyed one of the taller buildings longingly. "Are you sure you don't want to stay?"

"It's only two o'clock in the afternoon. We should keep moving."

He packed the food with our other supplies then climbed into the driver's seat.

I was probably making a mistake. Eros's men scouted the area and decided we should stay here, but Eros would also break up the journey as much as possible. I wanted to make sure we had plenty of time once we reached the mountain.

The road narrowed terribly. In places I wasn't sure we could pass between the jagged mountain walls, but Titus kept going while I held my breath. Eventually we passed into a wider valley, where the shrubbery had lost its leaves, and the grass was spotted with snow. Trees became scarce.

"Can we get there before dark?" I asked.

"I'll do my best," Titus replied. The road was pocked and rough, but he kept us climbing. Fortunately, it had been awhile since the last snow, so the roadway was partially clear.

We rounded a sharp corner with the SUV hugging the mountain wall. On my side the rocks fell away into oblivion. I gasped without meaning to and buried my face in the seatback.

Titus threw me a momentary glance. "Are you...? You're afraid of heights?"

That one glance over the cliff made me nauseous. I turned my eyes toward him and the nice, solid mountain on his side. "Yeah."

"Great," he replied flatly.

"I can climb. I just can't look down."

The road bounced us a few inches closer to the cliff, and I grabbed Titus's arm. He told me to put my head down and close my eyes. "I'll tell you when we get there."

I did as I was told because I was too terrified to pretend I could sit there like a normal person. I climbed into the back seat, ducked below the windows and closed my eyes.

"Hey, Sleeping Beauty, you're going to miss the ball." Titus shook my shoulder.

I sat up. We were stopped. There were streaks of daylight in the distant sky, but mountains on all sides blocked the rays. "We made it?" Here, at least, it felt like December. Ice was caked into the hubs of the SUV, and my breath showed in white puffs as I climbed out of the SUV and pulled on my parka.

"Only one person in town speaks English. He told me there is a small inn at the edge of town. We're lucky. It has indoor plumbing."

"And the yaks?"

Titus chuckled. "They're everywhere." Opening the back, he offered me a backpack, which I pulled onto my shoulders. He shouldered the other one, and we each carried a bag of food. "Ah, there is one thing."

"What?"

"We have to share a room."

"They don't have two rooms?" I doubted the inn was hosting many guests this time of year.

"They have rooms, but only one comes with beds. It has two cots. There is a toilet and sink in a partitioned corner. It's primitive, but at least there is a fireplace and plenty of firewood."

"Fine." I threw him a glance. "If you behave. You are a man, after all."

At this he laughed. "I'm not the reason I made you lock the door." We reached the inn, and Titus opened the door to our room.

Primitive was putting it mildly. The room had stone walls and a dirt floor. The window had a single thin pane and would have drafted terribly if it hadn't been shuttered from the outside. One thing in the room made up for its other deficiencies. There was a black kettle on a swing arm over the fireplace. As soon as we had a fire blazing, we dumped our meat into the kettle and let it brown before adding vegetables and two bottles of water.

Titus dug through the rest of our supplies trying to see if there was something else to flavor our stew. He made a stack of plastic bags which held foil pouches.

"Hey," I said, recognizing the MRE packets we were carrying for our climb, "those packages should have salt and utensils. Each meal has one."

"You've eaten these before?"

"My dad used to take me camping." One night when a storm hit before we could get a solid fire going, we were stuck in the tent with no way to heat the packets. Dad told me to put it in my armpit. When I refused, he offered to put it in his. I couldn't help cracking a smile at the memory. Even at nine, I preferred a cold dinner to one that had been in an armpit. "You'll hate the spaghetti," I told Titus. "You'd better stick with the beef stroganoff or chicken and vegetables." I took one of the packages and opened the plastic wrapper. It contained a foil pouch, fork and salt packet. "They don't need salt. There's enough sodium in these things to give you high-blood pressure." I opened three more packages and poured the salt into our soup, then repacked the MREs into the backpack.

Titus looked at me curiously. "So, you're used to roughing it, but you're afraid of heights?" When I nodded, he chuckled and shook his head, "And I can climb just about anything..."

"...but you're used to a palace," I finished for him. "Well, if the cot gives you fleas, I'll take you to a vet."

Now there was serious alarm in his eyes. "Maybe the floor is better."

"Oh, I seriously doubt that. Who knows what crawls around here at night?"

He shivered visibly. "Fleas," he muttered to himself.

"Just put your sleeping bag down. You'll be fine."

We lit a kerosene lamp and spread our travel papers on a cot. The itinerary said we were supposed to set up a base camp in a valley at roughly 10,000 feet. It was our destination tomorrow. We could take the yak that far. A villager would walk with us to the location and bring the yak back down.

"It's not going to take us all day to set up camp. Why is that the only thing on the itinerary for tomorrow?"

"We have to acclimate," Titus replied. "The instructions are very specific on this point. We need to spend an entire day and night at the base camp before moving on."

I found a climbing pamphlet among the papers. It was government issued and in English. "It looks like we can still have a campfire at base camp if we haul in our own wood." That was good news. The best thing about camping was getting warm by the fire.

We were carrying three tents. The largest was for base camp. It was large enough to sleep six and had two zip-down partitions. That way Titus and I could share a single tent and have separate rooms. The two lighter tents were for higher elevations. They were small, but tough. If a storm hit while we were on the face of the mountain, winds could gust over seventy miles an hour, and the temperature could easily drop to thirty below zero. Up there we would not have a fire. There was no dry ground upon which to build one, and it was too dangerous to build a fire on a glacier. We might have carried a kerosene stove, but we were traveling light from the base camp up. We had a small, battery-operated pot to boil water. This we would use to heat our food. Above base camp was a leave no trace area. That meant that everything we carried in, we had to carry out.

We counted our food packets and rationed them out, so we knew we would have enough without digging into our packs later to check. Eros had equipped us well. Most of our meals had a full MRE entrée, side dish and dessert, each packaged separately. Titus and I decided to stash the side dishes and desserts into the outer pockets of the packs in case we wanted them for snacks or light meals during the day. We also had dried fruit, nuts, jerky, water bottles and lots of energy drink powder.

By the time we packed it all away, even Titus was satisfied that we both had the maps memorized. Our GPS system would help us to stay on the trail, but if it failed, we knew the way.

The last item I repacked was the wooden box. Titus noticed it, and ran his finger over the carved rose. "This is what you're taking to the messenger?"

"Yes. At the final destination, a woman will have the key." I turned the box around so he could see the gold lock.

Titus lifted it with his finger, and his eyes turned worried. I wondered if he knew something about the lock that he wasn't telling me. The look lasted only a moment. "We'll make sure it's well cushioned on the climb, so it won't get broken if we take a spill." Reluctantly, he rolled his sleeping bag onto the filthy cot. "I sent a text to Eros this afternoon."

"To tell him I didn't stay where I was supposed to?"

"And that you tried to ditch me at the hotel." He offered his satellite phone to me. "I thought you might want to see the reply."

**She infiltrated the Fortress, faced Theron, was beaten nearly to death and still completed two tasks. Did you think for one moment a woman like that would take orders from you? Remember your place, Titus. And give her my love.**

I tossed the phone back to him. "So, he knows we're here."

"He always knows where you are."

"How?"

Titus tapped his watch. I looked at the matching one on my wrist. It must contain a GPS beacon. In other circumstances I might have been irritated, but on this journey it was comforting to know that no matter where I wandered, Eros could find me.

After climbing into his sleeping bag, Titus pulled off his sweatshirt and T-shirt.

"Titus!" It was bad enough we had to share a room. "Do you think you can keep your clothes on?"

He grumbled, "We never wear shirts in our world. I can't sleep with it on."

"It's going to get cold," I warned. Unless one of us woke in the night to add wood to the fire, it would burn out, and the room would be freezing by morning.

"But, I'm not cold now," he complained.

I slid into my sleeping bag across the room. "Fine, if you answer one question." When he nodded, I asked, "Why don't you have hair in your armpits?"

His brow furrowed. "We don't have body hair."

"None of you?"

"We don't grow beards either. Not until we're old men."

I laid back and stared at the ceiling. "That would explain why Aeas didn't pack me a razor."

I heard Titus chuckle. "I'll put it on the list of things we need for the way home."

Our local guide was waiting for us at dawn. We loaded his poor yak with everything except our backpacks and water bottles, but the beast didn't seem to mind. Our guide did not speak a word of English, Italian, French, Spanish, Latin, Greek, or any other language that Titus knew. Titus finally stopped bugging the poor man and let him walk in peace.

The trail was wide enough that Titus and I could hike side by side. We talked about Italy and warmer weather. Titus was not a fan of winter, but he seemed to be reveling in this adventure. He was surprisingly open, even when I pried into his personal life. He had never bestowed his pendant on any woman, but had some romantic experience with mortals. "Aphrodite encouraged that," he explained. "She'd rather her servants were unmarried, and she expects them to mingle with mortals. She views mortals as toys, so you can imagine her complete outrage when her only son decided to marry one."

"You're terrible," I told him, "going around seducing mortals and then disappearing."

He stopped me. "I'm not what you assume I am. I didn't leave little Titus's all over Italy. I just enjoyed the company of mortal women. I dated and tried very hard not to inflict heartache on any of them."

"Yeah, sure." I kept walking.

For some reason, the yak took a liking to me. Whenever I got slow on the trail, the beast would speed up and rub his head on me. If he were an ordinary steer, I probably wouldn't have minded, but the yak stank, so I tried to keep my distance.

The road was steep, but before long we reached an open plateau between four peaks. The guide shouted at us. When we turned around, we found him stopped and waving his arms.

Titus pulled the GPS device from his pocket and checked our location. "Oh," he said, "we're here."

The area designated for our camp was flat, hard ground. Titus looked around disappointed. "It isn't much, is it?"

"It's flat, and it's dirt." The snow had melted off and the dirt was dry, so we didn't have to pitch our tent in mud. There was circle of ashes and rocks that had been scattered. We were above the tree line, but to the north was a small cliff, which partially sheltered us from the wind.

After unloading the yak, our guide made a gesture of good-bye and started his descent, probably hoping to get home in time for a hot lunch. Titus turned to me visibly bewildered, so I had him circle the stones of the fire pit and build a fire.

While he stacked the wood and broke smaller pieces into kindling, I unloaded the large tent from his pack, rolled it out on the ground and unfolded until it made a rectangle seven feet wide by twelve feet long. I began pounding the stakes into the frozen ground with a mallet. The fire now burning, Titus stood over me and watched.

"I feel worthless," he confessed.

I stomped on a stubborn stake with my foot until it finally dug into the earth. "I can pitch the tent alone." With a grin I added, "I'll just make you give me a foot massage later."

Titus nodded unconsciously the way Aeas did. "Is there anything I can do?"

I showed him how to put the supports together and thread them through the tent's body. When it was standing securely, I laid down basic tent rules. "No boots in the tent. Sit down at the door and take them off, so we don't have mud and snow everywhere." I hauled both our packs into the center room of the tent and designated a bedroom for each of us. After unrolling our sleeping bags, we boiled water on the fire and heated our lunch packets. The sun was shining and there was no wind. Even though the temperature was near freezing, it felt warm.

"It's a long way from a five-star restaurant." I used a pair of pliers to pull a foil packet out of the boiling water and onto Titus's plate. We were having mashed potatoes with bacon bits for lunch and fruit cobbler for dessert. After removing the packets, I put apple cider powder into the water and split it between our tin cups.

He waited for me before he ate. It took me three meals to realize that he did this, but I came to understand it was the nature of our relationship. "It's definitely not as good as the food we had at the hotel," he confessed, "but it's not as bad as I thought it would be."

"The dehydrated ones my dad used to buy were worse. They never absorbed water like they were supposed to, and there were always crunchy spots. This is much better."

While he ate, Titus started to blink more often than usual. He seemed to be panting, too.

"Headache?"

"Yes."

"It's the altitude. Take a deep breath and hold it. Your body needs to absorb more oxygen from the air."

After a few long breaths, he turned to me. "Why aren't you sick?"

"You live at sea level. I live in the mountains. I'm only five thousand feet above what I'm used to. It's double that for you." I took his plate and trash. "You should rest. Use as little energy as possible until you adjust."

"That's good advice for both of us." He unzipped the tent door and motioned me inside. There was nothing else to do besides sit in the tent and talk. I had the feeling I was going to know Titus very well before this was all over. We left the tent door unzipped. There was only one advantage to winter camping—no bugs.

Titus reached out and took hold of my ankle.

Startled, I tried to pull away. "What do you think you're doing?"

"I owe you." He pulled off my sock.

"I was joking."

Titus paused, his head cocked to the side and his expression unmoved. "I'm a servant. This is what I do."

"I don't like to be touched," I persisted.

With his thumb, he began massaging the ball of my foot. "I've been advised of that."

"And, I'm ticklish. I might kick you," I warned.

He continued undaunted. "No, you won't. There's a pressure point here on your foot. If I keep my thumb on it, it disables that reflex."

This was a fight I was not going to win. Relenting, I lay back against the pack. "You did this for Aphrodite?"

"On occasion, but she's *very* particular. Anyone who touches her has to do it perfectly, so I've spent a great deal of time practicing on her maid Fauna."

"Interesting. Who usually gives her massages?"

"Theron, of course."

"*Him?* You've got to be joking."

"You've only seen the violent side of Theron. When he wants to be, he is as gentle as a summer breeze. She wouldn't have kept him all these ages if it weren't so." He rubbed my toes, which tickled. "He could probably seduce you given the chance."

I let out a growl. "Not as long as there was breath in me to refuse."

Titus set my foot into his lap and moved onto the next. Minutes passed in silence. It felt awkward. Titus looked up only once when a breeze tossed the tent door, then he went back to rubbing my feet as if he enjoyed it.

"Do you think Eros will find me again before we start climbing?" I asked him.

With a wicked grin, Titus asked, "Would you rather he stayed away?"

I considered kicking him in the chest, but I didn't. "If I never see him again, I want him to know I don't have any regrets."

Titus's eyebrows arched as he looked down at my foot. "None?"

"I could have done without spilling the dust and having him throw me off a balcony, but other than that..." I shrugged.

Shaking out my socks and slipping them back over my feet, Titus finally looked up. "I think I'm going to lie down like you suggested. You should do the same." He didn't move until I got up and went through the partition to my sleeping area. Then he went into his side and zipped it closed.

The zipper on my sleeping bag was down, and it lay open, which was not how I left it. I pulled off my sweatshirt and dropped it at the head of the sleeping bag to use as a pillow. The sweatshirt didn't fall to the ground. It stopped, draped over an unseen object. How long had Eros been here listening? Titus had seen him, that much I knew.

I stretched out on the sleeping bag as Eros's arm drew me into the hollow of his shoulder. "I'm glad you didn't let him keep you away," I murmured.

He kissed my temple. For awhile, we just lay there in the silent tent. Eventually Eros stirred. When he returned he had my sketchbook and a pencil. I could see them, so he must have had them unveiled inside a veiled bag. The pencil seemed to stand up on its own as he wrote on the blank page.

*In case you have time for therapy.*

"Unfortunately, I can't see my favorite subject." I thumbed through the pages, and stopped on a clean white page. "Come with me." At the tent door I pulled on my boots and went outside. I turned a circle before I found the landscape I wanted to draw. The afternoon sun began to fall, beautifully illuminating the peaks to the east. I sat in the dirt and felt Eros settle next to me. While I sketched, he toyed with my hair, then made a pile of stones and scattered them. When the sketch was finished, I turned the page toward him. "What do you think?"

He took the pencil and sketchbook from my hands. I thought he was writing a note, but when he turned the page around, it was a sketch of me—a very good one.

"That's amazing. You did that in less than a minute."

The book still facing me, the pages fanned to the back. Eros started about ten pages from the end and showed me the sketches there. In the first sketch I lay asleep in my own bed. In the second I was sitting on the bed with books spread around me. They looked like black and white snapshots, detailed down to the pattern on the comforter. He continued through them showing me each one, then stopped a page before the end and closed the book.

"You missed one," I said.

Eros set the book in my lap and laid his head on it.

"I want to see the last drawing."

He put my hand on his forehead and shook his head.

With a gulp, I asked, "Have you been watching me shower?"

He chuckled and didn't try to stifle it. The sound sent my spirit soaring. To my relief, he shook his head again.

"Okay," I relented. "Don't show me the last drawing. I'll look at it when you're not around. Instead, show me what happened to Theron after he beat me."

Eros laughed again and got up. He moved so that he was behind me with his legs on either side of mine. Resting his chin on my shoulder, he opened the book as it lay in my lap and started to draw with his left hand. These were different from his previous drawings. They were caricatures with the people represented in scarce detail, but recognizable from their features. On the first clean page he drew a bed and a body lying in it.

"That's me."

He drew a second person nearby, and I recognized him by the way he drew his hair. With a sigh, he drew teardrops on the face.

"That's you crying over me."

He kissed my cheek and turned the page. The next scene took me a while to recognize. It was a square room full of boxes and tools. In the corner he drew a bow hanging on the wall.

"It's a garage. My dad's hunting bow?"

Eros nodded. At the bottom of the page, he drew a close-up of an arrow. It wasn't the kind of arrow he had in his quill at the palace. It was the kind my dad used to hunt elk—aluminum shafted and razor tipped. He turned the page and quickly sketched an island with steep cliffs above the water—the Fortress.

The next scene was of a man and a woman together on a balcony. The curvy caricature Eros drew of his mother was hilarious. He over emphasized her mouth, so that she was pouting.

The next scene was of Theron on the beach with four arrows in his body. There was one in each shoulder and one in each leg.

"Ouch!" I slit my finger on an arrow once. It took five stitches to close the cut.

On the final drawing, Eros took his time. It unfolded like a Sunday morning comic. He drew a bathtub and Theron wailing, his arms and legs hanging over the sides, while a servant dumped a barrel marked "Ambrosia" into the tub. Aphrodite stood nearby pulling her hair and stomping her feet. In a text balloon over her head she screamed, *EROOOOOS!!!*

I fell back against him laughing.

He closed the sketchbook and wrapped his arms around me.

"Thank you," I whispered.

"Are you two going to sit out there all night?" Titus stood just outside the tent door, his coat unzipped and no boots on. He opened his arms to the west. The sun was down and the light waned.

I stood, clutching the sketchbook to my chest and took Eros by the hand. "Are you going to stay with me tonight?"

He squeezed my hand.

"We'll behave," I said to Titus.

"Not my business," Titus replied.

"Correct." I tugged on Eros's hand. "I might end up liking Titus after all."

I woke to a rock falling on my chest. At least I thought it was a rock until my hand found it and realized it had square edges and was wrapped in paper. The body that kept me warm all night was no longer beside me.

Without opening my eyes, I muttered, "You're up already, and you didn't make me breakfast?" I loved teasing him when he couldn't say a word. "You probably can't even fry eggs. Spoiled little prince." I sat up just as a granola bar whizzed across the tent and smacked me in the forehead. It landed in my lap with the box.

Inside the small, heavy package was an iPod loaded with music. After I'd opened it, Eros tossed a second package into my lap. It was identical, but had a small card on top. Written in Eros's script were the words: *for Titus.*

The little curtain to my sleeping area parted.

"Hey, wait! Are you leaving?" I jumped to my feet and followed him. I realized it was fully light, and yes, it was time for Titus and me to start climbing, but I didn't want Eros to go.

I stood there trying to find the right words to say to him. He had shown me the kind of pure adoration I never expected to feel, and there weren't words to express my gratitude. If I failed to get up the mountain on time, or if I didn't make it down alive, I wanted him to know it was worth it. I stumbled over my thoughts, and all that I managed to express was my doubt. "What if I can't make it?" I whispered.

He wrapped his arms around me and pulled me to his chest. He ran his fingers through my hair, kissed my forehead, then held me close. I rested my nose on his warm neck, inhaled his skin and let the memories of our stolen time together swim into my mind. I wished I could stay in his arms and forget about Aphrodite's contract. Sensing my weakness, Eros stepped back from me, lightly kissed my lips and unzipped the tent door.

"I'll meet you here in a few days with Aphrodite's reward." I forced determination into my voice.

He opened my hand and placed an invisible object into it. Its shape was familiar. Even without seeing it I knew it was the ring from his first finger. I tried it on my thumb and my first finger, but each of my fingers was too narrow. It slipped right off. I needed a chain. Titus wore a chain around his neck.

Unzipping his side of the tent, I found that his sleeping bag had disappeared with him. "Hey, Titus. Wake up, so I can see you."

"Huh?" He still didn't appear.

"You veil when you sleep. Did you know that?"

Now he appeared, shirtless with the sleeping bag knotted around him. "No, I didn't know that."

I lifted the chain that lay against his neck. "Does this necklace have deep personal meaning?"

"It's just a chain."

"Can I borrow it?"

"Sure, why?" He rolled his shoulders grumbling, "I hate sleeping on the ground."

I opened my hand and showed him the ring. "I can't see it now, but when he gets far enough away, and unveils himself, it should appear, right?"

Titus nodded and took the ring from my palm. "It's inscribed."

"Some sort of hieroglyphics. I don't know what it says."

As Titus slipped the ring onto his chain and began to fasten it around my neck, it became visible to my sight. A moment later my satellite phone beeped the reception of a text message.

**The ring was given to me by a man the Mayans esteemed as a prophet. The inscription says, "May wisdom and safety be your companions."**

I sent a thank you reply, then clapped Titus on the back. "Pack up. We've got climbing to do."

Before leaving camp, I showed Titus how to use his iPod. I strapped it around his bicep and threaded the earphone cord through his shirt so it wouldn't interfere with his movement. He nearly shouted for joy when the music began to play.

"What's on there?" I stole one of his earphones to listen. It was an opera in Italian.

"What's on yours?" He tugged on my earphone and brought it to his ear, only to wince when I turned on the sound. The first song that played was the one I had been caught dancing to at the palace—Eros's own little joke.

After checking one last time to make sure I had the wooden box, we hefted our packs and bid good-bye to base camp.

# CHAPTER 24

Mountain climbing was a test of will more than anything else. As the air grew thinner and glaciers rose unending before us, the most difficult obstacle was simply putting one foot in front of the other on the faith that eventually we would reach a destination. We believed we could see the meeting point above us where two cliffs rose together creating a triangular cave opening. However, we could not take a direct path to it. Between us and the cliffs was a wide crevasse in the glacier hundreds of feet deep. We were forced to go far beyond the location to the end of the glacier, cross over, and back track on the other side. Getting to the other side of the glacier was the first day's journey. Once there, we would leave the protective shield of the cliffs and climb the spine of the mountain to the meeting point. When we passed out of the cliffs' protection, there was only one area where we could camp, and it was just below the meeting point. We had to time our climb carefully so that we could reach it in daylight and with good weather. If we couldn't, we would have to climb back down to the shelter of the cliffs and start again the next day.

Titus and I were tied together for safety, but I had to wonder about it. If I fell, I would probably take him down with me; and if he fell, I didn't have a chance of staying on my feet. He outweighed me by about sixty pounds. Still, he insisted. Both of us wore ropes tied around our waists, and they were clipped to another, longer one, which tethered us together. About an hour into our climb, I realized this tether served a second purpose. When I got sluggish, Titus pulled me. He struggled with the altitude, but he was strong. If he just kept walking, I had no choice but to follow.

Monotony arrived as enemy number one. Exhaustion pulled in second. And third. Running a tight race for fourth were cold and numb.

We climbed for two hours on a relatively easy grade before the terrain shifted and we faced steep hills. At the base of the first really challenging climb, Titus stopped. "Sit," he said. "It's icy, and we need the spikes." He meant the crampons we had dangling from our packs.

I was grateful for the chance to rest, unload the pack from my aching shoulders and down as much food as possible. We had gained distance, but not much altitude. This afternoon we would travel about a mile, but we would gain over three thousand feet in altitude. I was admittedly nervous about this. I could handle the long climbs, the boredom and the cold. A face of sheer ice was a different story. Now there would be cliffs and the possibility of falling.

On the other hand, Titus was thrilled. "Now, we can have some real fun," he said as he eyed the way before us.

With the crampons securely on our boots and ice axes in each of our gloved hands, we started again. I watched Titus and tried to mimic his skill. He had not done a lot of high climbing, but he was naturally athletic, and he enjoyed climbing the cliffs around the Fortress. "Of course," he added, "when you fall there, you just make a big splash." We didn't have that luxury here.

By kicking hard and digging in the toes of my boots, I could make footholds in the ice. The axes I used for balance on the milder grades and for hand hold as it got steeper. We were moving slower now, and the rhythm of the music in my ears began to irritate me. I switched it off and pulled the ear buds out so they dangled from the collar of my coat.

Ahead of me, Titus was slashing through the snow and humming a melody. I moved faster so I could hear him. At the song change, he began to sing quietly. His voice was a smooth tenor that moved through the notes with ease. I had to wonder if he didn't sound better than the voice in his ears. That was the thing about these immortals. They were all so multifaceted. Though they varied from one another greatly, each seemed to have extraordinary talents. Aeas could do almost any mathematical calculation in his head. After attending my school for a single day, he could name every student who spoke up during class. Not all immortals received the same education. Their knowledge varied by class and necessity, but they all seemed to know more than me. A girl had to wonder why one of them would want to be with the likes of her.

We crested a steep climb and met some flat ground. Ahead of me, Titus seemed to be pulling harder. I looked up and saw an ice face directly ahead. As we drew near, it seemed to grow before my eyes. It was double my height—at least twelve feet—all compacted snow and ice with nothing to offer handholds.

"How are we going to climb that?"

Titus pulled more rope from his belt and lengthened the tether between us. "I'm going to climb it, and then you will. Watch carefully."

He reached high overhead and dug an ax in hard. Then he stepped up with the toe of his boot, digging in with the spike and pulling himself up. With the other hand he made a second, higher stab with the ax. "Hand, foot, hand, foot," he said. "Just like crawling."

"Crawling," I muttered. "Straight up."

It took him all of a minute to reach the top and pull himself over the ledge. Then he stood, adjusting the ropes. "Come on, *Bellezza*. Up."

While I climbed, he sang, and when I slipped, he pulled hard on the rope, so I didn't lose any ground. I couldn't get my toes to dig in far enough to offer a strong foothold, so I ended up doing most of the work with my arms. I pulled myself up by the axes and used my toes to keep me from sliding. Once I got my arms over the top of the face, Titus grabbed the back of my coat and pulled me the rest of the way up. I collapsed in the snow panting, while his song reached the crescendo. He stood, his arms out to the side, holding the last note. Then he pulled the earphones from his ears with a playful grin. "That's good stuff."

"You're going to cause an avalanche," I replied. "But, yes, you sing very well."

He offered me his hand. "A compliment. I'm touched." He pulled me to my feet. "Enjoy the view for a moment."

I turned and looked. Below us were the face we had just climbed and our footprints in the snow. Beyond that everything fell away. Far below was the village where we spent the night and the peaks that sheltered it. Farther out I could see a fine line that was the paved highway running east to west. My stomach did a somersault, and I used Titus's shoulder to steady me. "It's beautiful." I turned away. "But it makes me sick."

We were less than halfway to our designated camp for the night, so I started walking.

"Sometimes I don't understand you," Titus said catching up with me.

"I talk like a hick?"

He hung his axes on his arm and pulled off one glove. With the bare hand, he unzipped an exterior pocket on my pack and found a package of dried fruit and nuts. In the short distance before the next big climb, we shared the snack. "I understand your words perfectly. I don't always understand what's behind them."

"I'm fairly honest," I countered.

"Yes, that much I know. Why aren't you mad at him?"

"Eros? Why would I be? It's my fault we're in this mess. I betrayed him."

Titus shook his head. "He hid from you, and he threw you off a balcony. You're afraid of *heights*."

Admittedly, it was a terrible moment—that fall—but I had never been mad because I was too devastated that he threw me out. "Pixis caught me. And it was dark, so I couldn't see anything below."

"That makes it all right?"

"Neither of us was right that night, Titus. It doesn't matter anymore."

He stepped in front of me and stopped. "It does matter."

I didn't have to explain myself to Titus, but a confession had been a long time in coming, so it was a relief to get it off my chest. "I was the coward that night, Titus. I could have demanded to see him. I could have told him I would leave and never come back if he didn't show me his face, but I didn't. I betrayed him because *I* was afraid—afraid that he was a monster, but more afraid that if he showed himself to me and he was hideous, that I wouldn't love him anymore." I pushed past him again and climbed harder than before.

It may have been cowardice that drove me to betray Eros, but it wouldn't keep me from seeing him again. Whatever waited for me in the cave, I was going to face it and finish the task.

While the sun shined, it was cold. When it turned overcast, it got much colder. Bitter wind threw shards of snow and ice into our faces. Dark clouds hung on the peaks to the north.

"We have to move faster if we're going to make it before that storm hits," Titus told me, but I was moving as fast as I could with the wind beating me back at every step.

I cursed the mountain, Aphrodite and her contract a thousand times over. We reached another ice face, double the size of the last. Exhausted, I couldn't help crumpling to the ground.

"Don't give up. We only have to get over this face and around the break in the crevasse, then we can camp anywhere along the other side." He forced a smile. "Think of warm food and a sleeping bag." Titus was playing tough, but he was cold, too. He had trouble fastening his harness, and he beat his gloved hand against his leg before trying to sink the first screw into the face.

I shook my head to flick ice off my face. "The MREs are probably frozen." I was harnessed, too; and as he clipped off to the first screw, I became his safety net, my weight and strength the only things able to catch him if he slipped. He had tied a loop in the end of the rope, and I wrapped it around my bum, which I figured was the heaviest part of me.

Three-fourths of the way up the face, Titus did slip and slid three feet before the rope tightened and nearly jerked me off my feet. I sat against it and resisted as best I could. He gathered his balance again and kept climbing with the wind beating at his back. I adjusted the rope to keep it taut, then ducked my head against the coming storm.

"Your turn," he shouted down at me.

I raised my head to see him kneeling at the edge above.

"I've got you clipped off up here, and I'm tied to you, so you won't fall." He instructed me on how to clip off to the bolts as I climbed and then unclip from the lower one. Aside from that, I had to climb it the same way we climbed the last face—with axes for handholds and toes for footholds.

Any experienced climber would have rebuked us. We didn't really know what we were doing, and we were on a dangerous mountain. We had all the right equipment, but we were learning as we went.

The footholds still gave me trouble, but I worked hard to get a solid dig into the ice before pulling up on the ax with my arms. Still, it took me three times as long to climb the face as it took Titus. With two feet left, my arms felt so weak, I was afraid they would give out and drop me. I dug my right foot hard into the ice and managed to get my arms and shoulders over the ledge. "Help me," I moaned.

Titus grabbed my arm, dug his crampons into the ice and pushed back with his legs. He pulled me over the ledge right into his lap. Instead of scrambling up quickly, like I thought he would, he lay there gasping for breath. "I'm beat," he confessed as the wind blew over our nearly frozen bodies.

It was just a short hike to the crossing. We could see the chasm growing narrower to our right. "Race you to the other side." I said.

"You'll lose," he wheezed.

I rolled to my feet and started to push into the wind, but I was stopped by the harness. Titus was still on the ground chuckling. The rope that tethered us together was bolted into the ice so we created a pulley. He pulled the bolt out and unclipped it, but kept hold of the rope, so I couldn't take off without him. Finally, he rolled to his feet and said, "Go!"

We were too exhausted to run hard. All I could manage was a weak jog, and with a few long strides, Titus passed me and headed toward the crevasse. He stumbled along the edge for five or six steps, then leaped across. "Titus!" I screamed.

Safely on the other side, he grinned. "It's narrow enough here. Jump it." He tugged on the rope attached to my waist. "I've got you."

On an ordinary day jumping the gap in the ice might not have seemed like a monumental task, but my head was thick from lack of oxygen, my body completely tapped out, and I was carrying a thirty-pound pack. I wanted rest more than anything else, and it lay on the other side of the glacier. With a quick inspection of the distance, I drew back, took a running start and leaped across. As soon as I landed, I doubled over panting. "No problem," I wheezed. "Let's find a place to camp."

We ended up hiking another half hour before finding a place sheltered enough from the coming storm. By the time we shrugged off our packs and dug out the tents, the wind was whipping relentlessly. Titus used the ax to drive the stakes of the first tent while I put together the cross supports, which threatened to blow away before I could get them secured. Snow and hail pounded down on us. With another ax, I secured the tie-downs, barely able to see the stakes as I struck them. Titus was about to unpack the second tent, but I stopped him. "Just get inside before we both freeze."

We kicked off as much snow as we could, then ducked inside boots and all. It was a tight squeeze, the two of us and all our gear inside the tiny tent, but I didn't care. Neither of us moved to unpack our sleeping bags or food.

"When I can feel my fingers again, I'll find some hand warmers," Titus said. His teeth chattered, and his lips were a shade of purple.

I braved the cold for moment to pull off one glove, check my watch, and stick my hand inside my coat. "The watch says it's two degrees."

"Without the wind chill," he added. The hair hanging out of his cap was cluttered with ice. We had only an hour of daylight left, then it would get even colder.

"Okay," I said finally. "Haul your pack over here. I think I can unzip it now and find what we need." First I found a hand warmer and broke it against my leg before dropping it between Titus's shaking hands. Then I dug out our battery-operated cooking pot and a non-flammable heat cell. We discovered that all our water bottles were frozen. "What we need is a nice chunk of ice," I said regretfully.

"I'll get it," Titus replied. He pulled his gloves back on and braved the storm again. While he was gone, I found the sleeping bags, some MRE packets and hot chocolate powder.

Titus unzipped the tent door and handed in a chunk of ice just large enough to fill our pot, then shook himself off as he came inside. "I put two more outside the door." He zipped the tent closed with a shiver. "It does feel a little warmer in here."

The heat cell would only last a few hours. After that, we had our sleeping bags to keep us warm and another cell to help us thaw in the morning. With some warm food and hot chocolate in us we were finally able to slip off our boots, coats and snow pants and climb into the sleeping bags.

The sleeping bags were rated to fifty degrees below zero, but I still felt cold. There was no way I was parting with my jeans or sweatshirt, despite the fact that I had long underwear underneath. I pulled the top of the sleeping bag over my head and sat up, like a caterpillar in a giant cocoon.

Titus stacked our packs atop one another and rested against them with his legs in his sleeping bag and his hands wrapped around a cup of rapidly cooling hot chocolate.

"Can I sketch you?" I asked.

"You draw?"

"Not very well, but I enjoy it. I have to warn you, though. Portraits aren't my strong suit."

"Go ahead," he answered. "It's not like I want to move anytime soon."

I opened my sketchbook to a clean page. My fingers were half-frozen, and holding the pencil was difficult, but sketching helped take my mind off our suffering. When the light faded, we put a lamp between us, and I packed the pencil away. The shading would have to wait.

"So, you sketch often?" Titus asked.

"It's a school assignment. My art teacher said I would never master still lives and perspectives until I learned to harness the chaos in my head. He assigned me to fill a sketchbook with my own personal therapy, and he would give me a good grade."

This piqued his curiosity. "And that book is full of the things in your head?"

"Sort of. The process of drawing relaxes me."

"Will you show me your drawings?"

I shrugged. "They aren't anything great." I moved beside him and looked at each page as he went through them.

Titus spent a great deal of time on the first few sketches—my many starts and stops trying to draw Eros and a few random scenes from the palace. Then he came to Eros's self-portrait. "Wow. That looks just like him. You drew this?"

"No, he saw me struggling with the others, and he finally gave me what I was looking for. I colored it, because it wasn't right without the violet eyes."

Titus went through the rest of my sketches until he found the caricatures Eros drew for me the night before. When I explained what they were, Titus threw his head back and laughed. "Oh, I wish I could have seen it. I can imagine this scene perfectly." He turned to me with a smile. "Your drawings are good, even the one of me," he said.

"Not as good as these." I turned to the back of the book and showed him the sketches Eros had done.

"He's very well trained." A smile tugged at his lips as I turned each page. "They're all of you."

"They're all of me when I didn't know he was watching." I stopped when I reached the final sketch Eros showed me the night before. "So, there's one more that he wouldn't let me see last night."

"Turn the page. Let's look," he prompted.

I wondered if it was a mistake to look at all, much less let Titus see it, but I turned the page. The drawing there was a close up of Eros and me. My head was tilted back and my eyes closed. His face was tilted down, his nose against my jaw and his open mouth kissing my neck. Our bare shoulders touched. "Oh...I... uh... didn't pose for this."

Titus threw me a glance, then studied the sketch. "It's..." He searched for the right word and finally said, "hot."

"Yeah."

"And, look." Titus turned the page and showed me ragged edges behind it. "I bet they got hotter. That's why he took them out."

"You could send him a text and ask him?"

"No, *you* should send him a text and ask him." Titus set his empty cup aside and slid farther into his sleeping bag. "Tell him we're camped for the night." He closed his eyes.

I dug out the phone and composed a text: **There seem to be sketches missing from my book. Were they more revealing than the last?**

The reply I received was a colon and parentheses smiley face. I expected as much, so I gave him our report.

**We're camped for the night. It's stormy. It will probably be twenty below later.**

After dimming the light, I lay back and closed my eyes. If I were warm I would have fallen asleep immediately, but my whole body was cold. A moment later the phone beeped the receipt of a message. I opened Eros's reply.

**I believe Titus to be an honorable and trustworthy man. Use him if you must.**

"What did he say?" Titus murmured.

"Nothing," I replied. "He's good at being evasive."

I had lain perfectly still for hours, my body too tired to move and too cold to let me sleep. Titus hadn't stirred either, but he was still visible, so I wondered if he was awake. The storm howled around us. It rocked the tent relentlessly. Our heat cell went out, and it was much colder. When I raised my face above the sleeping bag, the moisture inside my nose began to freeze after a single breath. I could never remember a time when I had been this cold, not even when Dad's truck broke down in the mountains while we were hunting and we had to walk all the way back to the main road. It had been close to zero degrees that day, and I complained the whole way, but that cold was nothing compared to this. I understood the nature of winter well enough to know that when I stopped feeling cold tonight, it would probably mean I was dying.

"Titus," I whispered. "Are you awake?"

He raised his head from under the sleeping bag. "Yes."

"I'm still cold, even in my sleeping bag. How about you?"

"Freezing," he replied.

Where was Eros when I needed him? Probably in Kathmandu in a luxury suite or at Apollo's palace in Olympus with a roaring fire to keep him warm. I really did not want to blur the lines of my relationship with Titus, but what difference would it make if we were both frozen in the morning? "Do you want to share?" I said finally.

"Yes," he answered, his voice a little shaken. "Please." He unzipped his sleeping bag and ushered me inside. He was shivering, and his hands were icy. We each struggled out of our sweatshirts, unwilling to take off much, but knowing that the fewer layers between us, the better. When I snuggled in beside him, he wrapped his arms around me with a sigh. "Warmth. Finally."

We pulled the other sleeping bag over the top of us and hoped that the double layer plus our body heat would be enough to keep us from freezing to death in the night.

Though it was awkward, I was grateful to be warm. "You know how you said you didn't understand me?"

"Uh huh." He was still shaking.

"I don't understand you either."

"I explained why I took an oath to serve you." He forced a lightness into his voice. "But now wouldn't be a good time to ask me if I regret it."

"You said I was beautiful."

"Aren't you?"

"But, you're not attracted to me." If he was, I still couldn't see it. We had been together two days, and the only time I saw a hungry glimmer in Titus's eyes was when the waiter at the hotel laid a plate of spaghetti in front of him.

He raised his head and scowled at me. "That bothers you?"

"No, it's just unusual."

Titus let his head fall back and stared at the billowing tent ceiling. "You've never met a man who wasn't attracted to you?"

"Not really."

Now he seemed genuinely confused. "Even Aeas?"

I let out a snort. "Aeas is a Stoic. I can't get him to smile half the time. He doesn't count."

"He does count, as much as me at least. I'm used to being around beautiful women who don't belong to me. I can appreciate that you're beautiful without wanting you for myself." Titus shivered again, and shook me in the process. "And anyway, you're not really my type."

Curious, I asked, "And your type is...?"

"Dark hair, olive skin, generous curves."

I laughed. "I'm *really* not your type." But in all seriousness, I needed to know for sure. I propped myself up so I could see his face. "So, I'm safe with you?"

Titus looked directly into my eyes and answered, "Completely."

Satisfied, I lay my head on his chest. "Thank you."

He rubbed his hands on my back, still trying to warm them. "No, thank *you* for keeping me from freezing to death."

The storm was still beating the tent when Titus startled himself awake. "This isn't what it looks like," he murmured.

I had been sound asleep and felt him jump. He started to push me away, but must have awakened, because I heard him sigh and felt his body relax. "I'm giving you nightmares," I mumbled.

He pulled the sleeping bag tighter around us. "You're fine," he replied. "I'm sorry."

"It's morning?"

"It doesn't matter," he said. "We're still pinned down by the storm. Sleep as long as you like."

I planned to open my eyes, but I couldn't because I was warm and still too tired to move. Without realizing it, I slipped back to sleep and resurfaced later to hear Titus talking softly.

"The wind has stopped, but it's still snowing. If the trail is as treacherous as it says on the instructions, there's no way we can attempt it in this weather. She's going to have a hard enough time when it's clear." He waited for the reply before speaking again. "We have another day. You planned for bad weather. It should be fine."

He was talking to Eros on the satellite phone. I pretended to sleep, so they wouldn't hang up.

"She's tougher than I thought she was," Titus said. "I honestly didn't think we would make it up here yesterday, but she wouldn't quit." He touched my hair softly. "Uh..." He stammered like he didn't want to answer. "Yeah, she's fine." I felt him wince and wondered if Eros was digging for information that Titus didn't want to give. "And if that were the case?"

He stopped breathing for a moment. "Of course." There was a defensive note in his voice. "I'll let you know when we're moving again." He disconnected the call and let out a slow breath.

"Did you tell him I gave you nightmares?"

"No, I left that part out." He raised up on his elbows. "I'm glad you're awake. I need to take a walk, and I didn't want to wake you."

I sat up and groaned in pain. Every muscle in my body ached. My shoulders hurt from carrying the pack. My arms and legs ached from climbing. My lower back hurt from sleeping on the ground. As Titus moved toward the door, I collapsed back on the ground. The ceiling of the tent was coated white with tiny icicles, the moisture from our breath that had frozen as it rose into the air and clung to the ceiling.

"What's wrong with you?" Before going out, he put a hunk of ice from outside into our cooking pot.

"Aren't you sore?" I replied.

"I'm immortal, Psyche. Any damage I did to my body yesterday healed over night."

I rubbed my aching shoulders. "Lucky you."

"When I get back, I'll take care of that." He ducked outside.

I found the first aid kit, but to my utter disappointment the only medicine it contained was a single package of acetaminophen. I swallowed them without water, since everything had frozen again overnight. I turned on the pot so we could have a warm breakfast. Without the wind, the temperature had risen to a whopping fifteen degrees. Still, it made a difference. Inside the tent it wasn't as bitterly cold as it had been overnight. I set a couple of packets of scrambled eggs on top of the melting ice in the pot.

Before Titus returned, I moved into my own sleeping bag, which was cold. Now that our lives were no longer in danger, it was wise to put some space between Titus and me.

I had a headache. I wasn't sure if it was the altitude or the strain I'd put my body through, but I felt miserable. I lay down, trying to find some position that didn't hurt.

Titus came in shaking snow from his hair. He slipped off his boots at the doorway. In the pack he found some body wipes that were our only baths for the duration of our hike. He had to shake ice out of them before wiping down his hands and face. When he offered them to me I declined. I would rather be dirty than any colder.

He knelt beside me. "Roll over on your belly," he said.

"No, thanks."

Titus let out an irritated sigh. "You're in pain. Let me help."

"Because you're a servant," I muttered. "It's what you do."

"You're mocking me," he replied. "Your feet are nothing. This is what I'm best at. Give me two minutes, and I'll have you convinced."

"I'm okay."

"We're most likely stuck in this tent until tomorrow. I thought you trusted me?" He blew on his hands and rubbed them together.

I relented because I was in too much pain to argue coherently. I rolled over and used my sweatshirt as a pillow as I lay face down in the sleeping bag. My long-sleeved undershirt and T-shirt didn't feel warm enough and in two minutes I was going to put my sweatshirt back on and tell him to leave me alone.

"First I inspect, then I fix," Titus said. He placed two fingers over my spine just above the waistline of my jeans.

"Hey!" I protested when he slid those fingers under my shirt.

"The friction on your skin will keep you warmer," he countered.

I clenched my teeth to keep from growling at him. Which part of not liking to be touched didn't he understand?

He slid his fingers along my spine all the way up to my neck. As he dragged his fingers down my neck, I flinched. "That hurts?"

"Everything hurts." I started counting down from a hundred in my head. When I reached one, he was going to get his hands off me.

He started at the base of my skull, rubbing so gently I could barely feel the pressure. Then he moved down my sore neck and over one shoulder blade. With his strong palm he soothed the knotted muscle where the strap of the pack placed a strain.

Somehow I lost count of the seconds. My head hurt less as the tension in my muscles released. I had to hand it to Aphrodite. She trained her servants well. "You swore to stay with me until my dying breath?" I mumbled.

"Yes."

"Awesome."

"I told you I was good." Good was an understatement.

Once I went to a spa with Savannah. It was her sixteenth birthday present from her parents. We drove to Boulder Hot Springs and stayed at the resort. We enjoyed facials, the sauna, and pedicures. Both nights before going to bed, we scheduled massages. Of course, the masseuse had been a woman, so lying there with nothing but a towel over my behind wasn't a big deal. Still, I had enjoyed the sauna more than the massages. If the massage at the spa had felt like this, I would have stayed on that table all day.

"Are you still awake?"

My reply didn't quite make it past my throat. It sounded like a weak groan.

"Do I pass?" Titus teased.

"Oh, yes," I said. "Is this going to give you nightmares?"

"No, I'm comfortable with this," he said lightly. "It might give you nightmares, though."

"Maybe you should teach this to Eros," I offered.

"Not a chance," he replied. "Then I'd be out of a job." He had me sit up while he massaged the muscles in my arms and shoulders. "What will you draw today?"

I shrugged, which no longer hurt. "Whatever you choose."

He thought for a moment. "An animal. You don't have a single animal in your book."

"Except the caricature of Theron." I pulled away from him. Though it felt good to have him work the pain out of my muscles, I still wasn't comfortable with his hands on me. I didn't understand the boundaries between a mistress and her servant. How much of me did he think he could touch?

He took this rejection without comment. Instead he sat beside me and watched me draw.

"I will draw the most beautiful animal I've ever seen." It wouldn't be difficult. I used to have a book that was all about drawing horses in various actions. I drew Pixis rearing with his wings unfurled, the way he'd shown himself to Savannah.

It snowed until well after noon, and by then we didn't have enough daylight left to reach the next camp site. We had to stay where we were for another night and hope we could finish the journey tomorrow. We ate more food than we should have, but Titus assured me we would need the energy tomorrow. I knew the way was going to be more difficult, and I was dreading the climb.

Eventually, we just lay side by side in our sleeping bags listening to music. We split the headphones and listened to the operas on Titus's iPod, which he translated in between humming the melodies. Afterward, we listened to the music on mine. At first he balked at it, but eventually, his fingers began tapping on his chest. "Play that one again," he would say, and he would hum along the second time through.

I was glad when night fell with no wind. It brought colder temperatures, but also the hope that tomorrow our journey would be finished. We turned on another heat cell, which warmed the tent and allowed us to fall asleep. I didn't offer to share Titus's sleeping bag again. Even if I was cold, I would sleep alone.

He didn't have trouble sleeping that night either, because when I woke in the night and looked around, he had disappeared, sleeping bag and all. If I listened carefully, I could hear him breathing.

I lay there in the stillness. We seemed so utterly alone up here. For some reason, a junior high school retreat came to mind.

A group of us were selected to attend an overnight camp one weekend. Five or six teachers, the principal and the school counselor went with us. They taught us all about peer pressure and how to be leaders, then they spent the weekend taking us through trust-building activities. We led a partner around the camp blind-folded. We stood in a circle and the person in the center allowed himself to fall backward on the faith that we would catch him. We played games and shared our fears. Then we returned to school. I remember passing a few of those students in the hallways and thinking, "I know them deep down," but at school, we were still strangers, who belonged to different groups of friends and whose paths did not intersect.

This climb with Titus was like one, big, trust-building journey, and I wondered when we returned to Eros if Titus and I would still be friends, or would we pass one another, nod and move on like strangers? He helped me feel safe on this dangerous mountain, but once we reached the cave, that would be gone. I would be on my own again. This time Eros wouldn't be watching over me, and Titus wouldn't be there to catch me. Rory wouldn't be using his friends to help me, and Aeas wouldn't be standing by ready to heal my wounds. I would be utterly alone.

Through my mind flashed images of Theron and his flying fist, the crowd outside the Kappa Sig house, and a pack of hungry wolves. I shivered and bit down on my lip to keep from whimpering. This task would be worse than anything I had faced thus far, and terror so dark and formidable shook me to the very soul. I said one silent prayer. If I couldn't beat the enemy that waited, I wanted to die quickly.

# CHAPTER 25

I t was barely light when Titus knelt beside me and laid his hand over my forehead. "Psyche, we should pack up camp."

I opened my eyes to see him already dressed in his snow gear with his pack loaded.

"I've warmed you some breakfast and apple cider. While you eat, I'll take down the tent."

Shaking myself awake, I looked at my watch. It wasn't even six a.m., but I knew this was our one and only chance to finish the journey. It was better to get an early start than risk running out of daylight before we reached the top. I pulled on my snow pants, coat and boots. During the night I'd ended up wearing my sweatshirt instead of using it for a pillow.

"Did you sleep all right?" Titus asked.

"Fine," I replied.

"Really? Because, you don't look well-rested."

"I'll be fine." I dragged my pack outside and leaned against it while I wolfed down the warm meat and potato mixture and apple cider. My muscles were mostly recovered, all except my legs, which I wouldn't let Titus touch. Still, I knew once we got moving the soreness would wear off.

The sky was clear. It would be a bright and calm day, a perfect day for climbing. With the tent packed, Titus loaded it into his own pack.

"That one is mine," I protested.

"I'll carry it."

My pack was much lighter than it had been before. He'd taken the heavy gear out of my pack and replaced it with light, bulky items like the sleeping bags. It was a bad sign. He didn't think I could make it with the heavier pack.

With everything loaded, Titus checked our safety ropes and made sure the knots were tight. The first leg of the journey was a gentle slope running along the crevasse. Luckily, we already knew where the drop-off was, because it had drifted over during the storm. An unknowing climber might try to cross the fragile shelf and fall to his death. Our navigation system, however, kept us on a safe path.

Over three feet of powder had fallen during the storm, and we were forced to use snow shoes. Stuffing my boots into the bindings and tightening them down, I took a few trial steps around camp to make sure I wouldn't fall on my face in the deep snow. Once I got the hang of the shoes, I hefted the pack onto my shoulders and waited until Titus had done the same.

Snowshoeing was hard work, but it was easier than sinking deep into the snow with every step. After only a few hundred feet I was breathing hard and my muscles were complaining, but I pushed forward knowing it was only going to get worse. We were on relatively flat ground and once we reached the cliffs, the glaciers would lay below us, and we would be climbing the rocks.

We broke from the cliffs in less than two hours, just as the sun fully appeared on the eastern horizon. The snow around us was set aflame by the sun's rays. It nearly blinded us. Titus found our tinted goggles, and we traded snowshoes for crampons. The rocks were icy, and the way before us was steep.

For much of the morning, we climbed the rocks like icy steps that lead into the sky. The rise seemed gradual, but when I looked over my shoulder, I froze with fear. Realizing I'd stopped, Titus tugged on the rope at my waist and rebuked me. "Don't look down again!"

I faced the mountain and kept climbing. I forced myself not to think about the nothingness that lay behind me. I climbed with firm determination until the sun rose high overhead warming my back and lifting my spirits. I was succeeding. It wasn't that hard. I could do it. With this cheerful attitude, I reached the spot where Titus had stopped.

He stood at the peak of the section we had just finished climbing, and he gazed across the way before. As I crested the peak, I tugged on his pant leg triumphantly.

"I made it!" I exclaimed.

He turned with worried eyes. "Don't stand up," he said. He blocked my view as he helped me over the last ledge and sat beside me. "This looks like a good place to stop for lunch."

I leaned around him to see what he was hiding. The mountain's spine lay before us. While I'd envisioned the spine of a horse, a narrow line between two gradual slopes, this was a rocky twelve-to-fourteen-inch path with steep drops on either side. The spine wasn't like standing on the edge of a cliff; it was like walking a pencil line between two of them. Maybe if I hadn't been afraid of heights, if it hadn't been snowy, and if I had been a more experienced climber, the walk across the spine would have been doable. As it was, Aphrodite could not have chosen a more difficult mountain for me if she had picked one double in size. I dropped my face into my hands, the anguish of fear and disappointment crushing all my optimism.

"I can't do it," I cried.

Titus dropped food packets onto the ground between us. We didn't bother to heat them while we were climbing. "You *can* do it. And you will."

He didn't understand. It wasn't just fear. It was terror that gave me vertigo. I would get dizzy and be unable to keep my balance. I would fall, and I would take him with me. I would kill us both.

While we ate, Titus tried to soothe me. "The cave is straight ahead. It's maybe half a mile away. That trail is all that lies between you and finishing this task. It's an easy grade. Some of it is even downhill. If that trail lay in a valley, you would skip across it in a quarter of an hour."

"But it's not in a valley."

"You've come halfway across the world. You can't quit now."

"Titus, I can't do it!"

Angry, he reached into my open pack and pulled out the sketchbook. He laid it open on my lap, and Eros's face looked back at me. "Do you want to see him again? Do you ever want to hear him tell you that he loves you?"

I couldn't hold back tears. I promised myself I wouldn't quit, no matter the cost.

"That trail is no worse than looking into Theron's eyes and knowing he wants to kill you. It's no worse than nearly freezing to death in a storm."

"If I fall, I'll take you with me," I said.

"You'll go first, so I can see you. You just look at the trail, and ignore what's beside it. You focus on walking. Just walking. It isn't as hard as it seems." He put his arm around me. "You must at least try."

I took a deep breath and thought of my dad, his tireless hard work and his courage to face any task great or small. How hard must it have been for him raise a daughter alone? How much harder must it have been when she turned out to be so beautiful that every man he met wanted her? I wondered if he had spent the last six years walking a trail more terrifying than this one so I would make it safely to adulthood.

"I can't carry a pack," I said. "Leave behind everything we don't have to have. Put all the essentials into your pack. Tie the rest down here, so we can get them on the way down. Whatever you do, don't forget the box."

In one of the pockets of the pack there was a small satchel for day hikes. I stuffed a few energy bars and a water bottle into it and slung it over my shoulders. Titus wrapped the gear we were leaving behind in a piece of canvas from the extra tent and staked it into the ground. He lifted his pack onto his shoulders and shortened the tether between us.

"As long as you don't take me by surprise, I'm strong enough to catch you if you fall. So... well, scream if you lose your balance."

"I don't think that will be a problem."

He helped me stand, and I had to close my eyes to stop the spinning in my head. While we stood there, Titus slid a finger down my neck and came up with his chain and Eros's ring. "He gave you wisdom and safety." Titus kissed my forehead. "Now take courage and go."

The first five steps were the hardest. Leaving the safety of the small plateau and stepping away from Titus's firm grip brought on a new wave of nausea. It literally felt like I was walking in the air. Of course, there were rocks below to kill me if I fell. I had to find a way to walk the trail without seeing them.

It is possible to trick the mind and make something three dimensional look two dimensional to your eyes. I'd done it hundreds of times when drawing. Now I forced my mind to see the way before me two dimensionally. The trail became my only focus, and everything around it fell into a plane equal with it. I didn't look back, and I didn't wait for Titus. I walked slowly, coaxing my body to put one foot in front of the other.

My head began to feel thick, and I realized I wasn't breathing. After that I inhaled as I set my right foot down, and exhaled with the left. I didn't allow myself to think or feel anything along the way. The warm sunshine and the cold air ceased to exist. The farther I went, the more at ease my steps became until I felt my shoulders relaxing and my gait flowing more naturally. Still, I didn't allow myself to lose the visual focus of a two-dimensional trail, because without it, I would be helpless and afraid again.

I walked and walked and then the trail broke off. It ended inches from my feet and fell away. Blinking, I looked ahead. I was only about a hundred yards from the end of the spine. There the ground widened into the area where we would camp. Just above it was the opening to the cave where I would meet Aphrodite's messenger. I looked down at my feet again. The trail had collapsed leaving a gap about three feet wide.

"You'll have to jump it," a voice said.

Startled, I looked back and found Titus standing there. He rested a hand on my shoulder. I had walked in lonely silence all across the spine. I had forgotten he was following and that I was wearing a rope which bound me to him.

"It's only a few feet, not much wider than the crevasse you jumped the other night. And you're much stronger today."

"I could fall."

"You won't," he said confidently.

I looked down and grew woozy, suddenly aware that I was standing on a trail only fifteen inches wide and thousands of feet above flat ground. I felt all my resolve starting to crumble. Tears threatened my eyes again. I bit down hard on my fear and leaped. My right foot landed and kept me moving forward until my left foot landed. I crouched to the ground to keep from falling off the edge.

"Perfectly done," Titus praised. He took a step back and leaped. His foot landed almost exactly where mine had, but as it did the rock groaned and crumbled. He landed his second foot, and there the trail fell away also. Fear shot through his eyes, and I screamed.

I straddled the trail and dug my knees into the rock knowing he would pull me off the cliff when he fell.

Titus threw his body forward as his legs fell from underneath him. I reached out and caught his hand, only to have his glove come off in my fingers. Then he slid. The momentum of the collapse and weight of the pack pulled him down. I braced myself for his weight, but it didn't come.

Shaking, I inched forward, afraid I would further collapse the trail if I went too far. The rope had fallen to the side of the trail. I looked down and found him hanging by one bare hand, trying hard to reach for a foothold.

"Pull!" he yelled.

I pulled. I took up all the slack of the rope and pulled as hard as my arms could. Then I wrapped the rope around my body, leaned back and pulled harder. Below me he grunted, and a second hand appeared on the ledge. He pulled himself around the side of the ledge and climbed the rocks until he surfaced on the trail between me and the cave.

Panting, he wrapped both arms around me and rested his face in my hair until he gathered his composure. "Good thing you pulled off my glove," he said finally. "Let's keep moving." He probably hoped I wouldn't notice that his hands were shaking, and there was a slight glisten to his eyes.

I managed to stand and follow him. It was harder now that the mountain had tried to kill us again. The trail widened slightly, so I didn't have to watch my feet every step. Instead I watched Titus's back as he navigated the rest of the spine. When we reached the end of the trail, the ground spread out and flattened into a long, narrow dale which bowed before the cave. Along each side were waist-high stones that looked too symmetrical to have occurred naturally. Titus surveyed this warily.

"We should just camp in the cave tonight," I said. "Might as well use the shelter."

"Maybe," he replied, dumping his pack on the ground. He looked mostly recovered from his fall, but he was stepping lightly wherever he walked.

I unclipped from the tether and moved toward the cave.

"No, Psyche, wait!"

Because he ran after me, I jogged ahead. I ran a very slow fifty-meter dash and crested the rise to the mouth of the cave only moments before Titus caught me. I pulled in a deep breath and held it. Running at this altitude was an inch short of downright stupid.

The cave was about fifteen feet deep and equally wide with a peaked ceiling at least double the breadth. At the back was a solid stone wall. There were small hollows in the cliff walls as they rose, but other than that, the entire cave was visible, and it was empty.

I faced Titus and raised my arms in triumph. "I made it with seventeen hours to spare!"

"I knew you could." He smiled as he approached and was about to hug me until he looked over my shoulder, and his immortal eyes saw something that was veiled from mine. His expression fell. He grabbed my arm, pulled me away from the cave's mouth and literally dragged me all the way back to where his pack lay on the ground. "No," he murmured to himself, "it can't be. I didn't want to believe it."

"Titus, what did you see?"

"We can't camp up there. We must stay as far from the cave as possible." He dug through his pockets with shaking hands until he found the satellite phone and used the speed dial to make a call. He paced as he waited, growing more agitated with every step. Finally, he barked into the voice mail, "Where *are* you? We've arrived, and it's exactly what you feared." With his back to me, he dropped his face into his hands.

"Titus?"

He turned around with a forced calm. "We need to pitch the tent and get you inside. I want you out of sight."

I didn't move. I wasn't going to do anything until he told me what was in that cave. My voice was stern and determined this time. "I command you to tell me the truth. What did you see?"

He didn't hide the sadness in his voice. "A portal," he answered, "into the Underworld."

# CHAPTER 26

We camped in the center of the valley as far from the cave as possible. We didn't know for sure how much of the valley lay on solid ground and how much might be glacial ice. In silence we pitched our tent.

Titus refused to say more until he spoke with Eros, and while I had hundreds of questions, it was pointless to ask them. With the tent standing, we climbed inside. I unrolled both sleeping bags, which seemed futile. I doubted either of us would sleep tonight.

Titus looked too sick to move, until I tried to go outside and get ice for our pot. Then he jumped to his feet and told me to stay put until he returned. I unpacked MREs with little appetite. I wanted to know what lay ahead, but I was afraid that knowing might be worse.

While Titus was outside, the phone rang. The caller ID blinked that it was Eros calling. I pressed the send button and quickly said, "Don't speak. He's outside. Just wait."

I unzipped the tent and found Titus already coming toward the door. "It's him," I said.

He took the phone from my hand and walked away so I couldn't hear him as he explained what he'd seen. He shook his head, and I could tell by his stance that he was pleading with Eros.

I ducked back inside, where I warmed our frozen water bottles in the cooking pot before heating the meals. While I waited, I sketched the spine the way I had forced myself to see it all afternoon. The two dimensions took depth on the page, so that when I held it away from me, I saw the scene that had inspired so much fear—the steep drops and the jagged rocks on either side of the narrow path. Glad to have the image out of my head, I sketched the valley with the cave above. I was just getting to the formidable stone perimeter when Titus appeared.

He didn't look at me as he spoke. "Your survival will depend on your ability to resist temptation of every kind and follow my instructions exactly. One small mistake, and you will belong to Persephone. You'll be lost forever."

"I'll die." I'd accepted death as a very real possibility, so it didn't sound so terrible now.

"No." Titus's eyes grew moist. "The darklings are immortal. They won't kill you. They'll enslave you."

"I thought the Underworld was the Land of the Dead?"

"Your mythology joined our Underworld to your version of Hell. It is a place of eternal suffering inasmuch as we live an eternity compared to you. But it is not a final resting place for souls. It's a prison. Hades and his wife, Persephone, are guardians of the prison, but they've become corrupted. They are as wicked and despicable as those whom they punish. The Underworld is filled with suffering beyond imagination. A mere glimpse is enough to give you nightmares, and you will have to travel all the way into the depths of Hades to meet Persephone at the palace."

"How will I know the way?"

"She will send a guide, but you cannot trust him. He'll be one of her subjects. It's clear that the whole purpose of this task is to get rid of you. Aphrodite doesn't expect you to escape Hades."

"What about Eros?"

"He said this is why he sent me with you instead of Aeas. I've been to the palace in Hades. I know what will befall you there. I know what you will see. I'm to prepare you as best I can and give you the knowledge you need to escape their snares."

I tossed him a water bottle and a warm meal. "It's a good thing we have all night. You can start by explaining to me who is in the Underworld and how they got there."

Titus took a long drink before explaining, "When my parents were children, Olympus was a very different place. Robbers roamed the land in bands. They plundered the villages, raped women, murdered people and burned their fields. Then they would retreat into the mountains where they hid and built underground strongholds. No kingdom was immune from their violence. That is when the Council was first formed. All the kingdoms banded together and declared war upon the bandits. They tried to go into the mountains and fight them, but the robbers were well hidden, and each time the armies attacked, they suffered great losses without prevailing.

"This went on for several annum. Whenever the armies would retreat, the bandits would fall upon a poorly guarded village, kill every person in it and burn it to the ground after stealing the stores of grain and gold.

"It was Zeus who devised the plan for conquering the robbers. The kingdoms brought every soldier they could find and surrounded the mountains. They spent all winter piling wood and hay around the foot of the mountain range, a circular barricade to cage the robbers. The bandits thought they were merely trying to hedge them in and believed they had supplies to outlast the soldiers. When summer came, Zeus ordered the captains to set fire to the barricade and burn the entire mountain range. It would be the equivalent of the U.S. burning all the mountains between California and Colorado. He ordered legions of soldiers into the air, and they showered burning arrows down upon the rugged land."

Titus paused for a moment and downed half his meal, then continued, "Olympus lost sixty percent of its timber in that fire. The entire face of the continent was covered with haze from the smoke. When the robbers realized there was no place for retreat, they gathered themselves into one body, fought their way through the fire and attacked the nearest kingdom. They were greatly outnumbered, but the battle lasted two weeks before their leader was slain and they finally surrendered. The ones who survived were cast into the depths of the earth as punishment for their crimes. Hades was appointed ruler of the dominion. Since that time, all criminals from Olympus have been sent to Hades for punishment.

"Zeus became the Ruling Judge of the Council of Olympus. Your world knows the council as the Olympian Household, which is only partially correct. A few of his children do sit at the heads of kingdoms, but the council is not a single family with Zeus as patriarch. Aphrodite, however, is his daughter. Eros is his grandson."

"Eros is part of the Council?" I asked.

Titus shook his head. "Eros's kingdom was made up of portions of two existing kingdoms. Plus, he was just a child. He was offered a place at the council as an advisory vote, but not a ruling vote. Everyone expected him to marry into a kingdom with a ruling vote. His mother encouraged this most of all." He crumpled up the foil from his dinner and stowed it in the pouch were we kept our trash.

"And instead, he fell for a mortal."

"Eros doesn't care for power as long as the Council is ruling in fairness and doling out justice in equity."

"If Hades is a place for criminals," I asked, "why have you been there?"

He shrugged off his coat. "I know you don't like me touching you, but would you mind?" He motioned me to sit between his legs. "I need to use my hands. It helps me relax."

Reluctantly, I slipped off my coat and moved toward him.

He started rubbing knots out of my shoulders. "Five ages ago Aphrodite became enamored with a mortal named Thomas. She took him as a lover. She would steal away from the kingdom to visit him, and on one occasion Eros followed her. When he found them together, he demanded she give Thomas up, or Eros would tell her husband."

"Hephaestus?" I asked, testing my knowledge of Greek mythology.

"Yes. Aphrodite agreed, but she had no intention of leaving Thomas alone for good. Knowing that his youth wouldn't outlast Eros's resolve to reform her, she opened a portal for Thomas so he could collect the sacred fruit."

"She immortalized him?"

"But that wasn't enough for Thomas. He traveled to her palace and sneaked in during the night with the intention of removing from her the obstacles that kept them apart—her husband, her son and her other lover."

"He knew about Theron?"

"No, but he knew she had another. Theron and the palace guards realized there was an intruder. They searched everywhere for him. Thomas stole into the forge. My father was Hephaestus's bodyguard. Thomas murdered my father and stabbed Hephaestus before Theron and the others caught him. Thomas was tried before the Council and sentenced to the Underworld. Because he tried to kill Hephaestus, a member of the Ruling Council, Zeus himself travelled with armed guards to deliver Thomas to Hades. I was nearly fifteen, and Zeus had me accompany the party as a witness to my family that justice had been served."

"You made the journey, and you survived," I said optimistically. "So, I should be able to do the same. There are lots of stories about mortals who travelled to Hades and returned. Odysseus and Aeneas..."

"They are all fiction. Aeneas never existed. Eros is Aphrodite's only child. Only one mortal has been to Hades and lived to write about it. You might have read his work. He was Italian."

"We don't read Italian writers," I replied, "except Dante."

Titus squeezed my shoulder.

"Oh, you've got to be kidding me!" I exclaimed.

"He embellished a great deal. Some of the other myths contain elements of truth also. You will descend far into the earth until you reach the river Styx. You have to pay a toll to get across. I will give you the Olympian coins that you need, one for the toll in and one for the toll out. Put the coin under your tongue, and Charon, the boatman, will take it from your lips." Titus smoothed down the fabric of my sleeves. "It will be hot in Hades, but it's best if you keep your skin covered. The inhabitants of Hades are immortal, but they're cold. If they feel your warmth, they will assume you're Olympian. Do not tell anyone you are mortal. I assume your guide will know what you are, and so will Persephone, but no one else. See that it stays that way. There is a hierarchy among us. We, Olympians, are above the demons, but any immortal considers himself above you. There are guardsmen and punishers in Hades. In their kingdom they are basically free men, and they dole out violence to others. If one of them figures out you are a red-blood, they will fight to claim you. Death is merciful compared to what they will do to you." Titus shivered and wrapped his arms around me. "I'm afraid for you," he whispered.

I was afraid for me, too. "Tell me more," I prompted.

"You'll have to pass Cerberus, the three-headed dog. He likes treats, so you feed him and slip by while he eats. Then you must walk all the way down to the palace. All around you will be scenes of torture and suffering. See as little as possible. Keep your focus on your guide. He will take you through the gates of the city to the palace. In the city, speak to no one. It will go against your nature, but do not be fooled into trying to help someone who seems to be hurt or starving. The demons can transform themselves. A frail old woman might actually be a guardsman, and your mercy would be punished. Once you reach the palace, don't assume you are safe. The men at court are just as dangerous as any in the kingdom, and the palace guard more so.

"When you meet Persephone, you must remember two things. First, she is the queen of deception, so you cannot lie to her, and you cannot assume she tells the truth. Second, never anger her. In everything you say, be meek and polite. Be grateful if she's generous and humble if she's not. Remember that of everyone you meet in that forsaken place, Persephone is the most dangerous of all." Titus moved to face me and took my face into his hands. "Of all the things I tell you, this is the most important. Do not eat anything or drink anything while you are in Hades. To partake of their feast is to become a part of the kingdom. No matter how hungry you get, no matter how thirsty, do not let one drop of wine touch your tongue, not a single crumb of food. Do you understand?"

"I understand. Don't let them touch me. Don't help anyone. Don't eat or drink anything. Don't believe their lies. Be polite. Feed the dog. Pay with a coin from my lips. Don't let them know my blood is red. Anything else?"

"Just one more thing. Persephone is big on seduction. Life with Aphrodite is a cakewalk compared to Persephone's household. Don't have sex with a demon."

"Not going to happen," I said emphatically.

"Her attendants are well-schooled in their arts. Submit to one, and she will own your will and your body." Sheepishly, Titus admitted, "She nearly caught me. One of her maids came to me in the night. I didn't know why she was there, but I allowed her to tempt me. Luckily, the guard outside my room awakened, put a sword to my neck and commanded the girl to leave. Afterward he explained what I had almost done. It was perhaps the most terrifying moment of my life. Right up there with almost falling off a cliff."

"I'm not going to let anyone to touch me, right?"

"Your guide—the one man who knows you're mortal—he'll be the one you need to watch. He'll try to get you alone, and he'll try to tempt you. Resist him no matter the cost. As long as you say no, you remain free."

"You mean, even if he rapes me?"

"That's what I mean."

I tried to hide the shudder that shook me involuntarily, but I was sure Titus felt it. Every imaginable nightmare awaited me on the other side of that portal. "I doubt I'll be able to sleep tonight," I said.

Titus forced a smile. "I'll put you to sleep, and I'll watch over you in the night. Tonight, at least, you can rest knowing that you are perfectly safe."

In the hours before dark, I took what comfort I could from a man who was not my beloved. I allowed Titus to massage my back, shoulders and feet. He offered lighthearted conversation, and he sang to me softly while I tried to sketch. When night came, he kept me warm and held me while I cried. Then he softly caressed my temples until, unwillingly, I slipped into deep sleep. Without being conscious of dreams, I startled myself awake to find Titus still holding me and awake as he promised.

"Shhh," he murmured. "I'm still here for you." He stroked my face, and lulled me back to sleep.

Thanks to Titus, I slept long and deeply. When I finally woke it was after ten and he was gone. I thought for a moment he abandoned me, then I heard him talking softly outside the tent.

"I can hardly bear to let her go," he said. After a pause, he asked, "What did Zeus say? Will he free her from the contract?"

I stopped moving so I could hear every word now.

"Then I guess we have no choice. I've told her everything I know. I've warned her of all the perils I could think of. I'll wait for her here. The journey to the palace should only take a few hours. With any luck, she will be back by nightfall." He listened awhile, then said, "Goodness, I hope you're wrong. The longer she's gone the hungrier she is going to get."

Realizing I might be facing hours without food and water, I dug through the pack and counted how many rations were left. If I ate two meals, it would leave Titus enough for three full days without me. Hopefully, if I didn't come back by then, he would start climbing down before he ran out. We left some supplies at our base camp, and I was sure he could make that journey in a day, so he was supplied for at least a week. I was also pretty sure I wouldn't be able to resist water for a week if Persephone kept me that long.

I found what ice we had left and warmed it. The pot was heating slower now than when we started. The battery cell was running low. We had a second battery, but we left it on the other side of the spine.

Because I feared thirst more than hunger, I drank as much as I could. If it was hot and I couldn't drink, it wouldn't take long for me to get dehydrated and weak.

All too soon I found myself climbing with Titus toward the cave. Aphrodite's box was in the satchel slung over my shoulders. Titus had added my GPS watch to the satchel, too, so he would see my signal when I reappeared. The bag also contained food for Cerberus and an Olympian coin. Another coin was already under my tongue, so I wouldn't have to dig for it when I reached the river Styx. Outwardly, it seemed that all possible preparations had been made. Titus had wisely kept my tennis shoes in his pack, so I didn't have to wear heavy snow boots on the journey into Hades. All along he and Eros believed this was my destination, and they had planned for it while hoping they were wrong. I wore a long-sleeved undershirt beneath my T-shirt and my own comfortable jeans. Once Titus took my coat at the portal, I would look like I was heading off to school, ponytail and all.

School seemed like another lifetime now. I wondered how many units behind in Calculus I had fallen. This journey had probably doused all hopes I had of graduating in the spring. Failing my senior year of high school might have seemed monumental two months ago. Now it was the least of my concerns. Trying not to be made an immortal slave to some monstrous darkling was foremost in my mind.

Just as we reached the mouth of the cave, the wind whipped behind us. I ducked my face to keep from being sprayed with snow, but Titus smiled into the wind. "He came to see you off," Titus murmured. "He won't touch you. You're to pretend you don't know he's here."

Tears filled my eyes. "The next time you see Eros," I said, "tell him that no matter what happens, I will always love him."

Titus hugged me. "Be brave. You saved my life yesterday. You can save yourself today." He helped me out of my coat and moved me toward the open portal, which I still could not see. "The portal is guarded by two sentries. They are enormous, disfigured, monsters of men. Just walk past them as if they are not there. Your guide is waiting beyond them and... Oh, Merciful Heaven." He clutched my shoulders and wouldn't let me go.

"Titus?"

He laid his forehead on my shoulder and whispered. "It's Thomas. He's your guide."

I swallowed the terror that threatened to make me scream. "I'll be all right."

"No," he said. "I can't hand you off to that killer." But an unseen hand tugged on Titus's shoulder. He looked up, and beheld the face I couldn't. Looking sick, Titus stepped away from me, knelt on one knee and kissed my hand. "Go safely," he said. "I will be here when you return."

I ruffled his hair. "Try not to freeze to death." Then I turned, took a steadying breath and walked into Hades.

# CHAPTER 27

The moment I passed through the wall of the cave, I felt warm air hit my face. I ignored the towering figures on either side of the portal and approached my guide. "You're Thomas?"

"I am." He was not a formidable person. I matched his height, and though his chest and arms were muscled, he was slightly built. His brown hair was short enough that it merely lay back. He had a nice chin, a narrow nose and beautiful brown eyes. The color was warm and flecked with gold, although the light had gone out of them. He inspired none of the fear I felt when I looked into Theron's eyes. The eyes before me betrayed a soul given to deep sorrow. From under his arm, he unfurled a cloak very much like the one I'd worn in Eros's kingdom. "You're to wear this for protection. Your clothes will stand out here."

Thomas wore a black waist-to-knee robe similar to the ones in Eros's kingdom. Over his right shoulder he wore a scarlet sash, which was belted at the waist with a gold cord. Around his left bicep, he wore a thick gold band which bore a crest. Unlike the gold arm cuff Eros gave me, the band on Thomas was smaller than his bicep, and would not come off without being cut.

Without argument I donned the cloak and followed close behind him as he descended a staircase that led into the Underworld. The steps were driven into the walls of the hollow mountain, so that as we descended, we traveled the circumference of the circular chamber twice. Torches on the walls lit our way. We were in the belly of a huge volcano. The hot air stank of sulfur.

At the bottom of the staircase we met flat ground. The hard, barren earth formed a narrow shore for the river Styx. It was a river inasmuch as it was a body of moving water, but the water was thick and murky, the shores steep and covered with black slime. As we drew near, I realized there were bodies in the water. They looked like lifeless corpses floating down the river until they butted into one another. Then the bodies suddenly sprang to life and attacked each other. All of them had ghostly pale skin that was wrinkled and peeling. Sentries in black robes walked along the banks with whips in their hands. If some desperate soul climbed too far toward the shore, the sentries whipped him until he fell into the water.

As we stood at the dock, the people in the water called out to us. They wailed and pleaded with us. Some tried to grab our legs. Coming across the water was the boatman Charon. The bodies did not move for him, and his skiff plowed over them and pushed them under the filthy water.

I stayed very close to Thomas and pretended not to notice the scene. He seemed to be observing me as much as I was trying not to observe my surroundings. When Charon landed at the dock, Thomas said, "You'll need to pay a toll to cross." From his pocket, Thomas took a coin and offered it to the boatman. They exchanged it hand to hand, but I refused to be fooled. Titus had been specific about how I was to pay the toll. I moved the coin from under my tongue and slid it forward on my lips.

Charon plucked the coin from my lips without touching my skin. Then he allowed us aboard. While we crossed the river, I sat in the middle of the boat so no one in the water could grab me, and I kept my eyes on the coming shore. At the dock Thomas rose and offered me his hand. Since he already knew what I was, I allowed him to help me ashore, and this pleased him.

Immediately past the bank of the river Styx was a stone gateway announcing the entrance to the kingdom of Hades. There, just inside the gate, was the three-headed dog, Cerberus, who wore a metal collar with a monstrous chain staked into the middle of the roadway. When Titus said "dog," he failed to mention that Cerberus was not only vicious and three-headed, but as big as an elephant. A single tooth in the hound's mouth was as long as my forearm.

At the sight of the dog Thomas grumbled, "Worthless mutt." Just outside the gate was a pile of raw meat, which he divided into thirds. One third he offered to me. "Throw it hard, or the first head will eat everything, and the other two will try to take dinner out of our hides."

We timed our throws together, and I threw the meat as hard as I could. It went all the way beyond the third head where Thomas's throws landed. The dog moved to face the meat, the heads already fighting, and we slipped by its tail. As soon as we passed, Thomas threw me a glance. I wasn't sure if it was approval or just plain curiosity, but a slight smile tugged at his lips.

From there we started downhill again, this time on a long dirt road. Though the path descended, it was always the high ground. On both sides were steep slopes that led into various pits and valleys. As we moved farther toward the city, the air became so foul, I had trouble breathing. It wasn't sulfur. It was something else, but I didn't recognize it. The pits beside the road were full of people receiving assorted brutal punishments. In one pit the captives were on their knees and chained by the wrists between two poles. They cried for mercy, while punishers in black robes walked among them with hot irons. Seeing my attention caught by the scene, Thomas murmured, "Traitors. They're branded."

A guardsman pressed the iron into a man's chest. The stench of burning flesh made me gag. I turned to Thomas, whose handsome face was a welcome sight among so much brutality. "How many times?"

"As many as they can bear. Then they're dumped into the Pool of Blood." He pointed. The pool lay between several pits. It was just as filthy as the river Styx. "There's ambrosia in the water. When their wounds heal, they're taken back to the poles."

"What's the punishment for murder?" I asked.

His eyes grew colder. "Depends on the murder." We continued on, and Thomas showed me the kingdom in all its gore. "Those are the abusers. Some of them killed their wives. They are flogged and beaten just as they beat those who loved them." He directed my attention to another pit where the captives were brawling. Every person punched and kicked at every other person. "Cowards. They must fight for every morsel of food and drop of water they receive." He eyed a trio of black-robed guards at the edge of the pit. "That's guardsmen entertainment. Throw a steak into the cowards and watch them beat each other for it."

As we drew closer to the city, the stench became even more foul, and the pits more deplorable. The last pit held metal platforms, each with a large stake jutting up through it. The platforms were surrounded by dry sticks and wood. Some were being prepared, while others were burning. Standing on each burning platform was a suffering immortal. The flames licked their skin, and the metal seared their feet as they screamed in agony. Two guardsmen carried a body from one of the platforms.

"Is he dead?" I asked.

"No, but he wishes he was," Thomas replied flatly. "He'll be healed in the Pool of Blood and burned again."

"What did he do?"

Thomas let out a hard snort. "Probably nothing. The fire is reserved for those who displease the Queen. He may have dropped a piece of bread or served her breakfast cold."

"They're all men." I'd never heard a man scream like that. "She is never displeased with her maids?"

The road turned and descended toward the city. "When the maids displease her, she just sets the guards loose on them. Most of the maids would prefer the fire."

No wonder there were tears in Titus's eyes when he told me they might enslave me. He had seen all this cruelty and depravation. He understood fully the cost if I failed at this task.

I was sweating profusely now. It was probably ninety degrees at the bottom of the kingdom. The air was filled with smoke so foul breathing was painful. As the fumes rose, they took on a red glow. The whole city looked bathed in blood, which was ironic since everyone here had clear blood except me.

Enormous sentinels in black robes and gruesome masks guarded the gates to the city. When Titus called them demons, it was an apt description. The streets were crowded, and here it seemed that at least a portion of the people of Hades lived free of torture.

"Are these people innocent?" I asked.

"If the King and Queen feel they have fully paid for their crimes, they may be granted a work assignment in the city. The guardsmen and the court have to be fed. Someone has to work. A few are children of Hades. Both of their parents are workers, and they were born here."

I walked closer to him in the crowd. As we passed an intersection of narrow streets, a dirty, nearly starving child caught hold of my cloak. Startled, I stepped into Thomas and touched his arm, which was cold despite the heat.

When he saw the child clinging to my cloak, Thomas lifted his foot and kicked it square in the face. It fell away hissing and transformed into a narrow-faced man about our age. "That's a child of

Hades. Only they can transform like that. If you see a snake, make sure you step on its head."

He steered me through the streets until I lost all sense of direction. No sooner had I reached this point of confusion than Thomas turned me into a narrow alley where the buildings on either side rose and joined above us. The light from the street was blotted out. He took me by the arm and he pulled me through the darkness.

I instinctively resisted, but it was a futile struggle. Even if Thomas had laid a trap for me, leaving him was far more dangerous. The passageway grew narrower. Only a small window of red light illuminated the exit far ahead.

Just before he reached the opening, he stopped. "We've arrived." He cordially offered me his arm, and though I was leery, I took it. We stepped through the smoke onto a cobblestone road. Before us rose an enormous castle at least double the size of Eros's palace. It was medieval in design with tall spires atop several round turrets. Stone gargoyles and roaring lions adorned the upper decks. A wide moat surrounded the palace, which we crossed on a stone bridge. The moat flowed with molten lava. The lava gave off such severe heat that my skin stung just crossing the bridge.

The open gates allowed us entry into an enormous foyer with stairways that led to the upper levels and a grand entrance into what was probably the great hall, but Thomas steered me to a side staircase and took me to an empty upper hallway.

"Where are we going?"

He didn't answer, so I stopped, still holding his arm, and stopped him, too.

"I'm supposed to see Persephone," I persisted.

"You will." He led me to a tall wooden door much like the upper room to which Theron had taken me to see Aphrodite. Perhaps Persephone wanted to see me privately.

I entered the room and found that it was indeed an enormous bedchamber, but it was empty. Thomas followed me into the room and locked the door behind us.

I faced him. "I'm here to see Persephone. I demand you take me to her."

"I will take you to Persephone, but not looking like that." He unclasped the cloak and pulled it from my shoulders. "You're filthy, and you stink."

We'd just walked miles through pits that reeked of burning flesh, and he thought I stank? "It took me a week to get here. I camped four nights in the snow. I didn't exactly have luxury accommodations."

"I'll draw you a bath." He moved across the room to another door and motioned me to follow. "If there's one thing we have plenty of here in the Underworld, it's hot water."

The bathroom was bigger than my bedroom back home. At the center of the room a circular tub was sunken into the stone floor. Thomas merely opened a valve over the tub and steaming water rushed out. He went to a cupboard and returned with two bottles and a bar of soap. He set one bottle on the edge of the tub. "For your hair." The other bottle he uncorked and poured into the water as the tub filled. It was Underworld bubble bath, and fortunately, it smelled like pomegranates, not burning flesh.

"I'll gather some fresh clothing." He left the door open a crack on his way out.

I was dirty, and a hot bath sounded wonderful. I felt guilty as I slipped into the steaming water. Back in the mortal world, Titus was shivering in the tent trying to keep from freezing.

No sooner had I dropped under the bubbles when Thomas returned.

"Hey!" I exclaimed. "A little privacy here."

He ignored me and filled a bucket with hot water and soap. He dropped my clothes into the bucket. On the back of the bathroom door he hung a gown. It was like the gowns of Eros's kingdom, but it was red. The bodice was embroidered with gold leaves, and from the neckline hung a delicate chain of gold leaves. A golden belt hung at the waist. Unlike the gowns in Eros's kingdom, the red one had a slit that reached high up the skirt on the right side.

"I'm not wearing that," I told Thomas.

"You will if you want to meet the Queen," he replied as he left the room again.

Irritated, I scrubbed a week's worth of sweat and grime from my body. I ducked my head under the water to wet my hair, and when I came up, Thomas was standing at the foot of the tub. Startled, I sucked bubbles up my nose and started sputtering.

He held several sandals in his hands. "I need to size your feet."

I lifted one foot above the bubbles, and he held a sandal up to it. The sandal was way too small, so he set it aside and held up another. With the third he seemed satisfied and slipped it onto my wet foot. He frowned and ran his finger over the forest of hair that had grown since the last time I had a razor. "This will give you away." He looked up. "Show me your underarm."

Careful to keep myself covered, I raised my arm.

"That will definitely give you away."

"I don't suppose you have a razor?"

"I'll find one." He pulled the sandal off my foot and disappeared. While he was gone I washed my hair and wrung it out.

The razor he found was an old-fashioned straight blade. Thomas sharpened it on a leather strap before holding out his hand. "Give me your foot."

"No way."

He offered me the razor handle first. "I'm surprised at you. It looked as if you had a man servant."

"Did you recognize him?" I wanted him to leave, but he wouldn't. Most likely he had orders not to leave me alone.

Thomas lowered his eyes. "Yes, it was Titus." Behind him scarlet curtains hung floor-to-ceiling on either side of a narrow stained glass window. Firelight flickered from the other side of the colored panes.

I studied the razor briefly then propped my left foot up on the side of the tub and pressed the razor against my skin. It seemed simple enough, just drag the blade up my leg. When I did this, it didn't scratch the hair away. It peeled away a section of skin an inch wide and six inches long. Blood gushed to cover the wound.

"Stop!" Thomas shrieked. "You stubborn girl. You're going to get me cast into the fire!" He grabbed a towel and blotted the blood. Then he rummaged through a cupboard and found a jar of balm. "Give me that razor," he demanded.

I relinquished it willingly, as Thomas smoothed balm over the cut. It itched, but the bleeding stopped and within minutes, the skin healed. After rinsing blood and skin off the blade, he gripped my foot. When I shied away, he held on tighter and muttered, "Don't move," through gritted teeth.

Not many things were more terrible than having a demon shave my legs with a straight razor. When he reached my knee, he slid the blade right over it and up about four inches. Seeing I'd gone completely rigid, he relaxed his grip on my foot. "I'm not going to hurt you. You can trust me."

My body didn't relax. "Says the demon from Hades," I muttered.

He shook the razor under the water and made another pass up my leg. "You've been well warned."

"Not well enough, obviously." I made sure plenty of bubbles covered me before I let him near my arms. He didn't so much as nick me as he scraped the hair from my underarms. It was mortifying as much as terrifying. Demon or not, Thomas was still a guy, and I had really hairy armpits. Being raised by a man somehow had not prepared me for male servants. Between Aeas, Titus, and now Thomas, I'd be lucky to escape with any dignity at all.

When he was done, I sank far into the water, but Thomas lingered. Finally, I came up and said, "I'm ready to get out."

He held a towel like he expected me to step into it. Not a chance.

I snatched it from his hands. "I can dry myself. Wait in the other room." As soon as he left, I hopped out and dressed in a hurry, afraid that he'd come back.

My satchel lay on the counter where my clothes had been. I carefully took out the box from Aphrodite then looked for a place to hide the satchel. If they wanted to keep me here, all they had to do was steal my exit plan, and I would be stuck.

I snooped around the bathroom until I found a loose cupboard. I managed to stow the satchel in the space between the cupboard and the stone wall.

"Much better," Thomas said, when I returned to the bedroom. "The dress is stunning on you." After inspecting me he said, "You should braid your hair. All the women here wear braids." Then he touched the chain around my neck and the ring that hung upon it. "Take that off."

"No," I said firmly. "It belongs to Eros. I will wear it when I meet Persephone. As for my hair, I don't know how to braid." I held up the box from Aphrodite. "I want to see the Queen now."

"I could send for a maid," he offered, still looking at my hair.

I wasn't going to let anyone else touch me.

Frustrated, Thomas went to the dresser and came back with a brush and comb. He took the box from my hand and motioned me to sit beside it on the bed. "I'll braid your hair," he said.

I laughed without meaning to. "You? Come on."

"I've been with Persephone for five ages. I sleep at her feet. Sometimes she doesn't care for maids, so she's taught me all sorts of tedious things." He drew the comb across my scalp and parted the hair, then brushed the divided sides before braiding my hair into a crown that circled my head. I could see him in the dresser mirror as he deftly worked his way from side to side. "Why don't you know how to braid?"

"I never really had a mother." I didn't feel like explaining Jill to him.

"My mortal parents died before I was grown. I survived on the charity of our neighbors. I worked the fields alongside their children, and they fed me." He looked at me in the mirror. "That's all I remember of my mortal life before Aphrodite found me." The braiding done, he pushed the ends into the crown with the point of the comb.

I fingered the finished work and tipped my head to see it in the mirror. "It's beautiful."

"Now you're fit to meet Persephone."

The Queen's throne was located in the opposite wing of the palace. The throne room was rectangular with high, vaulted ceilings and red tapestries draped between the buttresses. Stone floors and walls kept the castle cool despite the heat outside. As we stood at the doors waiting to be admitted, Thomas put out his hand shoulder high. "Don't hold onto me. Just rest your hand on mine," he instructed. Persephone's court followed strict protocol, and if I wanted to gain her favor, I had to follow their customs flawlessly.

In my other hand I carried the box I received from Theron at the beginning of the task. It had come all the way from my modest hometown in Montana to the most awe-inspiring mountains in the mortal world, and into the depths of the earth to be handed over to Persephone, the Queen of Hades. A sentry announced me, and Thomas led me slowly down the long, red carpet that ended at her feet.

Persephone had dark, flowing hair that reached past her elbows. She wore a headdress of feathers and woven gold, which shifted like dancing flames as she moved. Her dress was red like mine, but far more intricately embroidered. Up each arm she wore bracelets of gold, and around her neck she wore her husband's pendant. While Aphrodite's pride kept her aloof, Persephone was beguilingly friendly. As I approached, she greeted me with a smile.

"The mortal Psyche, my Queen," Thomas said, "delivered without harm, as instructed." As I curtsied—a movement I practiced four dozen times upstairs before Thomas was satisfied I could do it right—he took his place beside the Queen's throne. He knelt and rested his forehead upon her knee.

Persephone ran her hand over his hair, petting him like a dog, while she considered me. "The mortal beauty I've heard so much about."

"I was instructed to bring this to you, Queen Persephone." It was appropriate for me to approach her standing, but to curtsy again as I offered her the box.

She took it from my hands and set it on the arm of the throne. "Well done, my dear. You have completed the third task, and by so doing, you have won the right to see Eros again. To celebrate, I hold a feast in your honor."

A feast.

I remembered well Titus's warning about food. Worse, I was hungry. Very hungry. It had been hours since I ate those half-frozen MREs, but I refused to lose my composure or to anger Persephone. "You are very kind," I said. "Thank you."

This pleased her. "Come, Thomas. Escort our guest into the banquet hall." She rose, her bracelets jingling as she moved, and came toward me. "I hope you're hungry," she said, then led the way out of the throne room.

Thomas appeared beside me and offered his arm.

"I can't go into a crowd," I murmured. The skin on my arms and back was exposed. Anyone who brushed against me would feel my warmth.

"You must not displease the Queen," he answered.

Despite Persephone's claim, the task was incomplete. She hadn't opened the box. Persephone had to unlock the metal clasp on the box and reveal Aphrodite's reward before I could return with it to the mortal world. I was forced to keep playing the cordial guest until she allowed me to leave the palace with the open box. I had fulfilled my end of the task, and now I was at her mercy.

We crossed the enormous corridors of the castle to a room as big as my high school's gymnasium. Around the perimeter were throngs of guests, dressed in fine robes and awaiting their Queen. In one corner were musicians, their instruments idle as they stood with folded hands, also waiting. On the far side of the room were several maids and man servants, all dressed in black and waiting for their duties to begin. Long, empty tables stood along one side of the room. Along the other side on a raised platform were two ornate chairs for the reigning couple and half a dozen smaller chairs for their guests. Long, empty tables stood in front of these seats also.

Persephone waited for the sentries to announce her. The already hushed room fell absolutely silent as we walked to the chairs on the platform.

"You will sit here beside me, Psyche," she said softly. "Thomas, you may sit on her other side." Persephone raised her arms. "Let the celebration begin!"

The room burst into motion. The musicians began to play. The waiting guests filled the dance floor and began to move in unison. A set of doors was thrown open, and each maid and man servant fetched a tray of food for the long tables.

Because we sat with the queen, we were served first. A cracked peppercorn roast adorned with sprigs of rosemary was brought to our table. The succulent aroma of roasted beef and hints of garlic made me salivate. One of the man servants sliced off generous portions and slid them onto plates the size of serving platters. Next, he spooned wild rice. By the time he finished, my platter contained meat and rice, steamed beans, a thick slice of bread, a slice of cake, a small bowl of pudding, three strawberries, a slice of orange and a sprig of parsley. It was simply beautiful, and I could not taste one morsel, or I'd be condemned to a life of slavery in Persephone's court.

I sat on my hands to keep them from betraying me. My belly rumbled, and I tried to breathe through my mouth, so I couldn't smell the food.

Persephone ate, so did Thomas. The guests filled their plates and moved to round dining tables beyond the dance floor. A couple paused halfway to their seats. The man fed his companion a strawberry from his plate. She accepted it enthusiastically, and made a great show of licking his finger as she took it.

Thomas leaned toward me, a small bowl of pudding in his right hand. "This is my favorite dessert here at court. They don't make it often."

"You can have mine," I replied.

He dipped his spoon into the pudding and held it toward me. "You don't want to try it?"

I felt his eyes mocking me, but I replied, "No, thank you."

The room rose into a jovial din. When all the guests had full plates, the large doors opened again, and five man servants rolled out an enormous fountain. After moving it to a prominent location near the dance floor, one servant went around the back and cranked the pump until the fountain flowed with wine. A cheer rose from around the room.

Guests crowded to fill their glasses. Three more servants poured kegs of wine into the fountain until it nearly overflowed.

Thomas rose, took the three glasses from our table and filled them, serving Persephone's, then mine, then his own. As he settled into his seat, he savored the wine. "It's very good," he told me.

I slid my glass closer to his plate and tried not to notice that my throat was scratchy.

By far the most handsome group in the room were eleven young men who stood together at one end of the ballroom. All of them wore clothing identical to Thomas—black robe, scarlet sash, a gold cord at the waist, and a golden band around the left bicep. They ate standing and remained apart from the rest of the guests. They varied greatly in appearance. Some were dark while others were blonde. All were muscular, although a few of them were slighter than the rest. Even among the immortals, they held a singular beauty. I realized that if Thomas stood among them, he would match their form and beauty perfectly.

"Who are they?" I asked him, raising only my chin to point.

"Persephone's attendants, the Royal Guard." When I eyed them again, Thomas asked, "Is there one among them that you fancy above the others?"

"They are all beautiful."

He leaned closer and murmured, "You could choose any one of them, and she would give him to you for tonight."

I was stunned that he offered this so freely as if I expected it. "To entertain me?"

"Of course."

I sat back in my chair, and looked into Thomas's worried eyes. "I was under the impression you were assigned to entertain me?"

He bowed his head. "If you don't like me, she will give you someone else."

I tried hard not to grin. "Is there anyone in particular you'd recommend?"

As he sipped wine, his eyes went carefully over the entire guard, then to me. "No," he said finally, "there isn't."

I sighed dramatically. "Then, I guess I'm stuck with you."

He realized then I was teasing him, and he chuckled softly. His teeth were perfectly straight and made his smile brilliant.

From the corner of my eye, I saw Persephone watching us.

Thomas offered me his hand. "Will you dance with me?"

The dance floor was crowded with couples stepping and spinning to the music. I'd only danced with a man once. It was my dad, and we were at his foreman's wedding. I was thirteen maybe. All I remembered was feeling awkward through the whole song.

"I don't know how to dance like that," I protested.

"I'll lead," Thomas replied.

"But there are so many people...."

He knew I didn't want anyone to touch me even accidentally. "They will give us room, I assure you." Then he leaned forward and whispered, "It will get you away from the table."

I took his offered hand. He led me down the steps of the platform. By the time we reached the dance floor, all of the couples moved aside and created a corridor of bodies with an open circle in the center of the floor.

Every eye in the room was on us when Thomas brought me to face him on the dance floor. He slid his right hand around my waist, and I tried not to shudder when the skin on my arm touched his. His body was so cold. He drew me nearer. "It's just like walking to music."

As the tune started, Thomas pulled me a step forward with his hand, and then pressed me back again. On the next step, he turned, leading me by the hand. We danced four complete repetitions of the same steps before he spoke. "You lied to me."

"I did not," I replied, still very conscious of the audience surrounding us.

"You said you couldn't dance."

"I've done a lot of dancing. I've just never danced like this before. As a couple."

"They don't dance where you're from?"

In my mind flashed images of high school dances, the blaring music, thumping bass and slow songs, where couples hugged on the dance floor barely moving. Then I thought of my dad's friends and barn dances, sawdust on the floor, the country swing and line dancing. "It's different."

The steps mimicked a waltz, and while I'd never waltzed before, I did know the box step and how to turn at the corner to change direction. Thomas was doing six steps—one forward, one back, then two turns. Each turn contained two steps. Once I understood where the next turn was going, the dance was simple.

"You learn quickly," he replied. When the music ended, Thomas murmured in my ear before letting me go. "Curtsy to me and then to the Queen."

I curtsied to him as he bowed to me. Then he took me by the hand and bowed to the queen as I curtsied again.

As he led me through the throng of guests to the table, I heard someone whisper, "Who is she?"

Another guest replied, "She is Eros's bride."

I shot a look over my shoulder to see who spoke. It was a pair of young women. When they saw my glance, both turned their eyes away. "They know?" I asked Thomas.

"They know who you are, not what you are," he replied.

"They speak English." I expected it from Thomas. It was probably his native tongue, but why would people of the court speak English? The explanation he offered was sickening.

"Most of the women here were once mortals. There are far more men than women in Hades, so the king allows the sentries to go into the mortal world and collect women for the court. Most of Hades speaks English now. I taught it to all the Royal Guard myself."

"They *collect* women from the mortal world?" That was a nice way of saying they kidnapped girls, brought them to Hell and forced them to live as slaves. Everything about this place was inhuman.

After we took our seats, Persephone turned to the Royal Guard and gestured toward the dance floor. Immediately they dispersed through the crowd. A moment later, they arrived on the floor in three straight lines, each man holding a young woman by the hand. A gap was left in their formation because Thomas stayed with me.

The women seemed delighted to have been chosen, and they all knew the steps, even though the bulk of the dance was done by the men. It reminded me of movies I'd seen of Victorian English dances. The group moved from one formation to another. However, the dance was powerfully seductive and would have had the Victorians fainting in droves. The exquisite beauty of the Guard, so much of their perfect bodies exposed, quickened my pulse.

I looked down, only to find the platter of food taunting me. Watching the seductive Royal Guard was safer. At least they were across the room.

One of the men caught my eye. For most of the dance he was near the front at the center. He was dark skinned with captivating blue eyes. He completed the dance as if his partner was invisible. His eyes never strayed from the face of the queen.

When the music ended, Persephone applauded. All of the other guests followed her example, and so did I, but our praise was lost on the one attendant who still looked only at the queen. Finally, she smiled at him. She beckoned him forward with one finger.

His excuse to his partner was brief at best. A few short strides and he'd scaled the platform and taken a knee before Persephone. She touched his hair, then lifted his face by the chin. He looked briefly into her eyes, then kissed her hand before resting his forehead on her knee again. She stroked his hair. "Welcome home," she said softly.

I turned to Thomas for an explanation.

He whispered very softly into my ear, "He fell out of favor with the queen eight days ago, and has just returned."

"From where?"

He turned away, but there was no mistaking the tightening in his jaw.

The attendant was oblivious to my curiosity as he rubbed his forehead back and forth across Persephone's knee. Probably no one else could see that his hand had moved from the floor to her calf where he stroked her skin. Finally, the truth struck me. He never left the kingdom. He just returned from the fire.

A gasp of revulsion stuck in my throat. He was so beautiful and so meek. His shoulders and hands, so perfectly smooth, had been burned and healed only to be disfigured again.

I dared to look into Persephone's eyes and found her smiling triumphantly back at me.

My eyelid twitched.

*Oh, no*, I thought. *Not now.*

# CHAPTER 28

Thomas grabbed my arm and pulled me to my feet. "You look tired. I'll take you to your room.

I couldn't speak.

He begged pardon of the queen, who seemed pleased to have him take me upstairs.

Mercifully, he didn't parade me across the room to the main entrance but pulled me discreetly through the servants' quarters and up a back staircase.

My legs seemed to melt beneath me. I could barely stumble down the hallway. Fear and disgust combined with my hunger and threatened to tear me apart at the seams.

Thomas nudged me through the doorway of the bedroom. The candles in the sconces flickered as he closed the door. When he secured the lock, I could no longer hold back.

Tears blurred my vision as I staggered away, but escape was impossible. There was no where to run, and no one safe to run to. I steadied myself against the bedpost, but the pain didn't bloom in my chest. I willed it away. I faced Theron. I crossed the spine. I vowed never to be disabled by panic again. Whatever Thomas planned to do to me, I would survive it, and I would return to Eros.

"My answer is no, Thomas. Titus said no matter what you do to me, as long as I refuse, I'm still free." I imagined giant hands in my chest packing strips of fear into a ball of courage. I stood straighter and pulled strength from Eros's love, my father's devotion, and Titus's loyalty.

"He's right," Thomas said.

I braced myself for what was next—hands where I didn't want them and that hungry look in his eyes. I tried to prepare my mind to survive being defiled. I squeezed my eyes closed, not wanting to see Thomas turn ugly and mean as he came for me.

"Sit." Thomas opened the drawer on the nightstand. As he drew out two small bottles, I shuddered. He didn't close the drawer fast enough, and I saw what else it held—a pair of golden shackles and a long strip of black cloth, a blindfold.

I swallowed the knot in my throat and sat on the velvet comforter of the bed. The room was deceptively beautiful. On a chiffonier stood a tall vase filled with long-stemmed red roses. Behind the roses was a mirror in a hand-carved wooden frame. The candlelight threw soft shadows on the plush velvet and satin pillows of the bed. The pillows were black satin and red velvet. Some had gold tassels hanging from the corners.

He did touch me, but not like I expected. When I opened my eyes, Thomas was kneeling at my feet and untying my sandals. He anointed his hands with both oils then took my right foot in his hand. He held it exactly the way Titus did and began massaging.

I was so confused by his submissiveness that I didn't know what to say. "You learned that at Aphrodite's feet," I said finally.

He thought for a moment. "I guess I did. Why?"

"Titus does it exactly like that, too."

"You like Titus." It wasn't a question.

"He is honest and trustworthy and loyal." Those were qualities one simply could not find around here.

Thomas dribbled more oil on my toes and rubbed it in. "I'm deeply sorry that he lost his father."

"You're sorry that he lost him, or you're sorry that you killed him?" I would not pretend I didn't know why Thomas was here in the Underworld.

He moved to the other foot. "I'm sorry he's dead, and that justice isn't always just."

Maybe it was true. Centuries of slavery was a severe punishment, but Thomas slept in a palace and dined with a queen, while Titus's father had long ago rotted in a grave.

Thomas's hands moved up my calf.

"Don't!" I tried to pull my foot away, but Thomas held on, and he had a firm grip.

"You don't let Titus rub your legs?"

"It's bad enough he's always rubbing my shoulders."

Thomas looked up, utterly confused. "You should let him. Your muscles are knotted."

"Thomas," I said firmly. "You may not touch my legs above the knee."

"As you wish, Lady." He poured oil on my shins and rubbed it in. It smelled of lavender and cinnamon. "I'm a slave, you know." He gestured to the gold band around his bicep. "You can require anything of me. Have I nothing that you want?"

"Nope." It sounded pretty harsh, but this was the Underworld, after all.

Thomas bit his lip and rubbed more intently. It wasn't the knots in my legs that bothered him.

"Why do I get the feeling I have something you want?"

"You do," he replied, and a cold chill ran down my spine. "But it's not what you think."

"Amaze me," I said flatly.

"May I touch your hand?" he asked. When I didn't answer, he assumed it was permission. He took my hand, turned it palm up and set it against his cheek. He let out a low murmur, and his eyes closed in pleasure. "You're so warm. I'd forgotten what it was like to be near a woman who wasn't cold."

"Why are you cold?"

"Human warmth comes from within. We don't have it here. I was warm like you when I arrived, but now I'm as cold as the rest of them." He lifted his head and stood. He tugged on my hand until I stood before him. "If I swear on my allegiance to my Queen that I won't press you, will you allow me to hold you?"

I shook my head.

"I'll stop the moment you ask me to." He bowed his head. "Just for a little while, I want to be warm again."

Cautious as I was, somehow I couldn't refuse him. Most likely I was being beguiled, but some innate sympathy made it impossible for me to be unkind to him.

"Don't let this scare you." He untied the cord at his waist and freed the scarlet sash. He dropped them on the floor, a pool of crimson and a golden snake next to our feet. He shook with anticipation and he tentatively stepped forward and slid his arms around my waist.

Touching him was like being doused with cold water. I gasped as he pressed me against his bare chest.

"It's a shock, isn't it? I remember that about the first time I... uh... *attended* Persephone. She was positively giddy over my warmth." He sighed and dropped his head so his cheek rested on my shoulder. "Now I know why."

"How does it leave you?" Giddy wasn't the word I would use to describe Thomas. He was enthralled. He took my hands in his and moved our arms so that they touched from shoulder to wrist. He even put his neck against mine.

"It slips away little by little," he explained. "Every time you're beaten or burned. Every time you lie with a woman who doesn't belong to you. Every time you speak falsely or seduce a maid, you get a little colder. Then one night you realize you're just like all of them, worse maybe, and your blood is clear, but it's cold."

Truthfully, I was hot after the banquet, and he cooled me off. I was less faint, and surprisingly, less afraid. When he finally let me go, I saw the change in Thomas's face. A hint of sparkle shone in the gold flecks of his eyes. Human warmth was a powerful thing. Kindness even more so.

"You look exhausted," he observed. "Will you sleep?"

"Not with you here."

"I won't harm you, and I see you have no interest in using me."

"You make it sound like what I want matters." Though I was no longer terrified, I still had to be careful.

Thomas pulled back the covers on the bed and fluffed the pillows. "You are unlike any woman I have ever been sent to attend. Everyone who comes here wants something from Persephone. Some come seeking riches. Others want to learn to be powerful. Maids come to learn the art of seduction so they can unlawfully ensnare their masters. She treats all her guests the same. She hosts a banquet for them; she offers her best wine and her attendants to fulfill their every desire. However, they all fail to grasp this one simple truth: to deny themselves is to gain what they want most, and if they cannot deny themselves pleasure for a single night, then they belong here with the rest of us." He gestured me into the bed. "I've rarely seduced a guest. On the contrary, they command me, and I obey."

"So, I can command you to leave?"

Thomas dropped to his knees at my feet. "Please, don't do that! It will make her unhappy." He gathered my knees into his hands and pressed his forehead against my kneecap. "Please, let me stay."

I stood at a dangerous crossroads. I couldn't willingly send him to be burned. However, letting Thomas stay put me in grave danger. I stepped out of his embrace and sat on the bed to think. I didn't know what to do.

"You're just trying to lower my defenses," I said.

He shook his head. "I would rather burn than destroy such strength and innocence." He kissed the hem of my dress. "And, I know what awaits you if you fail tonight. Let me stay, and I will pay you in honesty."

I wasn't the real prize. Persephone hoped Thomas's charm would make me falter in my determination to return to Eros. Once declared property of the Hades court, I was to be beaten and used by the Royal Guard. When word reached Eros, Persephone knew he would come to bargain for my freedom. She wouldn't be able to keep him forever since he was an advisor to the Ruling Council, but she could submit him to her will. He would allow himself to be degraded and abused to keep me from further harm. In fact, Thomas informed me, Eros already had permission from Zeus to buy my freedom if I failed to return by the end of the week.

I slumped against the pillows. My body was exhausted, but how could I sleep in a place like this? All around me lay pain and deceit.

In the high pitch of the ceiling was a mural of a battle with mountains burning in the background. It was the overthrowing of the bandits, the battle that led to the creation of the Underworld. I looked up at the billowing smoke, so real it seemed to reach down to me, and I was so grateful that Eros had sent Titus to prepare me for this journey.

"You really should sleep," Thomas offered. When I shook my head, he asked, "Do you mind if I do?"

"Go ahead."

He crawled to the foot of the bed and curled up next to my feet. When he said he slept at Persephone's feet, I didn't know he meant it literally. I was willing to bet he was a light sleeper, too. One couldn't exist in a realm such as this and not have very deep-seated defenses. "No, Thomas." I leaned against the headboard and set a pillow in my lap.

"Merciful beauty," Thomas murmured and snuggled close to me.

I thumped him on the head. "Just go to sleep, and don't tell anyone I babied you."

I nodded off only to be awakened by the giving way of the bolt on the door. Someone was coming into the room. Thomas was still sound asleep with his hand resting on my knee. I set a hand on his shoulder, but he didn't awaken.

The guard who entered the room was the one who was welcomed home last night. His mouth dropped open in surprise when he saw me sitting up and Thomas sound asleep.

"My lady, Psyche. It looks as if you haven't slept."

"Is it... morning?" Without the sun, how could they tell?

"The queen is up, if that is what you mean." He couldn't take his eyes off Thomas, still sound asleep with his head in my lap.

I shook Thomas's shoulder, and he woke with a start. He greeted the guard with a nod. "Are you back in her favor?"

"I am. She's awake."

Thomas rubbed his eyes. "We'll be down." He waited until the guard was gone, then he turned to me with a yawn. "Congratulations. You've won your freedom." As he put on his sash and corded belt, he chattered cheerfully. "You'll never guess what I dreamed about last night."

"You're a guy," I said flatly, "Gee, let me think."

He ignored my sarcasm. "You and I were walking through a valley full of flowers. The grass was so deeply green, and it was damp from dew. I could feel the sun warming my skin." He closed his eyes for a moment. "I'd forgotten how beautiful the sun was."

The dream didn't depress him. On the contrary, it lifted his spirits. Now dressed, he kissed my hand. "You are such a beautiful woman, and it has nothing to do with that pretty face."

"I'll be right back," I told him. I went to the bathroom to find my own clothes. After he washed them, Thomas hung them on hooks to dry, but they were gone.

I searched behind the loose cupboard for my satchel. My fingers found the strap, and I pulled it from its hiding place. To my relief, it still contained the coin, my GPS watch and the food.

"Psyche?" Thomas knocked on the door, then slid it open. When I told him my clothes were missing, he said, "That's not surprising. The maids would have taken them while we were at the banquet."

"Will I get them back?"

"I doubt it. We should go now. It's rude to keep the queen waiting."

This time Thomas led me through the main hallway and down the grand staircase at the center of the castle. There were no sentries outside the throne room, but when Thomas opened the doors, we found the entire Royal Guard waiting with Persephone. My knees wobbled. Thomas took hold of my hand and led me down the long red carpet to Persephone's throne.

Persephone stood. I couldn't read the expression on her face. Was she angry or merely disappointed? Would she order the guards to take me captive anyway?

I tried to curtsy, my body somewhat numb. At my side Thomas knelt on one knee.

"Arise, Thomas," Persephone commanded.

He obeyed, and she came forward. The queen took his face in her hand and brought his eyes to meet hers. Persephone turned to me. "My dear girl, I sent you my favorite attendant. Look what you've done. Instead of letting him tempt you, you've warmed him to the very soul." She touched my hand. Her skin was like ice. "Now, touch him." She placed my hand on Thomas's arm. It was cool, but not cold.

Thomas trembled very slightly, and my heart ached for him. He had protected me, and now he would be punished.

I fell to my knees at Persephone's feet. "Please don't punish him. It isn't his fault. I didn't mean to anger you."

She laughed and tugged on my shoulders. "Angry? I'm delighted. You are welcome in my house anytime." She instructed an attendant to fetch the wooden box. As he placed it into her hands, I noticed the golden lock was missing. She opened the box and offered it to me. "Aphrodite's reward."

Inside the box was a vial of clear liquid. Atop the cork was a rose carved from frosted glass. "What is it?"

"Ambrosia. Drink and be immortal."

I took the box and thanked her, but closed the lid. "I didn't ask to be immortal. I just want to see Eros again. I'll take the box and this vial to him, and I'll let him choose my fate."

"That's a lot of faith to put in a man," Persephone said flatly. She dispersed the guard, except for Thomas, and bade me to sit with her awhile.

The only other chair in the room was the king's throne. "Yes, sit there," she commanded. "He never uses it anyway." Thomas stood beside her, and she brought his hand to her cheek and felt of his warmth. "I want to give you a gift," she declared. "What will you have?"

"I'd like Thomas to give me safe passage to the portal."

"That's all? I'll only let him go as far as the river Styx, but your request is granted. Tell me about your journey."

I told her how we flew by jet to Nepal and stayed in the city. I wasn't sure how familiar she was with the modern mortal world, so I tried to explain as best I could. Thomas was absolutely captivated. The world had changed a great deal since he tilled the earth as a child.

"I'm very surprised that Aphrodite sent Titus to accompany you," the queen said.

"She didn't. Titus abandoned his post. He grew tired of Theron's jealousy and his punishments."

Persephone nodded. "Would you like to trade?"

Confused, I clarified, "Thomas for Titus?" Knowing I couldn't lie to her, I had to speak carefully so I didn't offend her. "Titus has been with me a single week. I've only begun to explore his talents. And he's committed no crime."

Persephone gazed up at Thomas, who rubbed her shoulders "The innocent ones stay warm the longest. It took Thomas a full two ages before he went cold."

If I understood her correctly, she just admitted Thomas was innocent of the crime for which he was sent here. If she knew he was innocent, why wouldn't she set him free? Of course, the answer stood right there in front of me. Thomas was her favorite. Knowing he was undeserving of his fate probably made her like him more.

If an innocent man had been punished for the murder, what happened to the killer? I looked up at the soft light in Thomas's eyes. I should have known the first moment I saw him that he was innocent. The man who killed Titus's father had always been free. He'd nearly killed Titus, and he'd nearly killed me.

To Persephone I said, "You probably wouldn't enjoy Titus all that much. I'm led to believe he's not Aphrodite's best student. If you want the real prize, it's Theron you're after."

This piqued her interest. "Oh? What dealings have you had with Theron?"

"I've met him after each task. He's volatile, to be sure, but..." I repeated Titus's words exactly, so that it wasn't a lie. "...when he wants to be, he's as gentle as a summer breeze. At least, that's what I'm told."

She made me recount all my dealings with Theron from our first meeting at the Fortress. I worried she would find me insincere, so I was as honest as possible. I explained how I was sick from the dust when I went to get the second task, and that Theron had a small feast waiting for me. I told her that he offered me the white fruit if I accepted his bed, and that when I refused, he beat me so severely I could barely call for help.

She made me recount the story a second time and repeat to her every word exchanged between us. I was embarrassed to tell her that I called Theron a "boy toy," especially with Thomas standing right there. Surprisingly, he wasn't angry. He just shook his head and muttered, "Suicide."

"So, let me make sure I understand you," Persephone said. "He offered you the sacred fruit with the condition that you allow him to consummate the bargain?" When I nodded, she asked, "Do you have any idea what you've just told me?"

I shrugged. "He wanted what most guys want."

"I see." She turned to Thomas. "Our guest has been through quite an ordeal, and it looks as if she's hardly slept. I think you should escort her back now." She asked what was in my satchel.

"An Olympian coin and food for the mutt," I replied. I carefully stowed Aphrodite's box in the satchel, too.

"Go, then." She squeezed my hand in a friendly way. "I look forward to hearing the news of your wedding."

When we were out the gates of the city, I asked Thomas what happened the night of the murder, and I wasn't surprised by the story he told. He had stolen into the palace, desperate to see Aphrodite. She neglected him for months, and he didn't know why. He went to the palace unarmed hoping to sneak into the upper rooms and catch her alone, but the palace guards were alerted of an intruder before he cleared the main level. He fled down a dark set of stairs. It led into a forge, where Thomas found a man pounding steel into a breastplate.

Beyond the forge were cave passages. Thomas fled into these, but by then two of the guards were after him. When they caught him, he expected to be killed, but the tall blond guard stabbed the older man, then dragged Thomas back into the forge, where the rest of the palace guards were waiting. They all knelt around the unconscious blacksmith, who had been stabbed in the back three times.

"I caught him," Theron said. "Here is the murderer."

The trial before Zeus boiled down to Theron's word against a mortal, and Thomas was declared guilty.

"Is there any way you could be freed from this place?" I asked.

"Not unless Zeus himself ordered my release." Thomas kicked at the dirt sadly. "You know what I would wish for if I could leave?"

"Revenge on Theron?"

Thomas shook his head. "I would return to my homeland, grow old and die when it was my time. Death isn't so bad, you know." His eyes roamed across the scenes of suffering around us. "It can't be worse than this."

We reached the burning platforms, and the foul stench wrenched my empty belly. Thomas offered me his sash, and I held it over my nose until we reached the giant dog, Cerberus. Once past him, Thomas stopped me. He took a coin from the satchel and placed it carefully under my tongue. His fingers lingered on my lips, and he leaned forward and kissed my cheek. "Thank you," he whispered, "for bringing me back to life."

"I won't forget you, Thomas."

I paid the boatman Charon with the coin from my lips. As he ferried me across the river Styx, Thomas stood on the bank and watched me go. I raised my hand and waved good-bye.

As we docked on the other side of the river, an icy hand reached far out of the water. The fingers were narrow and bony with overly long, broken nails. When I tried to step onto the dock, the hand grasped my foot. The fingernails cut into my skin.

I jerked my foot away, but the damage was done.

I looked down at the person in the water, who showed his red-marked hand to the others. They all began to shout in a frenzy. "Red-blood! Red-blood!"

The sentries turned abruptly, whips in hand.

"RUN!" Thomas screamed from the other shore. *"RUN!"*

# CHAPTER 29

Both black-clothed sentries started toward me. I jumped from the dock and ran for the giant staircase, where I took the stairs two at a time.

One sentry pushed the other out of the way and took the lead in the chase. He was faster than me and gained ground with every turn of the stairs.

I pulled the satchel over one shoulder and used my hands to push me up the steps faster, but I was pulled to my knees. The sentry caught my feet and tried to pull me down to the shore.

I kicked furiously, freed my feet and left my sandals in his hands. Barefoot, I could move faster. My feet gripped the warm stone. I pulled up the cumbersome dress so I could take longer strides.

Would the portal still be open when I reached it?

Both sentries clamoring at my heels, I reached the platform, where cold wind signaled the opening to the frozen mortal world. All that lay between me and freedom were the enormous monsters who stood guard at the portal. I slowed to a walk and started toward the portal, ignoring the guards as I did on the way in. Behind me rose a shout. "Don't let the girl escape. She's a red-blood!"

Now alert, the sentries stepped together so they barred the exit. Each held a long, spear-tipped staff.

Panting up the stairs behind me was the river sentry. Once he got his hands on me, I would be doomed. Spears were the better option. I moved toward the portal just as the river guard reached the landing. "Grab her," he commanded.

One of the monsters stepped from the doorway and swung at me with an enormous paw of a hand. I dove between his legs and slid into the snow.

Now past the portal, my eyes saw only the stone of the cave's wall. My skin immediately stung from the cold. I was barefoot in a sleeveless dress, and it was storming beyond the cave. If Titus wasn't nearby, I would freeze to death in minutes.

While I couldn't see the sentries anymore, I could still hear their voices. "Let us pass!" they demanded. "No one will know we left the boundaries of the kingdom. Look! She's right there. We'll grab her and bring her back."

A second voice added, "We'll share her with you. When we've taken what we want from her, we'll dump her body in the Styx."

Storm or no storm, I got up and ran. Their heavy footsteps followed. As soon as I stepped from the mouth of the cave, I was blind. It was snowing so hard I couldn't see the tent at the end of the dale. I couldn't even see the forbidding stone wall around the valley. I stumbled and fell. My body rolled off the slope, and I sprawled into the snow disoriented.

"There she is! Hurry and grab her!"

I pulled myself up and staggered forward. The ice under my feet felt like knives shredding my skin. Where was Titus? If I reached the tent, could he save me from the sentries?

A dark figure appeared before me. It had to be him. I ran harder, only to reach the figure and realize it was a jagged stone pillar. Beyond it, the mountain fell away into oblivion. I had run the wrong way. I wasn't anywhere near the tent. I was on the outer perimeter, and in this weather, Titus couldn't see me. Worse, the demons were veiled.

"She's on the fence," the sentry said. They moved closer.

I rummaged through the satchel for Aphrodite's box. I couldn't dodge an enemy that I couldn't see. Ambrosia would give me immortal eyes.

The voice that spoke next was just an arm's reach away. "Come away from the fence, girl. You don't want to freeze out here. We'll take you inside where it's nice and warm."

Footsteps crunched closer, but the falling snow was too thick for me to distinguish them.

"That's not solid ground under your feet. It's an ice shelf. Come back to us, and we'll save you," the sentry said.

I could no longer feel my feet or my nose. If it was ambrosia I held in my hands, it would heal my body. It would show me the immortals hunting me. It would possibly save me long enough to find my way to the tent and my boots and my coat.

"Grab her now!"

I put the vial to my lips and drank.

Icy hands grabbed me around the waist and pulled me off my feet, but the sentry didn't appear in my sight. He threw me over his invisible shoulder.

Something was terribly wrong. My lungs constricted, and my muscles flailed into a spasm. I choked. No air came when I tried to breathe.

The ground moaned beneath the guard and me. He took another step toward the cave, and the ice shook. With a thunderous snap, the shelf gave way. The sentry roared, but it was too late. We fell through the air. Far below and coming too fast was the floor of the crevasse. Mercifully, the poison pulled me into unconsciousness before we landed.

Eros shouted my name. I wasn't dreaming, just floating somewhere in darkness, unable to surface, unable to sink. He shook my shoulders, then poured sweet liquid into my mouth. "Wake up! You can't do this to me now!" More liquid ran over my lips. He gave me another hard shake. "Psyche, open your eyes!" His voice was frantic. "Please," he begged, "come back to me."

I willed my eyes to open, just to please him. All I managed was a flutter that gave me a glimpse of his worried face. I murmured his name as he lifted me into his arms, and I slumped against him, weak and mostly lifeless, as he hefted me onto a wet, furry back that I knew was Pixis. "Get us off this mountain," he said. The horse's strides rocked us as we gained momentum and launched into the air.

I found myself in Theron's house, but I didn't know how I'd gotten there. Men were crowded in the foyer and the living room, all murmuring and stealing hungry looks at me. The Hades sentries were there, some with whips in their hands, others wore masks like they did at the gates of the city. Theron paraded me through the throng, his iron grip bruising my arm. When I tried to pull away, he squeezed tighter. He forced me upstairs, and suddenly we were standing on a cliff. Theron dragged me to the edge and made me look down. Eros lay below, his limbs contorted, his body lifeless. Through my mind echoed demonic laughter.

"NO!" The sound of my own voice woke me. I thrashed against ropes that held me bound, only to realize they were sheets and a blanket.

"Finally," Eros murmured. "You've been out for hours."

My heart pounded. The ceiling fan spun slowly above and the fragrance of exotic flowers floated through the open window. It was night, and the lights were off, but a soft glow came from the adjoining bathroom. We were at the cottage in Hawaii.

I blinked at the ceiling. "What happened?"

"You drank poison."

"I saw you." Even in my grogginess, I remembered that glimpse of violet eyes.

"You think so?" He reached over and took my hand, then held it up so I could see my fingers intertwined with his. The ring was back on his finger, and it shimmered in the dim light.

I closed my eyes, unwilling to turn my head and look at his face. "The sentry? I fell…"

"The fall killed him instantly, which is why you're still alive. Your body is fine." That irresistible chuckle escaped him. "I poured enough ambrosia down you to cure cancer."

I bolted up. "You didn't! It will make me…"

"More beautiful. I didn't think it possible, but it did." He tugged on my hand. "Psyche, aren't you going to look?"

I couldn't explain my reluctance. I had seen him before, but now I didn't want anything between us to change. I understood that what I felt for him on sight might be caused by the dust, and I only wanted what was real.

Slowly I turned to face him, and he smiled. Every ounce of worry melted. Warm affection and indescribable love shivered through me. I grew dizzy. I forgot to breathe when he smiled.

"It was torture not touching you while you slept. You are such a temptation."

"It's just the dust," I countered. "It made you sick, too."

"Didn't Aeas tell you? I'm immune to the dust, just like my mother. The first time I came to your school, I spilled it on myself. I fell in love with you, and I convinced myself the dust did it. But all along it was just you."

"Well, I spilled it on myself, and you said…"

He covered my lips with his fingers and sighed. "I was wrong. I knew you were afraid, but I hid from you, convinced that you should love me blindly. I also knew you loved me, which made your betrayal painful, but you were right. It was unfair of me to hide when you'd already offered so much of yourself to me."

I leaned back on one elbow. "How many times did you practice that speech?"

"Hundreds. Was it good enough?" His eyes sparkled mischievously. The strange color and the intensity of his gaze fit so well with the voice and personality I loved.

"I suppose it will do."

"Anyway..." He twirled a lock of my hair around his finger. "The effects of the dust won't survive a bout with Firelake poison, so you're cured."

"Is that why I'm not attracted to you anymore?" I asked innocently.

Shock drained the color from his face. "You're... not..."

I could only hold a serious expression for a moment, but in that instant, I saw in his eyes uncertainty and grief. I couldn't torture him. I broke into laughter, and his mouth drew a hard line.

He rolled over and pinned me under his body. He dug his fingers into my sides and made me squirm. "You horrible, horrible girl! I'll tickle you until you cry for mercy."

"Mercy!" I howled.

"I want tears." He grabbed for my foot.

I wiggled one arm free and pulled his face toward mine. "Mercy," I whispered, my lips grazing his.

"Cheater," he replied before he kissed me. His arms snaked around me and held me tight.

"Wait!" I pushed away. "I'm not fainting."

"Ambrosia," he muttered, pulling me back.

The door burst open. "I bought all the steak they had at the... Oh, she's awake," Aeas said.

I tried to pull away, but Eros wouldn't let me go. He kissed me until I gave in completely, then pulled back an inch and licked his lips. "We're busy."

I set my palms against his chest. "Did he say steak?"

Eros rolled his eyes and relinquished his grip. "We'll go broke trying to feed this girl. I'll have to double the size of my herds."

"I don't eat mutton," I replied as I swung my legs over the side of bed

"You'd eat it if Eudora cooked it," Eros said. "She does wonders with mutton."

I was positively famished. If Aeas had ten steaks downstairs, I could probably eat all of them. When we reached the kitchen, Eros gave my shoulder a shove and sent me staggering to the side. "Out of the way. The spoiled prince can broil steaks."

Aeas's eyebrows arched. "You called him a spoiled prince?" He turned to Eros, amused. "Want me to throw her in the dungeon?"

"You have a dungeon?" After all I'd seen in Hades, the thought made me shiver. "Please tell me you don't actually put people into it."

Eros set five steaks on a broiler pan and put them in the oven. "I might put you in it."

I rummaged through the grocery bag, where I found a bunch of bananas. "Some God of Love you turned out to be."

Eros leaned so close our cheeks touched. He whispered, "Stay with me through another storm and find out." He smiled at the flush that ran up my neck and into my cheeks.

I avoided his eyes. "Where's Titus?"

"Probably still in the bathtub," Aeas replied. "That's where he's been all night."

"Will you tell him I'm awake, and I'd like to see him?"

Aeas left the room, and I turned to Eros once again. "Was he waiting for me in the tent?"

"Yes, he was half-frozen this morning when I arrived. I tried to send him to Apollo, but he wouldn't leave until I was ready to abandon hope of your return."

"Thomas told me you were prepared to bargain for my release if I couldn't return."

Eros took me into his arms. "Surrendering myself to Persephone would be less torture than watching you suffer." He kissed me until someone at the doorway coughed.

It was Titus, of course. He leaned against the door post, and when I approached, he threw an uneasy glance at Eros, then grabbed me. He hugged me hard. "You made it. I can't believe you actually made it." He let me go and kissed my hand.

"Such little faith in your mistress," I said, and Titus grinned. He was still my friend, and he'd won not only my trust, but Eros's, too. "Sounds like you tried to die on me."

He waved my concern away with his hand. "So, you're one of us now. We're headed to the palace in Eros's kingdom?"

I shook my head. "No, I need to go home."

"Not tonight," Eros answered. "The poison is still in your system. You have to stay awake or you'll spend the night in relentless nightmares."

"But my dad…"

"…received a text from you this afternoon," Eros said. "You apologized for running away and said you'd be home tomorrow."

Much as I missed my dad, I didn't mind avoiding him for another night. The reunion wouldn't be pretty. "He's going to ground me until I die."

Titus shook his head in disbelief. "You can't send her home. Not looking like that."

Instinctively, I touched my face. "What's wrong with me?"

"She's a riot waiting to happen," Titus muttered.

Eros dropped a kiss onto my hair. "Her father will be reasonable, I'm sure."

"I can't go home?" I persisted.

"You can go home, but you probably don't want anyone but your dad to see you." Eros's eyes softened. "It was the only way to save your life. I couldn't lose you again."

I slid my hand into his. "You're burning the steaks."

# CHAPTER 30

I was so tired my vision blurred, but Eros wouldn't let me sleep. It was almost three in the morning. Aeas had been gone for hours. He bolted out the door the moment Eros said he could return to the kingdom, and he took Titus with him. They crossed into Olympus and were flying home on horseback.

Eros and I sat on the same bed where I awoke earlier. I had taken a long bath and changed clothes. I no longer had to worry about invisible intruders. The ambrosia gave me immortal eyes. I could see Eros even if he was veiled.

"There are things I still don't understand about your world," I said.

"Sit up and look at me, so you don't fall asleep, and I'll tell you whatever you want to know."

I scooted away from the wall, crossed my legs and sat knee to knee with him. "What if I still nod off?"

He ran his hand over my knee. "Then I'll resort to more underhanded methods of keeping you awake."

I shook my head. "Forbidden fruit."

From his pocket he drew out a chain and familiar pendant. "Not anymore."

"Do you still want me for a wife?" I asked.

He fastened the pendant around my head and secured the second chain so that it stayed in place. "More than ever."

I yawned. "Why did Gina choose a mortal life? Aeas wouldn't say anything except that she had no right to send me to Aphrodite. Gina said she misses Aeas every day."

His expression saddened. "Yes, I suppose she does, but he won't visit her. Before he was just too stubborn. Now I think he's afraid. He can't bring himself to see her as an old woman."

"Was he in love with her?" My head sagged wearily to the side, and I could barely keep my eyes on him as he spoke.

Finally relenting, Eros stretched out his legs and pulled me between them, then tucked my head under his chin so I could rest against his chest. "No, it wasn't that kind of love. She's his sister. His twin."

"Why did she leave your world?" All my strength fled. If it weren't for his arms around me, I'd have fallen over.

"Her love was killed, and she wanted to die." He hugged me tighter. "I never understood her choice until today."

"I can't stay awake," I murmured.

"You can sleep now. I'll wake you if you tremble in your dreams."

"One more question," I mumbled, barely coherent. "Where are your wings?"

"On Pixis." He shrugged. "I've never understood why your mythology gave wings to me and no one else. Every immortal with a horse can fly..." His voice slipped away as my eyes fell closed.

I awoke but didn't open my eyes, too afraid the memories surfacing were imagined and I would find myself home in my bedroom, sketchbook in my hands and an imperfect resemblance of Eros on the page. I lay perfectly still and listened for my dad in the kitchen or the neighbor's dog barking. Instead I heard a sleepy groan and felt a body shift beside me. The seams of our jeans caught as he rolled over. A hand found my belly and rested there. I opened my eyes.

Eros was still there, asleep and glorious in the sunlight, his hair tousled and his T-shirt rumpled. I drew the hair back from his forehead and pressed my lips there. He didn't stir. I didn't know if I would ever get used to looking at him. He would never cease to thrill me. I ran my fingers over the skin on his muscular arm. I still couldn't believe I could see him while I touched his so-familiar skin.

On the floor outside the bathroom was a duffle bag full of Eros's clothes. Handled paper bags next to it held women's clothes with tags printed in Italian. There was a silk camisole, a cashmere sweater and stylish wool slacks, all sized 4 tall. A smaller plastic bag held socks, a modest pair of panties and a bra, which was the right size. I didn't even want to know how he came upon that knowledge. A shoebox at the bottom held a gorgeous pair of leather slip-ons. I knew enough fashion to recognize the designer and the expensive leather. Eros was prepared for everything, it seemed. And he had amazing taste.

I stole into the bathroom to change. I was thrilled by the clothes. Savannah would have been so proud—and jealous, of course. I had never bought clothes like this for myself. I had never wanted to turn heads or flatter my figure. Today I was delighted to slip into the outfit and beautiful shoes knowing Eros bought them just for me.

When I came out of the bathroom, he was sitting up in bed rubbing his eyes. "Now there's a sight to wake up to."

I turned a practiced circle. "When were you in Italy?"

"Last week, getting the task from my mother."

I smoothed the wool of the pants with my fingers. "I'm so proud of you."

"...for getting the sizes right," he finished.

"For not buying skimpy underwear," I countered.

He laughed as he rose and stretched. While he showered, I scrambled eggs and cut fruit for breakfast. I had just set two plates on the table when Eros came downstairs wearing slacks and a dress shirt. He laid a wool blazer over the back of a chair.

He buttoned the cuffs on his shirt. "Do I look fit to meet my future father-in-law?"

"You're going to let him see you?" I should have been flattered that he would allow my dad to see him, and of course, it would prove I didn't invent Erik in the first place, but the thought of introducing my dad to a real boyfriend after having run away for a week didn't seem like a good idea.

Eros took my hands. "He'll be sensible."

"Easy for you to say." I pushed the plates aside, no longer hungry.

Eros sat me at the table and scooted a plate in front of me. He took the other plate and sat beside me. Undaunted, he forked eggs into his mouth and waited until I did the same. "He'll only have to take one look at you to realize I'm right about taking you away."

"What about finishing high school and going to college?" I asked.

"You were planning to move to a campus full of hungry young men without your dad, and you thought that would make you happy?" His tone was cutting.

"I like learning. I don't want to spend my life being ignorant."
I was already at a disadvantage with Eros without being a high
school drop-out.

"What were you planning to study?"

I shrugged. "Business, maybe."

He set his fork down. "You wanted to learn about business
more than anything else?"

"Well, no, but a business degree is pretty safe when it comes to
finding a job."

Eros shook his head. "Learning isn't the same as finding a job.
If you could study whatever you wanted without worrying about
finding a job later, what would you study?"

I could see where this was going. "Art. I'd learn to draw things
as I see them. Learn to paint like the murals in your palace."

"I can offer you more than any university: master artisans and
craftsmen, the history of two worlds, every concept of math and science in your world and mine." He nibbled on an orange and smiled
playfully. "And later, if you still want a job, I'll send you out to
herd sheep."

"Gee, how could I refuse?"

"Plus, I'll be with you every day, and we'll never have to hide."
He took my hand. "Tell me that's worth more than a high school
diploma."

"I'll have to learn your language first."

"Yes." He leaned over and murmured in my ear a phrase I'd
heard him speak before while I lay in his arms. He pressed his lips
to my hand and translated, "My heart and soul."

The six-hour flight wasn't nearly long enough. I was so worried
about seeing my dad that I was ready to take off to Olympus and
avoid the whole thing completely. Eros, however, was dead set on
asking for my hand in marriage, so he insisted we go to my father's
house as soon as we landed in Montana.

When the anxiety over this meeting threatened to drive me
crazy, Eros took me into the stateroom and distracted me. Before I
realized it, we were landing.

He drove me home in my own car, which had been sitting
inside the jet's hanger. I offered to drive so he could disappear,
but he refused. Usually he wore blue contacts if he had to be seen

anywhere in the mortal word, but today he left them out, ready to show my dad his face as it really was. Eros's eyes were proof that he was no mere mortal.

The afternoon was growing gray as we left the airport. After so many extraordinary adventures, this short drive together seemed so normal. He reached across the center console and took my hand while he hummed with the radio. I wondered if this was why he had fallen in love with me and no one else. I understood the part of him which so enjoyed this mortal world, its flaws and its wonderful technology.

My dad's pickup was not at the curb when we arrived. Eros climbed out of the car with a stern order for me to stay where I was, then he came around and opened the door for me. That sort of chivalry made me feel foolish, but I allowed it. We walked hand in hand up the sidewalk.

The neighborhood was deserted. The neighbor's old Jeep was in her driveway, and across the street was an '82 pickup that never moved. I doubted it even ran anymore. My fifteen minutes of fame was over, and even the paparazzi had finally moved on.

Inside we waited. Eros sat calmly on the couch leaning forward with his fingertips pressed together while I paced. He followed me with his eyes, back and forth. At last he sighed, stood and crossed into the kitchen. He came back and offered me the phone. "Call him and tell him you're home."

All I managed to say after the single ring was, "Dad, it's me."

Dad replied, "I'm on my way," and hung up. Seven excruciating minutes later his truck rumbled up the block.

I turned to Eros, terrified. "Maybe you should... disappear."

Before my eyes he turned a little fuzzy. Not understanding what happened, I looked around, but everything else was clear.

Eros rested his hands on my shoulders. "He can't see me."

When the door swung open, I saw a mixture of fury and fear in my dad's face. His eyes narrowed as he slowly closed the door and stepped toward me.

Guilt made me want to hide, but Eros gave me a shove and I stumbled forward, right into my dad's open arms. I couldn't remember the last time he really hugged me, but he squeezed me in his tough arms, the smell of cold weather and sweat on his coat. When he stepped back and looked at my face, really looked, he put his hands on my cheeks and his forehead puckered in confusion. "What happened to you?"

"Dad, there's someone I want you to meet. This is Eros."

He looked over my shoulder and instinctively shoved me to the side, ready to put himself between me and the danger. Then he blinked, more confused. "You?"

"Hello, Ron," Eros replied.

"Wait a minute. You guys know each other?" I demanded.

"We met once..." Eros began.

"...a long time ago," Dad finished. He looked at me then back to Eros. "It was you? You're Erik?"

Eros nodded, no trace of shame in his admission.

I nearly burst for fury. "You said you didn't believe me! You were going to ship me off to a mental hospital!"

"He only saw me once, Psyche," Eros explained. "He didn't know about my world or the portal."

"You left her out in the snow." Dad's eyes grew angry.

"About that," Eros replied, "can I say one thing in my defense before you try to kill me?"

Dad folded his arms across his chest.

"Her car was ten feet away. The keys were in the ignition. I had no idea she'd sit out in the cold all night like an imbecile."

"Hey, whose side are you on?" I exclaimed.

"On this one issue," Eros said, "his." He took my hand and made no effort to hide the gesture from my father.

"Where have you been for the past week and a half?" He eyed the two of us warily.

I didn't know how to explain wolves, flying to Nepal, nearly freezing to death on a mountain, and then travelling into the belly of the earth to find the kingdom of Hades. From Eros, I learned some things are better left unsaid. "I've been trying to win his mother's approval."

Dad's eyebrows shot up. "Did you?"

Before I could scoff, Eros said, "Yes, she succeeded. Now it's my turn." He drew something from his pocket and kept it covered in his fist until my dad put out his hand. Eros dropped a velvet pouch into Dad's palm.

Dad opened the pouch and poured out its lone content: a ring. It was a rectangular diamond swirled in an intricate gold setting.

To one side was a figure clearly representing Eros with a quill full of arrows slung across his back. He reached across the diamond and touched a gold heart, which was set in the stone's center. On the other side, reaching back, was a maid with flowing hair. Their hands met over the heart. Though the entire setting was no bigger than my thumbnail, the detail of the people was lifelike down to their eyelashes and fingernails. "My mother's husband made it for us."

After studying it, Dad slid it back into the pouch. "She's too young for this." He dropped the pouch into Eros's hand.

"I'll give her all the time she wants, but not here. She isn't safe outside your home. Let me take her to a place where no one will stare at her or make her feel afraid."

I could see the war in my Dad's eyes. "You'll never come back?" he asked.

"Of course I'll come back, Dad. I'll come every Thanksgiving and Father's Day. I'll come home every time I have a craving for a good steak and homemade lemonade."

"What if I need to talk to you?"

Eros offered him a card with a cell phone number printed on it. "Just call me. The voice mail says Erik Savage, but it's me. I check my messages every couple of days." He threw me a sideways glance. "That is, if she'll let me leave long enough to check them."

"Psyche, go upstairs while I talk to Eros alone."

I left the room, but stayed on the bottom step where I could hear them.

"Do you really love her?" Dad asked.

Eros sank onto the arm of the recliner. "So much it makes me sick."

Dad chuckled. "I think that was my line. I was only seventeen, and you said I didn't have anything you wanted in return for that favor."

"Back then you didn't have anything I wanted. How was I to know your daughter would be the only woman in two worlds who could win my heart?"

"Did you trick her?"

"You mean did I dust her the way I dusted Patricia so she wanted you?"

The name stuck in my mind. Patricia was my dad's high school sweetheart, the cheerleader who dumped him in front of the trophy case, the same woman who married a cheating lawyer and later divorced.

"No. I didn't even let her see me. And I told you back then it would only last a few weeks. I didn't lie. Everything that happened afterward was real."

Dad stuffed his hands into his jeans pockets. "It was too long ago."

Eros's voice was sympathetic. "Psyche has made me a believer in second chances."

I peeked my head around the wall, and Eros saw me. He glared and motioned me upstairs, so I went reluctantly to my room and looked around. If I was leaving for good, what should I take? I pulled out one of my suitcases. My clothes were mostly useless in Eros's world, so I took only the two designer dresses I bought in Italy. I packed toiletries and the photo album from my childhood, which was filled with pictures of my dad and me. An additional album held photos of my friends, mostly Savannah, and a few stray certificates from school. I stuffed it on top. I left behind my modeling portfolio, my yearbooks and my current textbooks, which were still in my backpack. I didn't know what Dad would tell people. Maybe he would say I went away to boarding school or that I went back to Europe. It didn't matter what excuse he made.

I took one last look out the window to the back yard where I played since I was three. So many of my memories were of summer evenings spent there with my dad. Leaving was harder than I imagined.

Downstairs I found Dad and Eros at the bar sharing a plate of nachos. It was odd and completely unexpected. They sat there and talked like old friends. "Why are you still so young?" my dad asked.

Eros wiped his fingers on a towel. "I'm immortal."

"Psyche will be, too?"

"Yes, she is a little already." Eros didn't explain why, but Dad guessed at the proof.

"That's why she's prettier today."

When I came into the room, Eros stood. "You're ready to go?"

My throat felt dry. I didn't want to cry. "Yeah."

Dad hugged me again, then apologized. "I can't even send you off with a Christmas present. I haven't done any shopping."

Christmas Eve was only days away, and my sudden and unexpected absence showed in the fact that Dad hadn't put up a tree or hung a single string of lights. "It's okay, Dad. All I want is your blessing."

He put his arm around my shoulders. "You've got it." When he offered his hand to Eros, he said, "Take care of my girl."

Dad held on until Eros answered, "Every day of my life."

On the front porch I took a deep breath and looked into Eros's beautiful eyes. "Give me the ring."

He slipped it on my finger. "Can we get in the car before your neighbors see me?"

When we were safely locked in the Subaru, I turned to him. "There's something I need to talk to you about before we get to Olympus." Once we reached the palace, we would be flocked by people. Who knew what the kingdom was planning to celebrate our soon-to-be wedding?

"Titus already told me I have to buy you a horse of your own."

I wished it was that simple. "Do you think Zeus will give me a gift for our wedding?"

"He most assuredly will." Eros put the Subaru into gear and drove out of the neighborhood. "Considering the burden you're taking off his hands, I expect it will be something very expensive."

"I don't want something expensive. I want something priceless."

Now I drew real concern from him. "Speak, Psyche."

"You have to promise not to tell Titus. I want a man's life."

# CHAPTER 31

I sat before a gold-framed mirror on the upper level of the palace. A maid newly brought from the village braided my hair. She was sixteen and gorgeous. I picked her myself. I didn't understand a single word she said, but I saw in her a gentle temperament and a strong will. However, that was not why I picked her to be my maid. She had dark, wavy hair and skin a shade darker than the golden complexion of our kingdom. Her eyes were green, and she was well-built—shorter than me and curvy. Titus was with me in the village when I first saw her. He couldn't keep his eyes off her.

The following week, he pressed Eros to give him a pendant. Since he had given up his place in another kingdom, his citizenship had to be established by Eros's hand. Eros had assigned the gems, and the pendant was being forged, but it had to be ratified before the governing council of the kingdom before it became official. The moment Titus took possession of that pendant, I had no doubt he would hand it off to my maid if she would have it.

A soft knock came from the door, and Eudora appeared. "His Highness, Judge Zeus, has arrived."

I jumped to my feet. "Already? Where's Eros?"

"On his way up from the valley. He saw the horses flying in."

"Get Aeas for me."

Zeus had very few dealings with the mortal world anymore, so he didn't speak English. I needed a translator if I was to greet him. I hoped Titus was still in the village, where I sent him this morning.

With my new maid at my side, I descended to the foyer to greet Zeus. I was not at all surprised by his mighty stature or the grandeur of his personage. In our mythology, he was the king of the Gods. He was, in fact, the most powerful man in all of Olympus and had been for ages. Wisdom and kindness shone in his eyes. He was the first man in all of Eros's world that I had seen with a beard.

It was white and lightly waved. Atop his head were unruly white curls. He would have been blonde and stunning in his youth.

Standing at Zeus's shoulder was my wedding gift. He wore a scarlet cloak around his shoulders, a gift from Persephone I was sure. The black half-robe of Hades had been exchanged for a white, long-sleeved Olympian robe and warm boots from Apollo's kingdom, but he still wore a scarlet sash. His head bowed meekly as he waited for me to greet Zeus.

Aeas arrived at the foyer just as I reached the bottom of the stairs. I curtsied before the Judge, and bid him welcome. Aeas translated.

Zeus came and took me by the hands. "So this is the lovely Psyche, who caused so much commotion the past few months. I've heard of nothing but your goodness, your strength and your beauty."

"I'm sure Eros exaggerated," I replied.

"I never exaggerate," came the reply from across the room. Eros crossed the foyer toward us. He greeted Zeus with a firm hug. "It's been too long since I welcomed you into my house."

"Well, I plan to return in a few months to celebrate your marriage. Do you think you might be able to get that pendant off her head?"

Eros folded his arms across his chest. "I'm working on that."

Zeus stepped aside and motioned to the other man. "The gift you requested for your wedding hardly seems any gift at all. You've done me a service by righting a wrong. Persephone admitted fully that she's always known his innocence. And..." he added. "...no one can lie to Persephone."

Now acknowledged, Thomas moved forward, threw his arms around me and whispered, "I dined with Apollo last night. This morning I saw the sun rise over snow-capped mountains. How can I ever thank you?" His eyes glistened, but he held his tears.

"You don't have to thank me."

Thomas dropped to one knee before Eros, then took the hem of Eros's robe and kissed it. "My Lord."

"Thomas," Eros replied, "you're a free man. You don't have to bow to me. Psyche, take him upstairs."

I took Thomas to the bedroom that used to be mine. I was sharing Eros's now, even though we had not officially married. Since I brought no clothes of my own, I raided Aeas's closet downstairs for Thomas. I laid out for him a pair of jeans, a T-shirt and a button-down shirt. It was the stylish plaid one Aeas picked the day he came to stay with me. Aeas also gave Thomas a leather jacket since it was winter. Shoes were more difficult. Aeas's were too small, and Eros's were too big. I didn't dare take any of Titus's, so I gave Aeas instructions to stop for shoes before they left Bozeman.

"Your homeland has changed a great deal since you left, Thomas." In the duffle bag I packed for Thomas, I included two history books from Eros's library, a literature book and an art history book. "We didn't know where in England you were from, so we bought you a village in the north. It was the only one for sale right now."

"A village?" Thomas's eyes widened.

"Yes. You own all of it. Everyone who lives there will pay rent to you. That will be your living. There is also a nice caretaker's home on the property for you to live in. Aeas will be flying with you to England in the same jet that took me to Nepal. He'll see that you're settled and have everything you need."

He blinked in amazement. "You didn't have to do this for me. I just wanted to live free and die."

"And you will, but you'll live comfortably. Your freedom is my gift to you. The village is Eros's."

I waited in the hallway while he changed clothes. Then I walked him through all the toiletries in his bag—deodorant, shaving cream, modern razors, after shave, lotion and hair gel. I put gel in his hair and styled it so that he looked like a normal twenty-one year old. When I finished, I was looking at a guy who could easily send Holden Valentine to the unemployment office.

"Are you ready?" I asked.

"No." Thomas pulled me into his arms and kissed me on the mouth. His lips were cool, and I knew that given some time, he would be warm again. "Now I'm ready to leave Olympus."

Downstairs we found Zeus and Eros in the great hall. Aeas wore mortal clothes and was ready to take Thomas home. "She didn't tell me that," Aeas said, "but she might have told Titus."

I was about to ask what was going on when I heard a door slam in the kitchen. Titus stormed into the room. "So, it's true," he said.

"You had Zeus free my father's killer as a wedding gift?" His hands balled into fists. "How could you betray me like this?"

Eros moved closer to me, and at my shoulder, Thomas's body went taut. His looks were deceiving. He was a bodyguard as much as a lover.

"Titus," I said gently, "I want to speak with you about this privately."

"No!" He pulled the sash from his shoulder and threw it at my feet. "Release me from my oath."

"No," I replied firmly.

"Release me! I cannot serve you anymore."

"But you will," I answered. "Wait in the orchard. I will deal with you later."

He might not have obeyed if Zeus and Eros weren't standing nearby. As it was, he was compelled by his oath to do my will. He glared at Thomas then started back to the kitchen.

Thomas raised his voice loud enough for Titus to hear. "Maybe you should have sold him when you had the chance."

Titus spun around. "What did you say?"

"Queen Persephone offered Psyche a handsome price for you," Thomas replied.

I elbowed Thomas. "Handsome is a relative term."

"Is he lying?" Titus demanded.

"No. Persephone wanted you, and I wouldn't give you up."

Titus's demeanor changed. The fury gave way to shock. He left more quickly than he came.

I turned to Thomas. "Have a safe journey. I have to make amends with my man servant."

"Not just yet," Eros said. "I'm sorry, Psyche, but Zeus has brought with him serious legal charges from Persephone. Thomas will have to delay his journey another day. You will both be asked to speak at the trial."

"Me?" I exclaimed. "Why me?"

Eros continued, "Go make amends with Titus and bring him back. Aeas, I have an errand for you in the mortal world. Since he's already dressed, you can take Thomas if you like. He might enjoy seeing the town. It will make tomorrow's trip less of a shock."

I found Titus sitting on a stump pulling a twig into shards. When I said his name, he stood and prepared to bow. "Don't bother," I replied. "Just walk with me." I walked to the far end of the orchard. It stood on the same plateau as the palace, which dropped hundreds of feet to the valley. Here, free of the trees, you could see the village and miles of ocean. I had to hold onto a tree to keep from getting woozy. Even after my hike across the spine, I didn't like heights.

Titus stood silently beside me.

"If Thomas had killed your father, I would have done you a great injustice today."

"One night with him and you believe he's innocent? Come on, Psyche. He tricked you."

"Persephone told Zeus she's always known Thomas was innocent. There were three men in the cave that night. Your father, Theron, and Thomas. Your father was killed. Of the two that escaped, one was a killer, and one was not. You tell me, which one is the killer?"

"There's no proof."

"That's why I didn't ask Zeus to retry him. He was pardoned as a gift. It was the only way to set him free."

Titus's anger had simmered, but it wasn't gone. "I still don't believe it."

"Even if you don't, Thomas is a guest in our home, and you will treat him as such. Their journey is being delayed. Eros wants to see you about a legal matter. He didn't tell me exactly what it is, but he's going to force me to testify. I expect he'll tell you the same."

He turned to go.

"One more thing, Titus."

"Yes?"

"If you ever speak to me like that again in front of one of the Ruling Council, I'll have you thrown in the dungeon and left to rot."

He took my hand and kissed it. "That would be well deserved."

By nightfall Eudora was in the kitchen preparing for guests, and I sent my maid to help her. Aeas and Thomas returned from the mortal world. After delivering a manila envelope to Eros, which was his errand, Aeas took Thomas upstairs with a video game console and a handful of games. I heard Thomas's murmurs of amazement as Aeas plugged in the console and showed Thomas how to play. Soon they were whooping and jabbing each other competitively. A few hours later, I found Titus lingering tentatively at the doorway. Aeas finally convinced him to join them.

Alone, I went into the master bedroom and sat on the bed. The day had not turned out like I imagined it. I thought Zeus would quietly bring Thomas from Hades, and I would send him away with Aeas. When they were gone I planned to break the news to Titus. I knew he would be mad, but I expected him to understand.

Now we were all going to be paraded in front of the Zeus for who knew what? Eros still wouldn't tell me exactly what was going on, but he took Titus into his confidence, which irritated me.

A shadow shifted on the balcony, and I went to see what it was. Eros stood looking up at the stars with his arms folded across his chest. In front of him was a newly built, waist-high railing that enclosed the whole balcony.

"I thought you were downstairs with Zeus?" I said.

"He retires early." Something was bothering him. I stood awhile and waited. When he didn't speak, I turned back into the bedroom. "Are there things you can't tell me?" he said finally.

The question caught me off guard. "What do you mean?" There were still boundaries on my openness with him. I wasn't willing to discuss girl stuff.

His gaze stayed on the stars. "You never told me about your night with Thomas."

"I didn't know you wanted details. I'm not hiding anything. Do you think I betrayed you?"

He took my hand. "Of course not. If you had, you wouldn't be here. But, I felt blindsided by Zeus today. You're the reason Persephone filed charges against Theron. Is it true that he offered you ambrosia to sleep with him?"

"Yeah, so?"

"So? Psyche, if you had accepted that offer, you'd be Theron's wife. The contract you made with Aphrodite would have been voided. For him to immortalize and marry a mortal without Aphrodite's consent is a violation of his oath." Eros stepped forward and put his arm around my shoulder. "Is that why he beat you?"

"Yes."

"Why didn't you tell me?"

"Because it didn't matter. All that mattered was that you came back to me, and you loved me again." I let him nuzzle my cheek. He was freely affectionate, and I welcomed every touch. "I don't see how it matters anyway because I refused. Everyone is making a big deal out of this, and his real crimes sit like elephants in front of everyone. No one holds him accountable. He's a killer, and he's Aphrodite's lover. He betrays Hephaestus every day, and everyone looks the other way."

"Have a little faith, Psyche. Sometimes justice takes time."

I was afraid the entire Ruling Council was going to converge on our palace, but Zeus decided to deal with the charges privately. The trial was held in the great hall downstairs. An ornate chair sat on a wooden platform in the center of the longest wall. Zeus took this seat. Right next to him sat a scribe. Eros, Aeas, Thomas, Titus and I were instructed to stand to the right. When Aphrodite's entourage arrived, they would take the side to the left. I gave Titus strict instructions to translate every word spoken.

Aphrodite arrived with an uproar. We heard the clamor three rooms away, and when the party reached the great hall, I was surprised to find three prisoners in the custody of the guards, not one. Theron, another man, and a maid were all brought in chains. The maid was terrified. Her face was streaked, though her eyes were dry. When she saw Titus standing at my shoulder, she began to cry again.

"I demand that you release my servants this instant!" Aphrodite insisted. Her face turned to utter shock when she saw Thomas.

"Hold your peace, daughter. We wait upon another," Zeus replied. He sat silently until one of his guards appeared at the back of the hall and gave him a signal. Then he pointed to the maid and a guard brought her forward. She was forced to her knees before Zeus.

"That's Fauna," Titus whispered.

She was dressed like Aphrodite with excessive jewelry and flowers woven into her hair. Around her head she wore a pendant.

Zeus did not read charges against her. "Speak, girl."

"Please, don't send Atalo to Hades," she begged. "It wasn't his fault. I was afraid to ask permission from our mistress. I married him unlawfully. I kept it a secret, though he pressed me to admit it."

Aphrodite's already angry face grew harder. Her eyes narrowed on Fauna.

Zeus drew his fingers through his beard. "We might deal lightly with this crime in exchange for other testimony. Do you swear before the High Judge to speak the truth in all things asked of you?"

Fauna nodded. "Inasmuch as I do not betray my mistress."

"You are relieved of your oath to your mistress. You will speak the truth, or I'll send Atalo to Persephone!"

Fauna let out a cry and dropped her face into her hands. "I will speak the truth," she cried.

The guards brought Theron forward and forced him to his knees. "Serious charges have been made against this man, Theron. Fauna, to your knowledge has this man ever committed adultery with your mistress Aphrodite?"

Fauna's face drained of all color, and terror stopped her tears. She looked first at Aphrodite then at Theron.

"Speak the truth," Zeus demanded.

She choked on her answer. "Yes," Fauna squeaked. "I have seen them with my own eyes."

Theron shot her a look, and she shied away as if he struck her. When the guard pulled her to her feet, she clung to him, more afraid of Theron than of Zeus's justice.

Aphrodite stepped forward. "She's lying. She will say anything to save herself and this worthless man servant." She gestured toward Atalo, the other man in chains. "They are the traitors here, not Theron."

"Peace, Aphrodite. You will get your turn at the end," Zeus replied. "Titus."

Titus slipped around me. Aeas closed the gap and took up the translation. Since he wasn't a prisoner, Titus knelt briefly before Zeus, then stood to answer the questions laid to him.

"Why did you abandon your post in Aphrodite's household?" Zeus asked.

"I let the mortal Psyche into the Fortress. Later that night I was instructed to take her to the mainland. When I returned, Theron was waiting for me. He sought to punish me for my mistake. I feared for my life, so I left."

"Why did you fear for your life?" Zeus asked.

Titus's shoulders slumped slightly. "Theron and I fought. I couldn't prevail against him."

On his knees, Theron smirked, until Eros stepped forward with a manila envelope. "I have proof," Eros said. "These are called photographs. They use them in the mortal world. I took these pictures of Titus when he arrived here at the palace."

As Zeus looked over the photos, his eyes grew stern. He motioned Titus away and called my name. Titus took me by the hand and led me to the place where he stood a moment ago. He put himself between me and Theron and stayed to translate.

"My dear girl," Zeus began, "you have been through quite an ordeal these past few months. Only weeks ago you returned from the kingdom of Hades. At your request, the condemned murderer Thomas has been freed. While you were in Persephone's court, you told her of events that took place in the mortal world and a verbal contract offered to you by Theron. We all know that no one can lie to Persephone. Therefore, we deem her charges as correct, but we need to hear ourselves of this contract."

Titus set a reassuring hand on the back of my neck. "Just tell him the truth, and it's over."

I felt myself tremble, not only because Theron was a mere two feet away, but because I knew what else Eros must have in that envelope, and like Titus, I felt the humiliation of admitting I was a helpless victim. Still, I spoke the truth, just as I recounted it to Persephone. I repeated the insults I hurled at Theron and how he hurled me into a mirror in return. I let my eyes wander to Aphrodite when I spoke of the contract Theron offered me. For the first time, her anger seemed directed at Theron and not the rest of us.

Zeus stopped me with a raise of his hand and turned to Eros. "He assaulted your betrothed?"

Aeas stepped forward and explained how he found me and that he sent for medicine to heal my wounds. I held my breath as Eros pulled another stack of photos from the envelope and set them into Zeus's hands. Eros must have taken them while I was unconscious.

The old man's teeth clenched. He looked like a lion ready to roar. "Mortal or not, this is despicable!" He flung the photos onto the floor in front of Theron.

As they skated across the floor, Titus glimpsed for the first time my bloodied and disfigured face the night of the attack. He let out a groan and pulled me closer. "I'm so sorry," he whispered.

"This assault was never reported to the council," Zeus said.

Aphrodite stepped forward shaking a finger at her son. "Because he shot Theron full of arrows! He knew our laws wouldn't protect his mortal strumpet."

"Eros," Zeus said sternly, "revenge is never condoned by our law."

Eros held out his hands palms up. "Those weren't my arrows. They were her father's. He's mortal, and not bound by our laws."

Zeus wasn't fooled. He turned to me. "Does he speak the truth?"

"I didn't see the arrows that ended up in Theron," I replied, "but my father is a bow-hunter. He hunts big game every fall. His arrows are nearly always dark green with yellow feathers at the end and razor tipped to drop the kill quickly."

"Fauna," Zeus said, "did you see the arrows pulled from Theron's body?"

This time she stepped forward and spoke boldly. "They were green with yellow feathers on the end, and they had a vicious four-pronged razor tip."

Zeus nodded and dismissed me. "Then, we'll move on to the final matter." He turned to Thomas. "I believe you have something to say to this company?"

Thomas shook his head. "No one believed me then. I don't see that it would be any different now."

Zeus gave him an understanding smile and gestured to the guard at the back of the room, who went out the door and returned a moment later with another very large man.

The one who entered was mighty in stature like Zeus, but his gait was uncertain and his shoulders slumped. As he drew nearer, it became apparent that his face was not handsome. His nose was crooked and his mouth overly large.

"That's Hephaestus," Titus murmured. "He's a recluse. He hasn't left the forge in ages."

"Welcome, Lord Hephaestus," Zeus said. "You did not speak at the trial five ages ago because you were recovering from your wounds. I realize now we may have been hasty in our conviction. Would you please speak to the charges now?"

Hephaestus raised his hand and pointed to Thomas. "I ...re... remember, that boy." Each word was a struggle for him, but he continued, "H...h...he came into the f...f...forge, but he was...un... unarmed. Stavros ch...chased him into the caves. Then, someone st...st...stabbed me in the back. W... w...when I healed, they told me St...St...Stavros was dead, and the murderer was s...s...sent to Hades. I d...d...didn't know it was th...th...that boy they convicted." Hephaestus shook his head. "H...h...he didn't stab me. H...he was afraid."

Zeus turned his eyes back to Thomas. "You told the Council repeatedly that Theron killed Stavros. Is that still your account?"

"Yes," Thomas answered.

Zeus sighed. "I've heard enough. Aphrodite, now it is your turn to speak. Have you anything to say against the charges as they have been laid out?"

She stood trembling, her eyes a mix of fury and humiliation, but she held her peace.

"My lady!" Theron cried. "My love, save me! Psyche is lying. They are all lying. I have never betrayed you!"

His pleas fell on deaf ears. One of the photographs had spun as far as Aphrodite's feet. She was done covering his crimes, though Theron continued to call her name as the guards pulled him to his feet.

"Theron," Zeus said, "according to these accounts and the judgment of this High Councilor, you are found guilty of betraying Lord Hephaestus, abusing a subordinate servant, assaulting Eros's betrothed, violating your oath to Aphrodite, murdering Stavros and swearing falsely under oath before the High Council. You are a disgrace to the entire Olympian race, and I will personally see you delivered to Persephone's feet." He turned to the guard. "Hold him downstairs until we've finished the proceedings."

Theron fought hard against the guards as they dragged him toward the stairway to the dungeon. "Aphrodite! Don't let them send me to Hades! Please! Do something!"

When Theron was gone, Zeus turned to Aphrodite. "As for you, my daughter, you are forbidden from returning to the mortal world. The Fortress is hereby seized by the High Council. You will go home, and for once in your life, you will act like a wife." He bade Fauna and her lover Atalo brought forward. "The two of you are appointed caretakers of the Fortress. You are not banished to the mortal world, but are to live there and care for this Olympian property. You will report directly to the High Council. Now, Fauna, wear your pendant as it should be. If you cannot be proud of your husband's love, you don't deserve him."

Freed from their bonds, both Fauna and Atalo fell at Zeus's feet and thanked him.

Aphrodite threw a disconcerted glance at her husband, Hephaestus. With her two remaining maids, she followed him out the back door.

Zeus turned to Eros and yawned. "Holding court is exhausting. I hope Eudora has that mutton ready. It smells heavenly."

As Eros escorted the Judge to the dining room, I turned to Thomas. "What will happen to Theron in Hades?"

"He'll pay for each of his crimes separately. Persephone despises treachery most of all, so he'll go to the irons first, and he'll stay there awhile. Eventually, she'll take him into her guard, but she won't make it easy for him." He looked up at Titus. "She'll break him first."

By the time the sun went down, Eros and I found ourselves completely alone in the palace. Zeus and his guards left to deliver Theron to Persephone. Fauna and her husband took off to make merry in their new mansion. Titus volunteered to go with Aeas to England and see that Thomas was properly settled. An exhausted Eudora returned to her husband in the valley, and I sent my maid to stay with her parents for awhile.

Eros doused the lights on the upper level of the palace, and we stood on the balcony enjoying the cool breeze and the bright moonlight. "You've freed an innocent man, condemned a murderer to Hades, outted an adulteress, and reconciled Titus to the man he's hated for ages, can we *please* marry now?"

"Yes," I replied, "I'll let you marry me tonight, right after you help me do one last thing."

He let his head roll back with a groan.

"It's right up your alley, Eros. You're good at breaking and entering, right?"

"An expert," he replied, his mouth on my neck.

"We won't be gone long, and I promise, when we get back, I'm all yours."

"All right," he said. "Where are we going?" When I told him, he laughed. "Your timing is perfect. Do you know what tomorrow is in the mortal world?"

"No."

He kissed my mouth. "It's Valentine's Day."

# EPILOGUE

Rory lay awake and stared at the constellations he stuck on the ceiling years ago. The Big Dipper dimmed from view as the night wore on. He kicked off the covers and thought of Psyche. No one had heard from her in weeks. Her dad said she went back to Europe, but Rory called every airline with flights out of Bozeman the day she disappeared. Psyche Middleton wasn't on any of them. For the thousandth time, he prayed that she was all right—that the monster named Theron hadn't dragged her off and tortured her to death.

Rory had never seen Aeas again either.

As he drifted into restless sleep, he dreamed of Psyche's beautiful face. She stood over him, dressed in white with a crown of braids in her hair and a heavy cloak draped around her shoulders. She was even more stunning than he remembered. On her forehead was a jeweled pendant which sparkled in the moonlight. She drew a damp piece of gauze across his forehead and down his cheeks.

"What are you doing?" he asked the dream.

"Passing my curse on to someone else."

His face tingled, and he closed his eyes. "I worry about you."

"Don't worry. I'm happy now."

He didn't doubt it. She made it to heaven and come back as an angel, magnificent beyond human description. Psyche moved the cloth over his entire face, then squeezed the liquid onto his lips. He opened his eyes and tasted sugared nectar. The juice sharpened his vision. Behind her he saw a young man, but it wasn't Aeas. This guy was older, more strongly built, and when he looked at Psyche, his face lit in a way that made Rory ache for a love of his own.

Psyche bent and kissed Rory's forehead. "Remember, only the beauty in your heart matters." Rory squeezed her hand, then she vanished.

The next morning Rory woke to the buzzing of his alarm and rolled over trying to remember why he'd set it early. Clouds in his memory parted. He needed to double-check his calculus homework and reprint his term paper. Rory pulled himself out of bed and powered on the computer. He brought up the paper and hit print, then dragged himself to the shower.

With the mirror still foggy, he ran a comb clumsily through his hair, not really caring how it turned out. He dressed, piled books into his backpack and trudged down the stairs to the kitchen, where his mom was slicing oranges. She looked up, let the knife slip and sliced her finger.

"Mom!" Rory grabbed her hand and pressed his thumb on the cut. He dragged her to the sink and ran cold water over the wound.

Tears gathered in her eyes as she stared up at him. "My beautiful boy." She'd called him that a lot when he was little. He tolerated it until his body betrayed him in seventh grade and turned his face into a war zone. "I knew you'd grow out of it," his mom said. "No scars even."

Rory touched his face, but the bumps and ridges weren't there. He ran to the bathroom and threw on the light, then stared awestruck at his refection. "Only the beauty in your heart matters." He touched the glass. Psyche healed him. It was the face he'd always had under the acne, but he hadn't seen it in years.

Rory remembered the guy he used to be before the worst of it hit. He joked with girls, stood with his shoulders straight. It was later he started hiding in fantasy novels—when girls cringed to look at his face.

He grabbed his backpack and keys and ran toward the door. For once he wasn't going to sneak in right before the tardy bell. There was something he had wanted to do for months.

"Breakfast!" his mom called after him, but Rory could miss a meal for this.

He parked and jogged toward the nearest door, skipped going to his locker and headed straight to his first period class. Only one student was there. She sat in the front corner with a lock of dark hair tucked behind her ear. Her homework and calculus book were neatly stacked in the top corner of her desk, and she was hunched over a book.

"Hi, Vanessa."

"Hey, Rory." She didn't look up.

He knelt beside her desk and watched her eyes move back and forth across the page. "If I buy, do you think you could ditch Koontz for one day and have lunch with me?"

"Are you serious?" She looked up and went doe-eyed at the sight of his face. "What happened?"

"Do you believe in magic?"

"Not really."

Rory smiled and was surprised by the slight change in her eyes. She'd drawn a quick breath, too. "Then, I grew out of it. Isn't that what everyone says will happen?" He pulled the book from her hands. "I realize I'm not nearly as intriguing as Dean, but you have to eat."

She smiled into the faux wood grain of the desk. "If you don't mind being seen with me."

Rory touched her chin with the tip of his finger and drew her gaze to him. "I would love to be seen with you."

He blessed the gods of love and beauty.

# ACKNOWLEDGEMENTS

My journey as an author has been long, mostly uphill, and I would have fallen by the wayside long ago without the love and support of many wonderful people: my mom, Barbara Kerr, who read and loved all my novels, even the really bad ones; my husband, Nathan, who never resented the hours I spent writing and did his own laundry when the writing disease set in; Esther Davidson, Aimee Davidson, and Hank Wyborney for reading countless drafts and offering suggestions; Jessica Hansen, Emily Hansen, Janae' Hansen, Tiffany Coulson and Ashley Yorgesen for loving this story; Ashley Yorgesen, Keitra Calaway and Conner Coulson for the original cover photo; and to everyone who encouraged me to push on when the rejection letters piled up. Thank you. I needed you more than you know.

# ABOUT THE AUTHOR

Michelle A. Hansen grew up in Washington state. She earned her Bachelor of Arts degree in English Teaching and taught high school English for six years. She loves books, Pepsi and happy endings.

*Painted Blind* is her first novel.

Made in the USA
Middletown, DE
30 November 2018